MW00353023

Also by Kyell Gold

Argaea
Volle
Pendant of Fortune
The Prisoner's Release and Other Stories
Shadow of the Father
Weasel Presents

Out of Position
Out of Position
Isolation Play
Divisions
Uncovered
Over Time

Dangerous Spirits
Green Fairy
Red Devil
Black Angel

Other Books
Waterways
Bridges
Science Friction
Winter Games
The Mysterious Affair of Giles
Dude, Where's My Fox?
Losing My Religion
The Time He Desires
In the Doghouse of Justice
The Silver Citcle
X (editor)

LOVE MATCH

by Kyell Gold

Dallas, TX

Love Match

Production copyright FurPlanet Productions © 2017

Copyright © Kyell Gold 2017

Artwork © Rukis 2017
https://www.furaffinity.net/user/rukis/

Published by FurPlanet Productions
Dallas, Texas
www.FurPlanet.com

ISBN 978-1-61450-344-6

Printed in the United States of America
First Edition Trade Paperback 2017

Typeset in Garamond Pro and Montserrat

Table of Contents

For Rukis, who wanted a volleyball story. Sorry.

Prologue (2015)

Let's assume you've got a job. Okay, you're a call center employee or a concession stand worker or a guy who makes tennis balls in a factory or a system administrator. That's a real thing, right? My agent was talking to one when she was getting my website up. Whatever it is, you've got this job. Now suppose that every weekend—or every week in your case because you have weekends off, right?—every week, the way you do your job is compared to a hundred other people. Sometimes as many as two hundred if it's a big week.

Understand, you're not only being evaluated against people at your company. This is across the world. All the best tennis ball factory workers, all the best concession stand workers, all the best system administrators. And your salary is determined by how you do that week. If you come out on top, if you make the best tennis balls the fastest, or whip out hot dogs without an error or…administer the systems the best: big raise. Huge. You might be able to coast for a few months on that, or a year or two if it's a big week. If you finish in the middle, you keep plugging along. If you finish last, well, you can still do the job, but they stop paying you so much, or at all.

On top of that, every week some central office ranks you against all these other people. There are listings people can read in the paper that show that you are the 198th best system administrator in the world, or the 48th best call center employee. Your life starts to revolve around those numbers. Maybe if you're top-100, you can move to a better company. Maybe if you're top-50, you can get major endorsements. I guess you don't get endorsements, but maybe you would, like maybe some hot dog company would pay you to wear their logo while you serve hot dogs. And it's a pretty amazing thing, to be in the top 100 of all concession stand workers worldwide. Top 100, out of like 6 billion people! But all you can think about are those 80-90 guys ahead of you.

Welcome to professional tennis. I can tell you without fail what my ranking was at the end of each of my years as a professional (I'm currently in my fourth). I can tell you what it was for each of the last ten weeks. I can tell you what I was seeded at every major tournament I've entered (ha ha, that is a trick; I have only been seeded in two major tournaments ever). And I can tell you the names of the top ten players and my record against each one of them (2 wins, 8 losses, in the aggregate, because until this year I didn't get to play top ten players very much).

I remember the date I first beat a top-100 player (*July 18, 2012 at the Cuyahoga Open. It was overcast. Grigor Markov, a pine marten with a below-average serve and a wicked forehand, was ranked #75 in the world. I blew one service game and lost the first set 4-6, then figured out how to return his serve and took the next two 6-3, 6-2. He smiled at the net, shook my paw, and complimented me on my return game. The next time we played, he was #94 and I was #81 and I beat him 6-0, 6-1. We didn't speak at the net.*) and the date I first beat a top-50 player (*December 18, one week before Christmas 2012. Keiran Lubovic, a tall fennec thinner than I was with a great sense of humor. He joked on every changeover and had a great net game. I beat him in straight sets 6-4, 7-6, and at the net he asked for my autograph on a tennis ball.*) and the date I first beat a top ten player (*earlier this year, the wolf Dubro Bielovic, #9 in the world, 7-6, 6-7, 7-6. He shook my paw at the net and told me seriously that he would see me in a Major final one day*).

And here I am in the final of the 2015 States Open, only six months later. There are four Majors a year, tournaments the world watches with off-the-charts prize money where everyone competes to get in. Just being in a Major final puts you in an elite club, and I'm in that one now.

Right, the clubs. They're not formal, like, there's not a building you can go into if you're in the "top ten" club (people who have been ranked in the top ten in the world—after this tournament I'll be #12 at least, maybe #10 if I win). It's more like a class of player: you get lumped in with all the guys who have made it to that level and no farther. If you've made it to at least one Major final, that's a more exclusive club. Winning a Major final is another club, the first one that most casual tennis fans are aware of, and then after that you've got to do something crazy to make it into the last club, the "all time greats." You could win seventeen Major finals, the current record, or you could win each of the four Majors once (a "career Slam"), or you could win them all in the same year. When I say "you," here, I mean, obviously, not *you*, unless you're one of the three best tennis players who's ever lived. Winning all four majors in a year is called a "Grand Slam," and only three people in the modern history of tennis have done it.

That's what the guy across the net from me is chasing. Braden Longacre is a cross fox currently ranked #1 in the world, which is a thing that will happen when you've won the last three Majors. He lost here in the finals last year and then came back in January in great shape, improving his backhand and seeing the court better than ever. He's also got a better record in five-set matches than anyone else in the top ten (maybe the top 100 for all I know) because even when he loses the first two, he's analyzing his opponent, figuring out their weakness, and often that's enough for him to win the last three and therefore the match.

I'm not even sure I can take one set from him, let alone two, but I didn't get this far by doubting myself. Still, I know that he is the whole package for a tennis player: smart, in his prime (he'll be 26 in two weeks), and ridiculously talented.

He's also kind of a jerk.

Part One: Volleys (2008)

Chapter One (September 2008)

The twenty-three 8th grade students at the Palm Gables Tennis Center in Palm Gables in the state of Pensa in the Union of the States scrambled to get in line by height. Fortunately, in the few extra seconds it took me to process what "arrange by height" meant in English, a slim cheetah an inch taller than me grabbed my arm. "We're gonna be together," he said. "Just wait 'til everyone else sorts themselves out."

The cheetah's red t-shirt bore a black stencil of a bear with the word "OBEY" in big letters below. His paw tap-tapped against the loose black fabric of his shorts. My own white collared shirt and pleated pants, which most of the other cubs seemed to be wearing some variant of, felt stuffy and formal as I stayed by his side. We watched the other cubs compare heights, standing back to back or nose to nose, and when they'd arranged themselves into some semblance of a line, the cheetah tapped my arm. I followed him up to the back row, where we stood near the far right corner, only a rabbit and a giraffe taller than we were.

The white rabbit who'd introduced himself as "Coach Murphy" steadied his little camera. The flash went off.

"Dammit," he said. Some of us started to break the tight formation, and he roared, "Get back in line! Don't you move 'til I tell you to!"

"Can I scratch my ass even if you don't tell me to?" the cheetah murmured next to me. "Ass" was a word I knew, and I giggled.

Finally, Coach got the photo taken. "All right, now find a practice partner. Don't care who it is. You'll get to work with everyone in your class, but your partner will be the one you practice with after class. You don't have to stay with the same one, but you have to pick one to start with. Eventually you will all play each other."

The cheetah turned to me and stuck his paw out. "I'm Marquize," he said. "Wanna be practice partners?"

"Yes," I said, shaking his paw without hesitation. "I'm, uh…"

"Pleased to meet you, Uh," he said with a grin.

"No, I mean…" I had been speaking English since I was ten, but all four years of practice evaporated under the pressure of actual social interaction. "My name is Rochi, but my Ma says that is too hard for English speakers to pronounce. I was going to select an English name, but I have not decided between 'Bruce' and 'Wayne.'"

Marquize laughed and clapped me on the shoulder. "Shadow Knight fan. Awesome. First of all, you 'haven't' decided. Not 'have not.' Okay? You have to learn to use contractions." I nodded, and he said, "Say it."

"I haven't decided." I didn't like how I'd said it, so I tried again. "I haven't decided."

"Good. Second, Rochi," and he pronounced it perfectly, "is a great name. I'm not saying 'Bruce' and 'Wayne' aren't, but don't give up your name. If you want to make it easier to pronounce, go with Rocky. Okay?"

"Rocky." I tried it out. "You are sure it will be right?"

"'You're sure,'" he corrected me. "Say it."

"You're sure it will be right?"

"Yes, I'm sure. It's kick-ass." He grinned. "Where you from?"

"Lunda. We arrived here last month."

"Awesome!" He grinned and extended his paw again. "I came over from Madiyah when I was four." Then he said something in an African language I didn't understand, and I shook my head. "Aw. Say something in your language."

I said, "I am pleased to meet you," in Kikongo, and then again in Swahili.

"I don't know that one." His ears fell. "Dang, I was hoping we could talk without anyone understanding us."

"That was two languages," I said. "But I don't know yours either."

He lowered his voice and his tail lashed. "It's Arabic. Don't tell anyone I can speak it."

"I promise," I said. "Why did your family come over?"

"Better life over here. My parents' families saved up and paid for our passage. I think a lot of lions were killing cheetahs or something maybe. We were all naturalized a few years ago." He tapped his chest. "I'm a Union citizen. What about you?"

"I am not." I shook my head, wondering if there was some way Ma and I could become citizens faster than that.

He laughed. "No, I mean…how did you come over here?"

"Oh. For tennis. Ma has a friend with a video camera and she sent my video to twenty schools. This was the best one to say yes."

"Coach likes to take international players." Marquize nodded. "Was your country pretty peaceful?"

I shook my head. "Where I was, there was little danger. Mostly. But…" I spotted Ma as she came through the door. "There's my Ma. Come say hello."

"Hi," Marquize said, and I caught the corrective note in his voice.

"Come say hi," I repeated, and dragged him over.

Ma was trying to fit in, with a red dress that looked strange to me; I was used to seeing her in a simple shirt and brightly patterned homemade skirt, but then again I was more dressed up than my usual t-shirt and shorts, too.

Her English was better than mine because she was a teacher, but I wasn't afraid she would show me up. Ma wasn't like that. And indeed, she kept her greeting simple and addressed me in English when I told her Marquize had suggested "Rocky" as the English version of my name. "I like the sound of that," she said.

Marquize smiled and inclined his head. "You're jackals, right?"

"Black-backed jackals." I had learned that one almost right away. "Not striped or golden."

"But you can date those other ones?" Marquize winked slyly.

Ma did switch to Kikongo then, saying, "No dating!" to me.

"It is possible," I said to Marquize.

He pointed. "What did she say?"

I wished he and I had our own private language then so that I could tell him without Ma hearing. "I will tell you later," I settled for.

"'I'll tell you later'," he corrected, and made me repeat it. Ma wanted to know what was going on, and I wagged my tail and told her Marquize was going to help me with my English.

The one language all twenty-three of us spoke fluently was tennis. (We all spoke English, too, and my competent English was second worst to Yu, the red panda from Xiaodong who was one year older than me, but I vowed to get better.) Coach Murphy and his staff worked with us in classes designed to correct the problems with our mechanics—and we all had problems.

We had to learn to toss the ball properly, the right stroke to serve with, how to set our feet for strokes, follow-through and racket grip, all the things I thought I already knew and had to unlearn and relearn. And Coach made everything clear with me from day one of our individual sessions.

"I'm the one you need to impress," he said, his long ears straight up. His feet fidgeted when he was sitting and tapped the ground when he was standing, and he carried a paper cup full of steaming liquid in his left paw. I wrinkled my nose at the thick, strong coffee smell, and he saw it. "What's the matter? I don't smell good? Get used to it."

"Coffee," I said. "I'm sorry."

"You don't have coffee back in Lunda?"

"We do. It is for…I mean, it's for tourists. We do not—don't drink it."

He held the cup out toward me. "You want some?" When I shook my head, he nodded and pulled it back, situating it under his nose and inhaling deeply. "Some people say you cubs are too young for coffee, but you know what? They'll give you a case of Mountain Dew and that's got just as much caffeine and it's got sugar too. Coffee's better for you. Not for everyone, though." He shrugged and sipped it. "You find whatever you need to stay alert."

At the time, I wasn't sure what that meant, so I used the trick I had picked up quickly of nodding as though I did. "Yes, sir."

We were sitting in his office, a small room that smelled of the adjacent locker room under the thick coffee smell. The machine responsible for the coffee sat to his right, in easy reach, and above it on a shelf sat four trophies, polished to a high shine. On the desk between us, I read the titles of five books over and over: "Serve and Volley," "Tennis Fundamentals," "The Mental Game of Tennis," "Winning Ugly," and, oddly, a well-read copy of "Travel on a Budget."

The books sat in a pile to my left; on the desk between us, my file was open, and Coach Murphy rested his free paw on it, but he was looking right at me. His blue eyes met mine as he said, "Hey. Rocky."

I gave him my full attention: ears perked, sitting up straight, tail still, even though he couldn't see it over the desk. "Yes, sir?"

"There's gonna be a lot of people coming around to watch you play. There's going to be other cubs challenging you. There's going to be relatives and friends and reporters and sponsors. As long as you're here, you gotta remember one thing." He poked his own chest with a finger. "The only person you gotta impress is *me*."

I nodded sharply. "Yes, sir."

The poking finger turned to point straight up in the air. "You got a two-year scholarship. A year and a half from now, the Junior Tennis Federation asks me for a list of the players from your class ranked in order of talent. If you're in the top three, you're eligible for another two year scholarship here—if I recommend it."

"If I am in the top three," I asked, "will you recommend it?"

"Maybe." He held that paw up and put up a second and then a third finger. "If you're rich, like Braden Longacre, you don't need the scholarship. If you're hard to work with, like Mitch Dallion, I don't want you back." The three fingers stayed up. "If you're talented, in need, and easy to work with, that's how you get a second scholarship." The fingers came down, the coffee cup went up, and Coach Murphy leaned back in his chair. "Some years I don't recommend anyone. Lots of years, actually."

I nodded again. "I will do the best I can, sir."

"Okay. First thing: call me 'coach.' This ain't an army base."

"Yes, coach."

"Good." He smiled. "Now tell me why you want to play tennis."

I straightened. "Tennis gave me the opportunity to bring my mother out of Lunda to the States. We were poor—"

"No, no." He tapped the file on the desk with the bottom of the coffee cup. "That's all in here. Why did you start playing back in Lunda?"

"My sister found a tennis racket and gave it to me to play with when I was ten. In the nearby city there was a small tennis club and I went there to play." *Found a tennis racket* was the official story we'd told the Palm Gables reps. My sister, nine at the time, had been running with a group of cubs that stole luggage from the nearby international airport. She'd gotten a tennis racket out of one of the bags.

He leaned forward. "That's in the file too. Why did you *keep* playing?"

I blinked, and my ears folded down halfway. "My mother wanted me to. The tennis club was supervised, and—"

"Nah." He waved aside my explanation again. "Something about it got inside you. Why did *you*," he smacked the word at me, "keep playing?"

"It was something I could beat the other cubs at." I expected him to stop me again, but his mouth curved up into a smile, so I went on. "I was never the fastest, or the strongest, but with the racket, I could hit the ball past them. I could see it, I could react quickly, and even the bigger cubs I could beat."

"Good." He smoothed down his whiskers. "What do you love about the game itself?"

I thought about that, and he snapped his fingers at me. "Don't think. Answer. What do you love about it?"

"The lines," I blurted out.

He nodded and took another sip of coffee. I felt the need to explain. "I mean, I like playing to the lines," I clarified. "I did not say that well. I like that there are lines and there is..." I drew a line in the air with my paw. "In and out. This side good, this side bad."

"I understood." He chuckled. "You're good at hitting the lines?"

"I used to make a game with myself to see how close I could get."

He pointed at the file. "Says here you have very nice control of your strokes but not a lot of power."

I'd thought I was hitting the ball pretty hard, so my ears went down a little more. He kept going. "Some spin. Mediocre serve, no strategy to speak of. Hey. Get those ears up. This is the only other thing you have to learn."

What, I thought, that people are going to tell me my game is terrible? But I forced my ears up, and Coach said, "You deserve to be here. Because I decided you're worth my time, and until I say you're not, you have every right to be here. I don't care if you go out and lose every game to Marquize without scoring a point off him. Maybe he's that much better than you are. Maybe his game matches up real well with yours. The point is, until I tell you to go home, you've got as much potential as anyone here. Got that?"

"Yes, sir, coach." My ears stayed up more easily.

"All right. Most of this stuff," he waved a paw over the file, "is pretty standard for a cub your age. Nobody has strategy unless you're Braden Longacre and your parents raised you on a tennis court. Nobody has a good serve. Most cubs know how to put spin on the ball but not how to control it. You wouldn't be here if we didn't have anything to teach you. So you're gonna listen to us and we'll make you better. Got it?"

"Yes, coach." My tail wagged, and I matched his smile.

"You're here for two years, and at the end of that we'll evaluate you. A big part of that evaluation will be the school tournament, and you'll also enter the junior tournament at the States Open, the one that happens in a few weeks. You'll enroll every year—after this one, it's too late for this one now—and after the one in 2010, we'll sit down and decide whether we want to offer you another two years."

"The States Open—that's cubs from all over the world?"

"Yes. We don't expect you to win it, although one of our recent alumni did. But you're expected to make a good showing."

"And if I do, I'll stay another two years, and Ma can stay with me?"

His ears flopped forward as he nodded. "Any other questions?"

I put my paws on the edge of his desk. "When do we start playing?"

Chapter Two

Marquize and I were given a court that afternoon. Coach wasn't going to watch us himself, but one of his assistants, a ferret named Frio, sat by the court with a clipboard taking notes. Frio had a dark brown mask across his eyes and wore the same thing the other coaches did: a white polo shirt with the school logo on the right breast. He also wore shorts cut off at mid-thigh, higher than the knee-length shorts or full pants favored by the other coaches. He smiled more than they did too, and gripped our paws warmly when he introduced himself. "I'll be your primary coach. Anything you need," he said, "you can come to me."

We had both been given the option of having new rackets, which Marquize declined and I happily took. I'd always felt that the racket my sister had stolen wasn't properly mine, so it was nice to have one that was. But it felt strange in my paw, and I smacked several balls out of the court while we were warming up.

"Want to spend a little more time getting used to the racket?" Marquize asked.

I shook my head, crouched over, tail twitching. "Let's play."

It had been probably a month since my last game at the Lunda tennis center the day before we flew over. More than that, it had been years since I'd faced anyone competitive across the net. My "games" at the club had become exercises for myself to see whether I could dispatch an opponent without giving up any points. Or if I could let him get to 40-love before I came back and won the game. Or if I could win the game only hitting to his forehand. I had all sorts of tricks to make tennis harder, but in that first game against Marquize, I abandoned all of them. His serve came whistling across the net, and immediately the word "mediocre" seemed generous to describe mine. I returned the third serve long, and managed to get the fourth one back in play, at which point he promptly smashed a return down the line.

My serve, by contrast, he handled with ease, and I soon found myself down three games. In that fourth game, as I was serving, I thought I saw Marquize easing back, grinning the way I used to grin at the other cubs who couldn't come close to beating me. I'd been watching his serve and the way he slammed the racket into the ball, and on my first serve I mimicked his motion. The ball hit the line and skidded by him, and his eyes went wide with surprise.

I proceeded to double-fault and then lose that game as well, but that one moment made it worthwhile. My next service game I actually won, and ended up losing the set 6-1. But as we took a break, Marquize came over to tell me I was really getting used to the new racket. I didn't tell him that I was actually learning how to play better on the fly.

I lost the second set as well, but I won three games. When I was able to get the ball back in play, Marquize's style became decidedly looser. I studied him to figure out where I could hit the ball that would cause him the most problems; Marquize did not seem to be studying me at all. He raced around the court with his cheetah's speed, making up for mistakes by getting into position with time to spare, and it was hard for me to find a place I could hit it that he couldn't get to.

He met me at the cooler as we grabbed water bottles—the mid-afternoon heat and thick humid air had me panting two games in, but not worse than at home in Lunda—and told me I'd played really well. "You were better second set than the first," he said. "You gotta cut that out or you'll be beating me in a month."

We were standing near Frio, who made a few last notes on his clipboard. "It's pretty common for cubs who come here out of a foreign country to be overwhelmed the first week or two. Especially a poorer country, because you probably didn't face a lot of real competition the last year or so, right?"

That was to me, and I nodded. "I won every match for the last nineteen months. Even against players three years older."

"Thought so." The ferret grinned. "Felt weird playing someone at your level, huh?"

"A little," I admitted. "But I think Marquize is above my level."

I said it partly because it was true; he wasn't far above, but he was above. But I also said it to be nice to Marquize, because he was trying to be nice to me, and it worked. He got a big smile, and even though he said, "Nah, we're well matched," I could tell he believed what I'd said.

That was the other thing I liked about tennis. There were winners and losers. You could be nice to people and say they were better than you, and they might believe it even after you'd beaten them. But people believe many things that aren't true.

"I'm going to be your coach for the first year," Frio said, "so I'm going to be the one watching your games and giving you day to day instruction. Coach Murphy will be in charge still and will ultimately make the decision about your stay here, but he'll take my words with a lot of weight."

It felt weird to have so many people looking after me, but I nodded. Marquize looked bored. "Of course, a big part of that is also going to be your performance in the school tournaments. You guys know about the tournaments?"

Marquize nodded, and I didn't want to seem dumb, but I hesitated too long. Frio said, "There's a mid-year tournament and an end-of-year tournament here at the school. The end-year one is more important, but we'll be watching you through all of them. They're your first exposure to a real match-like environment. Then when you and your coaches think you're ready, you can start entering actual tournaments around the country. There are lots of junior tournaments, but of course the States Open is the big one."

"That's in Port City, right?" I said because I didn't want him to think I knew nothing about tennis. "Coach said we'd be entering that every year."

"Yep." Frio smiled, creasing his mask. "And you'll at least have the chance to enter every year. We might decide that you wouldn't benefit from it. Now, about me. I'm twenty-five and I went to Palm Gables. I was on the tour for a year. Couldn't even get into the top 200, but Coach Murphy always said I had a good eye for the game, so he asked me to come on board. I've coached here for four years and I'm gonna give you all my best advice."

We both nodded. I still felt strange about it, but Marquize was playing it cool, so I did too.

"Another thing, and this is especially for you, Rocky, is if you need anything, if you're homesick or having trouble adjusting, you can come to me and I'll do what I can." He grinned. "I've lived in this area almost my whole life and I know a lot of people here."

It felt like he was expecting me to say something, so I said, "Okay. Thank you."

"I've never had a student from your country—continent even— most of our international students come from Slavic countries, and we have a couple resource centers an hour away for them. I haven't had a chance to look for anything specific to your country, but I'm sure there's something around. It's a really international area. We've got OswaldWorld two hours away and they pull people from all over the world."

"Will we get to Oz?" Marquize looked interested for the first time.

Frio grinned at him. "Tournament winner each time gets to go for free, and anyone who can afford it can go along. That enough to get you interested in the tournament?"

"Heck yeah." The cheetah's tail lashed.

I knew a little about OswaldWorld, supposedly the "Land of a Million Smiles," the amusement park that was legendary even back in my town. "How much does it cost to go?" I blurted out.

"Not too much," Marquize said. "It's like eighty dollars to get in for the day."

I tried not to show my astonishment at how much that was, but Frio clearly noticed. "If you need money, there are things we can do to help you out." The ferret cleared his throat. "We want you to be able to concentrate on tennis. That's why you're here. So anything that takes your time away from that…" We both nodded, and he turned to me. "Rocky, your mother came over with you, right?"

"That's right."

Marquize grinned at me. "His mom is really invested in his tennis. I don't think she'll distract him."

Ma taught English back home, and there was an English as a Second Language class at Palm Gables, but they didn't need any more teachers. Still, she could substitute if one of the teachers was ill, as long as she was certified to teach in Florida. So she was studying for the certification test and was happy to leave my tennis instruction to the school.

Chapter Three

Life in the States felt at first like I'd stepped into a movie. What was most different was the greenery all around, between the houses and in the sidewalks—not that it was there, because we had greenery in Lunda, too. But there the greenery felt like part of the world we were coexisting with. Here it was managed and controlled, square yards in front of houses or bounded by concrete curbs in the middle of streets, sometimes given a large park to spread out in.

The houses were newer too, and the great shopping malls fascinated me; our first week there I wandered through them, breathing in the clean air and marveling at how people in the States smelled far less strong than the people of Lunda. I found out quickly that it was a product called Neutra-Scent that the malls piped into their air, which deadened the smells of the crowds so that sensitive-nosed people like me and Ma could walk around without being overwhelmed. But we were used to crowd scents, so it felt more unreal than comfortable to me at first. I was surprised how quickly I got used to it.

And last, of course, was the food. In Lunda we had what I had thought was a great variety of food, fruits and root vegetables and four different kinds of meat prepared many different ways; many kinds of bread and occasionally candy bars and chocolate. We had juice and Coke and Fanta, and I hadn't realized what I was missing until I stepped into a convenience store in the airport. The variety of sodas alone astounded me, and I think after five minutes of staring at them through the transparent doors of the cooler, I was ready for anything I might encounter in this country. Ma and I ate out often those first couple weeks and we tried every different kind of food the city had to offer: Coabanan, Sonoran, Xaiqinese, Yamatese, Gallian...it was all delicious.

Once I started school, my scholarship paid for my meals, and

Ma had a large stipend for groceries and other costs of living—we thought it was large until we went to a grocery store and saw how little we could get for what we thought of as a fortune. But like the sodas, the prices quickly became normal to me. I had a little stipend for expenses that I could use to help Ma with her groceries, and since I didn't know what else to spend it on at the time, that's what I did.

I didn't have much else to spend it on because I didn't have much time to do anything but school. I was there pretty much all day, morning to night, and only had a little bit of time free in the evenings.

My day typically started at seven a.m. with weight training or running in the morning for an hour and a half. Marquize and I exercised together, and while we were allowed to set our own program, Frio gave us a recommended list of exercises which we followed dutifully as the semester started. Then there was a breakfast at eight-thirty and our academic classes started at nine. I had Math first, then Natural Science, and then Social Studies until lunch. After lunch I had English for an hour and a half—I tested out of the ESL class—and then forty-five minutes of either Art or World Cultures, depending on what day it was. That took us up until three, when we broke into groups to go back to the tennis courts, and my favorite part of the day started.

Three days a week I had an elective tennis class. You could choose from things like Leadership, Nutrition, Business, Conditioning—stuff like that that you wouldn't get in the normal classes but which were important. My ma had chosen Leadership for me, but Marquize was doing Nutrition, "because you get snacks all the time," he said, and I vowed to take that one next term. Those classes lasted until about five, and then we had two hours on the courts with our buddies while the coaches rotated around to mentor us.

The other two days a week we worked on the courts from three to seven. Sometimes, Marquize said, the coaches organized matches when they had an idea of who would match up well, but as of the end of September they still hadn't done that. What they did was present short lessons on some aspect of tennis, and then have us run drills.

We were never tested, but if they saw us play and it looked like we weren't incorporating the lessons, we were pulled aside and told about it. This happened to Marquize more than once. "I know where to put my feet," he complained to me afterwards. "I've been doing this for half my life."

One of the other guys in our class, a wolf named Jess, overheard us and laughed. "You know better than the coaches, Spotty?"

"Hey," Marquize called back. "How do they know where to put my feet?"

"I'll show you where to put your feet." Jess pointed at the backside of Alan, his tennis partner.

Alan, a chunky zebra who'd been born about fifty miles away from the school, smacked at the wolf's muzzle as we all laughed. "Yeah, yeah," the zebra grumbled, "but with the way you place your feet on those lines you'd probably miss completely."

He said it like it was supposed to be funny, and I waited to see if anyone else would laugh, but nobody did. Marquize made a little fluttery motion and what looked like a kiss with his lips, and said, "Oh, unforced error," which is a tennis term for when you plain screw up, and not because your opponent did something good.

"Big words, soft serves," Alan said, which was an expression I picked up quickly because they used it all the time.

But that was how the tennis cubs were. That's what the other cubs called us—there were other cubs at Palm Gables who were there for other sports, or just for academics. Ma tried to explain it to me a few times, that in order to get the academic certification to attract good tennis players, they had to have other students, but it never made sense to me. If you wanted good tennis players, you got good tennis coaches, and Palm Gables had those.

Coach Murphy talked a lot about the former number-one-in-the-world players he'd coached, the top ten players, the Major final winners. Pictures on the hallway outside the locker room showed many of them, and some of those pictures were signed. For as long as I could remember, I'd watched tennis on the black-and-white TV at the community center, and later our color TV at home, and I'd seen many of these players play. The idea that they'd walked these halls when they were my age intoxicated me enough that every so often in that first month I would stop and put a paw on the wall and imagine another fourteen-year-old cub twenty years ago doing the same.

But the non-tennis cubs, they didn't care about the coaches or the players or the tennis history at all. They knew about tennis, and a couple times I heard one of them say things that only a tennis fan would say, but around us they acted bratty. Jess got into a fight once; one day he mouthed off when there were three of them and one of him. He managed to tear one cub's ear, but they bloodied his nose and broke his tail and bruised him pretty good all over. We got a lecture about fighting after that, and the other three cubs were suspended while Jess was not, which we felt pretty much showed them where the line was at Palm Gables.

It took me a while to get used to that. "Is it always this way?" I asked Marquize after our practice, the day we heard about the suspensions. We were one month into my stay at Palm Gables, and I had just won a set from Marquize for the first time.

"What?" He looked up at the dark mass of clouds. "Yeah, this time of year we always get four o'clock showers. In a couple years we'll rank high enough to get indoor courts."

"No, I mean…the tennis cubs against the others."

He patted me on the shoulder. "You're a tennis cub. So don't worry about it. Just remember: friends in the school, not on the court."

"Even us?"

He laughed and wrapped an arm around my shoulders. "Hey, Rock, you keep taking sets from me and I might have to find another partner."

I was pretty sure he was joking, but not completely, so I stayed quiet, even though I knew I could get better and win more from him. He squeezed my shoulder. "Hey, that's when you're supposed to say something like, 'you better start looking now, then.'"

Relief relaxed me. "You think I am—I'm going to start winning sets?"

He spun me around to face him. "Doesn't matter what I think," he said. "You gotta always be thinking you can be the best. You might not be, but you never will unless you think you are. Got it?"

"Yeah." I flattened my ears, unnerved by his sudden seriousness. The mood was gone as soon as it had come. He laughed and reached up to brush my head. "You canids and your ears. Love 'em."

Back home, the boys would hug and wrestle, but ears usually only got touched in fights. "So, uh," I said, trying to recover some composure, "I'll try not to win too many sets."

"What?" He looked startled.

"I like playing tennis with you. It's fun."

It would've taken too long to explain to him that I'd never had regular tennis partners back home, partly because the other boys got tired of losing to me, partly because the other boys often disappeared. Mostly the interminable wars in Lunda took place outside the capital Lundara, where I'd grown up; mostly the gangs stayed outside the Nguwe neighborhood where my family lived. The reason I'd taken up tennis was not only that I loved it; the tennis center was the only sporting center close to our house, save for a basketball court, and the few times I tried to play basketball, the lions who owned the ball wouldn't let me. So it was tennis, and for the last three years only a few of us younger jackals played there consistently.

Marquize didn't need to know that, and it didn't seem to matter to him. He said, "I like playing against you, too, so let's go again," and off we went.

I remember that conversation because it was shortly after that that Braden Longacre came back to Palm Gables for the first time. He'd graduated the previous year and already had climbed the ladder of the WTP circuit to break into the top 200.

That was about as foreign to me as Marquize's language the first time I heard it, so here's how he explained it to me then: there are two types of professional (that means winners get money) events, both put on by the Global Federation of Tennis Players (the GFTP). There's the World Tennis Champions, the WTC, which are the ones everyone watches on TV; they include the four majors and other top tier pro events as well as the Challenger circuit for players just below that tier, where Braden was mostly playing. Then there's the World Tennis Players, the WTP, which are the events for people outside about the top 200 GFTP rankings. Those are often called "Futures" events because they're for young players, but older players on their way down or still trying to break in also play in them.

Basically, you play WTP events to get enough points to be allowed into WTC events. That's how I explained it to Ma when she asked about Braden. Most of the people who graduate from Palm Gables, even Braden Longacre, go to Futures events first and work their way into the Challenger circuit.

We were all introduced to Braden, not only the tennis cubs but everyone, at a small assembly on Court One, the only court with bleachers for a large audience. Coach Murphy had told us that we had a special guest, and even though I knew this was the States, I flashed back to the tennis center back home, the time all the boys were called together and we stood out on the cracks and grass of our tennis court and shuffled our claws over the concrete we pretended was green like on TV, and a tall hyena came out in her crisp green uniform and surveyed us. She told us that we could not waste our time playing games, but that our tribe and country needed us. She took Pierre and Luongo and Peh-Peh, whose name was also Pierre so we had to call him something else. Her eyes lingered on me, but I was a jackal and I was scrawny; two of me would not have made one of Peh-Peh the lion. Those three boys were older and bigger, and they followed her out, and we never saw any of them again.

That had been years ago and half a world away, under a hot desert sun rather than muggy cloudy skies, but still my fists clenched on my knees. Even when this fox walked out in shorts and a white shirt with a yellow logo over the breast, I couldn't quite unclench myself. So I focused on his fur, because it wasn't normal fox red; he had darker brown fur between his ears and along his tail, with highlights of red rather than a full coat of it. His forearms and feet were just as brown as any of the foxes I'd met here, and so were his ears, and his throat and the tip of his tail were both the bright white of someone who washed every day.

He carried himself like the hyena sergeant, though. Muzzle up, ears up, back so stiff you could tell time by his shadow. His tail didn't even swing as he walked; he kept it arched and still. Chickens wouldn't shit on his feet—Ma used to say that before we moved to the States. We were all so quiet that the click click click of this fox's claws on the cement of the tennis court echoed in all of our ears.

"This is Braden Longacre." Coach Murphy couldn't keep the excitement out of his voice. "He left Palm Gables two years ago, and already he's ranked number one-ninety in the world. He had a feature on the Tennis Channel, he's been interviewed by Bud Nichols, and he's beaten Ludo Dragovic, the world's #9 player." That was for the non-tennis cubs; we tennis cubs knew all the top 20 players, although when Marquize and I checked later, we found that

Dragovic was only #15 when Braden beat him. Still impressive.

Anyway, Coach Murphy went on, but I kept staring at Braden. So military, so precise. Marquize leaned over and whispered, "I was wondering what they did with the tennis robot they made last year," and I broke down into giggles, which got him giggling too. Coach Murphy didn't stop, but his voice got louder, and when I looked back up, I saw that Braden was staring right at us.

His voice surprised me. "Thank you, Coach," he said when the rabbit stepped back, finally finished with the introductions. He held his vowels almost musically, and his voice reminded me of the old bat-eared fox who led the singing for our neighborhood in festivals. "It's a real pleasure to come back to Palm Gables. If you cubs take full advantage of the coaching and facilities here, you'll have every advantage I did."

"Except for the trust fund," Marquize muttered.

"What's a trust fund?" I whispered.

"Money. Lots of money. His family's loaded."

The crowd of students around us watched in their name-brand clothes, with their expensive perfumes and their professionally groomed fur. "I thought everyone's family was, in this country."

"Not everyone's." Marquize patted my knee. "Don't matter, though. We got talent. We got as much talent as that fox down there."

(I would later find out that Marquize was downplaying his family's wealth, if not, perhaps, his access to it. Of course, compared to the others at the school, maybe he really did think he was poor.)

The guy in front of us, a Geoffroy's cat named Malik, half-turned and smirked. "You think so? You gonna play him?"

"Will he play people? Us, I mean. Students?" My ears perked up. Braden was going on about something else, the importance of study or something like that. I tried to imagine him on the tennis court.

"Usually the guests Coach brings in will play a few sets with the older cubs, or at least hit a few balls with them," Marquize said. All the seventeen-year-olds sat up near the front, ears perked forward. "Who knows if this asshole will do that."

Malik, still listening, said, "I bet he will. Look at him, he thinks he's better'n all of us. Wants to prove it."

"By beating up on younger cubs?" When I played at home, I always went easy with the youngsters. I played all out against the older ones because they were supposed to be better.

"We're the future." Marquize included Malik in this with a wave of his paw. "He wants to know how good the future's going to be. We're the ones who are gonna be coming in at the end of his career to dethrone him."

"Or sooner than that." Malik grinned. "He ain't all that. That Dragovic match, he got lucky. Drago hurt his ankle in the fourth."

"He's still pretty good. You see him at the Ocie?"

"That's where I saw him!" I looked down again at Braden. On the black and white TV his markings hadn't been as distinctive, but now I remembered him. The announcers had mentioned his youth and his talent and I'd been impressed with how good his technique had been in the one match I saw.

Marquize and Malik continued to argue about Braden, while I watched the cross fox. Then, he had been fully focused on tennis. Now, as he watched Coach talk, he bore an arrogant smirk on his muzzle. It might have been one of the markings in his fur for as permanent as it seemed.

Chapter Four

Ma says she remembers the first time I played a match against an older cub. It depends on what you mean by 'older,' I guess. At that age, I counted anyone taller than me as older, and I'd been playing taller cubs for as long as I could remember, so I'm not sure which match she's talking about, the lion or the hyena or the other jackal or another one I don't remember. She doesn't remember the species, just that his name was Christian.

But I remember the last match I played against a younger cub. My sister Ori used to tag along with me and got good enough playing cubs her age that she challenged me one day. We'd just turned twelve and eleven, but she'd grown half a foot in the last year to get close to my eye level. She had found an old book about a "Battle of the Sexes" that had happened some forty years ago, male tennis player against female, and she wanted to re-enact it.

Ma wasn't there, and neither was Aunt Kamina, and even though I didn't want to play Ori, she was a pest. So finally I did.

Lots of the cubs at the center watched, I think because we were two of the best players, but also because there was only the one court. I knew that court well, knew which cracks would make the ball spin crazily and where I could hit a short lob that my opponent might trip running toward. When I started, I didn't want to beat Ori by a lot. I thought I might even let her win the match.

That idea lasted all of one serve. From the moment the ball hit the pavement for the first time, my generosity ebbed. I might let her win a set. Maybe four games. Finally, I was playing so that anything she won she'd have to take from me, and I had one year, six inches, and at least ten pounds of muscle advantage.

She started out chattering at me, but after losing three games she shut up, and when I won the second set without losing a single game, she dropped her racket and walked off the court. She didn't talk to me for a week and she didn't play tennis again while I lived in Lunda.

After that, I would hit balls with the younger cubs, and I'd practice with them, coach them when Coach Arrel wasn't available, watch some of the videos we'd gotten from the States (they were thirty years old, but we had no Internet until the year before I emigrated). But I never played an actual game against one.

Ori's staying with Aunt Kamina now. My special visa to stay in this country only covers me and one other person, to act as my guardian.

**

A bunch of us gathered around Coach after the talk. Braden was shorter than I would've thought, though he was taller than Coach even when both their ears were up. Marquize and I, standing at the back of the crowd, could see over all but the coyote and two stags at the front. "Listen up," Coach said. "I know you all want a chance to play Braden, and he's very generously agreed to spend two hours here, but that's not enough for everyone to get in, so we're going seniors first, then juniors, then sophomores."

"Why not go by tennis rank?" Malik, sixteen, was better than all the juniors and a couple of the seniors.

"The idea isn't to have a competitive game," Coach said. "The idea is to give you guys the privilege of playing against a real pro, and the seniors will be out there sooner. The rest of you will have a chance next year."

"One service game each way," Braden said. "That should give you an idea of what it's like out there."

"This guy thinks he's the only cub who ever graduated from a tennis academy," Marquize muttered.

I giggled and elbowed him. "Maybe playing him will give us an idea of what it's like to play an asshole."

It was bolder than I normally would have been, but I wanted Marquize to like me, and he responded with a laugh and an elbow back. "Like we don't know that already."

At that, a couple of the cubs in front of us turned around, and one of them said, "We sure know you two do."

"I dunno," Marquize said. "We haven't played you yet."

"Hey."

The sharp tone of Coach's voice always brought us to attention. Marquize and I looked up to see him staring at us. "You three," he said, waving a paw. "Go start your practice games. You're not getting time."

Marquize and I hadn't thought we were going to anyway, so it wasn't that big a deal. But Braden was looking right at me, and so I paused and looked back as Marquize turned to go, and before I knew it, Braden had put a paw on Coach's shoulder. "Now hold on," he said. "Why don't I play a little one-on-two to warm up?" He reached out a long, dark finger. "The coyote and cheetah there."

"I'm a jackal," I said loudly.

Coach's big white ears swiveled. "Rocky and Marquize? They're frosh—"

"It's okay." Braden pulled his lips back in a smile. "It won't take long."

Of course, with that buildup, everyone stuck around to watch us play. We were all dressed in tennis clothes already, so it was only about five minutes before Marquize and I were standing in doubles alignment staring down Braden Longacre on the other side of the court.

It was pretty exciting. I thought Marquize and I would be able to at least win our service game off him, even though we'd never played doubles together. I'd never actually played doubles at all. But it was two of us against one of him, and even if we weren't close to best in our class, didn't an extra racket make a huge difference?

"Follow my lead," Marquize told me. "When I'm serving, you go up to the net. Then cover the net and if you're going for a lob, call it. And if I call it, duck." He grinned. "That should work for a couple games."

So I stood up at the net, and Marquize unleashed his best spin serve. Braden, standing coolly on the other side of the net, smashed it back as though he'd been expecting it. I got a racket on it, but couldn't drop the shot; it sailed back toward mid-court, where Braden advanced on it and sent a laser down the line, landing in the corner, and not even in the doubles alley.

That's how the first game went. We lost four straight points. Then it was Braden's turn to serve, and Marquize and I alternated receiving. Each of us got his ball back over the net once, and we had one little three-shot rally before Braden smacked the ball between us, so that Marquize and I both stared at it as it bounced past us for the last point of the game.

"Well," Braden said, stretching, "that was a nice warm-up." He turned to Coach. "Who's first?"

Marquize turned to walk off the court, but I stared back at this fox with the dark white-tipped tail, the brown fur between his ears that accented his eyebrows so that he always looked a little bit angry, the haughty half-lidded eyes that had already turned away from us. "Hey," I said, "don't I get to serve?"

Coach and Braden and Marquize all turned to look at me. "You had two games," Coach began, but Braden held up a paw.

"It's okay," he said. "Let's see what you've got. What are you, fourteen?"

Fourteen is what I told people, but the truth was I didn't know for sure. Ma celebrated Ori's and my birthday on the same day, the first day of spring. By the time I was old enough to realize that we probably hadn't been born on the same day—let alone the same day as a few of our neighbors—Ma either couldn't remember or wouldn't tell us when our real birthdays were.

So I was probably fourteen, but I might've been thirteen, and there was an outside chance I was fifteen. When we came to the States, Ma was asked for my birth certificate as part of our documentation, and she just shrugged and said it had been destroyed in the war. So we went by memory, and legally my birthday was March 21 and in that fall of 2008, I was fourteen years old.

But I didn't say that to Braden. I said, "Does it matter?"

That was the first time I saw him react with anything other than his self-assured smirk. He raised his eyebrows and the angry expression vanished. "All right," he said, setting himself on the baseline. "Serve."

Of course, the first time I went for it, I double-faulted. As he crossed to the ad court, Braden had that smirk back, and I wanted to wipe it off. I'd watched him receiving Marquize's serve—very useful, because I could watch without worrying about my own serve mechanics. Braden's return was as clean and sharp as any of our teachers, but I also noticed that like we did, he always moved to take the serve from his forehand. And on the ad court, most of the serves

I could hit would be to that forehand.

I could serve down the middle pretty well, and I'd only the previous week started really learning to serve wide with velocity. Braden might not expect that; Marquize had tried and had hit it too wide, and one of the faults I'd made had been wide as well. So he might not expect me to try it again.

All of this went through my head in five seconds as I bounced the ball, so when I tossed it up over my head, I let the racket come around like I'd been practicing, and drilled the ball over a crouching Marquize, right onto the line on the far side of the service box.

Braden reacted a half-second too late. He lunged with his racket and clipped the ball, but only redirected it into the sideline. We all stood watching as he froze, staring at the line. Then he looked up at me and said, "Second serve," as he went back to his position.

"I think you mean, fifteen all." Marquize stood at the net.

The cross fox gestured with his racket. "It was off the line."

"It hit the line." Marquize looked back at me, but I didn't know what to do, so he appealed to Coach. "You guys were looking. Didn't you see it?"

Nobody spoke up. Malik met my eyes and looked down, and Coach said, "I wasn't really watching."

In the silence that followed that comment, Malik raised his head abruptly. "I think it might've been in," he said.

Braden ignored him. "Second serve," he repeated, and went into his crouch.

Fine, I thought, I'll do it again. So I tossed the ball up, reached back and slammed it forward, following through with terrific form and confidence, and the ball sailed two feet wide of the line.

"Love-thirty." Braden stalked to the deuce court.

I lost the game, of course. *We* lost the game, I mean. Afterwards I passed it off like it was no big deal, but inside I felt like if I'd scored that point I would've somehow beaten him. Marquize was furious, the other students sympathetic, and Coach was very loud and confident, telling me I'd done really well and complimenting me so heavily that I figured he knew what had really happened. Marquize wanted to stay up with me, but he had homework. "We'll go out for a night hit-around," he said. "Or we can play Spades if you don't want to hit." I did want to get back to the courts and hit again, but

instead, I called Ma from the dorm phone and asked if I could visit her even though it wasn't the weekend. I didn't explain why because it seemed too hard over the phone.

She was home, so half an hour later I stomped off the bus and up the stairs to her one bedroom apartment. I threw my bag against the wall inside the door and stalked past the small kitchen where Ma had turned from the stove to greet me.

Ma is about five foot, and since I was ten I've been taller than she is, but I don't feel taller. "Ro," she said, "what's wrong? What brings you home?"

"This *guy*." I kicked the couch, not hard.

She snapped at me anyway. "That is not ours. Did the furniture hurt you? Then leave it be."

So I smacked my fist into my palm and turned around. She'd come out to stand on the edge of the carpet that marked where the kitchen started, her brown ears perked, determination on her short, wide muzzle. I would never outgrow her ears; some of the other jackals back home said she had a fox's ears and sometimes she would say that her great-grandmother was a bat-eared fox. Our family had distinctive tan dots over the eyes and a ruff of black and silver fur that almost formed a collar, breaking only right at the hollow of our necks. I had more tan on my left paw than my right, where Ma's were both evenly tan; she said I'd gotten the dark right paw from my father.

Though our fur pattern looked mostly the same, our builds couldn't have been more different. Ma resembled Ori, a small, stout, full-chested jackal with thick legs and arms, in contrast to my stick-figure build. The coaches had told me I was going to have to add some muscle, though they were surprised at how strong I was.

Right now my muscles all felt tense enough to pop out of my skin. I clenched two fists and then let them go. "This guy, this fox who graduated from the school, he came back and I played him and I got an ace by him, but he said it was out and everyone just let him get away with it and I *lost!*"

Ma came forward to hold my wrists. "He's good, this fox?"

"Nobody else got a serve past him."

"Mm. He's proud?"

I nodded. "You should have seen him. He had a real shit-eating grin when he won."

Those were Marquize's words. I said them without thinking, and Ma lifted a paw and casually cuffed me across the muzzle. "Language, Ro," she said mildly.

I ducked my head and flattened my ears. "Sorry, Ma."

"So this boy, he had more to lose than you did."

I flicked my tail. "I guess."

"But you know you beat him."

"Uh-huh." At least on that one point.

"So." She spread her paws. "You know, and he knows. And now he must live with knowing."

I kicked at air, and she grabbed my tail and held it still. "Hey," she said. "You have fun?"

"Fun?" Honestly, I'd sort of lost track of fun in the excitement of proving myself. "I guess…I mean, teaming up with Marquize was fun…but that fox!"

She shook her head and went back to the kitchen. "Let the fox worry about the fox. All your teachers—"

"Coaches."

"All your coaches, your classmates, they will remind you to play hard. You must remind yourself to have fun."

I breathed out, and it felt like a big knot came undone in the middle of my chest and in my arms. My paws relaxed and I breathed again, and I nodded. "You're right. Sorry."

"Good. Come stir the pasta."

I walked into the little kitchen. Ma pulled down a jar of pasta sauce and opened it. "Ori says she is having trouble with the English chapter from your book. You will have time this weekend to work with her?"

"Sure. I'll come over Friday night."

"Nothing happens on the weekends still?"

"Tennis. But I can go back Saturday during the day. A lot of the guys go home."

"Tennis is important. It's why you're here."

"I know." I stirred the pasta, inhaling the steam. "And it's fun." But that wasn't the worm that was still gnawing at my gut, only partly quieted by Ma's words. I couldn't forget that if the school stopped thinking I was worth a scholarship, I wouldn't be the only one sent home.

Chapter Five

The following week, Frio took me aside during a practice session. He held out a small bag, embarrassment on his masked muzzle. "Hey," he said. "You played pretty well against Braden, and a few of the guys and I were thinking...y'know, since you go home on the weekends..."

I took the bag. My ears went askew because I was picking up on his confusion, but when I looked into the bag and saw the little box with a picture of a cell phone on it, my ears shot straight up.

"Seriously?" I dug the box out and dropped the bag on the bench.

"Yeah." He relaxed, his smile growing. "Now, uh, the school will pay for it as long as you don't go over the two hundred minutes of talking and fifty texts. We're rolling it into your scholarship money. So you have to keep your grades up and your tennis up, but if you keep going the way you have been, I don't see a problem with that. Officially it's to help you coordinate going home and stuff."

He seemed to be waiting for me to say something, so I said, "Thank you very much."

"You're welcome." He brought his muzzle closer to mine. "Unofficially, a couple of us wanted to do something nice since Braden was such a dick to you."

"It's all right," I said. "I had fun and he got to win. I'm over it." Marquize had taught me that phrase. Being "over" something meant it no longer had power over you, and while that might not be true, it was important to say it so that people didn't realize that you were still feeling threatened by it. I understood puffing yourself up for others perfectly well.

Frio, however, did not take my declaration of liberty from the memory of Braden as well as I'd hoped. "Don't be over it," he said. "You've got to take any incentive you can find to make you play harder. Play for revenge, play for pride, play for your mom, play for your dad."

"My father died in a war," I told him.

"Oh, I'm sorry. Play for his memory, then. Or play for your mom. She gave up a lot to come over here with you, didn't she?"

"I'm not sure about that. Anyway, she doesn't care how I play, only that I have fun."

"Hmph." He pursed his lips. "Okay, so maybe don't listen to her *too* much. About tennis, anyway."

Ma was plenty smart about a lot of things, tennis included, but I didn't want to argue with Frio when he'd given me such a nice gift. So I nodded and told him I'd let him know if I had any trouble setting up the phone, and I went back out to finish up my practice.

***

I didn't have any memories of my father. Until I got to the States, nobody really ever mentioned him much. Back home, if you had two parents, it meant that one of them worked in the government or military and could protect the other, or else your family was wealthy. I didn't know any of those families. They mostly lived in a secure neighborhood on the other side of the city. Ironically, I heard that crime was worse in the area around their neighborhood than it was in our little quarter, where mostly things stayed peaceful.

Ori and I only really talked about our father once, after the hyena took the three male cubs from the tennis club. We were walking home, our tails down, and she said, "Do you think they took our dad like that?"

"I don't know," I said. "Ma never said."

"I asked Miss Tonda about it and she said it happens here all the time."

"Wait." I put a paw on her shoulder. "What did you ask Miss Tonda about?"

"What battles happened right after I was born. He must have been in one of those, right?"

"I guess so." I hadn't really thought about it.

"I just want to know what happened to him." Her ears went down and she stared at the dirty ground, kicking a chunk of brick along in front of her. The sun was hot on our ears and the dust thick in our noses like it always was, but the orchards we walked by were flowering, and that as we crossed the street toward our house, Ngada the tailor had a new rack of red sarongs out. I remember looking at them and thinking that they looked like blood.

"Why won't Ma talk about him?" Ori wanted to know.

I didn't know that either, but I tried to explain it to her in a big brother kind of way. "Did you see how quiet everyone was when Pierre and Luongo and Peh-Peh went off with the hyena?"

"But we're talking about them now."

"But they're gone. If they don't come back…" I spread out my paws. "Then they're gone."

Ori thought about that and shook her head. "But if someone asked me about them, I would tell them what happened."

"Maybe Ma was alone for so long that she forgot."

"Maybe." Ori looked up at me. "You wouldn't ask her anyway."

I pushed her, but not hard, and she laughed. "You wouldn't!"

"I would," I said, but it was true; I hadn't asked Ma about our father at all. Maybe when I was younger, but I'd gotten the impression she didn't want to talk about him, so I'd stopped.

"I'm going to ask her," Ori decided. "It's been eleven years."

I didn't say anything, because I was torn between not wanting to upset Ma and finding out what had happened. But as it turned out, when we got home, Ori helped Ma with dinner and never brought up the subject of our father.

On our way to school I asked her what happened, and she said, "I just decided not to." Then she talked about the assignment she was presenting and I didn't push the issue.

That didn't mean I didn't think about my dad. When we saw video of battles on the news, footage of bodies covered in patches of blood that had attracted dust in clumps like a great beige fungus, I would search the images for jackal ears. When I was playing a game, especially when one of the older cubs threatened to beat me, I imagined my dad beside me telling me to fight on like he'd done—or was still doing, maybe.

When I was younger, I'd imagine he was a secret agent working on a spy mission, but when I was six, a teacher asked us to talk about our parents and I told the class, "My Ma teaches English and my dad is a spy." The next boy, Kiko, another jackal, said, "My dad disappeared when I was one and my Ma says he died."

I felt terrible, so I raised a paw and said, "I don't actually know where my dad is. He might be dead too."

Kiko looked grateful and the teacher said that if our parents were gone, it wasn't because they didn't love us, and that we should be thankful for the family we had. Some cubs had neither mother nor father and lived with an aunt, a grandmother, a cousin. After that day, I didn't tell anyone that dad was a spy. I just said he was gone.

***

I called Ori that night from my new phone, standing in Ma's kitchen while she retreated to the living room. I knew she could still hear me if she wanted to, but she had music on and her ears down so I trusted she wouldn't listen.

Ori was getting ready for school, so I talked to my aunt for a bit before my sister finally came on the line. "I got a new phone," I said. "As long as I keep the minutes down, we can talk for free for a little."

"Great!" She perked, and I could almost see her wagging her tail. "How did you get a phone?"

I told her how the teachers had given it to me after this match, and then I had to tell her about Braden, and about how arrogant he was and how much I wanted to beat him and…

"I get it," she said, amused. "You wanted to teach him a lesson."

"Yes. And I did! I got an ace down the outside line and he said it was out and nobody argued."

"So what?"

I breathed across the phone. "I'm afraid if I screw up they'll send me and Ma home."

"Aw, Ro." She laughed. "They ain't gonna send you home."

"'Ain't'? You're talking like a thug now Ma isn't there?"

She giggled again. "I told Kamina it was how everyone talked in America. You won't tell Ma, will you?"

"Just make sure you keep watching the good movies as well as the ones you like."

"So didn't your friend Marquize stand up for you?"

"He did, sort of. We were playing doubles. Ori, it was fun. When you come visit, I'll show you and we can play."

"I haven't played in years," she said, but her voice had a little slowness to it that she always got when she was lying.

"Kamina told Ma you were playing at the tennis center again," I guessed.

"Agh." She growled. "I told her not to."

"Why not? I think it's great."

"You know Ma. She will tell me that I should play as hard as you and maybe I will come to the States too. I want to have fun. I am happy here." She paused. "Except for Kamina."

"Is she making you walk to school with a friend again?"

"I wish it was only that." Ori paused and lowered her voice. "She made an appointment for me to go around to Miss Mareille's."

It felt like I was supposed to know what that was, but I didn't. "What does she do?"

"She arranges marriages."

I couldn't think of anything to say. Ori was only thirteen; none of the girls my age had been talking about marriage by the time I left. When I stayed silent, Ori went on. "She knows I'm young, but Miss Mareille can find a good match for me and by the time of the wedding, Kamina says I will be ready."

"Why?" I forced out.

"I don't know. I told her I didn't need to be married, and she said that I would be saving a life, that if a boy is married, they might not take him for the war."

"They took Father."

Ori didn't say anything to that right away. Finally she said, "I know. But Kamina says it's my Christian duty to be a mother and protect a family and help the jackal community grow. There are lions going around saying the lions should rule Lunda and Kamina says if they come into power then they might send more jackals to fight for them."

"What if a jackal came into power?"

She huffed softly into the phone. "Don't be silly."

"Well, why not? Over in Alharia they have a jackal president."

"In Alharia they don't have so many lions. It's jackals and fennecs and everyone else."

Alharia would be a good place for Ori except that they were all Muslim and spoke Arabic, so a Christian Kikongo-speaking jackal would not be very welcome there. "There just needs to be a good jackal leader," I said with the stubbornness of someone who had been learning World Cultures in a safe Pensa classroom for two months.

"Maybe I'll start training to do that." She laughed. "When I'm president, I will come over and visit you."

"You don't need to be married," I said. "I'm telling Ma."

"I think she already knows." Ori shifted around and when she spoke again, her voice sounded closer to the receiver. "I told Kamina that Ma didn't want me married, and she said, 'You're in my care now, and your Ma says I may decide your future.' I threatened to call Ma and she didn't care at all."

"Ma can't know. She'd never allow it."

"She knows."

"Hmph. I'm going to find out what's—"

My phone beeped, and I pulled it away from my ear to look at it. "Oh," I said. "My battery is low and we've been talking for thirty-six minutes."

"It's because you were so worked up over that fox," Ori said. "And I shouldn't have told you about the marriage. Really, Ro, don't worry about it. I can handle Kamina. I'll go along with it and I'll figure out a way out of it."

"I want to call you more often," I growled.

"You know what? Give me the number. I can call you from the school and that way it won't use your minutes up."

So I did, and hung up, then went inside to where Ma was sitting on the couch reading. "Ori's getting married," I said, standing there with my arms folded.

Ma flicked her ears and turned the page in her book. "Already?"

"You knew about this. You told Kamina to do it."

"No." She shook her head slowly. "I told Kamina to take care of Ori as best she could. She thinks Ori should be married, and I'm thousands of kilometers away. I'm in no position to argue, and it wouldn't be good for Ori for me to argue."

"She's still your daughter!"

"Lower your voice," Ma said. "Kamina knows the situation there and she's very smart. I trust her judgment."

"So you think it's all right for a girl to be betrothed at thirteen?"

At that, Ma did lower her book and look up at me. "I was," she said.

I curled my tail around my leg and sat down on the armrest of the couch. "What?"

"I was promised to your father at thirteen. My mother, God rest," she made the sign of the cross and looked up at the ceiling, "thought it would stabilize our family to be joined to his." Her ears flicked back and she brought one paw to the front of her muzzle. "Your father was seventeen and his father worked in the government."

I'd never met any of my grandparents. "What happened to—to my grandfather?"

"Heart attack." Ma slid a bookmark into her book, closed it, and set it on the end table. "He was dead before they got him out of the building."

My head ducked and I made the sign of the cross reflexively. In the tennis locker room, there was a defibrillator that I'd read the instructions to a couple weeks ago. I'd thought then that I'd never known anyone who'd died of a heart attack. "And grandmother?" I said softly.

Ma shook her head. "There's no point in going over all this. You just work as hard as you can and don't worry about your past."

"I can't worry about my past because I don't have any," I said, and swung my legs off the couch.

"Rochi," she called, but I was still thinking about Ori getting married, about shadowy grandparents and a father I'd never known, and I wondered what he would have thought about his daughter getting betrothed at thirteen. Had he insisted that he and Ma wait until she was sixteen before getting married? I knew that she had been roughly seventeen when she had me, but that was just a number, and it could also be a lie.

Ma didn't come after me when I went to the bedroom and lay down on her bed staring at the ceiling. I'd been feeling more at home at school, but this pushed me farther from the other cubs. None of them had a younger sister getting betrothed, or a dead father (though I hadn't told anyone here about my father, so they might be hiding dead fathers or mothers too).

But Ori...

I closed my eyes. I would just have to earn the money to fly her over here; that was all. When she was away from Kamina and back in Ma's custody, Ma would decide what was right for her.

Chapter Six

Back at school, one of the things I hadn't expected was the way that match against Braden changed other things. All the guys had seen my ace, even if none of them stood up for me, and I started getting more offers to play. "Hey Rocky," said a cougar named Bret over lunch, "bet you can't get an ace on me."

Yu, whose English was improving, offered to help me navigate the paperwork of being an international student. And Kim, a coyote in our class, cornered me and asked if I'd play her. "What," I said, thinking of my sister, "like a battle of the sexes?"

"Hah." She shook her head and her ears, as large as mine, flipped upright. "You wish."

Coyotes unsettled me because they looked so like jackals and yet the colorations were different. They had many of our mannerisms and the muzzles and ears matched exactly, more closely than the other canids at the school, none of which I'd encountered back in Lunda. Foxes were skinnier and more flamboyant, wolves stockier. I'd never met a maned wolf, but there was one named Veronica in our class and she looked like a fox who'd been stretched out. She and Kim hung around together a lot, but she was quieter; every now and then she would drop in a single smart comment.

Usually the boys and girls didn't play together, but there wasn't a rule saying we couldn't, so in the evenings following that visit from Braden, a bunch of us started hanging out around the courts. We'd get Bolts from the 7-11 down the street and would hit the ball back and forth, rarely scoring games, sometimes playing doubles (there's a thing called 'mixed doubles' where a guy and a girl on each side play each other), sometimes singles, occasionally one-on-two like Braden had done. And the ones who weren't playing sat around and talked. As we got closer to Christmas, a few couples coalesced out of the chaotic movements of our group.

I wasn't used to this world where you could date whatever girls you wanted to. The older boys back home joked about going to the "Pussy Hotel" (I'm translating, but it's about that crude) with girls, and I thought that was a real place until well into my first year in the States. But it was understood that Ma would find a nice jackal family with a daughter my age or younger (though not thirteen, like Ori was), and we'd get married, and if another family with an eligible daughter came along, I'd marry her too. There were a lot more girls than boys back home; it's not hard to figure out why.

But here, the whole thing was not only reversed but stood on end. Species wasn't important in the States—well, I guess it was to some people. Most of my friends had same-species parents, though Kim's parents were a coyote and a wolf, and Veronica's parents were a possum and a tiger.

Some really religious people believed that you should only date within your species. There was a bear named Loris, not a tennis cub, whom I heard lecturing people about dating their own species, and he had a cross around his neck. Malik got yelled at once by Loris when he was going around with Veronica. But he told me (Malik did, not Loris) that that attitude was "provincial" and "outdated," and if he did want to marry Veronica, there were thousands of adoption agencies and surrogates (that means that if they wanted a Geoffroy's Cat cub, he would find a girl to be the mother and they'd adopt her, and if they wanted a maned wolf cub, I guess they would find a maned wolf guy to sleep with Veronica). There was a Jewish wolf named March who told me another time that he could only date within his religion, but that different species couples were okay (and that while they didn't so much hold with adoption, surrogates were just fine).

We were Christians too, but when I asked Ma, she said that God wants us to have a family and love them, and He doesn't care what species they are. She said we marry within our species because we don't have the money to do surrogates (although we do have a lot of adoptions, but that's also because a lot of cubs are orphaned).

I guess this is a good time to talk about God. I always went to church with Ma back home, but here in the States they didn't have any ECC churches, so we prayed at home on Sundays. Some of the other cubs went to church on Sunday, but others, like Marquize, didn't worship publicly at all.

It took me a while to get my head around that, and I actually had a really good conversation with Marquize in mid-December. "You're not even going to church on Christmas?" I asked. Ma had found a nearby church that was something close to ours, not enough to go to weekly, but enough for Christmas services.

Marquize was sitting next to me against the fence as Veronica and Kim played on the court we'd recently vacated. Malik was watching the girls, and Yu was talking to his girlfriend, a lithe otter named Brittany whose giggle cut across the court like a fault call on a serve. Bret wasn't with us that night, and neither were Pom and Dom, who we called the fox twins even though Pom was a red fox from the northeast and Dom an arctic fox from the northwest. A cool breeze stirred the humid air and ruffled our fur, which felt good over my tongue as I panted. Marquize's shirt lay in a pile beside him and he brushed his paw through his chest fur as we talked. "Nah," he said. "Christmas is home with family."

"So you really don't go to church at all."

He grinned at me and let his tongue loll out in an imitation of my panting. I gulped my tongue back but a moment later it was out again, and he laughed. "In my case it'd be a mosque, but still...Nah, I told you. I'm not very religious."

I stretched one leg, then the other, trying not to show how annoyed I was at my tongue. "I hope you don't mind me asking, but then...how do you explain the world?"

"Science," he said with a shrug, and dug into his pocket for a tennis ball. He dropped it and caught it on the short bounce. "Gravity, light, all that."

"Yes, but..." I gestured up at the clouds. "Why?"

"Why what?"

"Why...why is everything here?"

He bounced the tennis ball again. "Why does there have to be a why?"

That one floored me. "Haven't you ever thought about that?"

"Not really." He pursed his lips. "The world just is, and we make of it what we make of it."

"Okay, but...if we weren't given the Earth for a purpose, then what purpose do we have?"

"I dunno." He grinned and held the fuzzy yellow ball in his paw.

"I guess we just figure it out as we go along."

"What if we're wrong?"

"Okay." He turned toward me. "What if there is a God, and He made the world and He wants me to do something, only He hasn't been able to tell me what in a way I could understand. What if I do the best I can with the information I have? Would He really be upset at me for that?"

Nobody had ever asked me to rule on a religious question before. I stammered out, "I—I mean—I don't—"

"God's forgiving, right?" I nodded. "So if there is no God, then I don't have to worry. And if there is, then He'll forgive me as long as I don't really fuck things up."

Malik used the f-word a lot, and Marquize had lately taken to it as well. I still couldn't bring myself to say it. "But what if you don't understand because you didn't try hard enough?" I asked.

"Well, whose fault is that?" he said, and laughed again, but then I guess I looked serious or something and he reached out to pat me on the leg. "I don't know," he said. "How do you know you've looked hard enough? You have to go by what you feel, right? I haven't felt anything, but I guess you have."

"Kind of." I wasn't sure what he'd think if I admitted it, but he looked encouraging so I went on. "Our church taught us that God has a plan for all of us and if we follow His rules and eventually the plan will be revealed to us."

"Hum." He nodded, and then looked toward the court. "So your plan is like, meet a nice jackal girl, have a family, support them with tennis?"

So I told him what Ma told me about not having to marry a jackal, and then added, "Our Church also teaches that I'm supposed to use my good fortune to help people in need. If I start making money, I will send some of it back home."

He leaned back against the fence and smiled. "I'm glad you don't have to marry a jackal. Might be a long time 'til you found one here in the States."

"There's a community down in Las Palmas." Ma had looked them up and we had both said we should visit them sometime, but neither of us had felt any particular urgency to do so. I think she was waiting for me to be ready to marry, and wanted me to know there were options. "And there's dating services on the Internet. Every time I check the news there's another ad for one. 'Find your perfect partner—exotics too!'"

Marquize laughed. "'Find your one in a hundred or one in a hundred thousand.' But you don't want just anyone, you know. You want someone in the life."

"What life?"

"The tennis life." He gestured to Veronica and Kim. "Someone who goes to tournaments and knows the pressure. You won't see each other all the time, but at least you'll be at some of the same places, going through the same things. Cubs on the junior circuit get together all the time."

That was another thing I was going to have to look forward to figuring out when I left the school to be a pro. Marquize went on. "You like Veronica or Kim? Probably they're the closest thing to a jackal here."

I glanced at him, then down at the girls, who were changing sides of the court. "They're okay," I said, because I couldn't tell if there was an answer he wanted me to give, and I honestly didn't really feel anything either way. They were nice, and I liked hanging out with them, but not as much as I liked spending time with Marquize. I knew what it meant to be in a relationship like Malik and Veronica were, but I hadn't felt that with anyone myself.

Which wasn't to say that I was unaware of sex. You would think it had been Marquize who'd first shown me how to get porn on the Internet, but actually it was Bret.

The cougar had been working on a math problem with me, both of us helping each other through the tangled mess of beginning trigonometry, making angles with our fingers and circles with our pencils. It had been more than an hour, and as we finished one online problem, he said, "Wanna see something?"

I said, "Sure," and in the time it took him to open a new browser window, I was staring at mostly-naked females of six different species. I remember the fox and the horse because the fox had her head thrown back and the rows of white teeth looked like a jackal's, and the horse's breasts were the unbelievable size of my head.

"Pretty cool, huh?" Bret's little black ears flicked forward, intent on the screen. "Check it out."

He clicked, and without warning we were watching a video of
a big male wolf pumping away at the backside of a raccoon as she
fondled her breasts. "You gotta pay to see the whole thing," he said a
little wistfully, "but the freebies aren't bad, huh?"

"Yeah," I choked out. I'd heard the phrase "porn on the Internet"
so constantly at Palm Gables that it had faded into the background,
a kind of uncharted territory that we cubs were warned against, that
we knew the boundaries of but not what lay beyond. And here was
this cougar, my classmate, taking me across the fence and squarely
into it, giving the words texture and meaning and lots of other sensa-
tions. I wanted to be that wolf; hell, I wanted to be that raccoon. I
just wanted to be involved in something like that.

"What's one of your favorite sites?" he asked, fingers poised.

"Oh, uh." My mind was a blank. I think even if I'd had a favorite site, I wouldn't have been able to say the words.

"You've looked at porn before, right?" Now he'd turned toward me and his eyes crinkled in amusement, the inevitable prelude to mockery.

"Sure," I said. "Porn is all over the Internet." The words, so familiar, had gained a new and immediate reality for me. Why would Bret have assumed I knew about it?

Oh. The previous week, he and Dom and Marquize and I had been talking about porn on the Internet. Dom had been talking about the pay site he liked—his parents didn't look at his credit card statement or he found one that would hide it or something. And Bret had said he liked the free sites and Marquize had agreed and I'd said, "Yeah, me too," or something, so as not to seem ignorant.

I thought back to our World Cultures lessons on using the Internet for research. "I, uh, I don't just go to one site. I search for what I'm looking for and then I try a bunch of sites until I get a picture of the…" I swallowed the word "truth" because that didn't really seem like what was happening on the screen. "Porn."

"True dat." He tapped his fingers over the keys. "So what do you search for usually?"

Why did he care so much? Now, looking back, I think he was probably bored with the sites he knew and wanted some variety, but at the time I felt cornered, tested. What would I search for? I'd honestly never thought about it. "Jackals," I blurted out. "Jackals having sex. With other people who aren't jackals." At that moment, that was the most daring thing I could think of.

Thank God for the Internet. He typed "jackal sex" into the search bar and about eight different sites came right up. I pointed at one. "That one's good," I said, saved by the maxim that when you are a fourteen-year-old boy, there is no such thing as bad porn.

We looked at two or three more sites, enough for me to calm down (in one respect) and to notice that the header of the browser window said, "Private." So when Bret was ready to go back to math, I said, "How do you get that 'private' at the top of your window?"

And that is how I learned to hide my browsing history. I wouldn't say I was addicted to porn after that, no more than most of my friends I talked to, but at least once a week I found some private time on a computer and looked at picture after picture. It helped that I was living in the private dorm room during the week, so I didn't even have to worry about Ma looking over my shoulder. And the next time Bret and I worked on an assignment together, I was the one to say, "Hey, I want to show you something."

Naturally, I shared some of my finds with Marquize, too, but he was cool on them, not nearly as interested as Bret. He didn't mind looking, but most of the sites I showed him were met with a shrug and a "that's pretty good," and his scent didn't change the way Bret's (and, I suspected, mine) did when we watched it. It wasn't until October that I started to guess why.

A lot of the students followed football—the States version, not the kind we played at home. I hadn't followed most other sports in the States; I was there to play tennis. But when my classmates talked baseball or football, I didn't want to be left out, so I picked up a little about those sports here and there. Baseball was about athleticism and finesse, a lot more like tennis: running fast, getting the ball past a bat, hitting the ball. Football was more like tennis mixed with boxing: you had to get a ball past a team of other people who could hit you and knock you down.

Anyway, in October one of the football players told everyone he was gay. By "everyone," I mean he was at a press conference and they said "Hey, are you gay?" and he said, "That's completely true." Or something like that.

I heard the story from Dom at lunch. The arctic fox had a bunch of friends back in the northwest who texted each other all the time, so basically he either had his racket or a phone in his paws at all times. At lunch, of course, it was the phone, his claws tapping while he ate with the other paw and our conversation went on around him. This time, though, he stopped to tell us all the news, as one of his friends was watching TV and it had just been reported.

Pom and Bret got their laptops out and connected, and pretty soon we were staring at the story and the face of this tiger, a player for a team called the Chevali Firebirds. They said he was a defensive player, but he didn't sound defensive to me at all, just very straightforward. I stayed quiet to hear what everyone else thought of this, and somewhat to my surprise, most of the guys said it was cool.

I knew what gay people were in the way that I knew what dingoes were: a kind of people different from me who lived somewhere else. The boys back in Lunda used 'gay' as a generic insult without even knowing what it meant. By fourteen, I understood that some boys wanted to date boys instead of girls, but I wasn't quite sure what that meant. Certainly the kinds of activity I'd been introduced to on the Internet would not be possible between two boys.

The other thing we occasionally heard about gay people was that they were evil and satanic. We had a pastor for a year who told us that we had to cast out gay people, but when Ori and I asked Ma about it, she said we didn't have to worry. And indeed, that pastor didn't last very long, and the next one didn't say anything about gay people. So at the time this tiger came out, I thought that gay people had something wrong with them, but they weren't evil, and that this tiger was kind of like a drug addict telling the world about his problem and vowing to get help.

And that was why I missed the significance of all my friends saying, "I wonder who his boyfriend is" and "hope they don't beat him up on the field," and into a lull in the conversation, I said, "He can still play?"

"Well, sure," Bret said. "Why wouldn't he?"

Everyone looked at me, and my ears went back. "I don't know," I said. "I don't know how long…I mean, will he take care of it after the championship?"

"Take care of what?"

Now I knew I'd said something wrong and I didn't know how to fix it. "Forget it," I mumbled.

The table was silent for about a week, as I recall, and then Pom said, "There's gotta be more of them in the league," and the conversation went on around me. The only thing I remember was when the boys turned to asking if anyone in our school was gay, and after a couple names were tossed around, Bret said, "You know who…" and they went quiet.

When I looked up, their eyes darted away from mine. I flushed even more; did they think I was gay? But then a moment later, Marquize sat down beside me with his lunch. "Hey," he said, "What's everyone talking about?"

They filled him in while I stayed quiet, and Marquize didn't say a lot either. "Good for him," was all, and then he turned to me. "Hey Rocky, I need to work on my passing shots. You game to play some net this afternoon?"

And that was it as far as Marquize was concerned. I thought he knew what I'd said somehow and didn't want to talk to me about it, so I was quiet all the rest of that day.

I asked Ma again that night about gay people, and she asked me if one of the other boys had "tried something" with me. I said it was about the football player and turned on our TV to the sports channel where it was all over: his face, his words, the press conference, every single wolf and bear and deer and rabbit giving their opinion on what it meant for him, for the sport, for everyone he played with.

"Rocky," she said, "you let people live their lives and you worry about your life. Don't listen to anyone who says different or who says God knows what they should tell other people to do."

"But it's a disease or something, isn't it? Like Pastor Portway said?"

She sighed. "Some people think that. Some people say it's evil. Some people say it's natural. You can't worry about that. All you can worry about is tennis."

So I did.

Chapter Seven

Tennis wasn't my only worry, though. Two weeks later the phone bill for my first month arrived, and I was shocked and ashamed to see how expensive it was. "But Ori called me," I protested when Ma showed me the bill. "It shouldn't cost me anything."

"Did you ask them?" Ma was unruffled as always.

"No…" But I thought I'd understood how phones worked.

She told me to stir the bean soup. "Next time you will know."

"Yes," I said, stirring. It smelled of home; somehow Ma was able to get the spices she knew and had found a place to buy the right kind of beans, or at least close enough. I closed my eyes and could almost feel Ori standing beside me asking if it was done yet. "But I still have to pay this now. Where will I get the money?"

"Talk to the school," she said.

My monthly stipend—outside of my meals—would barely cover the bill, and leave me nothing for the rest of the month. "But…"

"You made the problem." She checked the oven for her bread. "You fix the problem. Own up to it."

Talking to Ma was one thing. But going to Frio, who'd given me the phone and had instructed me to bring him the bill—that was something else. Days went by and I slunk around in the routine of the school, going to classes in the morning, playing tennis in the afternoons, practicing more in the evenings with the group who were becoming my friends. The phone bill hung over me every minute, a burning guilty shame, and finally after about three days Marquize took me aside after we'd finished a match.

"You suck," he said. "And I don't mean like that football player."

I didn't even think about what he meant by the last part because I knew the first part meant I wasn't playing well. And if I didn't play well, I wouldn't get to stay here and Ma and I would have to go back home. "Sorry," I said.

"I don't think you hit a first serve that whole set, your backhand was sitting up there, and you're reacting late to everything."

"I know."

He poked me in the chest. "So what's going on?"

I stumbled back and into one of the benches beside the court, where my legs gave way and I sat down hard on my tail. I yelped and pulled it free, and Marquize sat beside me. "Sorry," he said, tapping his head the way Coach did. "But tennis is up here."

"I know." I took a breath. "I spent too much money on my phone bill. I don't know what to do. I owe the company five hundred dollars."

He blinked at me. "Wow. Your ma doesn't have that?"

I shook my head miserably. "I can't go to Frio. He did such a nice thing getting me the phone, and I messed it up."

"Come on." He got to his feet in a quick motion and grabbed my upper arm with a paw, pulling me with him.

"Wait!" I squeaked, but he dragged me across the court to the ferret, who was trying to enter something on a small handheld computer.

"Hey, Frio," Marquize said. "Rocky needs to tell you something. Go easy on him."

The ferret put down the computer, looking glad for the distraction. "What's up, Rocky?"

I couldn't talk at first, but then he remembered about the phone and asked me and it all came spilling out. I got out the amount of the bill and how sorry I was and then as I started to ask him if I would have to go to jail, my throat closed up and the words got harder to force out.

"Dude," Marquize said, gripping my shoulder. "Whoa, hey, I didn't realize—you're not going to jail. We'll figure something out."

"Yeah, don't sweat it," Frio said. "Let me ask around. But what the hell happened?"

I explained the problem, and the ferret smacked his head. "Jeez, I just assumed you knew how cell phones work. No, no, anytime you're connected it counts as minutes. You should always call your sister, because then it's free for her, but yeah, you still have to keep it under two hundred minutes."

"I'm sorry," I said.

"Hey, don't be. I'm the one who feels like a jerk. We tried to do a nice thing for you and it got you in more trouble. I can't get you the money, but I think we can loan it to you and find a way for you to pay it back."

"Like a job?" Marquize squinted at him. "I thought Coach didn't want us taking jobs."

"What Coach don't know..." Frio rested a paw on my shoulder and squeezed. "Anyway, Rocky's talented enough and motivated enough. I know he won't use the job as an excuse to slack off."

"I won't!" I lifted my head. "I'll work. I'll do whatever it takes. Thank you so much..." I couldn't figure out how to express my relief at having found a way out of debt. Prison, forcible return home, an end to tennis: they all dissolved away.

"All right, all right." Frio laughed. "You wanna get back out there? I should have something by the end of the week."

I sprang back out on the court and played better than I had in days. When I got home, I helped Ma cheerfully and told her I'd resolved the cell phone problem. She was worried about the prospect of a job, but said she didn't think the coach would do anything that might harm my career.

Thursday, Frio took me aside and gave me an address to go to Friday night after practice. "Friend of mine runs a loading dock," he said. "Help them move some boxes four-five hours a night and they'll give you ten bucks an hour."

"That's...that's one hundred dollars a weekend?" I stared at him.

"Hey, you're good at math. Yeah." He seemed apologetic. "I know it'll take five or six weeks to pay it off, but my buddy will give you an advance so you can send it all at once."

"I can't believe I can make a hundred dollars in a weekend."

Frio laughed. "Rocky," he said, "if you graduate from Palm Gables, you won't cross the street to earn a hundred bucks in a weekend."

Later I asked Marquize what Frio had meant. "Why would I not cross the street for a hundred dollars?"

"What he meant was that you'll be earning so much more in a weekend that a hundred will seem like nothing," Marquize explained. "You know that when they say the major tournament prizes are in the millions, they mean dollars, right?"

We were sitting in plastic red chairs on the patio of our favorite fast-food place, Meat'n'Malt, both of us with steak sandwiches and thick milkshakes, his chocolate, mine strawberry. The steak sandwiches were my favorite States food, and close to my favorite thing ever: the browned meat, the greasy, dripping cheese, the bread, soft and chewy but firm enough to keep the sandwich together, and the glorious sweetness of the grilled onions on it. I always saved the strawberry milkshake for when I was done with the sandwich because I didn't want anything else in my mouth while I was eating it. Now I paused with the last bite of my sandwich held to my muzzle, and Marquize's gently teasing question made the sandwich bitter for a moment. "I know that," I snapped. "I just didn't…think of it."

"Okay, well, you'll be making thousands if you play well in tournaments even at the Futures level."

I hadn't thought about the junior tournaments much; they were the better part of a year away. I scarfed down (another expression Marquize had taught me after watching me eat my first steak sandwich) the last of my sandwich and reached for the shake. "What about the junior tournaments at majors?"

"Yeah, they have prize money, but it goes to your guardian. When you get onto the pro tour, the money belongs to you."

"I don't mind if it goes to Ma," I said. "She'll look out for me."

"You're lucky, then." Marquize took a bite of his own sandwich. "Most cubs can't wait to get the money away from their parents. Most cubs can't wait to get everything away from their parents."

"What about yours?"

"Oh, they're fine." He chewed on his sandwich and looked across the patio at the street, the parade of SUVs going by. "Look at all the soccer moms."

I followed his gaze. "Are they all taking their cubs to play soccer?"

"It's an expression. Moms who get cars that are too big so they can carry their three cubs and all the gear for whatever sport they're into."

I washed down the sandwich with the last of my Coke and then reached for my shake. "Do most cubs' moms not work?"

His hazel eyes turned on me. "Mine does. My parents run their business together. So, y'know." He shrugged. "I'll see them at fall break and on the holidays."

Before I could go on, he said, "It's cool. They're not smothering me, they're letting me do my thing. Not like Bret. You know he calls his parents every night? They want progress reports."

"Wow." Even though I still lived partly at Ma's place, there were days when I didn't call her.

"They say he's spending enough of their money that they want to make sure he's making good use of it."

"I guess that's fair," I said, but dubiously.

Marquize tore off a bite of his sandwich. "If they're going to send us here, they should trust us to want to be here. Bret works hard."

I nodded and said, "Yeah," but I was wondering inside whether maybe Bret worked harder because he had to report to his parents.

***

That Friday night, I went down to the address Frio had given me and found a large open space with three trucks backed up to it. When I poked my head around a corner, I saw a dozen guys, all at least one and a half times my weight (if not my height), either stacking boxes or loading them onto trucks. A big bear driving a forklift noticed me wandering around and said, "Hey, cub, can I help you?"

"My name's Rocky," I said. "I'm looking for Genten?"

"Gen!" the bear roared, so loud I jumped. "Cub here to see ya!"

I flicked my ears around and scanned the warehouse. Up on a metal catwalk halfway up the back wall, a stout wolf was looking at me. "You Frio's cub?" he called.

"Yeah." I waved up.

He gestured me up the metal stairs at the end of the catwalk. I hurried over and climbed them, ears folding at the clanging my steps made, and met Gen at the door of an office with a nameplate that read, "Genten Careyon, Shift Foreman," below one that read, "Lantz Mattock, General Manager." The wolf, a grey wolf with black-tipped ears and mussed fur, held the door and waved me in. "Bill," he yelled down from the catwalk, "when you're done with four-sixty, prep four-eighty for midnight."

I caught Bill's, "Ten-four," reply and filed it away as I walked in and sat down on a chair. Gen came in a moment later and sat down behind the big desk.

He picked up a pair of thin-rimmed glasses and hooked them behind his ears, looking down at a paper on his desk, and then picked up a pen and tapped it. "All right," he said. "Ten bucks an hour, max six hour shifts. That what Frio told you?"

"Yes," I said. "But I can work longer if I have to."

He grinned. "He told me you will show up here at nine, and I have to drive you home at three myself. Got it?"

"Yes, sir."

His smile got wider. "All right. Job's easy. Move boxes where me or Ralph—you'll meet Ralph—tell you. Sometimes you might just have to keep the floor clean. Sometimes I'll ask you to man the phones up here. It's easier for me if I can supervise the floor without worrying about people calling in. Most of the time they'll have messages with updated times. You write those down and get them to me on the floor. Got it?"

I nodded. "I can do whatever you need, sir."

"We might also ask you to go fetch food for the guys around one am, when we get a lunch break."

"From where?" My ears perked. I knew our Meat'n'Malt was open 24 hours, but it was a couple miles away and the buses didn't run after midnight.

Gen picked up a menu from the desk, and I read the words, "Sunshine Diner." "These guys know us," he said. "You ready to get started?"

"Yes, sir," I said with what I hoped was enough enthusiasm.

I knew I was strong enough to move boxes even if I didn't look it, but I only did that a few times, and only with the lightest boxes. My main job seemed to be to stay out of the way those first two nights. When Gen drove me home the second night, he gave me six one hundred-dollar bills. "There's your pay," he said, "and an advance for the next four weekends. Frio told you not to mention this to anyone, right?"

"Right," I said, though he'd only really said not to mention it to Coach.

"All right. See you next Saturday, then."

I thought it was great that he trusted me so much after just one weekend to advance me my pay for the next whole month. Frio only asked me about it the following Monday, when he said, "Everything go okay this weekend?" and I said it did, and he said, "Good," and he set me back to working on my drills.

The following weekend, I showed up right at nine Friday night, and Gen looked slightly confused to see me, like he didn't remember. "Hi, Rocky," he said after a moment. "Okay, why don't you go along and help Donno tonight?"

Donno, a big tiger who wore an eyepatch and talked with a broad Southern drawl, told me to grab a broom and keep clear the path his team was taking from the warehouse to the trucks. The floor was already spotless, but when I pointed this out, he said, "Make sure it stays that way."

After about an hour of leaning on my broom, I had plenty of time to figure out some things. Clearly I wasn't being paid for actual work. I'd heard many stories of workers in the States being lazy, of huge sums of money being paid out for labor worth a tenth of it, of people being paid for three jobs at once, having done none of them. In all the cases, I'd assumed that the person getting the money would have asked for it, would have made some arrangement whereby he could get paid for nothing. And yet here I was, willing to work honestly and being told to hold a broom and watch a floor for ten dollars an hour.

On the way home that night, I asked Gen, "What are you getting from Frio?"

The wolf didn't startle, but his ears flicked and he turned to me. "You don't need to know stuff like that."

I exhaled. "Okay. I don't care, really. But if I'm going to be paid, I don't want to stand around the warehouse holding a broom for six hours."

"Fine by me." He pulled up in front of Ma's apartment building. "You don't have to show up if you don't want to."

"No, I want to work." Then I yawned, which didn't help my case. "I want to load boxes and do stuff."

He rested his paws on the steering wheel, tapping it. His car smelled like wolf and fast food and more wolves: he had a wife, who usually sat where I was now, and at least two cubs, one pretty young. That wasn't from the scent; there was a car seat in back. "Look," he said, "you'd just be in the way."

"My Ma raised me to work for what I get," I said. The "my

mother raised me" phrase had been coming around school a lot lately, mostly in the "my mother didn't raise no fools" variant, but I thought it could be applied more broadly. "Would you want your cubs to just take handouts?"

"Jesus," he said, "you sound like one of them fuckin' radio assholes. Hell, yes, I'd want my cubs to take handouts. You don't get given much in this life, so you should take whatever you can."

"If you don't want me to work," I said, "I'll find some other way to pay you back."

"Rocky." He sounded like Coach Murphy trying to explain angles on the tennis court to Bret. "I been paid back already. You want to earn what you got, you work as hard as you can and make Frio look good so he can get a promotion. Okay?"

"I'm already doing that," I said. "I want to work for you. At least three more weekends."

His eyes met mine full on, and they shone with the reflection of the streetlamp outside. "Jesus Dog," he said. "Fine. Fine. Okay, you show up next Saturday and I'll find something for you to do. Something worth ten bucks an hour."

"Thank you," I said, and got out.

True to his word, when I came over next Friday night, he sat me down in front of his computer. "Okay," he said. "This shit takes me like two hours to do after we're finished loading, so you should be able to finish it in six. What I need you to do is take all these invoices and enter them into this program like this." He demonstrated which field corresponded to what. "Then when the team leads come up with a completed manifest, enter those into this half of the page like this." Another demonstration. "Then you double check what you entered and click 'Enter' down here. Got it?"

"So I should wait until a manifest comes up before entering the invoice?"

He thought about that. "Yeah, I guess so. Otherwise you'd get stuck entering a form and have to go to another one, right?"

When he'd left, I examined the program. I hadn't worked much with computers compared to most people in the States, but I'd used the one in our tennis center a lot, and Ma had gotten my help with the ones at the school when she couldn't figure something out. Ori and I were both good with them. After a little playing around, I figured out that you could actually enter stuff on one form and then start a new one without submitting the first one. So I entered all the invoices on his desk and then, when Donno brought up the first manifest, I found the invoice it corresponded to, entered it, and submitted the form.

Gen brought me a drink and I showed him what I'd done. "Well, I'll be," he said. "You're a smart one, ain'tcha?"

My tail wagged. "Do you have anything else for me to do?"

He found some other tasks he'd been putting off, and by the time I left Saturday morning at three a.m. I felt a lot better about myself. I think Gen felt better about me, too, because even after I'd paid off the six hundred he'd given me, he asked if I wanted to keep coming by and working.

Of course, the work at Palm Gables got harder in October and November, too. In September the coaches were putting us through our paces to see what we could do and where they needed to shore up our game. Once they'd figured that out, they drilled us over and over. Footwork, gameplay, even sportsmanship lessons took up our practice sessions. For example, any time our opponent made a good shot, we were taught to applaud them with our racket on a paw. Just a couple moments, an acknowledgment, but it made a lot of difference. The first time Marquize applauded a serve of mine, I flushed and felt even better than I had for scoring the point. Back home we didn't applaud, but we did shake paws after every game, said, "Good game" to each other whether we meant it or not, and always behaved civilly. Tennis, we'd been told, was a noble sport. I'd always loved the courtesy and ritual of it.

The rest of the instruction was harder. Some of the things they taught were the opposite of how I'd learned them, such as where to direct your shots. I had always simply aimed where my opponent was not, forcing him to run, but here the more skilled players positioned themselves so that they could cover a good deal of the court at once. Marquize had done this in our first game, pushing my attempts to pass him farther and farther until I made an error. I learned how to spot weaknesses in a forehand or backhand, how to aim shots precisely to my opponent's weakness, and more, to be able to predict where the shot would come back and already be moving to hit it before it even touched his racket.

Marquize and I, among the tallest, were also among the newest. Some of our classmates had been learning these techniques since they were six. So while our height gave us an advantage in the service game, we both sat far down in the overall hierarchy of the class. My ace against Braden was seen as an indication of my potential, but as late as Christmas break, Marquize and Jeff, the wolf, were the only students I won sets from on a regular basis.

Besides tennis, I had the other classes, and here Ma made sure I did not fall behind. She brought home stories of all her students from the three classes she substituted for, all the ones who had so much potential and failed to apply themselves. If those stories failed to motivate me (and sometimes I did grow numb and stubborn and say things like, "But those cubs can't hit a tennis ball for squat," being very proud of myself for having learned to substitute "squat" for "shit," which I would say around Marquize), she would tell me the stories of cubs back home for whom the ability to read and write could be the difference between sitting in a government office or lying dead on a hill. And most often then I would say that we weren't home anymore, and she would say, "For now," and I'd get angry or scared or both.

When I felt overwhelmed by my schoolwork and tennis and Ma wasn't helping, I'd tell her about Marquize, who barely ever heard from his parents, or Bret, who called his "the Anti-Fun League," and would point out that my grades generally surpassed both of theirs.

"You don't have to please them with your grades," Ma would inevitably say. "You have to please me."

Usually after one of those arguments I would call Ori and we would talk about how unreasonable Ma could be. Those were the times I felt closest to my sister, like we were calling only across a town and not an ocean. And those conversations would end with Ori saying, "But Ro, you know, you must do well in school and make money. I don't want to see you back here."

English was the hardest of my classes, which I was not used to. I'd excelled in English back home and expected the same here. But English here went beyond simple grammar and vocabulary. We were expected to read books and talk about them. I did very poorly on the first book, *The Scarlet Letter*, and when we moved on to *Huckleberry Finn*, the teacher asked me if I needed extra help. But Ma wouldn't pay for a tutor; she insisted on helping me herself.

That book was a struggle, because Ma insisted on making me work to look up the words neither of us knew, and I said that if she was going to help me, she should actually help me. So I failed the first test on the book, and when I came home that night I lay staring at the ceiling with visions in my head of a failing grade in English and Coach Murphy calling me into his office to shake his head regretfully and say, I'm sorry, we would love to keep you, but you just can't understand English.

I worked with Ma more after that, and it helped that the story was a good one, about a cub who'd run away from home and joined with an ex-slave on his journey. The slave was a jungle otter like the ones we'd known growing up, and the cub was a river otter like Brittany (only much poorer, of course), so it was easy to see how their friendship had come about. We talked in class about the abolition of slavery and how jungle and river otters, like jackals and coyotes, like cheetahs and cougars, formed friendships.

One day after that, Bret called me and Marquize "ex-slaves," and Frio heard it and told him it wasn't appropriate. Neither of us thought he meant it to be mean; after all, we all liked the character in the book, and he'd only said, "let's watch the ex-slaves play." But it was weird, we agreed, to think of people like us being enslaved just because we came from another place.

World Cultures was supposed to give us perspective (that was the word the teacher kept using), and each of us was supposed to prepare a report on the part of the world we'd come from, whether it was a state or a country. Here I spent two or three phone calls with Ori figuring out what we would tell States cubs about our home, and Ma helped by making some of our traditional food and by looking over my speech before I read it out. She made me put in more things about war than I wanted to, because, she said, "they don't live with that here and you should make them understand it."

I don't know that I did. When I talked about the cubs who were taken by the hyena general, everyone got really quiet, and afterwards they all said how much they loved the food. Nobody talked about the war except Marquize, who stopped in the middle of a game two days later.

"Did your friends really get drafted?" he asked, standing at the net with two tennis balls in one paw.

I nodded, because I'd come to understand that this word was the equivalent in this country, even though here it meant writing your name on a paper and giving it to the government, and that the process of being selected for war was a courteous and ritualized one, rather than a desperate conscription without regard for name or species. Did he think I'd been making things up?

"What happened to them?"

"I don't know." I let the tennis racket dangle from my paw. "They never came back."

He rolled the balls around with his fingers. "I'm really sorry about that."

"Thanks," I said awkwardly.

He walked back to the service line and said, "Ready?" and that was the end of it.

My tennis-specific class, Leadership, was me, Bret, Pom, and Dom, and mostly what we did seemed to be exercises in cooperation. None of us really was meant to lead the group, but we were supposed to figure out who was best at which individual task and how they all went together. The first few times there was a lot of talking and some boasting, but once we figured out that Bret was really good at math and Pom had a terrific memory and Dom could look up anything from his phone, we could attack most of the exercises easily. Those were a lot of fun when we got to that point, around November, and my only worry about it was that I wasn't the best at anything, really, so I always did whatever the other three wanted. I tried to mask it by figuring out what that would be first and volunteering for it, but I wasn't sure our teacher, a raccoon named Mr. Teva whose paws never held still, bought my deception.

When Mr. Teva wasn't giving us exercises, he lectured us on the kinds of people there were, and he told us that it was important not only to know what kind of people were around us, but what kind of person those people thought we were. Some of our exercises forced us to work in pairs, and at least there I was close to the best of the group. Pom and Dom loved to work together but also weren't very good when they did, because they spent all their time chatting. Bret tried too hard to make his partner work, and when he was paired with one of the foxes, more often than not the fox would get sullen and either go off on his own (Pom) or sit and talk to his friends on his phone (Dom).

But I still had tennis. And before Christmas break, we played a tournament for all the ninth graders. To get our seedings—the ranking for the tournament—the fourteen boys all played a set against each other and then switched partners, and the nine girls did the same. Then the coaches ranked us and determined the order of play such that the highest ranked player played the lowest, the second-highest played the second-lowest, and so on.

In the round robin, I beat Marquize and a marten named Nigel who wore clothes that had their own names and had a driver in a huge car come pick him up for breaks. Everyone else beat me, even Jeff, which made for a very depressing morning. Again I saw myself returning to the tennis center, the others whispering, "He couldn't make it in the States." But I knew Ma would hate to hear me think that way, so I thought about how I could make the best of this.

Being seeded twelfth meant I was scheduled to play a big groundhog named Verid who had blasted his way through much of the rest of the class with a killer serve and a laser-like forehand. When I'd played him in the round-robin, though, I'd noticed that he didn't seem very confident with his backhand. He'd always try to run around it and use his forehand instead, and in my last two service games I'd started trying to hit to his backhand. The problem was that he had great positioning on the court, so wherever I hit it, it seemed like he'd already be halfway around the shot.

I happened to be done early with one round-robin game while he was playing in the next court against the ram who would end up as the #1 seed. Perron hit with smooth, polished strokes and mixed in some drop shots, which I was still working on. Alone at the fence, I tried to imagine what Frio would tell me about Verid's game.

"Look how Perron's keeping him off balance," I imagined Frio saying. "Perron's anticipating a cross-court shot there, and that would go to his backhand, but Perron came down the other line. And look: here, Verid's going to unload with his forehand and Perron's already going back, anticipating it. If Verid had a dropshot, this is when he would use it. But he doesn't."

I had all of this in my head when we started the tournament match, and this was a real match, best of three sets. The ninth-graders were the youngest class to have a tournament, and the tenth and eleventh had one going on as well, but the younger cubs came to watch us because we were closest to them in age. So we had the biggest crowds, and the eleventh-graders had the second biggest, because the quality of tennis was the best there. Plus, people wanted to see what kind of graduates the school was going to turn out. Many of the students left for the Challengers tour after eleventh grade; Malik told us that the twelfth grade had never actually had enough good players to hold a tournament.

Of my friends, Marquize and I played at the same time; Bret had been seeded into the second half of the games. I wanted to watch Marquize, but the way the tournament went, if we both won, we'd play each other. This wasn't very likely, as the cubs we were playing were pretty good—I already talked about Verid, and Marquize's opponent was a quick rat named Don who was a grinder, a guy who stood back at the baseline and lined up his shot, always got into perfect position, and hit it back to you. He was a bad matchup for Marquize, because the cheetah was the exact opposite kind of player; he'd dash around and smack flamboyant balls all over the court. I'd figured out that to play him, I had to be steady and learn how to read him, but that was easier said than done for me. Don only had to play naturally.

How to face Verid, though, I had only an inkling. The first set went a lot like the round-robin set: he broke my serve twice and I never came close to breaking his. But I changed my patterns toward the end of the set, experimenting because nothing else was working. When I thought I should hit to his backhand, I lobbed the ball the other way. I caught him by surprise twice, which would have won me two points if I hadn't overcompensated and hit the ball out of bounds both times.

So in the second set, I kept up that tactic, focusing more on making my shots. Again, I heard Frio in my head: "Decide on your shot, then prepare for your shot, then make your shot." So I shut everything else out and did that.

And something magical happened while I was doing that. I watched my ball spin toward the place I sent it, and once it was away I could watch Verid. I saw where he planted his feet, and the future opened up for me. I could see the movement of his racket, watch the ball sizzle across the net, and see where I needed to be in order to send it back as clearly as if I was watching a movie of his next shot. I moved without thinking, decided where I wanted to send it, braced my feet, and when I swung my racket, it connected with the ball and I watched my shot zip down the line and spin away from Verid's lunging racket.

I'd already won some points, and got the same polite applause for this one as I had for the others. Verid clapped against his racket twice and then moved to receive the next serve. But inside I felt a wild elation, a surging of joy and confidence. It wasn't that this had never happened before, but it had never happened so quickly, and never against a player that skilled.

The turning point of the match came when I broke Verid's serve. I don't think he believed it when he lost the last point, because he looked up at the scoreboard like he was hoping he'd heard wrong. But I'd learned to handle his serve and my sense of where it was going was right enough that I was now playing competitively in his service games. I won the second set 6-4 and we went to a third.

Here, Verid started to break down. He clearly hadn't thought he would need three sets to dispatch me, and he double-faulted away one game, lost another when I fake-charged the net and he hurried his shot, and even though he did break my serve once, I won the set 6-3 and the match as well.

Marquize, who'd lost 6-2, 6-3, ran onto the court to congratulate me. I'd shaken Verid's paw at the net after the game when the yellow and black blur ran up to hug me, and my exultation jumped. Only then did I really take in the cheers all around, and my ears perked up and stayed up, my tail wagged, and Marquize grabbed my paw as we ran off the court.

In the match against Don, I tried the same tactic, and was pleased to find that I could predict his shots even more easily. With Don, though, it didn't matter. I kept telling myself to be patient and then patience wasn't working quickly enough and I'd smack the ball inches past the baseline.

Marquize and I watched the rest of the tournament together. Don ended up beating Perron in the final, which made us both feel better about losing to him. Afterwards, we went out for malts at Meat'N'Malt, and Marquize made me tell him about the whole match. When I told him about my magical moment, he shook his head. "That's what all the greats say happens for them. I keep waiting for it but it never happens to me." He reached across the table and put his paw on top of mine and said, "Rocky, you're gonna be a great tennis player."

And I went home that night and said, "Ma, I'm going to be a great tennis player."

She said, "I know. Now peel the carrots."

Part Two: Faults (2008-9)

Interlude (2015)

"It's a crisp, clear evening here in Port City's Brushing Gardens and we are set for the male final of the States Open, the last Major of the 2015 tennis season. I'm Daren Lido and with me is three-time Major champion Alastair Dogget-Wensley. Alastair, the fellow on one side of the net is no surprise, eh?"

"Absolutely not, Daren. Braden Longacre has ripped through the circuit this year, posting a record of 67 wins to an incredible three losses. Here at the States Open he has dropped only two sets, both of those to Milos Daryavic in the thrilling five-set semifinal. He's been absolutely dominant these two weeks; his serve is working, his return of serve, always his biggest weapon, has been even better here than I've seen all year."

"Hard to believe."

"Indeed. And what's really made the difference for the cross fox this year is his unpredictability."

"How's that, Alastair?"

"Well, you see, Braden was always a very by-the-book player. When you're learning the sport, and playing, and through experience, naturally, you learn what shot to hit in certain situations. And there was—I think someone actually made a composite picture of it last year, it was really astounding—you could see that Braden had these lines in his head and when an opponent was on one side of the line, he'd hit to the forehand; on the other side, he'd hit a backhand. In front of one line, a lob, in back of another, a drop shot."

"But isn't that something all players do?"

"Yes, but not with such startling regularity, something like eighty to ninety percent. It was almost as though a computer were playing on the other side, and this was a trend that had gotten worse over his career. But this year, he's loosened up quite a bit. He'll hit unexpected shots and he's varying his speeds and placement amazingly well. And I think you can see its effect on him. Look at these pictures from the Ocie Open this year, and then from 2013, the only other year he's won it."

"It's funny—if I didn't know he'd won it in '13, I wouldn't be able to tell from this picture."

"Exactly. He's so serious, so focused. And two years later, well, just look at that smile as he hits a winner."

"Certainly he's been on more magazine covers this year. And speaking of covers, his opponent in this match is someone who I think I can safely say has never graced one."

"No, although that's sure to change. Rocky N'guwe, who has given you Yanks the first all-Union final at the States open since McCardle and Barwin back in '82, has had an amazing tournament. His best finish at a Major before this week-end was losing in the quarterfinals of the Ocie, although he has won four smaller tournaments in 2015. He came into this Open seeded twenty-fourth, not a household name but familiar to those of us who follow tennis. He was also seeded twenty-fifth at the Gallic Open this year because of his strong clay court resume, but otherwise he's never entered a major tournament seeded."

"And he and Braden are both graduates of the Palm Gables academy."

"I'm sure Coach Murphy appreciates you mentioning that."

"Ha ha, of course he has turned out many stars, and this isn't the first time two of his graduates have faced each other in a Major final. Well, technically they didn't both graduate, but both of course benefited from the instruction there and have said many times what a big influence it was on their lives. But back to Rocky. How'd he get here?"

"Daren, his big match was against Phillippe Dubois, the marten who has accounted for two of Braden's three losses this year. I would say that Phillippe was not at the top of his game when he met Rocky, but I also don't want to take anything away from this young jackal. He played an extraordinary match and dispatched Dubois in four sets. Interesting note: Longacre has lost only two sets this whole tournament, as we mentioned, but N'guwe, though he has lost a set in all but two of his matches, has not been taken to five sets by anyone."

"That's amazing. How is he doing it?"

"Rocky has always had a gift for adapting his game to his

opponent. Here's a clip of that match against Dubois. We know Phillippe likes to rush the net, and here Rocky lets him come up, gets in perfect position, and unleashes that passing shot down the line."

"Beautiful shot."

"But here, in an earlier match, he was playing against Juan Navarro, a baseline pounder, and watch this sequence: Rocky works him to the right, to the right, to the right, and then a deep shot to the left, sending Navarro scrambling—"

"I can't believe he got to that."

"He gets to it, he's got incredible court coverage, but Rocky's already at the net waiting when it gets there. Easy put-away."

"So how is he going to play against Longacre?"

"Well, Longacre is much harder to predict, but these two do know each other well. N'guwe actually stayed with Longacre at Desmond Robin's house for the Ocie Open this year, and the two are good friends, probably from their Palm Gables days."

"Not tonight, though."

"Definitely not. I would guess that Rocky's going to see if there's any part of Braden's game that is off tonight. I'd expect him to do a lot of probing, testing his opponent, and zeroing in on any weakness. The problem is that if Braden's playing at his top level, well, there really isn't a weakness to exploit. He gets impatient sometimes, but not many players have been able to stay with him that long."

"And how will Longacre play N'guwe?"

"Well, the key to N'guwe is to attack his backhand. It isn't very strong. But he knows that and is very crafty in disguising it. I expect Braden will expose that weakness. The other trick with Rocky is to be unpredictable. He is a wonderful talent at finding the holes in your game, so if you can vary your style, he'll be caught off guard. That's how Daryavic beat him in the fourth round at Wimbledon this year."

"Alastair, thank you so much. We're going to go down to Bonnie Raymond now, who is courtside as the players warm up."

***

"Thanks, Daren. I'm here with Rocky N'guwe. Rocky, how does it feel to be in your first major final?"

"It's amazing, thank you Bonnie."

"And against a friend like Braden Longacre—you two are friends,

right?"

"Uh—yes, that's right. Well, off the court. On the court we're opponents, you know. We've played before."

"You have never beaten him, in fact."

"No."

"Do you think today will be the first time?"

"I can always hope. But he's having an amazing year, and really, I'm going to have to play my best and also hope he makes some mistakes."

"That doesn't happen very often."

"Not with Braden, no."

"He's very experienced in finals, of course, this being his seventh. Are you feeling the pressure of your first final?"

"It's funny. Not really, but what I'm feeling is, you know, I've never played this far into a weekend before. Heh. I'm used to going home sometime in the middle of the week. So this tournament feels like it's been going on forever."

"Ha ha, that's an interesting take on it. Well, I wish you the best of luck and hope we have a great final."

"Thanks, Bonnie."

"Daren and Alastair, Longacre as usual politely refused my request for an interview before the final, so I guess we'll only hear from N'guwe this time. Back to you in the booth."

***

"At the first changeover, this match has been extremely one-sided. Longacre leads five games to one, and N'guwe simply has no answer for the fox's passing shots. And—"

"Oh, what was that?"

"I don't—it looks like the two of them exchanged words on the sideline as they got up."

"Yes, Longacre said something to N'guwe, and the jackal set his ears back. I couldn't see what it was, could you?"

"No, we're looking at it on the replay and we can't see. Well, as we said, they do know each other, and maybe that was just something between friends."

"Longacre did not look happy."

"We're looking back to see if N'guwe did something on the

court…"

"Or maybe said something."

"I don't recall anything, Alastair, do you?"

"No, I don't. They've been very civil thus far."

"Well, perhaps Bonnie can find out after the match. Here we go, with N'guwe serving to stay in the set."

Chapter Eight (2008)

The excitement of the tournament passed almost immediately into the last day of classes and all my friends going home for Christmas break. Marquize promised to call; I had the numbers of all the guys and girls, and the first couple days we texted back and forth while I was at home. I had decided that texting was about the best thing ever, and I was going to keep working so that I could maybe get Ori a phone she could text to me with. But it also had to be not a nice phone like I had, not so nice that it would get stolen.

I thought texts should be about important stuff, but Bret texted me the day before Christmas with "OMG family has cartoon snow-wolf in front yard," with a picture of a pile of snow in the approximate shape of a wolf, with a piece of coal for a nose and—I squinted—tortilla chips for ears. And then Dom texted back, "Better than fox angels that glow," so Bret's message must have gone to everyone. An hour later, I'd figured out how to do that as well, and I was texting back asking what decorations we should get. I had a little spending money and so did Ma, but we were overwhelmed by the shelves and shelves of decorations: Santas in every species, angels in the twelve species of Jesus, snowflakes, trees, globes in a hundred different colors with silver and gold glitter, intricate glass and simple paper…how were we to decide what to do?

Christmas back home was a large gathering of our community, but there were fewer decorations and much more church. I called Ori the night before Christmas Eve—Christmas Eve morning her time—to ask her if she was playing a part in the hours-long nativity play.

"I'm singing in the choir all night." She was excited about this—the previous year she'd only been in the first choir during the story of the Garden of Eden. Neither of us were particularly good actors, but that didn't stop the people who actually played the parts of Adam and Eve, David and Goliath, Daniel, and especially Moses. The only parts Ori and I played were as the pair of jackals saved by Noah during the flood, and I was once one of the babies killed by King Herod, which was great because you could scream and flail around. For a couple seconds, at least.

"That's great," I told her. "I always said you sing well."

"What are you and Ma eating?" she wanted to know.

"We ordered a big piece of ham. But people don't just have dinner here. Everyone buys gifts for each other and all the stores here sell millions of dollars of stuff in December. Everything is presents and wrapping and Santa Claus."

We knew about Santa Claus, of course, from the movies, but I tried to explain how different it was living in a world that half-believed he was real even over the age of ten. Ma and I had chosen a Fox Santa from the store because there were no jackals, and I'm not sure how either of us would have felt about a jackal dressed in red and white with the kind of manically grinning muzzle many of them seemed to sport (when they weren't looking coyly to one side). The Fox we got at least just looked relaxed and happy.

"And we got a can of stuff that you spray it and white foam comes out which looks like snow. We put it on the windows."

"Is that until the real snow comes?"

I explained that in Pensa, there wouldn't be any snow, that the temperature still hovered around ten on the coldest days. "I knew that," Ori said, "but I thought all of the Union got snow. That's how all the movies are."

"Marquize doesn't even have snow yet," I said. He'd called to say that it was cold and dry and he was hitting tennis balls against a wall even though Frio had said we shouldn't do that anymore because it formed bad habits. Marquize said that he was working on consistency, which was a thing Frio focused on with him, by trying to hit the same spot on the wall over and over.

Then he asked what I was doing and I guiltily said I planned to go down to the courts and work on my serve even though I'd planned no such thing. He'd called me on it. "You're not going to practice," he'd said. "You hate practicing alone."

"I don't have a choice."

He'd laughed. "Rocky, you always have a choice. Look, you're doing great. Don't worry about practicing. There's parties there, right? Go find a Christmas party. Have some fun."

I'd promised I would, but in truth, I was going to help out at the warehouse that night. Gen had promised to give me some cash "for Christmas presents," and I liked the warehouse work. It wasn't tennis, but it was a nice change of pace and it certainly paid better, at least until I improved enough to start playing in tournaments (which wouldn't be long, I told myself; I'd beaten Verid, after all).

At the warehouse, everyone relaxed and joked a lot more than I was used to (later I would realize some of them had been drinking a little). I'd gotten to know a few of the guys close to my age, and so when we finished early and they gathered around a cooler someone had brought from a truck, this big, stocky wolf named Jazzy invited me to join them. "Have a beer, Rock," he said, holding out a bottle.

"He's underage." Merritt, another wolf but with all white fur, tried to block the bottle with a huge paw.

"So're you." Jazzy shoved the paw aside easily. "Here, Rock. Don't tell the cops."

I took the bottle as Merritt said, "Yeah, but he's like, really underage."

"So? He's not gonna drive. You got a car?"

"No," I said.

"You gonna get in trouble with your Ma?"

I shook my head. Merritt sighed and held out a small plastic box a little bigger than a postage stamp. "Here. Take these. Peppermint breath strips. They're strong and they'll make your eyes water, but they'll kill the beer smell enough to get you past your folks. Works for wolves so I guess it'll work for jackals."

The peppermint smell rose to my nose even as I thanked Merritt and put the strips in my pocket. I'd had beer before, and honestly Ma wouldn't care about me having one as long as I didn't go do something stupid after.

"What are you missing to be here?" Jazzy asked me as we sat around.

"Nothing. Everyone at my school is gone for the holiday." I tipped the beer bottle to my lips, because it felt very adult. This beer tasted watery compared to the ones Ma and Malik had shared with me. I wondered whether Marquize had had much beer. He talked about raiding his friends' parents' liquor cabinet, but he'd refused beers the times Malik had brought some around.

"Rich cubs' school," Merritt said.

"Rich cubs and Rocky." Jazzy punched my shoulder.

I grinned and nodded, and didn't rub the spot where he'd punched me. He went on. "We had to miss a party at this guy Marcus's place. His parents are down in Coral Beach until tomorrow afternoon, so he was having a party tonight. But it's two in the morning now and he didn't answer when I texted, so I guess it's all over."

"I'm gonna text Amy." Merritt took his phone out and thumbed letters.

"You guys throw parties much?" Jazzy asked.

I shook my head. "I live in the dorms. Ma lives in an apartment and a lot of the cubs I know are boarders so their parents don't live around here. We hang out on the tennis courts after school and have beer sometimes." Once, technically, when Bret snuck a beer in.

"Awesome. I'm in football at my school." He sighed and took a long drink of his beer. "Gonna miss those parties. One more semester and it's off to Delavon Vocational. Gonna be an electrician like my dad."

"Cool," I said.

Merritt's phone beeped. "Hey," he said, holding it up for Jazzy. "Amy says there's still like twenty people over there. Wanna go?"

"Shit, yeah. Let's bring the beer." Jazzy hefted the cooler. "Rocky, you wanna come?"

"Jaz, he's fourteen."

"He's gonna be a tennis star. Plus he's real mature. Aren't you?"

The prospect of getting into a party with a bunch of older cubs I didn't know scared me, but the beer warmed me, and what else was I going to do? Go home? Go hit a tennis ball against a wall at two in the morning? Besides, I could tell Marquize about it when we talked next. So I nodded, getting to my feet as well. "I'd like to go."

"There," the grey wolf said. "He wants to experience a real Union high school party. Anyway, isn't Marcus's little sister there? She's about his age. You like coyotes?"

That was to me. "Sure," I said.

Merritt sighed. "All right, but he ain't gonna follow us around all night, is he?" To me, he said, "Are you? I mean, if we bring you,

you're going to have a good time, meet Marcus's sister, dance a bit, maybe make out, but that's what we want to do too."

Jazzy laughed. "Don't worry about him ruining your chances with Lorrie. I think you did that yourself last week."

"Fuck you," Merritt said amiably.

Ten minutes later I was squeezed in between the two muscular wolves in the front seat of a truck bouncing over rough streets (I learned what a "pothole" was) toward my first "real" high school party. Despite the wolves being twice my bulk, I was as tall as either of them, my eyes at their eye level as we drove, which I think probably made them feel more comfortable about bringing me to their party.

Marcus's parents lived on a quiet street—at least, all the houses but theirs were quiet. When we made the turn, I could see right away which house had the party going on. All the lights were on and cars packed the driveway and street in front of it. Otherwise, there wasn't much to set it apart from the other houses: two stories, peaked roofs, five windows across on each floor with a large carport attached.

Jazzy and Merritt walked with me up to the front door and Merritt pushed confidently in without knocking. From inside the house we felt the throb of bass music coming through the floor, and Jazzy set the cooler down. He and Merritt each took a beer and offered me one, but I declined, and we made our way to the basement.

Through the basement door, pounding bass assaulted my ears over which a high-pitched voice sang words almost too fast for me to pick up. If I focused I could make them out, but the music wasn't what interested me. What interested me were the people.

All right, and the decorations. I admit that for the first five minutes I gaped at all the sparkly tinsel and Santas of various species, including a few female Santas showing a lot more fur than the male ones. Anatomically correct snow-wolves of both genders kissed in one cartoon, which looked to have been drawn by someone at the party. On another wall, I saw a cartoon deer in a similar style drinking a beer bottle.

But the people! At Palm Gables, the tennis cubs joked, we played, but always underneath there was the understanding that we were here not just to learn tennis, but to be great at it. The non-tennis cubs were there to get an education and then go on to do whatever you did when you weren't a tennis player. To the extent that I'd given them any thought at all, I suppose I'd imagined them filing out of school after graduation in a uniform line of white-shirted business-suited drones to fill in the foundations of the world I would play tennis on.

But these cubs—older cubs, most of them (like my co-workers) nearly full-on adults, they were anything but drones. I could see well enough in the dimly-lit basement; the reason I had to stop was for my nose to process everything that was going on. About six different kinds of alcohol, from beer that dripped from a keg and foamed sticky on the floor to bottled beer to tickles of sharper, richer, more vibrant aromas that tantalized me. The heady musk of a dozen different species, of twice that number of people, all crammed into a tiny room, sweat and lust and giddy excitement pervading every scent. And I could even smell the furnishings of the basement, the wood oils for the coffee table that looked far too expensive to be holding up three fallen beer bottles, six plastic cups with drinks of various shades, and a slender bobcat girl in a bright blue dress; the rich smell of the couch fabric struggling to be noticed through the smells of the two raccoons and the skunk and the marten all crammed into it (the marten had his? her? paw in one of the raccoons' lap; the skunk held cups in both paws).

Over by the music, a knot of activity whirled and bounced, dancers ricocheting off each other and back together. Two couples attempted to slow-dance together, paws roaming over each others' backs and sides. Next to them, a well-dressed coyote served drinks at the bar, and that was where Jazzy dragged me.

He put an arm around my shoulder as we got to the bar and the coyote looked up. "Hey Jaz," he said.

"Marcus." Jazzy squeezed my shoulder. "This is Rocky. He works with me an' Merritt."

"Okay." The coyote eyed me. "Hey Rocky."

"Hi." I was taller than he was, but he made me very aware of my simple t-shirt and jeans, dressed as he was in a snazzy blazer with a button-down shirt under it that seemed to shimmer in the colored lights. He moved with a confident economy to his motions that made me think he played tennis, or at least some sport: as we talked, he was pulling bottles down, mixing drinks into red plastic cups, distributing them to the people clustered around the little bar.

"Rocky, this is Marcus's parents' place, so if you see anyone trashing something, come tell him."

The warning was implicit: don't go trashing anything yourself. I nodded. "Marcus," Jazzy went on, "Rocky's a frosh, so don't serve him any alcohol."

Marcus didn't stop mixing his drinks. "First off, Jaz, of course I'm not going to serve alcohol to anyone I don't know. Second, if you think seniors drinking is somehow less illegal than frosh drinking, maybe you should study harder in civics. Third, Rocky's not a frosh from our school. Never seen him before."

"I didn't say he was," Jaz protested.

"And fourth, he's holding a beer, which I presume you gave him." Marcus turned away from Jazzy and gave me a smile. "Welcome to the party, Rocky. Have fun."

"Thanks." My throat was dry, but I felt self-conscious about drinking the beer in front of him after that speech, so I turned away and surveyed the room. Behind me, Jazzy said, "Beer's not alcohol. Hey, we brought a cooler. Where you want it…?"

What did one do at a party? I didn't want to go dance with a bunch of people I didn't know. I looked for Merritt, but he had already somehow disappeared in the small, crowded room. Plus I didn't want to go around the whole party looking for him after he'd specifically told me not to.

I heard my name again behind me and flicked my ears back reflexively to listen. "Rocky's cool," Jazzy was saying. "He works at the warehouse on weekends. Good guy."

"All right," Marcus said. "But—"

"Hey." Jazzy grabbed my shoulder again. Marcus was going on behind me but the wolf's voice drowned out the coyote's words. "Come on, I'll introduce you to Marcus's sister."

The wolf propelled me through the crowd to the edge of the circle of dancers, where a coyote a good foot shorter than me danced with abandon, throwing her elbows out every which way, her muzzle open in a gleeful smile. "Hey!" Jazzy tapped her on the shoulder. "Hey, Marcus's sister!"

She stopped and turned, and put her paws on her hips. "My name's Shawna," she said.

"Shawna, this is a friend of mine, Rocky. He's about your age."

She glared at him and then looked toward her brother at the bar. I didn't see what passed between them, but she turned and smiled at me. "I'm practically fifteen. So if Marcus told you I'm fourteen he was pretty much just lying."

"I'm almost fifteen too." I smiled. "I might be fifteen, actually. Ma doesn't know when my birthday was for sure."

"Really?" Her ears perked up. I was aware of Jazzy leaving, but paid it no mind. "How can she not know when your birthday is?"

"I was born in a hospital in Lunda where the weather is much the same all year. She only remembers that I was alive when she moved to the city to live with my father in the spring, so she said my birthday is the first day of spring."

"Why did you move to the States?"

So I told her about tennis, and she clapped her paws together. "I've only seen those tennis cubs when we drive by the courts. They all look so stuck up and rich, and Daddy says that school has caused nothing but trouble for us."

"Trouble?" This was the first I'd heard of it. "How?"

"Something about taxes." She giggled. "I don't really care. I think tennis players are sexy. Do you know Braden Longacre?"

"I've met him." I tried to keep my tone light. "He's kind of a jerk."

"Oh my god, you know, I saw an article about him and we saw him play four years ago on those courts. I remember because I thought he was so unusual—a cross fox, you don't see many of those."

"Do you see many jackals?" I asked, a bit cross myself.

She stopped and looked at me again, maybe seeing me for the first time. "No, I don't."

"So what is your school like?" I asked.

Her paw found mine. "Let's go upstairs."

I didn't think I could talk about school with someone for an hour, but we sat on the stairs of the house and she told me about her classes, how the popular girls didn't like coyotes even though her father had worked his whole life to become respectable, how she had tried to get them interested in her favorite video games but they didn't care, how the teachers didn't like her either (though I thought that might have something to do with the video games, to be honest), and how her brother was this great guy and all the teachers asked her why she couldn't be as smart as Marcus or why she couldn't play baseball like Marcus, or softball—there was no girls' baseball team, which I thought was odd. "Girls can play tennis just as well as guys," I said.

"But they don't play against them," Shawna pointed out.

I didn't bring up Ori's "Battle of the Sexes" because it didn't seem like the right time. "But it's the same game. They don't play with softer balls or bigger rackets."

She giggled again. "Don't you know anything? Softballs aren't soft. I mean, I guess they're soft-er. But they're bigger, and you pitch underhand, that's all."

I got annoyed again, because how was I expected to know that? But Shawna was the only person talking to me at the party, and we were having fun together, so I let it go. And I didn't mind letting it go. It was almost like when Marquize said something like that to me. I didn't mind so much because I knew he didn't mean it in a bad way, and I felt like Shawna was saying the same kind of thing.

People started leaving soon after that, and Merritt came up half-dragging Jazzy behind him. "We gotta go," he said. "Rocky, want us to drop you off?"

"Please, yeah. What time is it?" We all checked our phones. "Oh, no, four in the morning? It doesn't feel like it."

"For me neither," Shawna said, and smiled.

"All right, all right," Merritt said. "Give him your number so we can go."

What? A hundred romantic movies I'd watched flooded back to me. *Get her number.* That meant that she liked me, that we would have more conversations, that maybe we would…go out on dates? I'd been at ease the whole evening, but now, as our attention shifted to Shawna, my heart pounded and my ears flushed with heat. What if she said no?

"Oh." The coyote giggled softly and met my eyes. She didn't say anything for a moment, and I was certain she saw and enjoyed my anxiety. "Sure, I mean, if he wants it…"

"I do," I said, my phone already out. She dictated the number and I typed it in. "I'll call you."

"Call me now."

I wasn't sure what that meant. She'd taken out her own phone. "So I have your number too."

Merritt was making a motion with his head, but I didn't know why I shouldn't do that, so I called her, and she put the phone to her ear. "Hi, Rocky," she said. "I had a really nice night."

And then she leaned forward, phone still to her ear, and kissed me on the lips.

***

Marquize wasn't all that excited to hear about the party. "So you kissed a girl," he said. "Did that help you with your ad court serve?"

"You're the one who told me to go a party."

"Yeah, well, you don't have to tell me about it."

"You asked me to!"

He softened. "I guess I'm jealous. I didn't get to go anywhere fun."

I didn't tell Frio about the party, but he had his own complaint;

he had set out practice hours for me during the week and he kept asking whether I was skipping them or losing sleep because of the job. "I don't know why you're still there," he said the first week of January. "You're not going to need to be a computer operator once you start playing tournaments."

"It's fun," I told him, and left it at that. There was a little more to it, of course; I'd started a bank account and I enjoyed watching the money in it go up every week when I deposited my pay. I'd bought a nice spice rack for Ma's kitchen for Christmas that she really liked, and I'd bought myself a new tennis outfit that Marquize, at least, had said looked better than my old clothes. The other guys showed up with new shirts and shorts about every week, and while I thought that was silly, eventually I did figure I needed another change of clothing. So I went to the school shop and got a pair of white shirts and a nice white polo with the school crest embroidered on it in navy blue.

At one of our evening practice sessions, I mentioned the kiss to Bret, and he was a lot more enthusiastic. "Did you get your paw inside her dress?" he asked. When I shook my head, his ears drooped. "Not even her boobs?"

"No," I said. "We just talked and then she kissed me."

"Does she have nice boobs?"

I thought back. They certainly weren't like anything on the websites Bret and I had looked at, but I supposed they were attractive enough. What made for unattractive boobs? I wasn't sure. "Yeah," I said. "Real nice."

"Great." He showed the same smile he got when we watched porn together. "Is she gonna come by?"

"Uh, maybe." To tell the truth, Shawna and I had only talked twice in the two weeks since the Christmas party. Both of us were busy with school and starting a new semester. "We're going to a movie with her friends Thursday night, so she's going to pick me up here."

"She drives?"

"Her older brother does. He got a car for his birthday but part of the deal with his parents was that he had to take his sister places two nights a week. She said sometimes he's a pain about it but it was good that she was going to the movies with me, because he wanted to come along."

"A-ha." Bret grinned wider. "Chaperone."

Once he'd explained that word to me, I realized that that was probably Marcus's intention. For all that Shawna said they fought, they seemed to genuinely like each other. If Ori were here and some coyote guy wanted to take her out on a date, I'd sure want to go along and make sure she was safe.

That reminded me that there might be jackals asking her on dates even now. I'd only talked to her once since Christmas, and she hadn't mentioned Kamina's wedding plans for her at all. I'd told her about my bank account and she promised to find out how much it would cost to bring her over. I knew I'd be making more money in a few years, but I was afraid that would be too late; Ma said that we would bring Ori over when we had the money but wouldn't discuss details with me because she said that until I was playing professionally there wasn't anything I could do.

Shawna came by on Thursday around six with Marcus and two other friends of hers. She walked to the courts while the rest of them stayed in the car, so I got to introduce her to the others. I particularly wanted Marquize to like her, and he was very polite and smiled; Bret was a lot more enthusiastic, as was Pom. Of the girls, only Kim even said two words to her, but they're both coyotes so that was probably why.

The movie was fine, but what I liked most about that evening was sitting next to Shawna in the theater. In the car, Marcus made me ride up front while the three girls squeezed into the back, but in the movie theater he let me sit next to Shawna, and during the movie her paw reached over and clasped mine. And that was nice, but then she moved my paw to rest on her knee, and the hem of her skirt had slipped up so my fingers were on her bare fur, and touching her knee like that made me think of the porn on the Internet and I don't remember watching much of the movie.

We went out to a diner afterwards and talked about it, and Shawna's tail rested atop mine the whole time. Even though I hadn't paid a lot of attention to the movie, I'd gotten enough to be able to talk about it, and I was surprised at how much smarter Shawna was than her friends. Like, when I talked about one of the books we'd read in our World Cultures class, she and Marcus knew what I was talking about but her two friends had no idea. Maybe it was just coyotes being clever (her friends were a doe and a possum), but I think it was that Shawna was smart.

The more we talked, the more we had to talk about, and the longer our conversations went. I was careful to talk to her on the phone from Ma's apartment so I didn't go over my cel minutes again, but that meant that I went to Ma's apartment on the weeknights I wanted to talk and then had to go back to Palm Gables to sleep in the dorm. So if I hung out with my friends after school doing our extra practice sessions, I might not have a lot of time to talk to Shawna.

Those informal practices weren't that important, and as far as I could tell, I was still doing fine in my lessons, but Marquize told Frio every time I missed an hour or two the night before, and Frio drilled me harder that day.

"You beat Verid, and that was good, but you should be able to beat Don, too. You're just not going to do it with baseline strokes like that. Look how flat that is! Focus on where you want it to go. Give it some topspin, give it some zip. Take those quarter-seconds away from your opponent's reaction time. He wants to play the game at his pace; you have to make him play it at yours, and you can't do it with volleys like that."

"I can't aim it when I give it topspin," I complained. "And anyway, Verid couldn't catch up to it."

"Verid's slow, and between you and me, he's going to spend a couple years on the Challenger circuit and then quote-unquote retire to cash in on the story of the one time he took a top-fifty player to a third set." The ferret glared at me. "You have the chance to be better than that."

"As good as Braden Longacre?"

He laughed once and then patted me on the shoulder. "Maybe. You've got the tools. Do you have the focus?"

Ma was worried about that too. "No girlfriend tonight," she said, swatting my paw as I reached for the phone that Friday night. "I see more of you now but I feel like I see you less. You're visiting me, you can talk to me."

"Okay," I said. "Can I call her to tell her I'm not going to call tonight?"

"No."

"She's going to call here otherwise."

Ma smacked my arm again. "You gave her our number?"

I resisted the urge to smack her back. "Yes! So she can call me."

"Tchah!" She flattened her ears and spun away from me, tail arched. "Fine. Call and say you won't call tonight. After two minutes I'm coming to hang up that phone."

So I called Shawna to apologize to her, and she told me her parents got unreasonable too, and it was only when Ma came threateningly toward the phone that I said, "SorryIgottagobye!"

"You are here to play tennis," Ma said as I dropped the phone back in its cradle. "Not meet girls. You're too young."

"Oh." I put my paws on my hips. "But Ori's old enough? Is that it?"

"That is different. You want a girlfriend, you can go back to Lunda."

Our eyes locked, hard and stubborn. "I can play tennis and see Shawna. And she's not my 'girlfriend.'"

Ma shook her head and sat down in her armchair. "What do you have to talk about all night, every night?"

I swung my tail to the side and plopped down on the threadbare couch. "Just stuff. You wouldn't understand."

"You think I was never fourteen?" She flicked her ears. "Twelve, in my case."

"If you know, why are you asking me?"

"Because I want you to tell me that you're talking about nothing. I hear you on the phone in there, 'oh, Mary said that? What could that mean? Listen to what Brad said.'"

"Brant."

She waved her paw at me. "It is not about tennis. It is distracting and it is useless."

"She's not useless." I struggled to explain why I liked talking to Shawna. "She makes me feel…"

Ma inclined her head and did not help me. I discarded some of the more physical words that came to mind and settled on, "wanted."

"You think you are not wanted?" Ma barked a laugh.

"Wanted for me! She doesn't care how well I can hit a groundstroke or how low my backhand is. She likes talking to me. I tell her stories of home and she tells me stories from her life and we have fun!"

"Exactly!" Ma leaned forward in her chair. "Fun! You think you can afford to have fun?"

"It's a lot better than not having fun," I snapped back.

"I brought you here because you have potential—"

I got up from the couch. "I know. I hear about it all the time, from you, from Frio, from Marquize."

"What happened to being a great tennis player?"

I turned at the door of the kitchen and looked back at her. She sat there on the chair in her t-shirt and jeans, looking very modern, very States. "Great tennis players have girlfriends too," I said.

"So now she is your girlfriend?"

"No! I mean—look, I can handle it."

"Ro," she said, as I started into the kitchen. I stopped and flicked my ears back toward her. "I trust you can handle it. But if you can't, something has to go."

I was pretty sure I could handle it all; at least, I had been until that moment. With Ma's permission came the possibility that maybe I couldn't. I was certainly more tired that week than I could remember being, though until that moment I hadn't actually thought about it. Losing hours of sleep, losing practice time so I had to work harder to make Frio happy in school, all of that contributed. And when I was tired, I had less patience and perhaps I snapped more easily at people.

Or maybe everyone was on my case because I had a girl to come around and talk to. She wasn't taking up that much of my time, and as much as Frio was threatening me and Marquize was annoyed and Ma was worried, I hadn't noticed that my tennis was suffering.

Chapter Nine

February came in with five straight days of storms that drove the school inside for practice and left most of us restless and annoyed. There weren't enough indoor courts for everyone, for one thing, so some of us always had to stare at the people using the courts or else stare out the windows at the rain-soaked outdoor courts. "How hard would it be to put up a canvas tent?" we grumbled (okay, "we" in this case was Bret, but we were all thinking the same thing).

The coaches had us run shuttle sprints and do other boring exercises if we started grumbling too much, which we hated even more than standing around watching, but we didn't have a choice really. After the third day of shuttle sprints, though, Frio grabbed me and Marquize while we were waiting for the court and said, "Come on, let's shoot some hoops."

I followed the two of them, a little puzzled, and then understood what he meant when we arrived at the basketball court. "Rocky, you know how to play basketball, right?"

I eyed the orange metal hoops with the white nets dangling from them, then the orange ball Frio had gone to get. I had watched basketball games at home but never had the chance to play on the playground. Still, I'd learned that it was good to hide how much you knew at first. "You throw that in there?"

"Right." He laughed. "Okay, real quick. This is a layup." He stood under the basket and to one side and pushed the ball up into the air. It skimmed the board behind the net, bounced once on the hoop, and dropped in. He grabbed it and walked back to the edge of a painted rectangle that started under the basket. "This is the foul line. If someone makes excessive contact while you're shooting, you get a couple free shots from here." He lofted the ball toward the basket, and this time it went in without even a bump on the metal.

Marquize was waiting for it. "And when you've got the ball, you have to bounce it off the floor. That's dribbling." He bounced it down and back into his paws. "You can take like three steps without doing that, but then you have to either shoot the ball or pass it."

All of that made sense. "Okay."

"I'll take the two of you on myself," Frio said. "Play to twenty?"

"Sure." Marquize grinned. "Rocky, let me do the shooting."

There followed about twenty minutes of frenetic activity. Frio hadn't told me that he was allowed to reach in while I was dribbling and take the ball, which he managed to do several times before I learned how to guard against it. For the first ten minutes or so, the game was largely him against Marquize, while I followed them around and tried to get between them so Marquize could shoot. It wasn't easy; I guess you couldn't hit someone but you could keep an arm or hand on their midriff to try to control their movements, and Frio was keeping Marquize far from the basket. The cheetah got a few baskets in anyway, but Frio made nearly every shot he took. Also they hadn't told me that shots counted for two points, so after ten minutes Marquize and I were down twelve to six.

As we walked back down the court, Marquize murmured to me, "Next time we come down, run ahead of me and wait under the basket. I'll pass and you lay it in."

"Okay," I said. It sounded good and the layup had looked easy. Surely I could do that.

Frio made another shot and then followed Marquize down the court. The cheetah moved slowly, giving me time to run ahead, and when I was under the basket I turned to see the ball coming my way. I managed to catch it, but Frio was already running at me, so I heaved it desperately up as the ferret crashed into me.

"That's a foul!" Marquize yelled, running to retrieve the ball.

Frio had a paw on my side, steadying me. "You okay?" I nodded. "Okay, go to the line." He grinned.

I missed the first shot, throwing the ball too hard. Then I overcompensated on the second shot and didn't even get close to the hoop.

"It's not really fair," Marquize said as he tried to guard Frio, "because we've grown up playing, but Rocky never has."

"That's why you get him as a partner and I'm alone." The ferret grinned, faked a step forward, and when Marquize jumped back, he launched a ball on a lovely arc and into the basket. "Three pointer!" he crowed, raising his paws in the air. "That's seventeen."

Marquize took the ball and gave it to me. I understood what he meant: we'd do the same thing but in reverse. Frio understood it too, so instead of guarding me, he followed Marquize around, trying to keep him from getting into a position where I could throw him the ball. I got it near the foul line and Marquize was running around, keeping a couple steps ahead of Frio, but the ferret was great at cutting off his angles. And then I saw that they were running in a sort of pattern and without thinking, I tossed the ball to where Marquize was going to be, and he caught it right under the basket and put it in.

"Awesome," Frio said with a grin. "Now if you can do that six more times and stop me from scoring, you guys might win."

Needless to say, we didn't.

Afterwards, though, he stood between me and Marquize with his paws below our shoulders. "This wasn't just good exercise," he said. "Learning to pass is about angles and anticipation and it's not unlike tennis. That pass you made, Rocky, that was good. And guarding is about knowing where your opponent is going next. Marquize, you did great at that. So if you guys want to come down here and practice next time it's raining, I'm always up for a game."

Marquize and I got back in time to claim our time on the court, and though we were tired from running around for twenty minutes, it was better than shuttle sprints for sure.

"No practice tonight, I guess," he said when we were changed and looking out the window at the continuing rain and wind. "You want to work on homework?"

"Oh, I told Shawna I'd go out with her tonight." I took my phone out. "We're going to have dinner and it's kind of like our first date sort of."

"You've been out with her a million times." Marquize's tail flicked and he turned. "Whatever, have fun."

"Marcus isn't coming with us this time," I called after him, but he didn't stop walking.

Well, fine. It wasn't like he was coming on the date with me.

Going on a date with Shawna was a lot like playing that first basketball game. I knew the basics of what happened with boys and girls, but figuring out the patterns, the moves, the way you danced around each other: all that was a mystery. Shawna did play the instructor as enthusiastically as Frio had, with whispered admonitions behind her brother's back about where to put my paws (there was, as best I could determine, an acceptable area from about six inches below the waist to the edge of her skirt, and most of the arms were okay too, but nothing else unless she brushed me with her tail first and then I could pet that, which I enjoyed doing, so I would sometimes move into the way of her tail swinging).

For our first solo date, we'd decided to go to a movie and dinner. Shawna had taken to loaning me romantic comedy movies that I could watch to learn about dates. Ma watched them with me and usually ended each one by telling me how stupid one or both of the leads were. I thought the romance was exciting but I guessed I could see what Ma meant, because mostly the characters had nothing in the way of lives outside of each other even though they argued the whole movie until the end. Regardless, I did come away from them with an idea of what guys were supposed to do—or at least what Shawna expected her guys to do.

So I insisted on paying for the dinner and movie, another romantic comedy. I noticed that in all the movies she'd given me, the leads were the same species; oh, sometimes, like in this one, a wolf liked a coyote, but he or she always 'came to their senses' and picked the wolf by the end of the movie, and it was no different in this one. During the movie she leaned against me and I put a paw on her leg, but I found myself thinking about the species thing. Weren't there any movies where even a bobcat and lynx fell in love? Or a fox and coyote? I was sure I'd seen some movies like that back home. Maybe the same-species ones were the only ones Shawna was interested in.

Was she sending me a message that our relationship wasn't serious? I wondered that right as the wolf's best friend in this picture was telling her, "What's wrong with him? He's successful, he's gorgeous, and he's a wolf! You guys will have the most amazing cubs!" Was Shawna telling me she was going to dump me for a coyote? Was she—

Was she putting her paw in my lap?

Uh.

Yes she was.

I swallowed. The action on the screen was very far away all of a sudden compared to the warm pressure on an area that only I had touched, at least in the last ten years or so (except for—but that was just goofing around). Shawna's fingers rested there on my jeans, not pressing, though I was sure she could feel the reaction they were causing. Her eyes gleamed with the reflection of the movie, still watching it, not looking at me, as though her careless touch were nothing but an accident.

What did I do now? Was I supposed to reach over and touch her? Was she just trying to get a reaction out of me (done) or was this a prelude to something else? Was the something else going to happen in this movie theater? Frozen, I hung in my ignorant limbo, not even daring to shift, though the pressure against my pants was getting difficult to bear. I was worried that if I moved, I'd call attention to the touch, and maybe it would stop. Or maybe it wouldn't.

After a length of time I could only measure in my own thudding heartbeat, she moved her paw away. I risked another look at her, but she seemed totally engrossed in the movie. Had I failed some kind of test? Had she been waiting for me to reciprocate? I was pretty sure that counted as excessive contact. Did I get a free shot?

That last thought would have made me giggle if my pants hadn't still been feeling very confining. I tried to focus on the movie, but all I seemed to get were the parts where the girl was complaining that the guy didn't understand anything she wanted him to do.

By the time the movie ended, I'd recovered from the touch enough to stand up in the light without being embarrassed. I thought Shawna might say something about it, but all she said was, "That was a good movie, don't you think?"

"Uh," I gulped, "it was fun, yeah."

She gave me a long coyote smile, ears perked, and linked her arm through mine. "I'm glad you had fun. Walk me home?"

Of course I walked her to her house, and at the front door she said, "I had a good time tonight, Rocky. Maybe we can see another movie next week?"

"Yeah," I said, though of course I was not nearly as excited over the prospect of another movie as I was at the prospect of another dark theater, another casual paw, another touch. My groin already responded to the thought in a way that I was sure Shawna could smell, if not see, so I just said, "Definitely. I, uh, gotta get home. School tomorrow."

She smiled; she knew, of course she knew.

And so did Ma, somehow. I'd barely been home ten minutes before she confronted me, fists on her hips, her tail arched and eyes blazing. "So what happened during this movie?"

"Uh…" I gulped. "Well, this wolf, Jayson, he was a designer in a big company—"

She smacked me on the arm. "What happened in the theater while the movie was playing?"

I flinched. "Nothing!"

"Don't tell me nothing." She got her muzzle up under mine and pushed me in the chest. "Fooling around, that's what happened."

"How—nothing happened, Ma!" I choked the words out.

"You're a terrible liar," she said. Her eyes flicked down to my crotch and her nose twitched. "Just paws. Did she open your pants?"

"No!"

"Did you open hers? Get under her shirt?"

"Ma!"

"You listen to me, Ro." She stayed put as I backed up. "Don't you get involved with this girl."

I tried to recover my confidence. "You just don't like her because—because she's not a jackal."

She grabbed my paw and brought it to her nose. Her nostrils flared before I could yank my fingers back. "I don't like her," she said, "because she's not helping your tennis."

"Neither is my job." I fell back on the only argument I had.

"No," she agreed. "But if I get the permanent job next year then you will quit the job." Her ears flattened. "The girl doesn't do anything for you."

If only she knew. "Okay, Ma, but I like her. She keeps me happy."

"You're too young to be happy."

"Oh, but it's okay for Ori to be married?"

Ma set her teeth and turned her head to the side. "That has nothing to do with being happy."

"I thought you moved us here so we could have a better life. Shawna's part of that. I could never have met someone like her in Lunda, and we wouldn't be feeling like…" I struggled to articulate the feeling that the relationship was casual, with no pressure and all the freedom in the world to decide where it would go. Back in Lunda, if I were introduced to a girl, she would certainly be a jackal, and on our first date we would already know that we were intended to be married if the financial exchanges were settled properly.

"I moved us here so you could develop your tennis and become the best you can be. And, I hope, so we can bring Ori here as well. This coyote girl is no part of your future."

"It's harmless," I said. "Shawna, I mean. I can't get her pregnant, and—"

That got Ma's attention. "You better not even try."

"But—"

"You can get diseases from coyotes. You can make her brother angry. You're underage and if anything happens and then she goes to her family, you could be in trouble."

This was an exaggeration, I was sure, based on what Jazzy had told me went on at some of these parties, based on what I knew Malik and Veronica had done and had said some of the other students had done. Malik had told me that as long as you were within two years of the other person, you couldn't get in the worst kind of trouble for it. And anyway, that was the point of most mixed-species couples: to be able to do that kind of thing without worrying about getting pregnant. Apart from Loris the religious bear, very few of my classmates wanted to date within their species.

"But it isn't all of that. It's distracting you from tennis."

"No, it's not."

"Would your coaches say that if I asked them?"

"How would I know? They all say I'm doing fine."

She narrowed her eyes. "Maybe I will go ask them."

"You do that," I said, and walked into the kitchen, leaving her in the living room standing beside the couch, one paw resting on it, staring after me.

I was supposed to call Ori that night anyway, so I waited until Ma was in her bedroom with the door closed and music on. Ori wanted to tell me about the thunderstorm they'd had the night before, but I spent the first fifteen minutes ranting about Ma being unreasonable about my girlfriend (I had decided that yes, she was my girlfriend, based on her actions that night). Ori listened patiently and then said,

"She's right, though."

For a minute, I couldn't say anything. "She's right?"

"This isn't helping your tennis."

"It's not hurting it."

"Ro." Ori spoke patiently. "I love you, but you're a boy. You know what boys are like. You know boys are why Kamina pays Abbas to walk everywhere with us."

"Her neighbor?" Ori had only mentioned a couple times that she'd been escorted to the tennis center.

"He has a gun. He scares away the gangs."

I drew my knees up to my chest on the couch. "Has it gotten so much worse since I was there?"

"When you were here, you were my escort. You were big. And I wasn't old enough to be desirable yet."

"You're thirteen," I reminded her.

"Almost fourteen." She sighed. "And at least two of the boys in the tennis center found me desirable."

My ears shot up and I sat up fast. "What happened?"

"Nothing."

"What almost happened?"

"Millions of things almost happened."

"Ori!"

"Fine, but don't tell Ma. She can't do anything about it and she'd only worry. All that happened was that a couple of the younger lion boys just joined the club and they pushed me around a little before Mrs. Chrêtien came into the room and then it was fine."

My gut tightened. "You can't go back there."

She made an exasperated huff. "That's exactly what Ma would say."

"She'd be right! Ori, what if Mrs. Chrêtien doesn't come in next time?"

"I'm being more careful. Anyway, they wouldn't have done anything right there in the center."

I stood and paced back and forth. "Did you tell Kamina?"

"No, because then she wouldn't let me play tennis anymore." She said it as though I were stupid, and I guess I was for asking.

"You didn't even want to play tennis when I left."

"Yes, but now you're gone, I can beat most of the players there and they're all nice to me because I tell them about how you're doing in the States. So it's nice there, and it's much better than school and it gets me away from Kamina."

"You should find something more...more girly to do."

Her voice got sharper. "What about all the girls you play tennis with?"

"That's—they're not going to be attacked by the boys here."

"Neither am I," she said. "So stop worrying about it."

"If you're going to play tennis," I said, "then I'm going to keep dating Shawna."

"It's not the same thing," Ori said, and I knew she was right, but I didn't care.

Ma didn't talk to me much that night, so I figured if I kept my dates with Shawna quiet, she wouldn't have cause to complain about them. And if Frio could stay happy with my tennis, then Ma wouldn't have any reason to complain anyway. And as a last resort, I thought, I could always give up the job if it meant more time with Shawna.

At least, I thought that until I went to the ATM Saturday morning and found that I had only five dollars left in my account.

Clearly I couldn't quit my job, because I had to buy dinners and go to movies with Shawna. I asked Gen if I could work more for him, and he said I wasn't supposed to be working as much as I was, so I shut up quickly after that. Jaz and Merritt weren't any help, and I didn't really want to ask the other tennis students about how to earn more money. For one thing, of course, none of them needed to and it would make me look poor as well as being a waste of time. For another, it would indicate to them that I was getting distracted from tennis, which they would be delighted by. Verid in particular had dedicated himself to making sure I didn't beat him in another tournament, and whenever I passed him on the courts, he would catch my eye and then smack the ball so hard on his next hit that sometimes it sailed into the stands.

But nobody, not even Coach Murphy or Frio, rode me as hard as Marquize. Around the tournament and after it, I'd gotten to the point that I could beat him more than half the time, but as we rolled into March and the weather got better, he began to outpace me again.

"Weak," he snapped at me one day when I was trying to master topspin and my volley fluttered in front of him. He snapped it back at my feet; I got the racket down and the ball back over the net, in perfect position for him to slam it back at me.

"I'm practicing!" I yelled back.

"Not as much as you should be," he retorted. "Serve, and try to break a hundred."

The radar in our courts was set to km/h, not miles per hour, so a hundred was easy to do. I bristled and sliced a serve past him. The radar read "180."

"Better," he said.

"What do you care anyway?" I asked, rolling balls in my paw and thinking for a moment of Ori and the fresh balls at the center.

He crouched ready for the next serve. "Because I wanna go to the pros with you. I don't want to be playing in majors while you're struggling at the Futures level."

"I'll get to a major final before you do," I said, and served again.

We said that kind of thing to each other all the time, but while it still felt casual on my end, Marquize felt more serious about it. It bothered me, but there wasn't anyone I could talk to about it. Frio came to me to ask about the cheetah's attitude in mid-February, and a couple weeks later in March as well, and I appreciated him keeping an ear to the situation. He'd put an arm around my upper chest as I was a little too tall for him to reach my shoulders now—I'd grown to 6'3" by this point—and he'd said, "You know you can come to me with any problems."

What was I going to say? That my best friend was mad for reasons I couldn't quite figure out? I couldn't tell Frio I thought Marquize was jealous because I'd been skipping our after-practice dinners to go out with Shawna. I'd offered a couple times to take him with me and have Shawna find a girlfriend for him, but he'd said that if he wanted to go out with a girl, he'd find one in the tennis world. So I told Frio that I'd figure it out.

The second time, the ferret asked if it had anything to do with my girlfriend. I said, "How'd you know about Shawna?"

"Oh," he grinned, "you guys didn't think your evening practices were completely private, did you? But I didn't know her name. How's things going with her?"

That was a complicated question. Our next movie had passed

very chastely, though I still didn't hear most of it because my heart was pounding so hard. I wondered whether me not responding to her touch had been wrong, and if she wasn't going to try anymore because she thought I wasn't interested. I hoped that wasn't the case, but I couldn't think of a proper way to ask her. We went out to dinner several times and still had good talks, though I got distracted more often in them as I turned that question over in my head. I could hold her paw and give her a polite kiss goodnight, and then go back to the dorm and dream about the slender fingers brushing me.

The dorm, too, was a weird place. We all had individual bedrooms that let onto a large suite, and a shared bathroom. Normally after dinner and evening practice, Marquize and I would hang out in the suite doing schoolwork, and often several of the other boys from our class would join us. After dates with Shawna, I usually went back to Ma's because it was closer, but on the occasions when I did go back to Palm Gables, I found the suite empty, everyone back in their individual rooms studying.

The previous week we'd been to another movie, and this time Shawna had leaned over and her paw had come across the seat again. I'd tensed, but she'd just taken my paw. "Want to touch me?" she'd whispered.

"Yeah," I'd said back.

She'd taken my paw and placed it on her breast. I knew from the porn I'd watched on the Internet that breasts were desirable, and from talking to Bret and Malik that being allowed to touch them was quite rare for boys our age. And Shawna had pretty nice breasts (again, according to Bret and Malik). But when she held my fingers to them, mostly I thought, "soft." I'd rather have felt the curve of her hip, her rear just around her tail.

Still, I could tell that what she was doing was supposed to elicit more of a reaction, so I tried rubbing like I'd seen in some of the videos. Honestly, though, the movie was interesting, so I got distracted and then she pulled my paw away and dropped it. I wasn't sure if I'd done anything wrong, and after the movie she'd kissed me good night like usual and said she'd see me the next Tuesday evening.

So when Frio asked me how things were going, I said, "Okay, I guess."

"It's not that you can't handle having a relationship," he said. "It's

just a lot more work. It's one more thing to distract you from tennis."

"Am I still doing okay?"

"Well." He patted my side, keeping his arm around me. "You're doing okay. You could be doing better."

"I'll work harder," I said. Talking about Shawna while so close to Frio was a little weird, but that was ridiculous, of course. All the coaches put paws on us, and it didn't mean anything. It was the way sports worked in this country.

"Tell you what." Frio let me go. "I'll see if I can come up with some things to help motivate you."

With that nebulous promise, he sent me back to the locker room, where Marquize was almost done dressing. I went to my locker, next to his, and pulled my shirt off.

"You coming to practice or going out with your girl?" Marquize asked.

"Practice tonight," I said. "I'm seeing Shawna tomorrow."

"Great." He hefted his bag. I thought he might be heading out without me, but he waited while I got my shorts off, towel around my waist. "What did Frio say?"

"Oh…he said he was going to help me work harder. He said I'm doing fine."

"Huh." Marquize scratched his ear and nodded. "I'll meet you outside, then."

But he didn't leave right away. He was still there when I got out of the shower and got dressed. "Hey," he said as I fluffed out the fur of my tail. It wouldn't get dry for an hour but at least I could get it to the point where it didn't flop around behind me.

I tossed the towel away and pulled my shorts on. "Yes?"

"I want us to go to the majors together," Marquize said. "You know, I've been doing tennis clubs since I was five. I never got to do stuff after school with other cubs and none of them played tennis with me. I'd have friends here and there, but nothing stuck. My parents thought that coming here would be better for me. And, you know…" He looked down at the floor and then back up as I pulled my shirt on. "I like the other guys, but you're at my level. I mean, come on." His eyes met mine. "We both know we can be better than any of the other potzers here."

"Potzers" was a word Marquize had gotten from a movie, one I hadn't seen but he wanted to show me. I shut my locker and leaned back against it. "I didn't stop being your friend," I said. The sensation of feeling like Marquize was afraid of losing me was new, and I wasn't sure how to cope with it. I knew he'd been upset at me since I'd been dating Shawna, but I thought it was that he was worried about me. "I'm still going to the majors with you," I said. "But you told me to have fun, too. And you and I used to go out almost as much as I do with Shawna."

"Yeah, I know." He shrugged. "I guess if Frio's going to help motivate you then I shouldn't worry so much."

But his tail remained curled down and his ears weren't all the way up. I put a paw on his shoulder. "Hey," I said. "I'm having a birthday party in a couple weeks. I want everyone to come, but what if just you and me go to dinner before?"

It was gratifying to see a smile bloom on his muzzle. "Yeah," he said. "That would be nice."

Chapter Ten

The next week was a lot better. I even skipped a dinner with Shawna so I could practice with our class one evening. Marquize and I played doubles, of course; by this time we were a lot better than the time we'd played against Braden. We'd gotten used to each other and I didn't even realize how much that mattered; I set up to the left because I knew Marquize was drifting right behind me, or he'd duck out of the way of a ball I had a good shot on. The only doubles team that gave us problems was when Malik teamed up with Pom; the two of them meshed well, and when we wanted to play some games for fun after practice, we'd usually settle into that configuration.

This week at practice that's what we did, with Bret and Brittany nominally refereeing and everyone else chatting on the sidelines. We only played one set, which ended in a tiebreaker with Marquize and I losing 10-8. I expected the cheetah to say something about me having missed too many practices, but he only grinned and sat with me drinking water afterwards while everyone debated where to get dinner.

Dom drifted over to sit behind us on the bleachers as Pom plopped down near me. "No girl today?" the red fox asked me.

"Nah. I don't see her every day." I glanced at Marquize. He tipped the bottle back as though he hadn't heard me and started talking to Yu, on his other side, about a local tournament coming up.

"How far you get with her? Second base yet?" Pom's big black ears flicked.

"Um." I glanced again at Marquize, but he wasn't paying any attention.

Dom spoke up behind us. "Second base means you got to touch her tits through her clothes," he said.

Pom turned. "It doesn't mean clothes. It's just the breasts."

The arctic fox shook his head slowly, still looking down at his phone. "First base is kissing, open muzzle. Second base is petting through clothes. Third base is petting without clothes, blow jobs, whatever."

"No." Pom counted on his fingers. "First is kissing, second is *any* kind of petting above the waist, third base is below the waist. Including, ah, oral, you know."

At least I knew the term "blow job," or thought I did, again from the Internet, but the whole "base" thing was confusing as hell. I wasn't going to get any help from Marquize, so I leaned back and said, "Is this 'bases' like in baseball?"

Both foxes looked at me and then Pom laughed. "Sorry. Uh. Yeah. It's, I guess..." He scratched his ears. "It's like code? I guess so we can talk about it without, y'know, talking about it."

"Although," Dom pointed out, "we had to talk about it to confirm the definitions, which didn't agree, so it's not a very good code."

"Maybe it's different in the northwest." Pom shrugged. "Anyway, Rocky, what'cha say?"

"Um." I took another drink of water. The sun was right in my eyes, setting over the trees around the court and the buildings behind them. "I guess...somewhere between second and third?"

"Ha ha!" Pom laughed. "What, did she stop at the waist?"

Dom held his phone down to the red fox. "I think he means that he got to third base by one of our definitions but not the other. Look, here, we're both right according to Wikipedia."

The red fox ignored the phone. "So what happened? Come on, Rocky, we don't have girlfriends yet."

"I do," Dom said.

"We don't have girlfriends in this state." Pom snorted, and Dom stayed quiet.

So I told them a little haltingly about the theater and the groping, and in the middle of that, Marquize and Yu got up to go hit around again. The foxes listened eagerly, and so I felt comfortable transitioning into questions. "But listen, when she had my paw on her, uh, what was I supposed to do? Did I do something wrong?"

"Nah," Pom said. "I think you just hold it and like play with it a bit?"

I looked at Dom, but he was back looking at his phone. "Ask

Bret," he said. "He looks at porn all the time."

I didn't want to confess that I did too, because of the way he said it, so I just nodded. "Yeah, I guess."

"Just enjoy it," Pom said. "Don't be afraid of it. Wow. I'd be happy just getting to sit next to that pair."

Dom smacked him on the back of the head. "That's Rocky's girlfriend."

"What? I'm appreciating her." He turned to me, paws out. "You didn't get offended, did you?"

"Nah," I said, but I was wondering. I liked being around Shawna because she was fun to talk to, and the prospect of touching each other was exciting. But I didn't have that rapturous feeling Pom had when he talked about breasts, the way Bret would point out females in the porn he showed me. Then again, Dom didn't seem to care much about breasts either, nor did Marquize, so maybe it was just a thing some guys liked and others didn't. Or didn't *dis*like, but didn't get all wagging and drooling over.

"See?" Pom smacked Dom on the knee. The arctic fox didn't even react. Pom turned back to me. "You know, I figured you'd get a girl before us. I just thought it'd be one of the tennis girls. You and Marquize both got that exotic air."

I laughed at that, and the fox's ears flicked back. "What?"

"It's funny," I said. "Because I feel very common, but all of you, the foxes, and cougar, and red panda…you all feel exotic to me."

"Exotic, really?" Pom laughed, and his black ears came back up. "Foxes are so common here in the States. I mean, we're pretty, sure, but…nothing special."

"I think you're very handsome." If I'd known the word *striking* then, I would have used it, but all I was left with was handsome, which I knew was the equivalent of pretty but for guys. And it didn't seem to come with any romantic attachment—Ma had called me "handsome"—so I thought it was safe.

It did make Pom smile, and he said, "I like your fur, too. It's unusual and pretty cool."

"Careful," Dom said behind him. "Don't want to make your girlfriend jealous, Rocky."

"Ah, shut up," Pom said, and smacked the arctic fox again. "He's just jealous 'cause you didn't say his fur is handsome." It wasn't until later that I realized that Pom and I had exchanged compliments about our looks, and Dom had teased me about making Shawna jealous, without any of us saying we were creeped out or disgusted at the idea that guys could find each other attractive.

Dom, at the time, was shedding his white winter coat, and so even though he kept himself well groomed, he was bluish-brown with white guard hairs and patches of white fur and looked very much as though he had some kind of disease ("it's not mange," he'd said repeatedly when the shedding started). Pom, though he was also shedding, managed it much better, and his thicker coat had the same coloring as the undercoat, so it didn't look as odd.

I never grew out a winter coat and so I didn't shed, and both foxes had told me how lucky I was to come from a tropical climate. "But the long fur is good in winter, where you live, right?" I'd asked.

"Sure," Pom had said, "but you can always wear a jacket."

I had a good evening, and I didn't really miss Shawna at all; then again, I didn't miss the guys when I was with her. But I did miss the tennis. When we weren't "petting," that is.

The following Friday, after our afternoon classes, Frio told me he wanted to take me somewhere on Sunday. Marquize was dressing next to me, so I said, "Marquize too?"

"Sure," the ferret said. "You guys can both come. Be here at the school at eight a.m., okay?"

We exchanged looks, and both said, "Sure."

So Saturday night, instead of staying with Ma, I stayed at the dorm, and Marquize and I set alarms for 7:30 and walked down together Sunday morning. Frio was waiting with his car, a nice sedan, and Marquize waved me to sit in front. "You're the one who was invited," he said, but with a smile. And he sat behind me and rested his knees against my tail as we drove.

"Here." The ferret handed us two laminated badges on lanyards. They read, "Shady Open, All Access," and they had our pictures on them.

"We're going to the Shady next week, though," Marquize said as he took his badge. Our class knew about the Open, of course, because a bunch of the students above us were getting out of class to compete, and we were going down Tuesday and Wednesday and then next weekend to watch the matches.

"Yeah, but I arranged something special for Rocky here." Frio smiled and wouldn't tell us what it was, no matter how much we bugged him on the two and a half hour car ride down. He played his music, which was a lot of rap, and then asked us what we wanted to hear. Marquize asked for punk or alternative, and Frio had punk-pop, so we listened to Green Day and the Offspring and Less Than Jake (Frio claimed to have met one of the guys from that band).

When we arrived at the stadium, it was around eleven and the crowds had gathered already. Frio navigated us expertly to a side entrance marked, "Players and Media Only," where we flashed our badges to the lanky wolf in the blue security uniform.

Beyond that door, our claws clicked down a silent corridor. Only a few people passed us, talking in normal low tones. Marquize and I looked around, sniffing the Neutra-Scent and the age of the building below it, the old wood and cracked concrete and the carpeting that still held the scents of the feet that had walked over it. "Media Room," read one door we passed, from which floated the smell of coffee and pastries. "Administrative Offices" read two other doors, closed, no interesting scents hanging around them.

The door Frio stopped at was marked, "Players' Lounge." He opened it and ushered us inside. After a moment's hesitation, Marquize and I both followed, our tails curled close around us.

The large room held a number of comfortable-looking chairs, a table stacked with bottles of water, energy bars, fruit, what smelled like jerky, and some eggs, and an attendant ermine in a red uniform behind the table with his paws behind his back. Two of the chairs were occupied, both by female players: a tall fox and a slightly shorter cougar talking to each other, both dressed in bright white shirts and shorts, with two large equipment bags sitting beside the chairs.

"Have a seat," Frio said. "I'll be right back." He ran his pass over a magnetic scanner that unlocked a side door, and left through it.

We wandered halfway to the table, feeling out of place in our casual shorts and t-shirts, and then stopped. "You can help yourself," the ermine said.

"We're not playing," I said before I could stop myself.

"Don't worry about it." She smiled at us. "If you're allowed to be in here, you're allowed to eat the snacks."

The cougar looked up from her chair. "Palm Gables, right?" We nodded. "Yeah, you'll be playing here soon enough. Take the free food now, cubs." So we each grabbed a water and an energy bar and sat down to wait.

I'd barely finished my energy bar before Frio came back into the room. Behind him strode a fox with his ears down, a dark-furred fox with reddish highlights under his muzzle, a fox I'd last seen across a tennis court some months ago. If he had a winter coat like Pom and Dom, he'd brushed it all out or shaved it down. His sky-blue tight-fitting shirt clung to his sides above a pair of loose black shorts that hung to halfway down his thighs.

"Rocky," Frio said, "you remember Braden Longacre."

I stood, not sure what to say, but I held out a paw. I'd remembered him being taller, but he was a couple inches shorter than me. More muscular, though, from arms to thighs to calves. When he gripped my paw, I braced myself, but he shook it with a casual disinterest and released it quickly. "Hi," he said.

"Rocky hit that service—that serve against you when you came to play Palm Gables." Frio clearly had been going to say "service winner," which might have technically been true even though everyone was calling it my ace.

I looked, I hoped, appropriately modest. "You played really well," I said, which I thought was a fair compromise between crowing over the serve and buying into his lie that it had been out.

But it didn't matter; nothing flickered in Braden's brown eyes. His ears stayed upright and his expression stayed neutral. "Sure," he said in the same tone. "Course I remember."

He clearly didn't. I tried to keep my ears up, to be polite, and my tail up because I didn't want it to matter that I remembered him so well and he didn't remember me. I tried to think of something polite to say, because Frio had arranged this meeting and I didn't want to come off a total loser. "Good luck in the tournament."

Braden gave a quick nod. "Thanks." He shot a questioning gaze at Frio.

The ferret cleared his throat. "Rocky's having some questions about focus and work at Palm Gables. I thought it might be nice for you to take a couple minutes and tell him about your regimen there."

Braden shrugged. "I practiced every day. Some days I practiced until my legs and arm were sore. I focused on beating my classmates one by one until I was best in the class."

"Did you have a girlfriend?" Frio prompted him.

The cross fox frowned, his whiskers going back against his muzzle, and his eyes flicked down to the floor for a second. "No. No time. Couple of my friends had girlfriends."

"And are they in this tournament?"

Braden's headshake was as quick and decisive as his nod. "Nope. Two of them are still on the Futures circuit. None of the rest are playing pro. And the two on the Futures circuit aren't the ones who had girlfriends."

We stood there in silence, and after another glance at Frio, Braden went on. "Look. You want to get to this level, maybe you have the talent, maybe you don't. But nobody has enough talent to coast through life. You can have a girlfriend or you can have tournaments. It's either-or. Because if you don't spend every minute practicing to be the best you can, then sooner or later you're going to come up against someone who did. Like me."

I thought his chest puffed out a little when he said that. "I understand," I said. "But are you happy?"

He stared at me and I thought maybe that was the first time he really looked at me. "Happy?" he said. "The way you get happy is by winning titles. That's the point of everything you're doing. If you want to be happy, quit tennis and get a day job doing, I don't know, working fast food or stocking shelves somewhere. Have a girlfriend and go drinking on the weekends and watch the tournaments on TV. That's what happy is. Happy isn't for us, not until we win a title, and then it only lasts as long as the next tournament."

"Well," Marquize muttered from the chair he hadn't bothered to get up from, "that's cheery."

"I'm not here to make you feel better," Braden snapped. He pointed at Frio. "I'm here because he asked me to come help a cub, maybe impart some of my work ethic to him. What are you, his entourage?"

"I was his doubles partner when you played us," Marquize said.

"Yeah, well, I guess Frio isn't worried about *your* potential." Braden returned his gaze to me while Marquize sputtered behind me. "Look, I've got a match to prep for. Is that enough? You're at Palm Gables to play tennis. So play fucking tennis. Everything else is secondary. Everything."

And with that, he spun on his heel and walked back to the locker room.

We stood—and sat, in Marquize's case—in silence. The vixen and cougar, who'd listened to the whole thing, giggled, and then the cougar spoke up. "Hey," she said. "Just so you know, there are a bunch of people on the tour who aren't as intense as Mister Pricklebutt there."

"Yes." The vixen grinned, her thick accent Siberian. "Lots of them have partners on the tour. In fact, when you boys turn eighteen, if you're on the tour, you'll have your pick."

"Absolutely. Jackal and cheetah?" The cougar turned to the vixen. "Leila would be into spots."

"Oh my god, yes."

Frio coughed. "Thanks," he said. "I think Braden made a good point, though, and I am these boys' coach, so…"

"Sorry." The cougar stretched and got up. "Didn't know you were doing a Scared Straight thing here. Come on, Davina."

"So what now?" I asked. "Turn around and drive home?"

"No, no." Frio gestured to the door. "We're here, so let's watch some of the matches. These are the ones you guys will be hopefully playing in a few years from now."

And the guys we watched did not look so much older than we were. The way they played, though…I'd never watched tennis up close at a professional level. Even here, one circuit below the Champions level, the shots were crisper, the serves harder, the play faster than when my friends in the school—and me—played. Marquize and I sat silently while Frio talked in a low tone about various plays, how the players (an agile lemur a few years older than us and a veteran wolf who was 35) were setting their feet, elements of their swings, how the wolf shifted to anticipate the lemur's returns, and how the lemur was able to get around the ball to get better angles on it.

It was a lot to take in, but after a few of the games, I started to get it. We stayed for Braden's match, and of the four players we saw, he was by far the most impressive. He ran his opponent all over the court, dropping shots with precision, and his main weakness as far as we could tell was that he was taking a little too much time to decide where to hit the ball. On several occasions, as Frio pointed out to us, Braden hesitated a second, allowing his opponent to get into position to hit a winner back. But a lot of the time, enough to win the match, he played with a cool unflappability that his opponent, a younger rabbit, couldn't shake.

After he'd won, he headed back to the locker room. Frio hurried down to try to congratulate him, but Braden either didn't see the ferret or ignored him.

"Well," Frio said cheerfully when he got back to us, "Braden's pretty intense, you know, even after he just won a match. Probably went back to see who his next opponent is going to be so he can start studying him. You guys ready to go?"

We were. On the way back, I sat in the back with Marquize even though Frio complained that he felt like a chauffeur that way. I told him I needed time to think about stuff.

Over the music, Marquize talked to me in near-whispers. Frio's ears stayed perked forward, so I'm pretty sure he wasn't listening. "That was a lot to take in."

"Yeah." I remembered Marquize's talk from earlier in the week. "I'm glad you were there with me."

"Me too." He snorted. "Even if Bray-den didn't really notice me."

"What does he know?" I grinned. "He's an asshole."

"An asshole who's going to be a champion." Marquize sighed. "Are we ever going to be able to compete with someone like him who lives for nothing but tennis?"

"I guess we only have one way to find out."

Marquize flicked his tail and picked at the spots on his arm. "I dunno. I know I was on you about your girl, but I can't do tennis twenty-four-seven. None of us in the class does."

"No." I sighed. "But I probably should do more."

We rode in silence for several more miles, watching the pastel houses and roadside restaurants trundle by. "So," I said finally, "do you know how to break up with someone?"

Chapter Eleven

I had the conversation with Shawna about halfway through March, sitting in the front room of her house, both of us on the sofa, her parents and brother out back barbecuing in the nice spring weather. I tried to be nice about it, the way Marquize had told me to. "It isn't about you," I told her. "It's me. I need to spend all my time working on tennis."

There was a lot I still didn't know about girls. As nice as I was, she started crying and said a lot of things that made me feel really bad, about how she thought I was special and we could have had a really good time together. I started to tell her we could still hang out as friends and then stopped myself, but she kept crying and I didn't know when it would be right for me to leave. So I put my arm around her shoulders and I said, "If you want, we can still talk sometimes."

Then she snapped her head around and glared at me and pushed my arm away so fast my claws snagged her sweater. "Oh, no, Rocky," she said, "you do *not* get to use the 'let's be friends' line on me. Get out!"

Which at least made it easier for me to know when I should leave, even if I still felt bad about leaving her with tear tracks running down her muzzle and a pile of tissues scattered around her paws. I got up, walked slowly to the door, and looked back at her. She sniffed again, and when she saw me looking, she said, "Don't act *guilty* now. You're just a dumb jackal. I was only dating you out of pity. Nobody's going to want to go out with someone who doesn't even know how to sext!"

I stared at her blankly. She wiped her eyes and looked haughty. "Who doesn't even know what sexting *is*," she added. "Just get out already."

Back at the dorm, I was studying in the suite when Marquize

came by. "How'd it go?" he asked, plopping down in the plush arm-chair next to the couch I was on.

"She was sad. And then angry." I looked up at his nod. "What's 'sexting'?"

His tail froze and his hazel eyes stayed steady on mine. "Uh. Why?"

"Shawna said I didn't know how to do it."

He relaxed against the side of the chair. "It's role-playing sex over texts. Sometimes with pictures. Did she send you something like she wanted you to touch her, or…?"

"No." I searched my memory. "Oh. One time I was here and she texted that she was taking off her shirt."

"Uh-huh." Marquize settled back into the chair. "And what did you do?"

"Well, I…" My ears warmed and flattened. "I thought she was telling me what she was doing with her day. So I, uh, I told her I was doing my World Cultures homework."

He grinned. "And what did she say?"

"Nothing. I think she went to sleep."

He laughed and reached over to pat my arm. "Rocky, you're awesome. Don't change."

"So you think she wanted me to…to what?"

"I almost don't want to tell you."

"Mar!"

He drew his paw back. "All right, all right. She wanted you to text her that you wanted to touch her bare chest, probably. Or else text her that you were taking off your clothes, too."

"But I wasn't."

"She probably wasn't actually taking off her shirt."

"Then why did she text that to me?"

He shook his head. "One day you'll understand."

I growled and went back to my book. I wanted to understand now, and Marquize wasn't helping. But he stayed around, and later he asked for more details and told me I'd done a good job. "Nobody likes to get dumped," another word I'd just learned, "but you told her the truth, so she should be happy."

"In some of the movies she likes, the main character's adventure starts when someone breaks up with her." I tch'd at myself. "I should have told her that."

"Don't waste that on her," Marquize told me. "She's going to be mad at you no matter what you say. But now you get to focus on tennis. And you had to do it tonight. If you waited until next week then you'd have to have brought her to your birthday party."

***

Ma had seen enough movies and television shows with birthday parties to have an idea of what a States-style birthday party was, and she wanted to throw me one for my fifteenth. We could hold it by the tennis courts, she said, because she didn't want "all my friends" in her apartment and I didn't know if everyone could get into the dorms. At the time I'd been thinking about Shawna, but by the time I broke up with her, we'd already started planning. So Ma was going to bring a cake down to the public park with the tennis courts, and all the tennis cubs were going to sing Happy Birthday.

I was excited about it and a little nervous, and the nervousness was part of the excitement, too. When we'd come to the States everything had been a new experience, and every day had brought eagerness and a little terror. But the experiences were all good, like meeting Marquize and meeting Coach Murphy, and starting a job and playing doubles and all of it. And little by little I'd lost the terror, and along with it the eagerness. But here was another new thing, and even though I'd been to three birthday parties in the last year, I was going to be the center of attention at this one.

When the day finally came, I bounced along from the school to the courts and my tail flicked all over the place. Marquize noticed and elbowed me. "It's not a surprise," he said. "You know it's coming."

"Yeah, but I never really had a birthday party before." I wagged my tail. "Ma would make me and Ori a birthday dinner, but that was all."

"Did you call Ori?"

I nodded. "This morning. I wished her happy birthday and she wished me happy birthday."

"How is she doing?"

"Fine." She had still managed to avoid being attached to any of the people our aunt might have in mind, but she'd been forced to cut back on tennis because Kamina was making her learn cooking and sewing and a lot of things Ori either knew well enough or had no interest in. She'd decided that she wanted to help families who had lost fathers and sons to the war, but Kamina wouldn't let her spend too much time with the groups there that provided aid to those families. A lot of them were foreign-run (though they did employ native people), and Ori said that Kamina was worried she would "learn foreign customs" and be less desirable as a bride.

It wasn't worth going into all that with Marquize, though. My sister's troubles were hers and mine and Ma's to deal with. Anyway, when we rounded the corner of the campus where the courts were and I saw everyone gathered there, everything else flew out of my mind. The crowd was larger than normal: not only Bret and Yu, and Pom and Dom and Malik and Veronica and Brittany, but also Frio, and Jazzy and Merritt, and two or three other cubs from the school who were friends of mine.

Ma was hard to see in the middle of them, nearly a foot smaller than even the tallest one, but I could sense her presence there in the center. Everyone clustered around her, looking inward, and I caught snatches of words like "looks great" and "delicious." And when Marquize and I got there and they noticed us, everyone cheered and made room for me to come up to the little picnic table.

"Hey," Bret said, patting my shoulder. "Happy birthday! Your ma's great."

Brittany, next to him, chattered agreement. "It's so interesting hearing about where you came from. You know," she said to Ma, "Rocky doesn't talk a whole lot about it and when he does it seems so grim. But you made it sound so interesting, too, with the Great Marketplace and the river and the open country, and he never talks about any of that."

"Rocky," Ma said with a smile, "never went out to the country much. We lived in the city his whole life."

"That's too bad. It sounds like there's some wonderful areas."

While she went on, I looked down at the cake. Chocolate frosting, fifteen candles, and a little toy fox with a tennis racket standing there. I guess most of the stores around here wouldn't have jackal toys, and fox or coyote was close enough, but Ma had also tried to color the fox brown, and as a result it looked more like Braden Longacre than like me. I didn't mind, though; I knew what she was intending to do.

"Shall we sing now?" Ma asked everyone.

Veronica told her to light the candles first, so she did that carefully and then we all stood around, me and Ma at the center, and everyone sang happy birthday. I stood there and basked in the attention all through the song, and when it was over, I bent down and blew out all the candles. Everyone around me clapped. Ma and I pulled the candles out and she had just made the first cut in the cake when a voice cut through the crowd. "Hey! Jackal!"

Charging down the gentle slope from the street was Shawna's older brother Marcus. I laid my ears back and moved to put the table between me and the coyote. He slowed as he got near the group, stalking across the grass, but he never took his eyes off me. The tennis class parted to make way for him, half of them watching him and half staring at me. Ma took a step back, still holding the cake knife.

"Hey, Marcus," I said, then felt like an idiot because his ears were flat back and his teeth were showing. What did I expect him to do, stop and put his ears up and say hi back?

He did not do that. He came partway around the table, and when I edged around the opposite way, he slammed his paws down on it. "You fucking little prick," he said. "You think you can get away with doing that to my sister?"

Doing what? The only thing I'd done to her recently was break up. Oh, which she'd been really upset about. "Look," I said, "I know she didn't want to, but I had to do it."

"*Had* to?" He lunged to the side and I hurried to keep the table between us, yelling back across it.

"Yeah! I'm sorry! I had a really good time with her—"

"Oh, I bet you did." He stopped and ran the other way, and I changed directions as well.

"I'm sorry she was so upset about it! Marquize said I was as nice as possible!" I kept dodging around the table, but I was watching Marcus, too, and once I'd gotten over the shock of his attack I didn't think he was really a threat. I mean, Ma had always told me not to fight, but that was back home where people carried knives and guns and where outside our neighborhood Ori and I had twice seen a dead body in the street. Here in the States, or at least around Palm Gables, there wasn't a lot of violent crime. I was pretty sure Marcus

just wanted to punch me and maybe bite, and that wasn't a fight; that was a scrap.

Back home, those were something no young male of any species could avoid. They happened over food, over insults, over compliments even. Punches and claws were traded and then the matter was settled. I glanced at Ma, but she didn't seem worried. She did keep the cake knife up, though.

"Nice?" The coyote snarled at me, and then he did climb up the bench and try to jump over the table.

My blood had been racing from the time he came charging down toward me, but as I faced him it slowed and I calmed myself. When he leapt over the table, I slid sideways out of the way, no longer so worried.

Even though I'd been in plenty of scraps back home, I knew that here any kind of physical violence was considered a fight and I should avoid it. And I didn't even want to get into a scrap with Marcus anyway because he was sticking up for his sister. But when he came over the table I knew I could hold my own if it came down to that. He was three years older than me, but I was taller than and almost the same weight. If I'd wanted to I could've waited for him and grabbed his arm or leg and thrown him down. Instead, I scooted around to the side and was across the table from him by the time he got his footing.

"Stop running away, you little coward!" Marcus panted and set his paws on the table again.

"Hey." Marquize stepped forward up next to the coyote. "Leave him alone. He's a good guy."

"Good guy!" The coyote whirled on him and jabbed him in the shoulder. "You know what he did?"

"Yeah!" Marquize pushed him back.

I started to come around the table then. "Hey, cut it out," I said, but both of them ignored me.

"I told him how to do it!" The cheetah got up in his face. "And you need to chill out."

Marcus's expression changed; his lips curled and his eyes narrowed, and I saw what was going to happen a second too late to warn Marquize. The coyote's arm came back and shot forward, landing his fist square in Marquize's chest.

There was enough force and surprise behind it to send Marquize to the ground holding his side. And that was enough to get Frio and Yu to jump forward, but I was closer. Marcus hadn't quite recovered from his punch when I grabbed his arm and pulled, yanking him off his feet and sending him tumbling to the ground. Right away, I jumped on top of him (because that's what you do in a scrap) but Frio was there to pull me off by my shoulders. "I just broke up with her!" I yelled. "What the shit is your problem?"

Yu and Dom held Marcus down while Frio kept me back. The coyote twisted, glaring at me. "Yeah, but you tried to feel her up first. Pulled the button off her shirt!"

"What?" I stared at him.

"She showed me!"

"Hold on, hold on." Frio didn't loosen his grip on me. "Rocky, did you do—"

"No!" I glared back at Marcus. "You were with us on all those dates, you know me, how could you—"

"She's my sister!" he yelled back.

A vision of Ori burst into my head, and that calmed me down. If someone had hurt Ori, if she'd shown me a torn shirt—well, Ori could take care of herself, but I still would have wanted to punish whoever'd done it. "Listen to me," I said. "Nothing like that happened. I don't know why she told you that. I said I had to spend more time playing tennis and I couldn't keep seeing her and she got upset, and then she threw me out. I never touched her. I mean, I snagged a claw on her shirt, but that's it."

"Probably," Veronica said, "she wanted this guy to come beat you up."

Marcus had shut up now, though he was still looking straight at me. I wanted to tell him about Shawna touching me in the movie theater, but this wasn't the right time, so I tried to look honest and trustworthy. "It's a shitty thing to do," Veronica went on. "I saw it in a movie but I never knew anyone who actually did it."

Bret, behind me, muttered something about coyotes, and Marcus's ears flicked, but he didn't otherwise react. "Rocky's a good guy," Dom, kneeling on one of his arms, said down to him.

"I saw the shirt," Marcus said stubbornly back, but he stopped struggling so much.

"We know Rocky." Marquize struggled to sit up. "He would've told me if anything like that had happened."

"And you'd tell me, right? Of course." His eyes moved to Marquize and then up beyond the cheetah, to my right. "Hey, lotta help you guys are."

Jazzy's deep voice laughed. "Didn't look like you needed much help getting beat up by a fifteen year old cub."

"Fuck you," Marcus said.

"Watch your language," Frio said at my side, still holding onto me.

"Anyway," Jazzy said, "Rocky talked about your sister at work and he never said anything like that shit. He really liked her."

"I still do," I said, "and it's none of anyone's business but I swear to you I didn't do anything."

Marcus exhaled and then spoke more quietly. "Let me up," he said. "I'm not gonna hurt him."

Yu and Dom exchanged glances and then slowly let him go, watching warily as he rose fluidly to his feet and brushed himself off. He extended a paw down to Marquize. "Sorry," he said. "You okay?"

"My ribs hurt." The cheetah stood and pressed a paw to his side.

A smile flickered across Marcus's face. "Sorry," he repeated. "Next time stay out of fights that aren't yours."

"Any fight with my friend is mine," Marquize said, and his eyes slid over to me.

"I think you'd better get home now." Frio stepped forward. "We're not going to call the police about this."

I think that was meant to be a threat, but Marcus didn't flinch or look particularly bothered. He glared at Jazzy and Merritt one last time, then turned around and stalked away, tail arched and ears back, the way he'd come.

When he got up the rise to the road, everyone relaxed and started chattering amongst themselves. I shook off Frio's paws and went to Marquize immediately. "You okay?"

His paw remained at his side. "I'll be okay until I can get some painkillers," he said. "It hurts a bit when I breathe."

"Thanks," I said. "For helping. I really appreciate it."

"Doesn't look like you needed it." He smiled. "But that's what best friends do."

Our friends crowded around him, patting him and cheering him for sticking up for me. "It's probably a bruise," Veronica said. Pom asked to feel the bruise, and Frio told Mar to wait for the nurse on campus. I offered to walk him there, and he said he didn't want to interrupt my party and that he could stay for cake.

So Ma came back up with the knife to finish cutting the cake. Nearby, I heard Jazzy and Merritt talking about how they were going to tell the school about the "fight," and Bret and Malik talking about whether they thought I really did feel up Shawna. I tried to tune that out and watch Ma cut the cake. "Why didn't you help me?" I asked her finally.

"I knew you could handle him." She cut another slice and put it on a plate. "This little bit of anger over a story his sister made up—I told you she was no good—this was going to pass quickly. Besides." She brandished the knife. "If you did need me, I would be here. Now, go talk with your friends."

I enjoyed the rest of the party even though I was still on edge. There was something warm about having everyone stick up for me like that. I answered a lot of questions about Marcus (and Bret took me aside to ask, "really, did you try to touch her?" and then I felt comfortable telling him about what Shawna did in the theater, which got him to slap me on the back so hard I dropped my cup) but people mostly seemed to forget about it. Marquize kept holding his side all through the party, though by the end of it I thought he was playing it up for sympathy. Certainly it was getting him more attention than even I had.

I caught the scent of coyote behind me as things were winding down and I was standing by myself at the table watching Ma talk to Jazzy, trying not to focus my ears to hear what they were saying. The sandalwood that floated along with it told me it wasn't Marcus, and when I turned I found Kim there half-smiling.

"You're all alone," she said. "Not feeling neglected?"

I shook my head. "This whole party is really nice. I'm so glad people came out for it."

"My birthday's next month. You should come to the party."

"Thanks." I smiled.

She looked towards Marquize, who was gesturing in the air as Bret and Yu watched. "You know he didn't mean to take the attention off you, right?"

"He meant to take Marcus's attention."

"Yes." She laughed. "It was very brave of him. I thought you were doing well avoiding the fight."

I turned my attention back to Ma. "I was brought up not to fight if I could avoid it, but you know…" I was going to tell her that this wasn't a real fight, and then I was looking at Jazzy and remembered him telling me that I didn't always need to be a hundred percent honest. I wouldn't have cared for myself, but I thought if I made the fight sound less important than it was, it would make Marquize seem less impressive. So I finished the sentence with, "…sometimes people force you to do things you don't want to. Or friends to jump in for you."

Kim didn't follow my look at Marquize, her thoughts obviously elsewhere. "So, coyote girl, huh?"

I hadn't looked at her in that way before. She was attractive, with those big coyote ears and her wide smile turning up in mischievous curls at the back. There wasn't a spark like I'd had with Shawna, though; Kim was just a tennis practicing partner I hadn't talked to very much. "Yeah," I said. "But everyone tells me I can't have a girlfriend and a tennis career."

"You can't have a girlfriend outside of tennis," she said. "But look." Over by the chain link fence around the courts, Yu and Brittany rested shoulder to shoulder, holding paws, deep in conversation. "If a couple are both in tennis, it can work. You see it all the time in the professional level. Your mistake was going after a girl from the town."

"I didn't go *after* her. We just met. But I think it's a lot easier if I don't, y'know…"

Kim laughed. "Don't worry. I'm not asking you out. Not that you're not cute, but I guess I'm like you. I like it if it happens naturally."

"Me too." I coughed. "But just to be sure, you don't have an older brother, do you?"

She laughed, and I laughed too. We talked about Marcus a little more and I told her about Ori and her situation. That appalled her, that Ori would be forced into a marriage, and I told her that Ma and I were also opposed to it, but that was how things worked back home. "Probably she'll be courted by a merchant and she'll have a good home. It'll be fine, but we both think she's too young."

"Yes!" Kim said. "She's thirteen!"

"Fourteen now." I smiled.

"Right, you're fifteen. One more year and you can start learning to drive." She elbowed me.

I grinned. "Have to talk to Ma about getting a car, I guess."

And Kim smiled again, and then Pom came over and joined us, and I could tell he was interested in Kim, so I stayed quiet.

As the party wound down and people waved goodbye, Marquize came over and found me. "Hey," he said. "It still hurts. I'm going to get some painkillers. Can you get my homework in school tomorrow?"

"Sure." I looked down at his side. "Are you okay?"

"I'll be fine. Just bruised, I think."

"Okay." I gave him a smile. "Thanks again."

He grimaced. "I've got to learn to fight better. Maybe you can show me."

"Hope I don't have to," I said.

**

I collected Marquize's homework the next day through all our classes, and when it came time for after-school practice, Frio picked up a racket to hit with me even though Dom had offered. It was harder for him to observe me that way, but he still managed to comment on my topspin as he hit the ball back. In addition, he could interact with me as we hit back and forth. "You're getting better," he said at the end of it. "You're much more consistent now and getting more precision and strength with your backhand."

"How do you think I'll do in the tournament?" I asked. "Can I beat Don?"

"Probably not yet." He tapped his racket against his paw. "But I would've said you couldn't have beaten Verid either, so shows what I know. Go out and play your best and who knows what you can do."

"Right." I walked over to put my racket away, trying to figure out in my head what I would have to do to beat Don.

Marquize was asleep on his bed when I got back. I called his name, but he didn't even stir. So I dropped off the assignments that were paper (he'd already have gotten the e-mailed ones on his account) and then I was about to go when I caught sight of his laptop, closed on his desk.

We had some World Cultures research to do for a paper, and I'd been using his laptop to write on since otherwise I'd have to go to the library and use one of their computers. His laptop could access our online accounts and he'd set up a login for me; we couldn't use it at the same time, but we had enough other homework that we could share it without too much trouble.

"Mar," I hissed again, then repeated it louder. He didn't stir.

It wouldn't bother him if I did a little of my World Cultures work here, and it'd save me a trip to the library tonight. Most of the rest of my work I could do myself.

So I sat down at his desk and opened his laptop. It took a moment to recover from being asleep, and then it sprang to life with a full-screen picture of what I had come to know very well as porn. But it wasn't the kind of porn I was used to. I mean, I'd seen males taking females from behind before, but the female in this case, a slender coyote with a long, fluffy tail—well, wasn't female.

The tiger behind him was male for sure, and was doing the same thing I'd seen in a lot of porn pictures, except his thing was going into the other male under his tail. And the other male's thing was out, too, and stuff was dripping from it.

I couldn't stop staring at it. My pants felt very tight, making me squirm in my chair. I looked up and saw that this picture was on a webpage called "Hot Gay Action XXX" and in the top right was the name "M. Spots" next to the designation "Premium Member."

Marquize made a noise on the bed. I jumped in the chair and slammed the laptop closed.

Chapter Twelve

I shut the door to my room and sat cross-legged on the bed, very aware of the warm hardness between my legs. I'd known what gay people did—well, no—I'd known who they did it with, but I'd never thought about how—and was that how it was? With the—under the tail—and they both seemed—well, porn was always like that—was Marquize into it?

Was *I* into it?

My heart pounded. I licked my dry lips and reached down to hold the end of my tail, which I'd curled tightly around my waist. There wasn't much doubt about Marquize. It was on his laptop. He must have been browsing and gotten sleepy and forgotten about it. Or not thought that I'd be coming to use his laptop.

Maybe I was fascinated by how unusual it was and that was why my erection wasn't going down. I'd gotten used to regular porn and it still had the same effect, but not quite this long, usually. This was different.

But what about Marquize? That explained why he'd never been interested in having a girlfriend. And why a lot of the tennis cubs had been talking about him when that football player announced he was gay—

Wait. Did everyone but me know?

I felt stupid. Everyone must have known, and I was the only one who hadn't.

Waitwaitwait WAIT. Did everyone think me and Marquize were—just because we were best friends? Was that why everyone was so sure I hadn't tried to attack Shawna like her brother thought?

I spent probably half an hour meticulously analyzing my memory of the party, every word that had been said, for some clue that people thought Marquize and I did…stuff like the tiger and coyote in his picture. But no, most people had said that I was a "good guy," not that I was gay or anything like that. And at the end of that analysis, my sheath was back to normal, until my memory played back the picture, and then it started getting hard again.

I squeezed my eyes shut and thought about tennis, about the lessons Frio had gone over that day. That uncurled my tail and helped me breathe more easily. Distractions: that was what I needed. So I spread out the homework I could work on here and then, when I was done with that, I went to the library.

***

I didn't ask Marquize about the picture on his computer, but all that week I kept thinking about it at inopportune times, like when I was lying in bed trying to release the tension in my groin, a practice I'd learned when Bret showed me my first porn. I tried looking at other porn and thinking about that, but the females in the pictures all became male in my head late at night. Then I tried not giving myself release at all, but that kept me tossing and turning all night and the next day (well, the day after, really; when you get a bad night's sleep it hits you the day after).

I had it on my mind even when I called Ori that Friday night, with the vague idea that I could ask her if she'd heard of any gay tennis players. If I looked it up myself at the library, someone might see the record of it there where I had to log in with my school credentials.

It wasn't that I was afraid the school would throw me out or anything. Everyone in my class had been okay with the gay football player, but there had also been another feeling I was familiar with, that it was okay *over there*. Back home, we felt that about things like, say, the villages where some of our countryfolk still collected multiple wives. That was the tradition, it was their way, it was perfectly fine—for them. Over there. Not in the city, not for us.

So I didn't want to be seen as one of those people coming into the city with a parade of wives and inspiring disgust. Marquize, my role model and leader in most things cultural here, had felt the same, clearly, because he'd hidden it away from everyone.

But Ori drove that out of my head pretty much right away. "Don't call next week," she said.

"Why not?"

"Because I won't be here. Kamina's taking me out to meet this jackal."

I sat up straight on the couch in Ma's apartment, ears shooting up. "She means you to marry him?"

She didn't answer right away. "Ori!" I demanded.

"It isn't settled." She sounded uncertain though. "I'm going out so he can see me again and so Kamina can see his plantation. He owns a coffee plantation north of the city."

"You can't! You're—"

"I intend to ask if he'll let me do my work with the survivor families."

I flopped back onto the couch and stared at the ceiling. I'd never felt the distance between us more acutely than when I wanted to run out the door and down the street to grab her away from Kamina and bring her here. "You haven't asked already?"

"It—there wasn't a good time for it."

He wasn't going to let her. He was going to get her pregnant right away and that would be it. She would be a mother for the rest of her life. "How old is he?"

"He's forty-one."

"What?" I put pieces together. "How many wives does he already have?"

"Ro—"

"Ori."

She sighed. "He doesn't have any. His last wife died when his plantation was raided."

I rolled off the couch. "I'm getting Ma."

"Ro, don't."

"You can't go marry this guy."

"I'll handle it. Kamina says—"

"Ma!"

She looked up from the book she was reading in bed with a bemused expression. "Ori says Kamina wants to marry her to a guy who owns a coffee plantation whose wife was killed in a raid." I knew I wasn't putting those thoughts together in the best way, and I didn't care. "You have to forbid it."

In my ear, Ori was telling me to listen to her, that she could handle it. Ma looked back at me and then nodded once and stood, holding out her paw for the phone. I dropped it in her fingers and stood there.

"Ori?" She turned away from me and paced toward the kitchen, then back. "Please put Kamina on."

She listened for a moment. "I understand. But that is not yours to worry about. Put your aunt on."

I flicked my tail back and forth, watching, wishing I could hear. Ma turned back toward me. "Kamina? Tell me about this suitor you have found." Her ears flicked back and forward, and she listened intently, eyes staring ahead as though she could see her sister sitting in that chair in front of the TV. When she spoke again, it was in short phrases as my aunt spoke on the other end in between. "I understand. He sounds like a wealthy prospect. Yes, I do see. Kamina, you must understand—no, I do not think you do. I do not. No. If you had thought this through, you would not be taking my daughter to a plantation in such a dangerous place."

Her eyes flicked up to me. "I see. So his wife died from an 'unusual accident.' If I called François, he would say the same? I do. Yes. Maybe I should call him anyway to ask how he's doing. I haven't talked to him since I moved here.

"Oh, Ro is fine. Don't change the subject. Now, are you going to break it off with this coffee plantationer?" Her ears went still then, and she got that intent expression again. "Yes," she said slowly, and looked up at me. "Yes, that will work. All right, then. Thank you, Kamina. No, I believe Ro and Ori are done for the night. Good-bye."

She held the phone out to me, her ears down. "There. Ori will not go to that plantation."

"Thanks." I took the phone back. "What—why was she sending Ori there?"

Ma waved a paw. "It is no business of ours."

By "ours" of course, she meant "yours," but I knew her well enough not to push the issue. I took the phone and sat down next to Ma to watch TV for the rest of the night.

Chapter Thirteen

The worry about Ori faded to a background noise quickly. Ma had taken care of it and that would be that. If Kamina tried anything again, Ma would deal with her. Maybe in another year when Ori was fifteen, she'd be more suitable to a match. I was fifteen and the whole episode with Shawna made me leery of trying to have a girlfriend again, but I knew how our customs worked and that girls as young as thirteen were often promised. If anything, fifteen was the prime age and by the time Ori was seventeen, she would be too old.

The tangled mess of worry about the picture on Marquize's computer and what it meant about him and what it meant about me took longer to process. My anxiety never came back as acutely as it had the first day I found out about it, but it bothered me from time to time, and more than once I almost said something to Marquize. I didn't, though; if he wanted me to know about it, he'd tell me, and I didn't want to have found out by spying on him.

Anyway, in April and May our training got a lot more intense. The end-of-year tournament was a lot more important than the Christmas one, everyone told me. Often if you did well in the tournament, you'd be encouraged to start playing in Junior tournaments in preparation for joining the Futures circuit full time the following year. Sometimes agents attended and picked up students right away, but that was rare. Guess which name came up when Coach Murphy talked to us about that.

So I started taking Braden's advice and focused on individual players. I was already beating Marquize routinely, and the next students up ahead of me were Pom and Dom, the foxes. They were both about the same, but with wildly different styles, so they were a good challenge for me. At least, when I talked to Frio about it, that's what he said.

Pom played like Marquize, with great technique and little anticipation, relying on his athletic ability to get to shots. He had a better touch with the ball than Marquize and a pretty wicked forehand, but he'd spray his backhand wildly around if you got him off balance. That was easier said than done: Pom had great footwork and speed and he used his tail for balance better than any other fox I've seen since then, except for one (a lot of players keep their tails curled around them; some let them flop around). I had to plan a series of shots to draw him to one side of the court, fake going to the other one, and then, when he jumped in anticipation, place the ball right where he'd been.

That was the theory, anyway. It was easier to train for him by playing Marquize, who played the same way, but it was also harder because Pom was better, and I couldn't get my skills to the edge they needed to be by practicing against the cheetah. It was good for Marquize, though, because he kept getting better, and it wasn't like it was bad for me. I liked Marquize best of all the tennis cubs—to play against—because he and I studied together, so we sat down afterwards and talked about what we'd done right and wrong. Also, we'd played together for most of the year, so we couldn't surprise each other. We could try, but we knew each other's moves and tricks. "Your forehand's better," he'd say. "You got good spin on it and it's going farther."

Or I'd say, "You're doing a lot better with your backhand. When you keep both paws on the racket it's a great shot."

Or he'd say, "Your serve is light-years better than it was six months ago."

Or I'd say, "Great footwork there. You're a lot more decisive."

Pom and Dom never talked that much after our matches. They'd say, "Good shot," or would discuss some of the points of our instruction with me, but they were each other's practice partners and had the same history with each other that Marquize and I had. They were happy to mix up practices for the same reason I wanted to: to work with someone new and get more experience. For all I knew, they had lists of players to learn and beat just like I did; if so, I'd improved enough to be on those lists.

Though Dom was quieter and most of our class thought he wasn't quite as good as Pom, I found the arctic fox a tougher opponent. He didn't have the strength or speed of Pom or Marquize or even me, but he played a cerebral game. He'd lull you into thinking you had control of a point with easily handled forehands, only somehow the shot before you were going to put him away, he'd send a backhand down the line, or a floater into the corner, or he'd cut an impossible drop shot, easing the ball over the net so it had bounced twice before you could even get up to it.

I had to think while playing him, but I also had to look for that unpredictable shot, to consciously do the things my instinct wasn't telling me to. It was hard, and more than once I got trapped by indecision and didn't do anything at all. I lost a lot of games to Dom at first, so I had even more motivation to beat him, because if I didn't, he'd stop playing me. Fortunately, I spent a few evenings by myself practicing different reactions to situations I'd been in with him, and over the course of April, I got good enough to beat him two out of three sets, and after that he sought me out to play against.

(I never would have had the time to work on that if I'd still been dating Shawna, so there was that. Marquize was nice enough to only remind me of that once or twice.)

Going into May, the games with Dom were the most fun of all the people I played, because he learned my tendencies as quickly as I learned his. We never put it into words, but I had to discover new ways to play against him because he would figure out my moves sometimes within the same match. I expanded my repertoire, but slowly, and even with Marquize's help, it wasn't easy.

My games with the cheetah turned into more theoretical practices. We stopped keeping score and just worked on points. I tried to mimic Dom's style to test Marquize, but it was hard to do because I wasn't used to thinking that far ahead. The games weren't the important part for me, anyway. The important part was the talk afterwards.

I felt more comfortable with Marquize than any of the other players or coaches. For a couple weeks after I found that picture on his computer, I was really scared that I'd lose him. He would say things like, "Now that you don't have a girlfriend, your focus is better," and I'd wonder: is there another reason he's happy I don't have a girlfriend? Or, worse, as the weather got warmer we took off our shirts a lot. Sometimes I'd look over at him with his shirt off, and I don't know why but I'd see him as if he were in one of those pictures.

Then I was worried I'd get hard again and he'd notice under my tennis shorts, and for a minute or two I couldn't focus on anything.

If I'd had someone to talk to, it would've been easier. Like tennis—I was learning leaps and bounds about tennis. But I was afraid to look up anything about gay people at the library, or to ask any of my friends, or talk to Marquize. Once or twice I tried to bring up that football player again, but nobody was very interested in talking about him. Again I got that sense of "over there."

Things had settled down with Ori, but without the push of desperation, I couldn't bring myself to ask her about it either. "Hey Ori," I imagined myself saying, "do you know any boys who like boys?" She'd laugh and say no, or tell me it was a funny question, or ask me if one of my friends asked me on a date. She was still back home, where we didn't talk about such things, where some of the people in our church preached love for all while others preached love only for some, where we were not so far removed from countries where people like that were hunted down and killed.

Which left Ma. I would've said that I could talk to Ma about anything, especially after she stuck up for Ori against Kamina. But Ma was distracted, and there were other things going on with her, things that she wasn't talking to me about.

Chapter Fourteen

Since I'd dumped Shawna (I didn't like that word because it made me sound like a jerk, but that was the word that everyone used, and so maybe I had been a jerk and I should own up to it), things were smoother between me and Ma. I came home on weekends and talked to her during the week to tell her how tennis was going. She was studying for her qualifying examination to be certified as a full-time teacher in Pensa, so that explained some of why she was a little more distracted around me.

But a week into April, she looked up from the dinner she'd made and said, "Ro? Can you buy the groceries the next two weeks?"

"Sure." I'd started to build my bank account back up again, but groceries for two weeks were not much more than I made in a weekend. "Why?"

"Thank you," she said, and went back to eating.

I knew she'd heard me and was deliberately ignoring the question, so just to be annoying I asked again, "Why, Ma?"

"Because I asked you to." She lifted her head and her eyes met mine, her ears straight up.

There was a moment where I almost challenged her again. But I was working hard at school and I didn't get a lot of time with Ma because of my job, so I nodded, said, "Okay," and finished up dinner.

I did ask Ori if she knew if anything was going on, but she talked to Ma less than she talked to me. "I don't know what she's been doing," she said. "Everything sounds normal."

"And you? How are you doing? Playing tennis?"

She lowered her voice. "Don't tell Kamina. But there's a mosque near the center that does charity work with refugee families. So I tell Kamina I'm going to play tennis and then I go to the mosque and volunteer. There's one jackal there, she's really nice and she lets me help sort the clothes."

"Clothes?" I lowered my voice too, in case Ma was listening. "Don't get fleas."

"Tch." She laughed. "They're boiled and pressed and disinfected before I get to them. It's all fine. And I really like thinking that they're going to families who don't have any clothes."

"Well, that's nice. You couldn't find a charity at our church to join? Then you could at least tell Kamina about it."

"Oh, our church does some things but it's all paperwork and it's not at the right times, and anyway then she would want to come with me and be part of it and I really want to do this for myself."

And I was sure that she relished the time away from Kamina, too. I was quite happy with my arrangement with Ma, but Ori and I had grown up with her and I was at school for five days a week. If I had to live with Ma, I probably would take any opportunity to get away from her. There was an element of mischief, of getting away with things, which I understood.

"That guy with the coffee hasn't come back around, has he?"

"No, no." She spoke confidently. "Kamina told him he couldn't marry me and she said it in front of me to make sure I heard it."

That reassured me. I hadn't found out what was going on with Ma, but to be honest, I didn't mind paying for our groceries. I did wonder if it meant that Ma wasn't going to insist I quit the job when she got her full time one. I liked the job, though I was starting to find myself daydreaming about tennis moves and lessons when I was supposed to be working. Jazzy and Merritt didn't exactly ignore me, but since the birthday party they weren't as conversational as they'd been when I was dating Shawna. They did tell me that Marcus was pretty embarrassed about charging up and challenging me, especially when Shawna told him that she "might have exaggerated a little bit."

I was glad she'd confessed, because I felt like Marcus hadn't believed me, even though all my classmates did. Kim still teased me sometimes about liking coyote girls and I didn't know how to respond to her, but I found I liked talking to her, so that was one good thing that had come out of that incident.

But the job, yeah, wasn't challenging me anymore. It wasn't bad money and the guys all more or less liked me, but I was starting to dread going to the warehouse because it was going to be six boring hours, and I had tennis to play and sleep to catch up on. I'd been about to suggest to Ma that when I got my bank account back up to five hundred that maybe I could quit the job. But with the strange request about groceries, I figured I'd put off asking her for a while longer.

***

Meanwhile, our practices heated up with the weather. The tournament was scheduled for the beginning of June, and as May came around, the coaches started shuffling us around to different partners so we could experience different styles. I found that some of my work in learning to beat Pom and Dom paid off when I was playing someone else, but I also lost a lot of practice matches and the students were much less willing to talk about the matches afterwards. That might have been because a lot of them were more tired afterwards, especially Dom, who wasn't used to the heat, but I felt like they were pulling ahead of me.

I sat down with Frio and Coach Murphy to talk about it around the second week of May. "I was taking Braden's advice," I told them. "I concentrated on Pom and Dom and really tried to learn how to beat them."

Coach Murphy turned to Frio. "You knew about this?"

"Sure." Frio fidgeted. "I told you I wanted to take Rocky to see Braden. That's what Braden said. Rocky and I thought the foxes were closest to his skill level."

"Well, that might've worked for Braden, but…if you're going to play like that then you have to be able to evaluate someone right away, like in about one game, and figure out who they're like from your past." Coach's tall ears cupped toward me. "It's a slow way to start out, and you might be better served by working on your all-around game."

"But I learned a lot," I insisted.

"He got better than Pom really quickly," Frio added.

"Pom's a lot like Marquize. How he plays, I mean."

Coach nodded at me. "Still, you should be mastering the fundamentals before you start tailoring your game to individual players. You're seeing the reasons for that right now. It won't help you in the tournaments, school or professional."

"He's got a few years before hitting the professional circuit, don't you think?" Frio turned away from me, looking at Coach.

"Maybe, maybe not." Coach tapped his foot and examined me. "We'll see how the tournament goes, huh?"

Afterwards, Frio and Marquize and I sat down to talk about the two weeks before the tournament. "For you guys," Frio said, "the tournament isn't a huge deal. It's like a final exam, sure, but the coaches have been watching you all year. We're going to have a big meeting mid-June and we'll discuss what to do with you next year. It's rare for anyone to get dropped from the program after their first year; usually we really sit down and look at that decision after two. So I don't want you guys to worry too much about it. You've both done fine, and compared to the rest of your class, you're in great shape." He reached out and put a paw on each of our knees. "Relax, play your games, and I'll come up with some stuff for you to work on over the summer while you're away."

"I'm not going away," I said. "I guess I'll be living here with Ma."

"Wish I could live here," Marquize muttered.

Frio chuckled. "Well, Rocky, if you want to come by for lessons, we can work something out, but if you want a couple months away from the school, nobody will blame you."

At the moment, I didn't want to make Marquize feel bad for having to leave, but I absolutely wanted more lessons. I felt like everyone else still had an edge over me and I was going to have to work as hard as I could to make it up. I'd tell Marquize about it when it was happening, but there was no need to bring it up now. He'd tell me to do extra lessons, anyway.

As we got closer to the tournament, all of us took to walking by the hallway in the school where the past winners of school tournaments were listed, two for every year. There were three entries for Braden Longacre, and the most recent one for Donal Marcher. I stopped and stared at the names, and Marquize, who happened to be with me at the time, stopped too.

"You realize these tournaments don't mean anything, right?" He put a paw on my shoulder.

"They mean you get your name on the wall. And the coaches know you can really play."

"They know that." Marquize's tail flicked back and forth and hit the back of my leg. "In your case, anyway."

"You're as good as me, if not better."

"Nah." He hadn't grown quite as much as I had over the year and so I was now an inch taller or so, but our eyes were still around the same level. "That was maybe true in December, but hasn't been true for months now. It's okay. Gives me something to work toward."

"And me," I said.

"Huh?"

"Well, I'd have to beat you to win one of those, probably." I gestured up at the wall. "So you and I will just have to be the two best."

***

The seedings for the tournament got posted a week in advance, the day we came back from Memorial Day weekend. Of the fourteen ninth-grade boys, I'd risen in seeding from thirteenth in December to sixth, which I found exciting. I was behind Dom but ahead of Pom, who was seventh, and Marquize had risen from twelfth to eighth. A lot of the guys who'd fallen behind us were ones who weren't in our practice group, but Don and Verid had their own little group who made up four of the five spots ahead of me (Bret was fourth).

So I played Pom first. Walking out, he saluted me with his racket and grinned. "For real this time," he said, and I returned his salute.

The first few games, we played conservatively, testing each other. We both knew there were things we were going to do that we hadn't tried in practice and were on high alert for it, sometimes too much so. I got nervous on my serve and double-faulted, but then settled down and won the game. I tried a few of my tricks that he knew, to make him think that was all I was going to do, letting him push me back and forth around the court on his service game. I had figured out by then which balls to chase and which to let go, especially early in the match, but I was also aware of the stands around us that were not as empty as usual, that were filled with two rows of adults I didn't recognize, people who took notes on paper and laptop computers and watched us both intently. So I didn't want to look like I was slacking or lazy in front of them. I wished there was a way to tell them that I knew Pom and had figured out his style.

The best way to do that, of course, was to win the match. Pom on his side attacked everything with more energy, ramping up his speed to get to every shot. It got to me about midway through the first set, when I was trying to move him methodically to one side of the court to set up a cross-court shot and he kept running around the ball and slapping that forehand of his to the corners, which made it harder for me to hit it back where I wanted. On my serve, I could dictate the pace better, meaning I could keep him just off-balance enough to stop him from placing the ball exactly where he wanted to (and placement wasn't a big strength of Pom's anyway). But when he was smacking the ball back seemingly randomly and I couldn't get a feel for where it would go next, I started second-guessing myself and missed two or three easy points in a row.

I was frustrating Pom, too, usually after long baseline rallies. Standing back and hitting the ball to each other wasn't something either of us particularly liked; we both liked athletic, acrobatic moves. But in the seventh game of the set, tied at 3-3, I was again trying to set him up for a cross-court and kept putting it off for one more volley, one more volley…and his tail flicked, he fidgeted as he was setting up to wait for my return, and then he wound up and drilled the ball down the near sideline, trying to catch *me* off guard. It would've been a great shot if he'd managed to hit the line, but it was about a foot out.

After that, I started to mix up my play, trying to frustrate him with long rallies the way Dom and Don frustrated me, with more success. We went to a tiebreaker in the first set*, which I won 7-3 when he hit a ball back into the net**.

* *A tiebreaker is played when the set ends tied at 6-6. The player who would have served the next game serves first, then they alternate serving twice each. Every point counts for—well, one point, and the first one to get to 7 or higher and be two points ahead of the opponent wins the tiebreak and the set. Officially it's scored as a 7-6 set and the tiebreak score is added in parentheses afterwards, so: 7-6 (7-3). Also sometimes if the winner won by getting to 7 (as opposed to a final score of like 12-10) they will just put the losing score in parentheses, like: 7-6 (3). Tennis scoring is way more confusing than actually playing.*

****The truth about tennis is that for every point that would be a TV highlight, there are probably nine points won on mistakes or basic miscalculations—the ball landing a few inches out, hitting the net, or a mis-hit off the racket. But all of those points involve strategy, watching what the other player's doing, reacting to their shots and trying to* *force them to play your game. So "he hit the ball back into the net" was actually a result of me serving it a little farther to his right, which I was trying to do, and him being off balance and catching the ball a little off the sweet spot of the racket, so it didn't have quite enough power to get back over the net. There was a little strategy here, but it was also luck on my part; if I serve in that exact location a hundred times, Pom probably gets it back over the net seventy of them. In a lot of those cases, I'm well positioned to hit a winner because he's still lunging to his right and the court is wide open to his left, so say in fifteen of those seventy returns I get a winner right away. In the rest of the cases we settle into a new game, a back-and-forth of trying to get the other out of position. So, you say, why don't you just serve it to that spot all the time, if it gets you approximately a forty-five percent win right out of the gate? Well, I can try, but I might not hit that exact spot. If I miss six inches to my left (Pom's right), it's out; six inches to my right and it's a much easier return for him. Also, once I've hit it there a couple times, he'll be expecting it and he'll shift his position so that's no longer an ideal spot. Then there might be an ideal spot on the other side of the service box (the area that you're allowed to serve into), but I'd have to find it, and he might be expecting me to go for it, so he'll be guessing and maybe leaning toward that side to be ready for it. The better you know another player, the deeper that chess game goes, because they know you just as well.*

In the second set, he got more desperate and made several errors he shouldn't have. I broke his serve in the fourth game to go up 3-1 and then I broke him again to win the set at 6-2. We shook paws at the net, and Pom was actually grinning. "You stepped up better than I did. Mind if we go through it after? My mom filmed it."

He gestured toward the stands where a red fox in a Palm Gables t-shirt and jeans waved to him. She was smiling too, holding a small video camera up in her paw. "Sure," I said, and fleetingly wished the match had been later in the day so Ma could've gotten out of her class to come see me.

She did come the next day to see me play Don, the top seed who'd won his first set easily. This match was the opposite of my match against Pom, because the rat had gotten better with his shot placement than the last time I'd played him. Over and over he'd hit a topspin forehand right into the corner past me after we'd been rallying for what felt like forever. But I'd gotten better too, and I stayed

with him on the rallies this time. I even managed to break his serve in the fifth game of the first set by surprising him with a drop shot that amazingly went right where I wanted it. Sadly, I got too confident and tried it three more times (once into the net, twice in easy reach for Don to hit a winner right back) and as a result Don broke my serve twice and won the set at 6-4.

The problem for me was that I didn't know how Don played. I hadn't played him outside of tournaments and I hadn't studied his game. So a lot of that first set I had to learn his tendencies on the fly. In the next set, I played better and was able to anticipate some of his moves, but looking back on it, just cutting down on my mistakes got me to a tiebreaker. Don plodded along patiently with me through the first part of the tiebreak, exchanging mini-breaks until we were tied at ten. Then he hit a serve probably a little softer than he'd intended, and I stroked a winner down the opposite sideline. So here I was serving for the set against the best player in our class.

I looked at where he'd set up, and it was the exact same place he always set up for a serve from the deuce court. I knew he had the range to get my serve no matter which side I sent it to. So I decided I'd fire it right at him, straight into his body.

That he wasn't expecting. He jumped to one side, corrected in time, but didn't have the leverage to get much on the ball when he sent it back over. I leapt forward to the net, hit it deep, and when he had to run back to get it—and he did get to it, and still hit it back—I waited at the net. He knew that's where I'd be, so he tried to lob it over my head.

I'm pretty tall. I've got a good jump and reach, and his lob wasn't as good as some of the others he'd hit. I hopped back two steps, planted, and leapt. I caught the ball squarely on the racket, coming down, and it slammed into the court on his side of the net and bounced twenty feet in the air, arcing over toward the coaches. Don chased it, but didn't even get a racket on it.

7-6 (12-10) read the scoreboard. Marquize jumped up and down with Kim and Pom, and Ma stood to applaud. I'd applied my lessons in real time and beaten the guy our coaches thought was best in our class in a real set. All the lessons, all the training, everything had paid off. I felt as good as I ever had on the tennis court and practically floated back out for the third set.

I wish this story ended better, but in the third set Don seemed to have learned as much about me as I had about him. He stayed consistent and broke my serve on a fluky mishit, and won the set 6-4. I didn't break down or anything; he just didn't let the lost set get to him. He stayed consistent and a lucky break went his way.

I learned that lesson, too.

***

Don went on to win the whole tournament. Afterwards, he announced that he wouldn't be returning to school, but would be playing in Junior circuit tournaments with an eye to starting his career in the Futures series the following year. I got a chance to talk to him while we were all milling around afterwards with sodas and crackers.

"You should join me," he said, flicking his long tail. "You're good. You're not going to get better going to school."

"Isn't that what school is for?" I asked.

He laughed. "Playing tournaments is how you get better. The Junior ones don't offer money, but they give you real experience. I'm gonna lose a bunch, I know, but I'll learn. I'll be winning some by next year. Then with the Futures I'll start earning real money."

"Okay, so…" I tipped the soda bottle to my muzzle. Soda, unexpectedly, was one of the parts of this life that felt consistent and familiar with my childhood. Coke sent a lot of their product over to Lunda, and while our family was not rich, we could afford a Coke every now and then. The Cokes here tasted very close to the ones back home. The main difference here was that they came in a staggering variety of containers for different muzzle shapes, and that even small gatherings like this one featured a veritable mountain of bottles. I drank and tried to finish my question. "Do the tournaments pay for you to come play? If they have no prize?" If that was the case, then I might be able to get by with those tournaments.

"Oh, uh, no." Don's pointed muzzle dipped toward his own bottle, but he didn't touch his lips to the straw that poked out from its mouth. "I mean, I know my mom is buying my plane tickets. The agent says sometimes they'll pay for you to stay there."

"How much does it cost to fly? I know only how much it costs to fly here from Lunda, but it must be less than that."

"I don't know." He shook his head. "Mom always buys the tickets."

"Does the agent pay if your family can't?"

"I don't think so." He nodded his head toward where an older female rat was talking to a leopard in a slick business suit. "Vanz keeps talking about how we're going to make money together, but he says it'll be mostly next year when I start playing more tournaments, getting more well known. He's going to get my name out there." His head rose and his eyes seemed to be staring into the future. "I might get an endorsement from a clothing line, you know, have my picture in magazines."

I didn't know, but I didn't want to say that to him. I'd seen billboards and clothing models and athletes promoting products, of course. But those had always been among the best in the game, athletes who were in the finals of major tournaments, the people I admired, not a rat who was pretty good but who I'd beaten one set out of three that day.

Still, he was the one with the agent, and no agents had come over to talk to me or Ma. I knew I'd done better this tournament, but it wasn't good enough, apparently, and I felt like I wasn't making much progress. Ma said she was proud of me and she insisted we call Ori to tell her about how well I'd done. That was nice, but my heart still wasn't really in it.

***

So a few days later, during our last week of classes, I went to see Frio in his office. There was barely enough room for me to sit in front of his desk, unlike Coach Murphy's office which had room for like four people, and three or four behind his desk, but I sat in the wooden chair Frio pointed me to and waited while he wrote something on his computer. All over the walls were posters of male tennis stars, and below that a lot of photos of Frio with various students.

One of the posters held my attention. I knew the player: Allion Podiowksi, a pine marten who'd won one Major about ten years ago but had been a contender during most of the time I'd been watching tennis. This poster wasn't from a match, though; it was the marten, shirtless, leaning against a wall with a racket dangling from one paw and a smile stretched across his short muzzle.

"Good pic, isn't it?"

I snapped my attention back to Frio, ears flattening. "Oh, uh, yes…"

"I love the way Pod played, but you can't get posters of him playing anymore. He does a lot of those modeling gigs. Got the body for it, doesn't he?"

"I guess." The marten was certainly fit, and the way he was posed made for some appealing curves. I wasn't sure he was all that much more attractive than some of my classmates, but I didn't want to say that because that would take me back down the road of Marquize and his pictures and my feelings, and that wasn't why I was here.

"What can I do for you?" Frio leaned forward, elbows on his desk.

Right, right. I took a breath. "It's about the advice Braden gave me. About beating one player at a time? I'm just…I'm not sure how I can make it work. I focused on Pom and Dom, but then Don came up and I couldn't beat him right away. How will I ever win a tournament? Now Don's leaving and maybe I can beat anyone else in the class, but Don said I should be playing tournaments, but I don't know how I can do that, so…"

"Whoa, whoa." Frio laughed and held up his paws. "Settle down, Rocky. I see what you're getting at."

"What Braden said made sense, it did. And it worked for him, but I don't know how."

"Well." The ferret tapped fingers on his desk. "Do you want to call him?"

"Me?" I curled my tail in against myself and shook my head. "No, I couldn't. I don't even know his number, or what I'd say, or…"

"I can call him." Frio held up his phone. "Won't take a minute. I'm sure he wouldn't mind."

I hesitated. I really didn't want to bother Braden, and he'd been a jerk last time, so if I came back to him and said I didn't understand his advice, what would he say? He'd write me off like he did Marquize. "N-no," I said.

"Too late." Frio grinned and dialed, then put his phone on speaker and set it on the desk.

Braden Longacre was a busy tennis player, I thought. He'll never answer the phone. But the fourth ring cut off abruptly, and a moment later, the familiar sharp voice came over the line. "Jesus, you better not be calling about next week. I haven't even—"

"Hey, Braden," Frio interrupted loudly. "I'm here with Rocky N'guwe. The jackal, you remember?"

The line went silent. Then Braden said, "Yeah. Course I remember." I'd just thought to myself that he was pretending again when he said, "Has he dumped that girlfriend yet?"

Frio looked at me, so I said, "Yes."

"Good." Braden's voice crackled through the line. "So what now?"

Again, Frio urged me to go on. I scrambled to think of a way to ask my question that didn't sound like I couldn't figure out his advice. "I'm really sorry. I didn't want to bother you, but Frio said…" Frio stared at me and I switched subjects. "Anyway, you told me to learn every opponent until I could beat them, and I started doing that, and it worked. But there are always new opponents, and I guess I could learn them during the first set of a match, like I sort of did with Don, but then I've wasted a set, and…"

I ran out of steam there. Frio picked up for me. "I think Rocky's getting overwhelmed by the size of the tennis world. You remember getting that way too, right, Braden?"

"Yeah." The fox's voice remained gruff. "What's the matter, Frio? You trying to recruit me to teach there? I'm still playing, you know."

"This cub's special." When Braden didn't say anything, Frio leaned closer to the phone. "Come on, five minutes, fox."

Braden sighed. "Jackal, you have an e-mail?"

"I hardly ever use it," I said, but I read it out to him.

"Okay. Don't let Frio call me for you again." And he hung up.

I flattened my ears, but Frio smiled as he picked up his phone. "There you go!" he said, as though he'd planned it all along. "He's gonna e-mail you now. You know how to get to your e-mail, right?"

"Sure." I had to go to the library to do it, or use Marquize's laptop. I glanced again at the poster of the pine marten, and uncertainty burned in me. "Hey…can I ask you one more thing?"

"You can ask me anything." Frio smiled and clasped his paws together, elbows on the desk.

"Okay, well…" I swallowed. "Is it bad to be gay? I mean, in tennis?" Then I saw the way he looked at me and I stumbled over the words. "Not me! I mean, I saw—a friend of mine had a picture—but he didn't say anything to me about it—I haven't asked but he's, I mean, I'm worried about him and…" My words trailed off, and as Frio kept smiling I started to feel better.

"There's nothing wrong with it." The ferret reached over his desk to clasp my wrist. "Some people consider it a private thing, and that's their right."

"So he won't get in trouble? Will the other people beat him up?"

The ferret laughed. "Not in this neighborhood. I wouldn't go down to the Pines and start flirting with guys there, but around here you should be fine. I mean…" He winked. "*He* should be fine."

"It's not me," I insisted.

"Sorry. Slip of the tongue." The ferret let go of my wrist. "How was it considered in your home country?"

I shifted in my seat. "I don't really want to talk about it."

"Hey, no problem. But listen, there really is nothing wrong with it. There are some people around this country who still think it's unnatural, who might even hate gay people, but times are changing. It's not like it was ten or even four years ago. There's a football player who's out now, two of them."

"I know, I saw."

He smiled. "And things have changed a lot just in the, what, eight or nine months since then. So don't worry about your friend. It's okay to keep it private, so I wouldn't go telling anyone else his secret, but only because it's none of their business. And if he chooses to share it with you, that's a big gesture of trust and you shouldn't betray that. But until then…" He leaned back. "He'll be fine."

I thanked him and nodded, but I still felt a little uneasy as I left his office.

***

That last week of school was crazy. I said good-bye to everyone, making sure we all had each other's numbers, taking all our finals, and talking about the tournament. I got lots of pats on the back for my match against Don and a lot of people asking if I was going to leave to play the Junior tournaments. I didn't want to say that I couldn't afford to do that, so I said that I thought I still had a lot to learn and maybe next year I'd consider it.

A whole bunch of us went out to the Meat'n'Malt for dinner the last day of finals to celebrate: me, Marquize, Bret, Kim, Yu, Veronica, Brittany, Pom, and Dom. We pushed two tables together and filled them with fries and onion rings and burgers and malts and talked about what we were going to do over the summer. Yu and Brittany, a year ahead of us and already ranked in the top four in their class, were going to work on tennis together over the summer. They'd gotten Yu's parents to agree to let him stay near Brittany over the summer and share a privately hired tennis coach as long as he also worked on his studies. I think it helped that his English had improved a lot.

"Summer school," Pom scoffed. "Not for me. I'm going back home and I'm not gonna think about tennis for two months. Dad says travel is important, so he's taking me overseas to Anglia and Gallia."

"Original," Kim said. "Isn't everyone going there? I'm going to Joshua Tree National Park to camp and hike for a week, and then there's a summer tennis camp in Crystal City I got into."

"Wait." Yu put down his shake, his eyes so wide that the auburn mask around his eyes visibly bulged upward in a shock of fur. "You're going to Porter Colliere's tennis camp? How did you get in?"

"I applied." Kim's smile had a good bit of smug in it, though to be honest, coyote smiles always had at least a little smug.

"You're not even the best girl in the class." Brittany, who was not either, narrowed her eyes. "I heard that Porter likes canid girls and she'll take the pretty ones over more talented ones of other species, even when those talented ones really want to go. It was all over the forums and there was even a picture of her with her arm around this other girl."

"It's still really cool that you got in," Yu said, and then he jumped as Brittany elbowed him.

"Maybe she does like girls." Kim eyed the otter. "But she doesn't take the best girls. She takes the most teachable ones. Anyway, did you even apply? You're prettier than I am."

"No." Brittany tossed her head, but her little ears came back up and her expression lost its anger. "I don't want to get in somewhere just because I'm pretty. Veronica, did you apply?"

The maned wolf had been texting, probably to Malik, and at the sound of her name her ears perked up. "Apply to what?" When they told her, she grimaced and said, "I did. They turned me down."

"Well," Brittany said to Kim. "Maybe it really is just about tennis."

"I don't care either way." Kim grinned at me. "However I get to go, I'm going, and lots of people say it's really good."

"I didn't even know these camps existed," I said, because I was a little uncomfortable discussing girls who like girls, and Marquize was quiet next to me. "How do you know about them?"

They told me about some online forums for tennis cubs, though it sounded like the forums were mostly full of complaints or for cubs to make fun of people. Bret did say he'd exchanged messages with a girl in Yerba and even sent pics, but then she'd stopped writing him. "Scared her off, I guess," Pom said with a wicked smile, and everyone laughed at Bret's scowl, eventually even Bret.

"I guess I'll have to go check those out at the library when you're gone," I said to Marquize.

"You're staying here this summer?" Kim's large ears were pointed in my direction.

I nodded. "Ma's taking her test this week to be a full time teacher, and if she makes it, then she has to fill out a whole lot of paperwork and get recommendations from the school to allow her to stay in the country in case...uh."

My ears dipped, and nobody said anything until Marquize broke the silence. "In case you don't get picked up after next year at the school."

"Yeah."

The table chorused reassurance, and the people closest to me patted my paws and shoulders. Dom, down at the end of the table, chimed in that with Don gone, I'd be easily in the top two or three in the class. "Are you taking classes over the summer?"

"Yes. Frio said he'll keep my tennis lessons going." I hesitated, then went on. Everyone—in this group, anyway—was pretty nice about filling me in on things I didn't know. "Why isn't everyone? I mean, isn't tennis the most important thing? I get it if you're going to tennis camp," I nodded to Kim, "but just travel? Working in offices?"

"It's important to be well-rounded." Marquize leaned in. "Like in 'Searching for Bobby Fischer'—ah, okay, you have to watch that over the summer. I'll send you down a copy. Anyway, the cub gets obsessed with chess and his dad is too, but the dad eventually realizes it's better to be a good person than a great chess player."

"Heh." Everyone turned to Pom. "Not me. My dad says I'll never get to Wimbledon on my own, so he's going to take me now."

Pom hadn't talked about his family much, and I guess that was why. I joined in with the group's reassurance, but it didn't seem to have a big effect on the red fox. "Statistically," Dom said, "our best chances of going to Wimbledon would be as Juniors. Palm Gables has had thirty-six of its students play at Wimbledon as Juniors over the last ten years, but only eleven graduates so far have made it into the main draw. So probably three of our class will go as Juniors and only one as the main draw."

"Don," I said, and Veronica and Bret nodded.

"Brittany," Yu said.

The otter smiled and leaned against him. "You're only saying that to make up for earlier."

"No, no." He put an arm around her. "You came in second in the tournament, but your game is perfect for Wimbledon. You love to go to the net and your volleys are great. In a couple years you'll be winning tons of Junior tournaments."

She nosed him, clearly enjoying the flattery. "So will you."

"No," he said. "Why do you think I'm dating you? It's only because you're better than me."

We all laughed, and the rest of the evening was spent talking about all the usual things: whose game was best, who was going to leave the school next, who was dating whom outside of our group. It was almost as if we were going to go right back to school the next week.

*   *   *

Ma's test was the following Monday, so I spent the weekend in her apartment helping her study. With books open in front of me, I quizzed her on all the different subjects. If I hadn't known Ma was smarter than me before this, I sure knew it after. She knew all those subjects, knew English words that I didn't even know the Kikongo words for, and corrected me when I asked questions that wouldn't be on the test or read something poorly.

Still, she was quite nervous Monday morning when I walked

down to the test center with her. It was the opposite direction from the school, so I couldn't go practice while I was waiting for her. I spent the four hours mostly walking around the neighborhood, playing a game on my phone that Marquize had sent me, and reading the texts from everyone who'd arrived home.

Marquize, unlike most of our friends, was going to spend two and a half months at home. There was a tennis center near his house that he said he was going to practice in, and I told him he'd better. I said I'd write him if I learned anything cool over the summer, and he said that I could take video with the phone and send it to him if I wanted to show him some tennis moves. I thought that sounded neat and I promised to try. But his parents wanted him to help with their pawnshops during the day, so he wasn't going to have a lot of time.

I wondered if this was like Pom's case where they didn't believe he'd make it as a tennis professional, and when I read that text, I thought about Ma taking the test in there so she could stay with me in the country and make sure I learned tennis, and I felt warm in my chest and had to wipe my eyes.

The feeling was one I wanted to share with someone, and June had just started so I had plenty of minutes on my phone. I dialed Ori's number, and she picked up quickly.

"Ma's taking her test to be a teacher," I told her. "If she passes, chances are good she'll get to stay, because Pensa really needs teachers, I guess."

"That's great! She's smart, I'm sure she'll pass. Wish her luck for me!"

"I will." I wanted to tell Ori how great it was that Ma believed in me, but I found my mind wandering to another thing Ma had done. "What happened with that coffee farmer? Did you find out what Ma did?"

"No." Ori's voice went kind of flat. "I asked Kamina, but she told me it was none of my concern. I wondered if I would see him again, but I didn't."

"And she hasn't arranged any other suitors yet?"

"Not yet." My sister regained some of her spirits. "I met this lion at the mosque who is really nice and I think he likes me."

I barked a surprised laugh. "A lion? A Muslim lion?"

"I know," she said.

"Ori, if you want to give Kamina a heart attack, just jump out from behind a door at her."

"Don't be stupid, Ro. I'm not serious about him."

I clucked my tongue. "I know that tone. You want to be serious about him."

"*His* family wouldn't be happy either."

"Ah-ha," I said. "So the two of you have talked about it."

"Oh, hush!" She play-growled at me. "You've been around Ma too much. Yes, all right, we've talked about it, but he's only sixteen and he's not wealthy enough to pay for me, and his family wouldn't."

"So he likes you too?"

She paused and then said, slowly, "I think he does. I mean…you know how much trouble it could be, chasing a Christian jackal girl. Well, he's trying to convert me."

I snorted. "Would you have to take a test?"

"I'm not going to convert. *That* would give Kamina a heart attack."

I thought for some reason about Marquize and his pictures, and the way he kept himself apart from the social scene, how Bret talked openly about girls he'd met on forums and Yu and Brittany were dating and so were Veronica and Malik. "You know," I said, "if you like him, and he likes you…"

"Ro, stop it."

"No, really. Times are changing, and—"

"Not here."

That brought me up short. I leaned back against the wall, the sun warm on my fur like back home, but the air clung to my fur and the smells were of suburbia: car exhaust, but not diesel; trees and flowers, not throngs of people; concrete and asphalt, not dust and brick and wood. It felt artificial, unreal, and I longed to be back home, to breathe in the dusty, comforting smells of thousands of people, to hold Ori's paw and run through the market, past stalls of fruit and clothing. "One of my friends likes other boys."

"Like in that movie about the wedding?"

That was one of her favorites, but I could never understand why. I vaguely recalled that there'd been a male character in it who for some reason had acted effeminate sometimes, but Ori had watched the movie probably a dozen times more than I had. "I guess so."

"Does he like you?" She giggled. "Does he want you to convert, too?"

"No!" I shouldn't have said anything about it. "No, he doesn't know I know, I...I found out by accident."

"Well, you said it wasn't such a big deal there, right?"

"I didn't think so. I don't know. He doesn't talk about it and my coach said to keep it quiet, so maybe it is a big deal? I mean, maybe it's one of those things that's a big deal when it's happening to you, but not if it's happening to other people."

"Oh." She thought about that. "Like being Muslim."

"What?"

"Kamina doesn't mind there being Muslims out in the world. I think she'd be a little upset if she knew I was working at their mosque. But she would absolutely forbid me to become one."

"Sort of like that."

"If you're his friend, then eventually he'll tell you, won't he?"

"Maybe." I didn't know, honestly, and again I felt the frustration of being in this world where Bret and Marquize and Pom and Dom had grown up and knew all the rules, where they walked confidently while I stumbled and felt my way and tried not to make a fool of myself.

"You'll figure it out. You're a good guy."

"Thanks, Ori."

"And Ro? If he does want you to convert—I mean, if you want to—I know I can't, but it'd be okay for you."

"I don't," I said quickly, and then honesty won out. "Know, I mean. I don't know."

"I'm just saying it's okay. Love you, Ro."

"Love you, Ori."

And I hung up and put the phone away, and stood there in the sun and thought.

***

Ma came out of her test feeling confident, though not overly so. "I knew most of the questions," she said, "but I'm sure everyone else did, too."

"When do you find out?" I held her purse as she straightened the small sun hat she wore between her ears.

"They said I would receive the results in six weeks." She took her purse back. "At least it is over now."

"I bet you passed." I swung my tail confidently. "Ori does too. She sends her love and wishes you luck."

"Too late for luck now." The sharpness dropped from Ma's voice. "How is Ori doing?"

"She's good." I told her Ori was doing community work, leaving out the Muslim part and also the lion would-be boyfriend part, not because I thought Ma would disapprove, but because Ma would almost certainly feel obliged to tell Kamina.

She liked hearing that. "I'm glad you keep close to your sister. Kamina takes care of her, but family nourishes the soul."

"Kamina is family, too. She's your sister."

Ma sighed. "Not like you and Ori. We grew up with different mothers and there was always some competition between us. I tried to make sure that between you and Ori, you remembered love first before all else."

I nodded. "I do. I'll bring her over here. Once I'm playing tournaments and making money, I promise I will."

Ma didn't say anything as we crossed the street, and then pointed to a Coabanan restaurant. "Shall we try them for lunch?"

I agreed, and we sat down to an interesting meal of *ropa vieja* (shredded beef), black beans, rice, and plantains that felt close to our home food, but different enough to be an exotic treat. The plantains weren't as sweet and the beans and rice were saltier, but the differences weren't bad. I was used to things being sweeter and less salty here in the States, so it was a nice change.

The waiter was a species I didn't recognize, and Ma didn't either, but unlike me, she wasn't afraid to ask. The young fellow told us he was a hutia, a relative of capybaras and squirrels but native to Coabana. "You see?" Ma said to me as he walked away. "There is always something new to learn."

"That's why you make a good teacher and I make a good tennis player," I said, digging in my pocket for my wallet to pay for the meal.

That week, I packed up my things from the dorm to move in with Ma for the summer. Marquize was packing in our suite at the same time to go home; everyone else had left over the weekend, but he was delaying his departure. "I like it down here," he said, "and we can get in another few days of practice before I go to the Port City Pawnshop Valley of Death."

"It can't be that bad," I said.

He sighed. We were taking a break from packing out in the common area, sprawled out on the empty couches in the uncommonly silent space. "Pawnshops are depressing. It's where people trade things they love for money they need. So everything I see, I look at and wonder what happened to the person that they had to give it up."

"Maybe they didn't really love it and they were happy to get rid of it."

"Sometimes." He gestured to his laptop computer, one of the few things he hadn't packed. "In that case they mostly sell it on eBay. Pawnshops are for people who need money quickly and usually all they have is things they wouldn't normally sell. And when they come in they say, 'I'll be back for this in a week.' But they usually aren't."

Marquize had never talked about his parents' business much, and I was starting to see why. "But you're helping them." I tried to think of more positive things to say about pawnshops. The ones

I knew of in my home didn't feel as bad or depressing as the ones Marquize's parents owned. But then again, nobody in the States bartered for things the way we did back home. If I outgrew a pair of pants, for instance, we wouldn't take them to the pawnshop. We'd find another jackal family with a son a couple years younger than me and we'd trade them the pants for ten loaves of bread, or maybe a bicycle wheel, or whatever they had. Once Ma took our old black-and-white television and a bowl of *lituma* (baked plantain balls; Ma made wonderful ones) and three of Ori's old dresses and spent the day trading to return with a color television on which Ori and I could watch our movies.

"Helping, I guess." He smiled, though it wasn't a very happy smile. "It just feels sad."

"It's a job." I reached over to pat his paw. "You're earning money for your family. And someone has to do it, right?"

"That's right, I guess. But that's why I want to do well at tennis."

I thought about the reasons I wanted to do well at tennis, which revolved around Ori and Braden (in different ways) and Ma, and my father, sort of, and most of all myself. I couldn't imagine boiling those down to simply wanting to escape something. I wanted to be good at tennis because I wanted to be great, not just so I didn't have to go back home.

"Hey." Marquize grabbed my paw, startling me out of those thoughts. I turned to see him looking at me with a peculiar intensity.

"What?" Ori's question burned through my mind. Oh no, I thought, he's going to ask me—he's going to want to date me—

"This is kinda forward, but I really want to do it." His whiskers twitched and his ear flicked nervously.

Oh no oh no what am I going to say I can't do it but if he asks can I no I can't but do I want to I don't I don't I don't know…

I…

He took a breath. "I talked to my parents and told them my laptop died and the shop here couldn't fix it. So they're going to get me a new one and basically my pay this summer will cover that, maybe a little extra. It was about time for a new one anyway."

My eyes flicked to his open door, my scattered frantic thoughts derailed. "When did that happen?"

"It didn't." He smiled. "But you know, I'll be gone this summer

169

and I thought you could use a laptop."

My heart was still pounding from what I'd thought he was going to ask me, and I was uncomfortably aware that my sheath was also still...affected. So I didn't answer right away, and Marquize's eyebrows lowered, his smile vanishing. "I don't know what your culture is around giving gifts, but I didn't give you a birthday present. And it's an old laptop anyway, and I was going to get a new one...if it's awkward or something, though, I can take it home. I'll tell my parents it started working again. They don't understand computers."

"No!" I didn't care about the laptop, but I didn't want him to feel bad about doing something so nice. "No, it's—I didn't expect—it's really really nice of you! I didn't get you a birthday present either, though."

"My birthday's in October," he said, laughing. "We barely knew each other then."

"I'll come up with something for this year," I promised.

"You don't have to." He squeezed my paw. "Just keep writing to me over the summer so I don't go crazy. I already set you up as a user on the laptop so you should be good to go with it."

"I will." My tail thumped against the couch. "Thanks! I mean, it's really nice of you. Now I won't have to go to the library all the time."

"That's the idea." His smile was back. "Next year we can study together here. Or wherever they put us. I don't know if we come back to the same dorms."

"I'll ask and I'll write you." And then, because thanks didn't feel like enough, I hugged him. We'd hugged our other friends good-bye, so I was pretty sure it would be okay, and Marquize hugged back and it felt nice, not just the hug, but having a real friend like that. And I managed not to think about how I'd reacted to what I'd thought he was going to ask me.

As we were finishing up, someone knocked on our suite door. We looked at each other and then Marquize went to answer it.

Frio stood there, eyes widening as the door opened. "Oh! I didn't know you'd still be here. I came to see Rocky."

I walked up. "I'll be out of here by five o'clock. Did you need me out earlier?"

"No, no." The ferret stepped inside and let the door close. "Just wanted to talk to you about plans for the summer. Coach Murphy will be here on and off over the summer, but he won't be able to observe students personally. He does agree with me that you have a lot of potential, so he asked me to write up a summer plan for you, and I had a few ideas I wanted to get your feedback on."

"Oh. Thanks." I had a weird warm feeling at the "lot of potential" comment, kind of like how I felt when Ori said she loved me, or when Ma said I could be great.

"We'll have the Gallic and Wimbledon to watch. And there's a clay court place a couple hours north of here. During the school year, it's not worth going up, but over the summer we can take a few days. It's less busy then anyway. You can feel how the clay courts react differently. How does that sound?"

"I'd be interested in that. And can we analyze the Majors when we watch them?"

"Course," the ferret said. "That's the idea."

Marquize patted my shoulder. "You're going to have a busy summer."

I almost told him that I wished he'd be able to share it with me, but Frio was standing right there. A second later I felt even better about saying nothing, because I realized I didn't want to give Frio any clues as to which friend I'd been talking about when I told him about the gay picture. So I just said, "I'll tell you all about it," which at least was the next best thing.

Chapter Fifteen

With everyone gone, the neighborhood felt deserted, but if I strayed away from the Palm Gables campus, it felt more crowded. Cubs were everywhere: in the malls, on the streets, in restaurants with their parents. I did run into Marcus and Shawna once, walking past an Applebee's with Ma, and we eyed each other but didn't say anything. I thought Marcus looked like he wanted to come after me, so I hurried along.

Frio gave me a week off, which was unexpectedly and thoroughly boring. I hung around the public tennis courts, but everyone there was casual players, so even when someone did play me, they weren't much challenge. I found a wall, like Marquize had, and smacked balls against it for an hour, and then that was boring so I called Marquize and complained to him. He complained back; Port City was humid in a way that Palm Gables wasn't quite ("it smells," he said shortly), and he didn't have anyone to play tennis with either. He asked how the computer was working and I told him it was great.

I hadn't actually opened it up since he gave it to me, but that conversation reminded me of it, so I checked it that night and found an e-mail from Braden. That was a surprise. I'd checked the couple days after our talk, but he hadn't e-mailed, and I'd given up on it, figured he'd said that to get rid of me.

But there it was in my box, though I didn't figure out who "acefox1990" was until I opened the message.

Rocky,

Don't get the idea this is going to be a regular thing, but I had some guys help me out when I was coming up and if you've got specific questions about the tour and stuff like that, go ahead and send me an e-mail. I'm usually pretty busy but I can answer quick questions.

About trying to figure everyone out: don't bother. As you get better the number of people you'll really need to figure out will get smaller, and a lot of the people you play against you can beat just by playing your game. If you're good, that is. If that doesn't happen to you, then you don't need to worry about it anyway because you're never going to be at a level where it'll matter. But Frio seems to think you can be good, so there you go.

Speaking of, I want to make sure you know that he's only one guy, one coach. He's smart, but he's also not perfect. You can find other coaches to talk to, and you should, and you don't have to do whatever he says just because he's your coach. If you have problems with him and you don't feel like you want to go to Coach Murphy, you can e-mail me if you have to.

Braden Longacre

I know it was all stiff and formal, but it made me feel better. I mean, he'd taken enough of an interest in me to write that e-mail. He was still kind of a jerk, but he was good and important and it felt nice to have him take notice of me in that way. I sent him a quick thank you and assured him I wouldn't take up too much of his time.

Because of what he'd said about Frio, it didn't feel right to talk to the ferret about the e-mail. It felt like a secret between Braden and me. But that didn't mean I couldn't tell Marquize about it. I left out the part about Frio and just said Braden wrote to me. Marquize was impressed and, I think, a little bit jealous.

"He's not even as good as he thinks he is," the cheetah said when I called him. "And he has no idea how good you are. I bet you're better than he is, or you will be soon."

"I'm nowhere near as good. He's playing in tournaments."

"Check out his results, though. He only wins like two or three a year."

So I had to ask how to check his results, and that led Marquize to telling me how to bookmark webpages online, and that led to me spending hours on Ma's couch looking at the various players and tournament results. I'd seen video of some matches, but that was kept in the Palm Gables library and I didn't think I could get to it from my laptop. But the results—all those were publicly available online. I could find all the tournaments once I knew where to look, and I started to learn the names of the players who appeared in the semifinals and finals over and over again. Despite Marquize's jealousy, Braden was one of those, at least at the Challenger level. There were thirty or so tournaments a year, and as I reviewed the results and got an idea of who was competitive, there were only four or five names that came up more than Braden's.

I wanted that, wanted to see my name there and wanted to be playing and beating those other players.

When I started working with Frio the following week, we played some games so he could get a feel for me, he said. We'd only played occasionally, like that time Marcus bruised Marquize's ribs; he usually watched me play the other students and then gave us lessons based on what he'd seen.

Actually playing with him regularly was a whole different experience. He was surprisingly not as good as I thought he'd be, though he was still better than me. I'd seen enough video of players doing well in tournaments to recognize where I and he were slow, imprecise, and in many cases predictable. Frio was more predictable than I was; I figured him out within a few days.

But playing against him really helped. He pushed me during the games, yelling things like, "Line up your forehand, don't just hit it. Good follow through. Watch your feet, watch your feet. Where am I? Where am I going to be? Hit it where I can't get it, make me guess."

The chatter unsettled me at first, but once I got used to it, it helped. Over the first week, I felt like I hadn't made any progress at all from when I'd arrived at the school. Frio was correcting nearly everything I did. But by the second week, he started praising me more, and my confidence rose. Having a coach working one on one was even better than having one dedicated to a small group of us.

I told Marquize on the phone at the end of that week that I wished he was here, too, and I tried to tell him the things Frio was teaching me, though over the phone it didn't work as well. "Are you doing okay for money?" Marquize asked me toward the end of the conversation.

"Sure," I said. "I'm still working at the warehouse on Friday and Saturday night. I'm glad it's not in the day. It's so stuffy in there at night, we're all panting within an hour. The guys who move stuff sometimes just stand in front of the fans. Fur blows all over the place."

"I mean—" He paused. "I don't want to pry, but you're paying for the summer lessons, right? How much do you have left over?"

"Oh." I hadn't even thought about that. Frio and I were using the Palm Gables courts, we were using the school's equipment, and yet he hadn't mentioned paying for it. I'd assumed that my scholarship covered the summer, but now Marquize's question made that assumption seem ridiculous. "No, I'm fine, Ma's working too and we're covering everything."

"All right. You let me know if you need money, right? I know I can't send you much."

"Don't send me anything. You already gave me the laptop."

"Oh yeah!" He brightened. "My folks got me a new one so we can Skype now."

"What's Skype?"

So he explained how we could talk over the computer for free if we got the right kind of account, and that sounded too good to be true, but we both signed up for it right then and it worked. The quality wasn't great, but I could hear and mostly understand him, and he could hear and mostly understand me, and it was better than paying for the minutes I could be using to talk to Ori.

The following Monday, I asked Frio if I had to pay him anything for the summer, and he waved a paw and said, "Don't worry about it. Your scholarship covers it." Which made me feel better until I wondered why Marquize wouldn't have known that. I didn't want to make someone tell Frio he was wrong, but I did think that if my scholarship covered my work, then maybe Marquize's would too, and he'd be able to come down for the rest of the summer. He could stay with me and Ma, either on the couch with me...well...maybe that wasn't such a great idea...but I could sleep on the floor for a while, or get a sleeping bag.

I asked Ma about it, and she said that if it were only two months, she could live with it. So I called Marquize back and told him what Frio'd said, and he sounded a bit suspicious. "They told my parents that my tuition didn't cover the summer," he said. "But maybe your deal is different? Like, I don't have a scholarship."

"Maybe," I said. "I don't know how to ask. I mean, what if Frio was wrong and I go ask Coach Murphy and it turns out I do have to pay?"

"Don't do anything," Marquize said. "I'll be fine. You can teach me when I get back down there. And hey, my parents are talking about maybe going to the amusement park, so maybe you can slip away and join us for a day."

"Sounds great," I said, and stretched out on the couch, mostly satisfied.

***

In July, Frio finally got around to taking me up to that clay court club. Clay courts used to be the standard in the States until hard courts were developed, and a lot of countries still used them: Gallia, Espanya, and Etrusca, at least. The clay sapped speed from the balls, meaning you had to hit it harder to get the same effect. Your opponent—and you—had more time to get around shots and return them. The emphasis was on strength and defense, which were not my strong points, I thought. Frio thought I was doing fine and that a few sessions on clay would help. "We can go back up there in August, too," he said. "There's a tournament then for seniors, but you can still see how the ball moves."

Because it was a long drive, he'd booked a hotel room and said we'd stay two nights. "That'll give us one afternoon and a full day practice, and then we can come back Wednesday morning and get in a couple hours before the afternoon rains kick in."

The trip felt exciting and adventurous. Yes, I'd grown up halfway around the world, but I'd really only lived in two cities all my life. We'd studied World Cultures and I had friends from all over, and yet I'd never gone more than a half hour from Palm Gables in any direction. My friends were back in Port City and Pelagia and Crystal City, literally scattered to the four corners of the country, and now at least I would get the chance to explore a little bit.

Ma worried about the trip, but she said that it was because the prospect of me traveling a couple hours away back home would have been very worrying. She knew with her head that the States was different and that I'd be fine. And Ori was excited for me when I told her. She'd never seen a clay court and imagined that they were made of clay like from the riverbank. "Will your feet stick in the court?" she wanted to know.

"They don't on TV," I told her. "I don't think it's that kind of clay. But I'll tell you. How is your lion?"

"He's not my lion, Ro." She sounded pleased, though. "I don't know if you heard about the villages that were attacked two weeks ago."

"I haven't." I had been very bad at keeping up with news from my country. Partly it was easy to blame that on how difficult it was to get news, but mostly, to be honest, it was that I wasn't trying. I had tennis and Ma and work, and I felt sure Ma would let me know if anything serious happened.

"There were twenty families that came into our center last week. A lot of the people stayed all night to make sure they all got food and supplies and just someone to talk to, to tell them that they can have a normal life again. Raji did. I wanted to but I couldn't think of an excuse, so I had to go home. But when Kamina went to sleep, I snuck out for four hours, until dawn when I ran back."

"You shouldn't do that. What if she'd woken up and you were missing?"

"Oh, she never wakes up." Ori said it very offhandedly. "I'm always up before she is. And those people needed someone, Ro. I talked to a spotted hyena and her cub for two hours and let them tell me about their house. It burned down. I told them they'd get a new one somehow and by the time I left the cub was sleeping."

"How are you going to get them a new house?" I wasn't sure how she could promise things she had no control over.

"I didn't say *I* would get them one. I said they'd get one. People always do. There's relief aid from countries all around the world. If you believe good things will happen, then they do, sooner or later."

"I don't know about that." It took a lot of hard work to get good things to happen in the tennis world. Good thoughts probably had something to do with it, but Braden had gotten some success while being, so far as I could tell, mostly negative about everything and everyone. Except me, perhaps. That last letter had seemed somewhat favorably disposed toward me, though maybe that was only in comparison to Frio. Braden didn't like him but maybe felt obligated to him? I couldn't tell why someone who'd separated himself from the school so much and didn't like anyone would still respond to my coach.

"Ma always said good things would happen to us, and look

where you are now. Look where I am."

She sounded more positive and happy than I could ever remember, which was definitely a good thing. It was nice that she had this lion to be close to, and she was smart enough not to let it go further than it could. If she could just avoid being sold to another coffee plantation owner, she might find herself in a good situation.

I asked her about Skype, but she'd never heard of it and nobody she knew had a computer that she could use privately. So it would be phones for us still, at least for a little while. She promised to keep an eye out, and told me to work hard over the summer, saying maybe I could come back and visit.

But I wasn't going back to visit. I was going to bring her here to live.

***

The clay courts are actually not clay anymore. They're made of crushed red brick. That's what Ernesto, the zorro (a kind of Latin fox from Platania, greyer than Pom with salt-and-pepper fur and russet highlights here and there and a black tip to his tail) who showed us around the Pelotas Rojas club told us as I knelt to rub it between my fingers. It stained them red even after I brushed the dust out of my fur. "The texture stays drier but it gives the same feel, the same touch as the clay," he said lovingly, bouncing a tennis ball. "You see, look how she bounces here…" on the court, " and here…" on the concrete beside the court. "You States players play on this," pointing to the concrete. "She is hard and unforgiving. The ball flies away from her. But the ball loves our court, kisses it, wants to remain close to it."

"Can we play?" I hadn't expected to be so excited about this, but Ernesto's enthusiasm for his surface was infectious. I wanted to see how my serves reacted, how my spin changed, what this surface would do to my game.

"You and me?" Ernesto put a paw to his chest, next to the Pelotas Rojas logo on his white polo shirt. "I would be flattered! But would you not like to play with your coach?"

"Let him play someone who's a true master of the surface," Frio said. Probably that was flattery, because Ernesto hadn't been ranked in the pros for over a decade (I looked him up later, when we got home).

Ernesto beamed, and we went to fetch our rackets.

As it turned out, Ernesto was a better teacher than Frio was. Currently, he wasn't as skilled, but he had been once, so as we played, he told me things like, "Good shot! But ten years ago I return that for a winner. Hit the ball then pay attention to your court coverage." If Frio minded someone else taking charge of my education, he didn't let on.

The court didn't play as differently as I'd thought it would. Maybe my shots weren't strong enough for it to make much of a difference, or playing on dirt courts when the tennis center was closed had taught me about slower surfaces. Whatever the reason, after warming up and playing a couple games, I started to figure out what was different.

Ernesto and I played an informal set for which Frio kept score. I would have been winning 6-5 when he called a halt to it. "You are too springy for these old bones!" he cried with a laugh. "I withdraw. The match is yours, N'Guwe."

It felt good to hear that, even though we hadn't been playing properly. I thanked him, and so did Frio, and then he showed us around more of the courts. "It is mostly people who wish they had started playing at your age who come to me," he told me, one arm around my shoulder. "You have good talent. Four or five years, I will see you in finals on TV."

"I hope so." I beamed and kept my ears straight upright as I shook his paw. "Hopefully in the clay courts too."

He waved and trotted off to his other duties, and Frio patted my shoulder. "Don't let that go to your head," he said. "Ernesto will say nice things about everyone."

"I did pretty well, though, didn't I?"

"Well, he let you get away with a couple things. But I have to admit you adapted to the clay court better than I thought you would. Most States students struggle with it for a while. Did you have clay courts back home?"

I shook my head. "We played on dirt, though."

"Ah, well, maybe that's it." We'd come back to the first court, where I'd played Ernesto, and Frio picked up his racket. "Want to play a bit more?"

"You know it." I hefted mine and hurried to the far court.

By the time we got to the motel, I was pretty worn out and I think Frio was, too. I collapsed on the bed while he went to the bathroom to freshen up. "Hey," he called to me, "you want to shower before dinner?"

"I'm pretty hungry." I panted rather than sweated, unlike Frio, who'd been wiping his damp fur with his shirt after our match.

"Okay. I'll just change shirts and we can grab dinner. How's burgers sound?"

"Great. Can I have two?"

He laughed, came out rubbing his bare chest and back with a towel, and leaned against the dresser. "The first two are on me. The next ones you have to pay for."

"Oh, thanks!" I sat up, tail wagging. I liked the informality—no, the intimacy—of sharing a room with Frio. It had been strange at first, but on the drive up we'd talked about movies and music and he'd played some of his favorite bands for me, ones I'd never heard of but was interested in. These were the kinds of conversations I had with Marquize or my other friends, but I hadn't thought to approach Frio with them. "I was planning to pay anyway."

"Nah." He grinned and dropped the towel on the dresser, leaning back. "Ah, that feels good. Anyway, I'm dragging you up here. I'll pay for dinner."

"That's really nice," I said, and hurried into the bathroom.

When I came out, he had a clean t-shirt on with a band name on it, not the sort of thing he would've ever worn at Palm Gables, and we drove to dinner. I only had one big burger, though I did like it a lot, and Frio told me it was the best burger place in the county. I didn't know what all the other burger places were like, but I figured in the States, that had to be pretty good.

Frio had two beers, and I worried he might not be able to drive us back, but he didn't say anything about it and he seemed fine on the highway. I still worried, but tried not to let it show. I mean, in school and on TV and before movies, it seemed like every day we got some kind of warning about drinking and driving, pictures of bloody corpses in cars, people getting pulled over by police, weeping family members notified, until I couldn't fathom why anyone would risk drinking and then getting into a car. None of our class drank anyway, though I knew some of Shawna's friends had at the party and at other times.

But nothing bad happened on the way back to the motel, and maybe two beers wasn't enough to be drunk on. Frio did buy another beer from the cooler at the front of the burger place, but he didn't open it on the way home.

"Phew," he said when we got back to the air-conditioned motel room. "You wanna freshen up before I hop in the shower?"

"Yeah, sure." I gulped some water, took my shirt off and rubbed some powder into it to freshen myself up. I'd showered at Ma's and I didn't really need to more than once a week, though I had to wash my paws often.

Then Frio went in to use the shower and I turned on the TV because he hadn't. There wasn't anything good on, so I texted Marquize with the promise of telling him more about the clay courts the next time we talked.

"Rocky?"

My ears perked. I turned toward the bathroom. Frio had left the door cracked a bit. "Yeah?"

"I forgot my conditioner. Can you grab it out of my bag for me?"

"Um." I stood and looked around. Frio's duffel bag was on the floor by the dresser, so I padded over to it. It held clothes and not much more. "I can't find it."

"I mean my toiletries bag in here."

"Oh." I padded to the bathroom and tentatively pushed the door open. It felt weird going into the bathroom while someone else was showering—not another cub my age, I mean; we did that in the dorms all the time because that's how the showers were set up. But nobody ever talked to each other in the showers.

On the sink was Frio's little brown leather bag, which I guessed was what he meant. "It's the green bottle," he said as I approached it, and I realized with a start that he was watching me from the shower. The feeling of being wrong intensified.

The green bottle lay there in the bag, plain as day. I picked it up and turned, trying not to look at the shower, and put it on the edge of the tub.

"Thanks, Rocky," Frio said, and as the curtain rustled I caught a glimpse of tan fur, dripping water. Before I could see anything else, I closed my eyes and hurried back to my bed.

The TV was still going, but I didn't see any of it. I was trying to figure out what had just happened. Maybe Frio was casual about nudity. He'd wanted his fur conditioner and didn't want to get the bathroom floor wet. That was the most likely explanation. I probably would have gone ahead and gotten it wet, myself, but maybe he was more fastidious.

Then again, I had told him what I'd seen on Marquize's computer. What if he thought I wanted to see him naked, and maybe more? He was attractive enough, I guessed, but I'd never thought of him in that way, not like I had Marquize, even if I was gay, which I wasn't sure I was.

No, I was probably reading too much into it. Frio was a friendly guy, and he'd gone out of his way to arrange this trip for me. He'd forgotten to get his conditioner and he didn't want to drip water on the floor. That was all.

I was settling down and trying to focus on the TV again when my brain snapped another question at me, one I had no answer for.

Then why had he left the bathroom door cracked?

***

Frio didn't say anything when he came out of the bathroom, a towel wrapped around his waist, his fur disheveled and askew from drying. I didn't say anything either, but I'd already slipped under the covers and was watching TV propped up in bed.

Frio sat on his bed and watched for a bit, then said, "I'm gonna let my fur air dry a bit more. The dryers here are pretty bad. Do you mind?"

"No," I said, and stared as hard as I could at the television.

He took the towel off and tossed it on the floor near his bed, then stretched out on his back on the bed.

The temptation to look gnawed at me. He was clearly inviting me to, and there wouldn't be anything wrong with it, right? Except that he was a coach and I was a student, and there had been at least one news story about a local teacher who'd slept with a student— a year older than me, even—and everyone had been horrified. But she'd been thirty-something, and Frio was at least ten years younger than that.

Was it weird? Was it something people would read about in

the paper and go, "Ew," the way they had about that other story?
I didn't know. I turned onto my stomach and tried to hide the fact
that I—my body, at least—was getting excited. I didn't know what
that meant either.

"You going to sleep?" Frio asked a few minutes later.

"Yeah," I said without looking at him.

"Okay." He rustled in his bed.

Oh no, I thought, he's coming over here, he's going to slide in
next to me and what am I going to do?

But he just turned off the TV, then the light, and then got under
the covers in his own bed.

I think I lay awake for another hour before I finally fell asleep.

***

The following day wasn't quite as exciting. Frio was up and dressed
by the time I got up and didn't say anything about the previous
night. Looking back on it, I felt a little ashamed at how I'd reacted.
He hadn't meant anything by it, probably. I'd just assumed because I
had this secret that he knew about it and was trying to get a reaction
out of me, which was probably not true at all.

It didn't help that I didn't have anyone to talk to about it. I couldn't call Ma or Marquize because then I'd have to explain why I was so upset, why I felt targeted. Of all the people close to me, I could most easily envision telling Ori, but where would I find the time? I had to have breakfast with Frio and talk about clay courts all morning, so I couldn't even explain to myself how I felt about it.

The lack of sleep meant that my feet were dragging that day. We played more on the clay courts, and I tried to learn, but kept getting distracted. Frio remained patient with me and we got a lot of good work done anyway, and we were both exhausted when it came time for dinner.

He picked a pizza place that night, and it wasn't great, but even bad pizza was a pretty good meal. So I was full and tired by the time we got back to the motel room. Again, Frio let me freshen up, and again he took a shower, and again, he left the door cracked. But this time he didn't call me in to bring him anything, and I made sure to be under the covers when he came out.

He didn't even have the towel on this time, so when he walked in front of the TV I saw him all the way naked, tan back fur and ivory front fur and his sheath and balls. He was poking out of his sheath, too, I noticed, but he didn't seem self-conscious about it at all.

I closed my eyes and leaned back on my pillows, waiting for him to get under his covers. But he didn't get into bed right away. He pulled out the beer he'd gotten the previous night and twisted off the cap with a hiss, then drank from the bottle. It clunked on the wood as he set it down on the dresser, and then he said, "Going to sleep?"

"Yeah." I didn't open my eyes.

"Okay." He turned off the light. And then he sat down on the side of my bed.

I froze. There was only me and him in the room, and that was scary, but it was also invigorating in a way, because there was nobody here to tell me what to do or what not to do. His breath smelled like beer, and then he put a paw on my side, under the covers.

"Rocky," he said, "I think you're really special, you know that, right?"

I swallowed and didn't know how to answer. He waited a minute and then went on. "Well, I do. I don't—I don't go around doing this with all the boys. But you came to me when you were confused, and I appreciate that. I want to help you."

His paw felt not right. But it felt good, too, and I was confused. *I think you're special.* That built warmth in my chest, made me want to respond and smile, to reach out and touch his fur like he wanted me to. He was a coach, one of Coach Murphy's trusted assistants, and he'd come to think highly of me.

"I've been doing a lot of work to help you, too. Staying over the summer, coming up on this trip...you've got a lot of potential and I want to make sure you reach it." His paw began to rub up and down my side. "And there are a couple things we can do off the tennis court, too. Just you and me. You're grown up enough to know what I'm talking about, right?"

My throat felt dry as the riverbed in summer. "Sex."

"Yeah. I promise not to tell anyone. You're curious about guys, though. I could tell when you came to me that day. It's okay. I like guys too. So now you know my secret, and I know yours. We can keep each other's secrets, can't we?"

I wavered. The temptation was so strong, I wanted to pick up his paw and put it right where Shawna'd touched me. I knew he wouldn't stop the way she had. But there was still that part of me, the part that sounded like Ma, saying, *Hang on. Do you really want to do this now? With him?*

His paw moved again, and now it was getting closer, and I could do nothing and it would just happen. It wouldn't be my fault, it wouldn't, because I didn't do anything. Frio was the one telling me what to do.

You don't have to do whatever he says.

Braden's words flared brightly in my head, and Ma's voice backed them up. I jumped and pushed his paw away. "No! I mean—no. Thanks, it's really nice and no, I think you misunderstood, it was someone else, it was Don," I grasped for his name because he was gone and Frio wouldn't be able to check.

For a moment, he didn't move, and then he got up. "Okay," he said, and sat on his own bed. I could see him easily in the dark, his paw reaching between his own legs, and then he got up and went into the bathroom.

I turned over and pretended to sleep, heart racing, pillow over my ears so I couldn't hear anything, nose buried in the fabric so I couldn't smell anything. When he came out of the bathroom, he went straight to his bed without a word. About twenty minutes later, his breathing evened out.

All night, I tossed and turned. Every time I started to doze off, I imagined his weight on the edge of my bed and I jerked awake again. Eventually the windows lightened, and then the room grew brighter, and then Frio's alarm went off.

***

The only thing Frio said about that night was very casual, as we were getting into the car. "Hey, nobody has to know about last night, right? We're keeping each other's secrets, right?"

I didn't know whether he would really tell everyone about me being gay. Clearly he hadn't believed my lame excuse about it being Don. When I didn't say anything, Frio put an arm around my shoulder. "Look," he said, "I shouldn't have cracked open that last beer. I got a little more truthful with you than I should've. But I know you wouldn't say anything to anyone, so I felt safe with you."

I nodded noncommittally. He took his arm away. "Maybe you'll feel safe with me someday, too."

My head fell back against the seat. *Maybe when I'm eighteen*, I thought.

***

Frio shook me awake when we got to Palm Gables. I mumbled thanks to him, said the trip had been really helpful, and asked if I could take the afternoon off to rest up.

"Sure." He smiled. "Bright and early tomorrow, though."

"Uh-huh." I waved and walked away.

All the way to the bus and all the bus ride home, I kept thinking about that night. I wanted to tell someone, but who? I couldn't tell Marquize because eventually then he'd know I'd told Frio about finding the porn on his computer. And besides, what if Marquize was jealous that Frio had picked me and not him? He was already jealous about Braden. Bret and Dom had stayed in touch over the summer, but I couldn't tell them if I didn't tell Marquize.

I could tell Ori, but it was already late there and I wouldn't be able to call. Ori would tell me that I should stick up for myself and that things would be fine. I didn't know if I could convey to her how scared I'd been that last night in the hotel, or how worried I was about upsetting my summer lessons.

I couldn't tell Ma. She'd go after Frio right away if she thought he'd hurt me.

But I needed to talk to someone. Ma was the closest in many ways. I trusted her, and if I told her I had to keep working with Frio, maybe downplayed what he'd actually done, but talked to her about my confusion over my own feelings...maybe, just maybe, that would work.

Ma wasn't home when I got back. Even when school wasn't in session, she kept busy around the neighborhood with meetings and groups that I didn't keep track of. She'd told me she needed to be busy during the day, and when I got home we'd talk mostly about tennis and my life. Now I sat restlessly around the empty apartment wondering what she was doing and when she'd be back. When I started making money in the tournaments, I'd buy her a cell phone so we could talk and text back and forth.

I sat down on the couch and texted Marquize just to talk to someone. He was working today, but he could sometimes make the time to send a quick text when it was slow. Then I leaned back on the couch and closed my eyes.

***

Ma shook me awake. My tongue was hanging over the side of my muzzle and my neck had a little pinch in it. "It's not good for you to sleep like that," she said, glaring down at me with her ears up and paws on her hips.

"Sorry," I mumbled, wiping my mouth and getting up. "I was tired."

"How was your trip?"

"It was...uh. The clay courts were really interesting. I did pretty good on them."

"Pretty well."

"Pretty well," I echoed.

Ma put down her cloth bag on a table and walked to the kitchen. "What do you want for dinner?"

The memory of the night before didn't quite have the iron grip on my stomach it had had that morning. Maybe I was better rested, or maybe it was just a little further back in my memory. But the jumble of thoughts over how to talk about it had settled.

I followed Ma into the kitchen and said, "Something did happen...on the trip, I mean. I wanted to talk to you about it."

She put down the frozen steaks she'd taken out of the freezer and met my eyes. "What happened?"

"Well, uh." I flicked my tail and then curled it. "My coach—the ferret."

"Frio."

"Yes." Thinking about it enough to form the words to tell her brought back some of that uneasiness, the terror and desire of lying there with his paw on my side. "He...well...we were sharing a hotel room..."

I hadn't even finished the sentence before her lips drew back, her ears flattened. She slapped her paw on the counter with an impact that made me jump. "Ro. Did he force himself on you?"

She switched to Kikongo, which gave the conversation more urgency and intimacy. I followed her lead. "No. No, he just...he said he was interested, that's all."

Ma relaxed, though her ears didn't come up. "You didn't let him?"

"I said no."

"And he left you alone after that?"

I nodded. "He said we'd keep it secret, but...he didn't do anything else." I left out that he hadn't really had a chance.

Her expression had gone from angry to thoughtful. "You want to keep working with him?"

I hesitated, then nodded.

"All right." She took my arm and led me to the couch. "Sit."

We sat together and she held my paw. "This is difficult, Ro. Because in our country, you know, you would be an adult. If we had money, you could marry."

I thought of Ori and nodded. Ma went on. "But here in this country, it is different. I teach cubs who are sixteen, seventeen years old sometimes. We—the teachers—know they are having sex. We talk about it in the lounges. Girls get pregnant, the nurse has papers on diseases...it happens. But we are told over and over again that we must never engage in anything like that with the cubs, even though they are nearly adults. Do you know why?"

I shook my head and then thought of that story with the teacher. "It's gross?"

Ma squeezed my arm. "Because we as teachers have some power over them. We can affect their lives. So if we do anything with them while that relationship exists, it isn't fair to the cubs. We can manipulate them without even realizing it. Maybe this coach of yours really does feel affection for you."

You're special, he'd said.

"But he still has a lot of control over your life. So this was wrong of him to do. Are you all right?"

I nodded again. "I mean...it was really weird." Ma talking about it so rationally made it easier for me to distance myself from the feelings. "I didn't expect it and I didn't know what to do."

"Do you feel attracted to him?"

"No!"

"Okay." She studied me. "You might think that this is a silly thing to be upset about, because of where we come from and the life we've had there. But you're no longer only from Lunda. You're also now from Pensa and the States. You are part of this culture too, and in this culture, that might be a shocking thing. So it's okay to feel bad about it."

"I know." The rejoinder was almost reflexive, but that was because the words hadn't really registered with me. I was from here now? How could I be from here and also from there? But when I stopped thinking about the words and examined my feelings, I understood a little better what Ma meant. I had friends here, I had lived here almost a year now. If some older male at home had made advances toward me the way Frio had, well—it wouldn't have been so gentle, for one thing, and he wouldn't have taken a "no," for another. But back home I would have been more prepared for it.

"Here you feel safe," she went on. "Nobody is going to come to take you away to war. Another boy might come fight you, but probably not more than that. If you go to the wrong parts of town, there are people with guns, but the wrong parts of town are easy to avoid. This is a betrayal of trust, which is why it may feel strange."

"That's it!" Ma was able to articulate the problem better than I'd been able to think of it in my own head. "I trusted him. But...he did let me say no. And he said really nice things about me."

Her frown deepened at that, for some reason. She patted my knee. "You are a very good cub, Ro. I think that sometimes you see the best in people even when it isn't there."

I didn't feel like I did, but I didn't say anything. She went on. "One last thing you have to decide is whether to tell anyone else about this."

My answer came out almost as soon as she'd finished. "I really don't want to. I'm fine and I don't think he'll…ask again."

She held up her other paw. "But what if he goes around to other cubs? Others who might not be as well prepared as you?"

I bit my lip. I imagined Frio confronting Marquize, who always seemed so self-possessed but could also sink into insecurity easily. If Frio told him he was special, asked him to do things, would Marquize be able to say no? I thought he would. When it came down to it, he'd lied to his parents for me about the laptop, and he'd stood up to Braden, at least once. "What if," I said, "I tell someone about him and he says something about me and they send us home?"

"What would he say about you?"

"Oh, he…" I squirmed on the couch. "He could say that I was lying. Or that I—that I wanted it."

Again Ma looked at me silently, but this time I think she was thinking about the situation, not studying me. My heart still pounded, wondering if she'd catch me running around the edges of saying that part of me *did* want it. "Our position is not very stable," she said. "If I pass my test, then I will have a job, but I am still here as part of your visa. It's possible that this is just something that happened once. You are over six feet tall and a very handsome jackal." My ears warmed and flattened. "So you don't look fifteen."

"And I might be sixteen," I added.

"You're fifteen." She gave me a stern look and then a smile. "Don't wish so hard for adulthood, Ro. It will come soon enough, and then you'll be my age and looking back wishing you'd had another year between fifteen and sixteen."

My paws reached out and found my tail, and ruffled through its fur. "So what should I do?"

"From what you've told me…" Ma sighed. "I don't think it's worth jeopardizing your life for. But be very attentive. If he makes any more advances on you, or if you suspect something with one of your friends—"

"Of course," I said. "I'll do something about it."

She nodded, and then lifted her paw from my knee and wrapped it around my shoulders. "I'm so very proud of you, Ro. You did the right thing when you were scared and all alone."

"It wasn't that scary," I mumbled, leaning against her, but my tail smacked the couch with its wagging.

So I went back to Palm Gables the next day as if nothing had happened, and Frio greeted me as if nothing had happened, and I had a lesson. I practiced for a little bit on my own, then Frio and I got lunch at McDonald's. We talked about the thunderclouds rolling in, and whether we'd be able to get another lesson in before it started raining. We didn't; we played some basketball at the gym. "One on one," Frio called it, and here he was much better than me, although I was enjoying learning how to shoot. When he guarded me, I thought he stayed a little farther away than he had the last time we'd played, and it looked like he was being really careful about touching me.

And the next day, we had a lesson in the morning and one in the afternoon, and we didn't discuss the clay court weekend. Nor did we discuss it the next day, as my life slowly went back to normal. The only thing that was different was that before the trip, Frio would sometimes come inside with me when I went to my locker to pick up my bag. After the trip, he always said good-bye to me outside and never came in.

I talked to Marquize for an hour that week about the clay courts, and twice I almost mentioned what happened with Frio to him. But again, I worried that he would discover that I'd seen his porn and, worse, told someone else about it, so I left that out. It was nice talking through the trip with him, because it helped me remember the really good parts of it, which had been overshadowed by that last night. I told him I'd look into getting a bus up there and maybe we could go sometime during the school year.

On his laptop—my laptop—I looked up other stories about teachers and students, and what I found confused me more. Not as to whether it was right or wrong; that was pretty clear through every story where the older teacher was painted as a predator, the student as an innocent victim. But in one of the stories, the teacher said that "their love was real," and in another, the student hadn't been the one to press charges. So in some small number of the cases, especially when the student was close to eighteen, it looked like there was real affection there. Frio *might* just have had a crush on me.

After a week, I decided I had to let it go or it was going to distract me from tennis too much. But I did want to write a letter to Braden.

> *Dear Braden,*
> *You don't have to reply. I don't want to bother you. I just wanted to thank you for the advice you gave me. It was really helpful this summer.*
> *Thanks,*
> *Rocky N'Guwe*

I didn't expect an answer, and I didn't get one.

Chapter Sixteen

So July faded into August, a series of hot muggy days punctuated by blasts of rain and wind. I soaked up the lessons and kept my focus on tennis. Frio said I was getting further than he'd expected and hoped, I guess in at least all but one area. But the more the days dragged on, the more that incident at the clay courts seemed unreal, like a movie I'd seen. Ma checked with me once in a while to make sure Frio hadn't done anything, but even when she asked, she was very circumspect. "Everything is still okay with Frio?" she would ask. Or, "Frio is helping with your tennis?"

Meanwhile, Marquize and I talked several times a week. The cheetah still hated his parents' store, but he'd taken to bicycling down to the waterfront and all around as daily exercise. There was a recreational tennis league at the college there and he'd convinced them to let him join their practices. They were mostly stronger than him, though none were faster, and he had better improvisation than they did. "They're wild, all but three of them," he told me. "You can't predict what they're going to do because they don't even know, and half the time they're not in the right place or if they are, they're not ready. But the top three guys, they're pretty good. The four of us play doubles and we have some good rallies."

I told him about my lessons and about the weather down here. "At least the heat breaks every other day or so," I said. "I mean, it doesn't really because everything's humid all the time, but the hour after the rain is really nice."

"It's been a week without rain here," Marquize said, or sometimes, "It's been raining three straight days." Port City didn't seem to have the same balance of rain and sun that we did; it was either all or nothing. "You'll see when you come up here."

He'd gotten a letter from the school with a form for him to register for the junior tournament at the States Open in September, which was half an hour south of where his family lived. I hadn't, but I'd asked Frio and he'd said he would take care of it for me. "Can I come see your parents' store?" I asked.

"Why?"

"I'd like to see it."

"It's gross. It's depressing. I'll take you to a nice place when you come up. You'll get pizza here that's like nothing you can get down in Pensa."

We also talked about movies, and when one of us had seen a good movie, the other ran out to see it so we could talk about it. We loved sports movies and superheroes, and Marquize loved the big fantasy movies that were coming out, and I loved war movies. Ma didn't like any of them, so often when we were discussing one, she would interject, "Hmph," or, "learn to live real life before you start a fantasy one."

And Ma got a thick envelope at the end of the second week of August with the results of her qualification test (nearly a month late). She passed, of course, and that meant she was eligible for a permanent job. So the next week was full of phone calls to the school, a stack of paperwork that looked as thick as one of my textbooks, and two meetings at the school itself. And at the end of it—she still didn't have a job.

"They say they had to move forward on setting the teachers for this coming year." She stirred a pot of boiling water with pasta cooking in it as she told me, very calm.

"But they told you you could have a permanent job if you passed the test!"

She shrugged. "The test took longer to process than they thought."

"Are you going to look somewhere else?"

"Maybe." She stirred, took out a piece of pasta, and tasted it. "Most of the schools have already started, but maybe one of them will have a teacher leave. I'll send my information around."

"Stupid test people," I fumed. "This is their fault."

"And what good is complaining? Do you think if the test board sends a letter to the school that they will undo their plans because it was unfair that my results were late? We must make the best of what we have. And the pasta is ready."

I remember that conversation was a Friday night because it was the next morning that I went on a shopping errand to the mall to get new clothes for the new school year. I told Ma I could go by myself because I wanted to buy her something as a congratulations on passing the test: a nice blouse she could wear as a permanent teacher. From our trips to the mall, I knew the kind of thing she liked, and I found one in her size after a bit of walking around. It was nice to be by myself in the midst of all those shoppers, but it was also a little lonely. I called Ori to tell her what I was getting for Ma, and talked to her for the first few blocks back.

When we hung up, I happened to be near a park where I'd noticed a basketball court, or half of one. It had been empty when I'd walked to the mall, but now it was occupied with about seven cubs around my age playing an intense game. Since I didn't have to be home at any particular time, I stopped to watch, leaning on the fence outside.

All the things Frio taught us were evident there, plus a few more: guarding another player, swiping for the ball without losing your position or risking too much. There was one raccoon who clearly wanted to steal the ball every time and as a result, the guys he was guarding often waited for him to jump and then drove right by him. If that sounds like I understood the game intimately from the first time I saw it, well, no. It happened about three times right in front of me in the ten minutes I watched.

And then I happened to look up at one of the players as he grabbed a rebound, a tall, muscular coyote, and I recognized Shawna's brother Marcus.

I froze, and he did too, but he relaxed first. "Time," he called, and tossed the ball to another player.

The game stopped as a few of the guys ran for water, and others watched Marcus walk toward the gate. I thought about running, but I figured I could probably handle myself as long as the other guys stayed on their side of the fence, and anyway, around then Marcus said, "I'm glad you stopped by. I wanted to talk to you."

"Oh?" I stayed wary.

"Yeah." He wiped his paws on his shorts and looked down at the grass. "When I got back, after that party…I told Shawna what I did and she came after me…" He flicked one ear and I saw a newish scar there, near the tip. "Said she wanted me to scare you, not fight you. I don't know how she thought I'd know that, but...girls, huh?"

He looked up with an awkward smile and stuck his paw out. "Anyway. Sorry. Been wanting to say that for a while."

"Oh, well. Thanks." I grasped his paw.

After a few seconds of silence, he said, "Hey, uh, if you don't have anything to do, want to shoot some hoops? We're down one and if you join we could play four on four."

"I..." I didn't have anywhere to be, technically. "Yeah, I can play for a bit."

So we played two teams, Shirts and Fur. The first few minutes weren't great for me: I had one shot blocked, missed another badly, and then let a guy get by me for an easy layup. I saw a couple guys grumbling to Marcus, and he looked in my direction, so I figured I had to do something to prove I belonged in the game.

When Frio and Marquize and I had played, they said I was really good at passing. I was at least taller than most of these guys so I had a fighting chance at rebounds, and a minute later I got one off a missed layup. The rabbit who'd been bringing the ball up put his paws out for it, but beyond him I saw another of my teammates, a skinny maned wolf, free near the basket. His eye caught mine, so I faked it to the rabbit and then threw it as hard as I could down the court.

The maned wolf didn't quite catch it; it went off his paws and bounced away. He was fast enough, though, to recover it and spin around a defender to find Marcus, who buried a nice shot.

"Okay," the rabbit said to me as we hurried back to defend. "You play point. I'm better at shooting anyway."

And when the maned wolf caught up to me next time around, he patted me between the shoulders. "Next time I'll expect it," he said. "Great pass."

From then on, I had more fun. I brought the ball up and my teammates ran around, knowing I'd see the moment they were open and get them the ball. It didn't always work out, but I had a lot of fun being a point guard, and I even got to score a layup once. When the game broke up, Marcus and the maned wolf (whose name was Joaquin) both told me to come by again anytime I wanted to play. I walked home with a big smile and a satisfying tiredness.

***

The day we got to move back into our dorms, at the end of August, I was the first one in. I know because the wolf handing out keys told me as he slid over the map of the dorm and tapped a claw on my new suite, this one with only four rooms off it. I found it easily, set my bags on the bed and my laptop on the desk, and went out to explore.

Marquize's name was on the room across from mine, not adjacent, but that was okay. My tail wagged anyway. It looked like two of the other boys I didn't know as well were in the other two rooms, so I explored more and found the suite one over where Bret and Pom and Dom were going to be. I couldn't wait for everyone to get back, so I texted Marquize that we were in a suite together and when would he get here?

I got a text a little later telling me he'd be there in an hour and if I wanted to meet his parents, I could come down to the lobby. So I unpacked my room until my phone buzzed again, and then I hurried downstairs.

Marquize's parents were surprisingly a little on the heavy side, but both nearly as tall as their son. Marquize himself ran forward and hugged me when he saw me, which left me surprised, a little breathless, and wagging. When he stepped back, he presented me to his parents. "This is Rocky," he said.

"We've heard a lot about you." His mother stepped forward and offered me her paw. "I'm Halifa."

His father was there to shake my paw when his mother was done. "Aziz. Marquize says you're quite talented."

I flicked my ears and smiled. "Oh, he's really good too."

"Rocky got a leg up on me this summer though," Marquize said. "Getting to train with the coaches, some extra time…that's really helpful."

"Well," his father said, "that's nice if he can afford it."

"He said it didn't cost him anything." Marquize had his jaw set stubbornly.

I kept quiet because I didn't quite know what to say. The air was a little tense, like when I argued with Ma, but I didn't know how to navigate through this argument the way I did with Ma. So I asked Marquize if I could carry anything up for him, and he gave me a bag, and we all wound our way through the dorm in silence until Aziz said, "Different floor from last year."

"We're in a suite," I said, "like last year's pretty much but smaller."

"So Rocky, is your mother around?" Halifa asked as the cheetah unlocked his room.

I shook my head. "She helped me bring my bags over this morning."

"How'd you get here?" Marquize asked, opening the door.

"On the bus." I wasn't sure why he asked that, but when he looked at his parents, I realized it probably had something to do with him not being allowed to stay for the summer, maybe about how I had to ride the bus and was still allowed to stay here.

His mom asked me a few more questions about my family, while Marquize basically ignored his parents, setting up his new laptop while his father stood with his tail flicking back and forth and looking at nothing in particular. In the middle of me telling Halifa about my sister working for a Muslim refugee shelter, Aziz said abruptly, "If you don't need anything else from us, we should get over to the hotel."

"Oh." Halifa looked over. "Yes. We'll see you for dinner, Marquize?"

"Sure." He didn't even look up from his computer.

I walked out to the suite with them. "It was nice to meet you," I said.

"Our pleasure," Halifa said. "Tell your sister we admire her work."

Aziz didn't say anything as he stalked toward the stairs, his tail now flicking rather than lashing, his brow lowered and angry. I watched them go and then walked back into Marquize's room. When he didn't say anything, I sat on the bed. After checking a few more e-mails, he turned to me. "Are they gone?"

"Yeah."

"Good." He closed the laptop and leaned back in his desk chair. "God, it's good to be back here. I missed this place."

"I missed you too." My tail thumped against the bed. "Wanna go get a shake?"

"I have to have dinner with my parents." His smile vanished and he glowered at the floor.

I leaned back against the wall. "Oh yeah. I forgot. What happened?"

"Nothing happened," he said, "just the usual stuff, sitting in a car for twenty hours on the way down from Port City listening to their talk radio and the politics, the questions about what I learned over the summer." He kicked at his chair legs. "How's your Ma?"

"She's good. She passed her test, but they didn't send her the results until a month late and her school had already filled their post. So she's substituting again this year. But she can get a full time job if one opens up."

"Good." He regained a little bit of his smile. "Hey, how about if I meet you for that shake after dinner?"

"Sounds good." I leaned over the side of the bed to where his tennis bag was and pulled his racket out. "Feel like a bit of exercise?"

***

Marquize survived the dinner, and by the time we came back from our shakes, half the other students had shown up. By the next day, everyone was back, and we congregated in our suite to talk about how our summers had been. Everyone seemed to have had a pretty good time, and to my surprise they were mostly as jealous as Marquize had been about my private lessons over the summer.

The memory of that scary night with Frio had been pushed back into a part of my mind I was aware of but didn't go to very often, kind of like the laundry room in the dorm's basement. And just as the laundry room smells sometimes rose into the suite to remind me it was there, occasionally things would bring that memory back to the surface.

Sometimes they weren't little hints, either, like when Kim told us about her summer at Porter Colliere's camp and Bret said, "So…did she have any…extracurricular activities for you?"

"You can imagine whatever you like," Kim said loftily. "The junior girls talked about it a bit, but she only ever touched me in very professional ways."

"Like, 'prostitute' professional?" Bret persisted.

"She was terrific." Kim ignored him. "She helped me out a lot. Rocky spent the summer with Frio and you're not asking him if he got touched inappropriately."

Everyone looked at me and I wanted to crawl away. I knew I ought to say something, but I couldn't bring any words to mind.

The longer the silence dragged on, the weaker the smiles got and the more curious the eyes turned to me. "Well?" Pom said. "Did he?"

"Uh." I flattened my ears. "No. Of course not. I mean, you know, he corrects my movements. That's not inappropriate."

"Relax." Marquize put a paw on my shoulder. "You'd know if it was inappropriate."

Down the couch, Dom's little white ears perked up toward me. "If he does, Rocky, you know you should call the cops, right? He's like, what, twenty-four?"

None of us knew. "At least twenty-two," Dom went on. "He's been teaching here four years."

"How do you know that?" Pom asked.

The arctic fox blinked. "Didn't you read the bios of all the coaches before you came?"

"We didn't memorize them," Bret said.

"Oh. Well, neither did I, but I remember stuff." Dom's short muzzle dipped and he looked embarrassed, his ears going partway down.

"He's right, though," Pom said. "You know that, right, Rocky?"

I nodded hesitantly. "I guess so?"

"Aren't there laws in Lunda about older guys messing with underage boys?" Bret asked, a curl to his lip.

"Yes." I glared around at them. "In the cities. But…it's complicated. In our culture, girls can be married at twelve." It was helpful to go back to the facts and laws of my home country and change the subject away from Frio.

"Hey." Bret elbowed Veronica. "You and Malik could get married there and then he'd be a citizen."

"Of that country." Veronica sniffed. "It's barbaric, letting girls get married that young."

"My ma and I think the same," I said hurriedly. "My aunt was going to engage my sister, my younger sister, to this coffee plantation guy, but Ma stepped in and made her stop."

Again everyone looked at me, but differently. "Wow," Dom said. "Like, your actual sister?"

"Whose sister do you think?" Pom elbowed the arctic fox. "Damn, Rocky, makin' it a little too real."

"Sorry." It didn't come out very sincere, modulated by my relief not to be talking about Frio.

"Don't be." Marquize stepped in. "You can tell us stuff like that."

"Yeah," everyone choed, and my ears warmed.

"Well, it wasn't a big deal. I mean, it was, but it's over now." I looked around at them. "Thanks. Can we talk about something else? Like what diseases Bret caught in Anglia?"

And it was over. But not entirely.

Later that night, Marquize came to my room. "Laptop working okay?" he asked as I invited him in.

"Yeah, it's great. Thanks so much." I beamed. "I got a lot of work done on it this summer."

He crossed the room and sat on my bed, bringing his legs up and folding them under him and then curling his tail around his body. The tip flicked back and forth, and he reached down to hold it in one paw, playing with it. He had on loose athletic shorts and a stylish green Ultimate Fit t-shirt, one I admired both for its color and for the smooth way it lay over his fur. I planned to get one for myself, but they were thirty dollars and I could get three regular t-shirts for that price.

"I'm really glad everyone's back," I said, "and, uh, especially you. I got a lot done this summer, but it was pretty lonely."

"Yeah." He smiled. "I'm glad to be back too." But he still looked preoccupied and hesitant, like he couldn't figure out how to say what he wanted to, which was weird for Marquize. As long as I'd known him, he'd always been able to say exactly what he meant. Except maybe that time I was dating Shawna and he was upset about it. But this felt different.

"You wanna go get our textbooks tomorrow?"

He nodded. "Yeah, of course." He tugged at the hem of his shorts and then lifted his head. "Hey, Rocky, this is gonna be a weird question, and if it's—don't get mad at me for it, okay?"

I laughed. "I can't imagine getting mad at you." Last time, I reminded myself, he'd only asked me if I'd accept the gift of his laptop. This wasn't going to be anything bad.

"Okay." He shook his head. "Just…you were acting a little weird when Kim asked you about Frio, and…*did* anything happen this summer?"

"Oh. No," I said automatically, but it was a lot easier to lie to him over Skype or over text, and with him sitting right there two feet away from me, my resolution not to tell him crumbled. "I mean—look, you can't tell anyone about this. I promised not to."

He nodded and leaned forward, apprehensive. I had to look away from him. "So that time we went up to the clay courts…we were staying in a hotel room together. Nothing happened. But he said some stuff. I think if I'd wanted something to happen…" As I said the words I could feel myself cleaning up the night, and maybe trying to make the memory less scary. Part of me thought that was wrong; hadn't I faced deaths of my friends and Ori's arranged marriage? But really, nothing had happened, and nothing had happened the rest of the summer. "Anyway, I think he's gay and he liked me, but really, he didn't do anything."

Marquize nodded slowly. "You know all that stuff Dom said about him being twenty-four or whatever, that's all true, right? If he ever does anything to you, you should report him to the police."

"Yeah, I know." Marquize had believed my story, and that made me feel better about it. "I told Ma, too."

"Okay, good." He leaned back and let go of his tail, which started flicking again. "Frio, huh? I kinda thought…you know, I got a vibe off him."

"You did?"

"Yeah." He cupped his elbow. "He likes to correct our form more than the other coaches do. He touches a little longer. I think he thinks we don't notice, but when you start looking for it, it's pretty obvious." He shrugged. "It's harmless, right?"

"I guess."

"Okay, well." He smiled. "Thanks for telling me. I know it must've been weird, and I don't know if your country is any different, but again: that is not okay. I mean, if he starts to do anything to you."

"No, I know. Thanks. I mean, he basically—I told him no and that was the end of it."

Marquize shook his head. "You hear all these stories of students and teachers, but you never think it'll happen to someone you know, y'know?"

"Yeah." There was one more thing gnawing at me. "Hey, while I'm—while we're talking—uh."

The cheetah tilted his head, shifting on the bed. "Yeah?"

Here was another time when I had to make sure I was forming the words correctly in English, and then I knew I was going to have to say them all in a rush because if I stopped midway, I'd lose my nerve and they would all fall apart. I took a breath, started, then had to stop again.

"You okay?" Marquize asked, looking a little more alarmed.

"Yeah." I rested one paw on the closed laptop, its cool plastic solid and reassuring. "I just wanted to say, one time last year I was using your laptop and I saw some of the—pictures—the stuff you had on it and it's totally fine with me. I'm not—I don't care about it and I still want to be your friend and I hope you can talk to me about it. If you want to."

He didn't say anything. After a second, I risked a look at him and saw him staring fixedly at the laptop. "Marquize?"

"You saw…" He trailed off.

"Uh-huh. And look, it's fine. I don't think anyone else will care either, but I understand if you don't want to talk about it."

He kept staring at the laptop, and his tail had gone very still. He sat rigid as a statue, not even flicking an ear. "It was—those pictures, whatever you saw, that was—I mean, I was curious. That's all. I'm not—I don't know what you think, but it's not what I'm *into*."

"It's fine—"

He got up abruptly, unfolding and stepping down from the bed and then hesitating. "I gotta get some sleep. I'm really tired. I'll see you tomorrow, okay?"

"Sure." I started to get up from the chair, but he was already out the door. It clicked closed behind him and I was left alone in silence.

What had I done wrong? I'd thought I was being nice, understanding, a good friend. Should I not have mentioned it at all? But I'd told him about Frio, about one of my secrets (cleaning it up, I reminded myself), and I was hoping to give him the chance to open up to me as well. Friends shouldn't keep secrets from other friends, I'd thought (setting aside my confusion over my own feelings), so I was pretty sure I'd done the right thing. Had I ruined something in the process?

But in the morning, when we met to go get our textbooks, Marquize was friendly and talkative again, and nothing seemed out of the ordinary. We hung out together most of the day, got our textbooks and looked up the schedules for our classes, played a few more sets of tennis, and went to dinner.

(I had definitely gotten better than him over the summer. I was a lot more prepared for his frantic improvisations on the court and, though I hadn't realized it, had gotten better at disguising my own shots so he didn't have time to prepare. I won all three sets we played and it wasn't even close. I told Marquize he was just rusty from the summer, but he shook his head and told me he was going to have to work twice as hard to catch up with me now. I felt bad for him, but also good for myself. And guilty about Frio, who had, after all, put a lot of time and work in with me to help me get to that level.)

We'd gotten back to the dorm and were heading to bed for lights-out, with the first day of classes the next day. Marquize said good-night with everyone else, and then unexpectedly followed me into my room and shut the door.

"I'm sorry," he said when I turned around. "About last night. When you mentioned the pictures, it was—it caught me off guard. You didn't tell anyone else about them, did you? None of the guys?"

I flattened my ears. "No, I didn't tell the guys. I thought it was a private thing."

For a moment my heart felt tight, fluttering like a trapped bird, waiting for him to ask me, "What about Frio? Did you tell him?" But he didn't. He just nodded and said, "Thanks. I'm glad you told me about seeing it. I don't know what you must have thought about me."

"I told you," I said, "it's fine, whatever you're into—I mean, curious about—"

He exhaled and then reached out for me. I stepped forward, not sure what was happening, but he wrapped his arms around me and then released me. "Thanks, Rocky," he said. "You're a good friend. And when I'm ready to talk about it, you'll be the first one I come to, I promise. But I'm—I'm trying to work through a lot of stuff and I can't deal with it right now. I just want to go to school and play tennis. Okay?"

"Of course. Whatever you want—whatever you need. Just let me know."

"Thanks," he said again, and smiled back to the black teardrop marks on his muzzle. "G'night."

And then he was gone, back to his room, and I had to be satisfied with that.

Part Three: Rallies (2009-10)

Interlude (2015)

"Let's pause here after the first set and look back on this year that Braden Longacre has had."

"Oh, it's been a beaut, hasn't it. You see here his path through the Ocie Open, which he'd won once before, but really, Daren, I'd say this renaissance for him started last summer. He got to the semi-finals at Wimbledon, which is not his best surface, and did very well there losing to the eventual champion. And here at the States Open last year, he made it to the finals and many thought he was going to win."

"That's true, and I would say that was really the start of this current run. All last year he's been getting to semi-finals, even at the Gallic Open which was previously a tough one for him. And he broke out of that mini-slump he went into after winning the Ocie in 2013."

"I still think that run at Wimbledon was significant."

"He'd made it far there early on in his career, though."

"You may have a point there. All right, and then here we see the Gallic Open. He benefited from the injury withdrawal of Shari Lobro, who'd won it the two previous years and was favored to win it again, but I tell you, the way Longacre dispatched Gulan Robino in the final, I'm not sure Lobro would have beaten him."

"Lobro would probably have won at least one set."

"Oh, no doubt. Robino's going to be very good, but he's even less experienced than Rocky N'Guwe is here. Braden is usually very quick to dispatch inexperienced competitors, a pattern we're seeing again here today."

"Wimbledon, now, he was number two in the world at that point and he had a tough final against number one Geoffrey Bowson, who was trying to retain his ranking. Longacre prevailed in four sets and took over the number one spot."

"And that's when everyone started to realize something special might be going on. He wasn't expected to win Wimbledon, and when he did, with the only remaining major the one here, his home country where he has performed very well—"

"He grew up near here too, about an hour north of Port City, so I reckon a good number of friends and family are in attendance tonight."

"Exactly. The media started picking up the story and the pressure on him has just increased week on week. The two weeks here I don't think he's gone anywhere without at least ten reporters following him around. Every match is in prime time and the post-match conferences have been madhouses."

"Ha ha, I don't know if I'd use that word, but they certainly have been nearly impossible to get into. But he's handled the pressure exceptionally well. Of course, Braden is famously terse with the media, so all we really know is that nothing's changed there."

"And he's handling the match the same way, coming out strong as if this is just another match. First set is in the books at 6-1, and Longacre will serve to open the second set."

***

I try to come up with positives after that first set, and the only one I can get is "at least I won a game." But that service hold was tough, and I couldn't even win my last service game after what Braden said to me on the changeover. As if.

My coach is in the box behind me. Whenever I've looked up at him he's been still and expressionless, ears to muzzle. He's not allowed to give me any signs or coaching in the middle of the match. The idea behind that is that it's supposed to rest on me alone. Most of the time that's fine. Most of the time I believe in myself.

Coming out in my first major final and losing the first set 6-1, though, that's hard on the old ego. I knew intellectually that Braden was a better player, and that I was likely to lose the match. But I told myself I could take him to four sets, maybe five. I certainly wanted to at least stay on serve, take the first set to a tiebreak. Tiebreaks would favor me overall, because in a single game, fluky things can happen. In a tiebreak, a single point can decide an entire set.

That's looking more and more like wishful thinking now. Everything's coming easy to Braden, just like it usually does—

No, that's not fair. I know better. Anyway, this isn't about him, it's about me. Part of why everything's coming easy to Braden is because it's difficult for me. Shots that I made effortlessly in earlier matches are going astray, making me tighten up and second guess myself. It was that first service game: I didn't think I was nervous, but I must have been. Coach warned me about that, how the atmosphere of a Final is different from anything else. And then doing badly in that first game affected all my others. And then Braden's comment—though that wasn't gamesmanship. That was sincere.

So I've got to pull myself together. I've been through times when I doubted myself before, like back at Palm Gables. It took a lot of other people believing in me to get me to believe in myself then, but they were all right. And over the years, I've lost some of them from my life, but others always took their place. And what remained was my own confidence.

I look up and out onto the empty court. Braden, to my right, is putting away his water bottle and getting ready to go out again. I take one more drink from mine. When it comes down to it, it's just me and it's just him. That's what this is all about. So I'm going to have to go out there and be the best me I can be. I might not be able to win a set from him after all. I might lose this thing in straight sets. But I can't let that bother me. So I'll take it one game at a time and focus on holding serve in this set.

Chapter Seventeen (2009)

The first week everyone was back, they got thick manila envelopes in the mail from the junior tournament at the States Open—everyone except me. I went to see Frio to ask where my registration was. "Oh," he said, "didn't you get it yet?"

I shook my head. "And everyone else did."

"Tell you what," he said. "I'll give them a call."

But I had a sinking feeling from his expression that I wasn't going to go to the tournament, and indeed, the following day the ferret came up to me with a crestfallen expression that felt melodramatic and fake. "Gosh, Rocky," he said. "I don't know what happened. I could swear I sent it in. But they don't have your registration on file, and now it's too late to go. I'm really sorry."

"That's all right," I said. "Maybe I can go watch."

"You can if you want, but it would be at your own expense," he said. "Gosh, I'm sorry!"

"Thanks," I said again, though I wasn't sure why, and I went back to the dorms to tell my classmates the bad news.

Most of them were sympathetic. "You'd have kicked ass," Dom said, and Pom agreed.

"Can't you send them a note explaining what happened?" Bret asked.

"Get real." Kim scoffed at him. "They handle hundreds of registrations and you think they'll just pick up the phone for some random student and be like, 'oh yeah, your coach forgot to send in your registration, it happens all the time, no worries'?"

"They might," Bret snapped back, ears flat.

Marquize didn't say anything until we were alone in my room later, and then his voice had a bit of a growl to it. "It's because of what happened over the summer."

"I think maybe." I didn't want to believe it was true. But it all seemed too coincidental: he'd volunteered to take charge of it, told me not to worry about it, and then it hadn't gone through. And that had been a couple weeks after our trip, so maybe the incident was fresh in his mind. "Maybe he just forgot."

Marquize snorted. "Not likely. Watch out for him, Rocky."

"I will." I sat on my bed. "I'm sorry I won't get to try your pizza."

"Someday you will." He smiled. "We'll have next year, at least."

"Yeah, I won't let Frio do my registration next year, that's for sure."

Marquize came over and sat beside me. "Or maybe next year we'll be gone. This place can only teach us so much. We should be out there playing in tournaments."

"No. I'm not ready for that yet. Coach Murphy told me about cubs who left too soon, who entered tournaments and lost a bunch and got discouraged and quit. He wants to make sure I'm ready before I leave here so I have a good chance at a career."

"I bet Frio wouldn't mind seeing you gone." The cheetah's tail flicked back and forth, hitting mine and then flicking away again.

"It's fine. You go, have fun, play hard, and Skype me after."

He held out his paw. "Promise."

And he kept that promise. It sounded like the tournament wasn't a lot of fun for most of my class—all the boys lost their first match and Kim was the only one of the girls to win hers. She won two, actually, before losing to a Gallic skunk. And the students didn't have much chance to get in trouble in the city, traveling with chaperones and with a curfew. But they did get to watch the professional matches, and that's what I wish I could've been doing while I was the only tennis cub left in my morning classes. In the afternoons, I practiced with Frio, and I didn't say anything about where everyone else was. If he'd done it on purpose, I didn't want him to know it bothered me; if he hadn't, I didn't want to make him feel bad. But the more I thought about it, the more I thought Marquize was right and he had done it to get back at me.

That notwithstanding, he was working harder on his teaching, if anything. I needed to work on my discipline, he said, because as I'd gotten better I'd developed a tendency to jump ahead of myself, to decide what the right shot was before I let the play develop. This was a little confusing, because I had thought that thinking ahead was what I was supposed to do. "It is," he told me, "but you should be flexible in your plan. A good opponent is going to guess what you're trying to do, just as you're guessing what he's trying to do, and will move to cut off your options. These other students aren't doing that yet, but once you get out on tour your opponents there will."

After a few games showing me what he meant, I got it a lot more. "See," he said after he'd beaten me with a passing shot, "you were trying to get me to that corner, which was a good strategy, but you telegraphed it too early. I saw it and got around your shot."

Panting, I nodded. "I get it, I think."

He kept harping on discipline even after Marquize came back, giving the same lectures and playing a game against Marquize to demonstrate. "You guys think you can work on that with each other now?"

"Yeah." Marquize picked up his racket to take Frio's place on the court. We volleyed to warm him up, and then practiced the techniques we'd been working on. Frio watched for a little while and then wandered off.

"He likes you," Marquize said, serving wide.

I ran to backhand the serve, getting it cross court so he had to run for it too. Marquize always guarded the shot down the line too closely. "I don't want to talk about it."

The cheetah got to the ball and hit it to the corner I was already running towards. "I'm just saying. He played what, one game against me? He plays with you every other day to 'demonstrate' something."

I lined up a shot past Marquize, then saw that he was running to cut that off and switched to a drop shot, something I'd practiced over the summer. He's fast, and he can change direction better than I can, but not a lot better, and the drop shot was too much for him. He dove at it, catching it on the second bounce and flipping it back over the net.

"Maybe he's afraid I'll tell someone what happened. Maybe he feels bad about the States Open," I said softly, grabbing the ball in a paw. Marquize was close enough to the net to hear me, and he stayed there, dropping one paw to the net cord.

"Maybe," he said, and when I tossed the ball to him, he didn't move. I turned to walk back to my baseline, and he said, "Rocky."

When I looked over my shoulder, his expression was serious. "I'd keep an eye out. He might not have given up, is what I mean."

"Okay," I said. "Thanks for helping me watch out."

"Sure." That got a smile out of him. "Anytime. Come on, let's hit another point. I'd like to see you drop one on me again."

Whatever Marquize's concerns, Frio didn't try anything for the first month of school. It helped that we weren't ever in a situation where he could. When I was in the locker room, there were other boys around, even when my whole class was up in Port City. Frio avoided me when I was changing, which made me wonder about what Marquize had said. In fact, the first time I saw him outside the courts that whole year was at Marquize's birthday party, and that was only for about two minutes.

We'd decided to have a little party in Marquize's room, Bret and Pom and Dom along with Brittany and Kim. Yu and Malik had an exam to study for, so came by to drop off presents and then left quickly. Brittany had the same exam but was more confident. "I know Math backwards and forwards," she said. "Come on, who brought the booze?"

Bret brought a bottle of rum sheepishly out of his backpack. "How'd you know?"

"Sweet sixteen," the otter said, grabbing it from him and cracking it open. "And I'm going to make sure none of you gets sick on it. Any first-time drinkers here?"

Marquize and Dom raised their paws, and after a moment Pom did too. I didn't, because I wasn't going to have any, so it wasn't going to be my first time drinking. "Right, let's get some Cokes out here then."

She was pouring the fifth rum and Coke when the knock came at the door. Quick as a fox, Brittany capped the rum and slid it under the bed, then grabbed a water bottle, dousing her webbed paw as she signaled to Marquize to open the door.

"Hey," Frio said at the door. "Happy birthday." He gave Marquize an envelope and craned his neck to look inside. "Little party going on?"

"Just a little one," Marquize said, taking the card and holding it awkwardly, not sure whether to let the ferret into the room or not.

I might have been imagining it, but I thought Frio's glance skipped over me when he scanned the room. "Well, keep it quiet, in bed by eleven, and…" He sniffed. "You guys don't have alcohol in here, do you?"

Brittany held up her paw. "Sorry. I was putting some rubbing alcohol on my paw. I cut it today and it opened up again."

Frio laughed. "All right, good. Just don't let the fumes get so thick that you're hung over tomorrow." He winked at the room in general and then closed the door.

I was a little on edge after that, expecting him to come back in. I remembered the beers he'd drunk and how he claimed they'd made him say things he normally wouldn't, and it didn't seem improbable that he'd come back, maybe when he thought we'd all have drunk a little bit, maybe ask to join in the party. As a coach, he wasn't supposed to, of course, but he had already demonstrated how much he could blur that line when he wanted to.

I didn't like feeling that way about Frio, but it cemented my resolve not to drink, so when Brittany offered me a cup, I turned it down. The fumes were already making me a little lightheaded, and I noticed the foxes sitting back from the bottle of rum, too, so I joined them on Marquize's bed.

"What'd you get him?" Pom asked me in a low voice, looking at the stack of presents Marquize hadn't opened yet.

"Oh, a…" I glanced down at my paws and matched his tone. "A money clip that's a sword, like from "Lord of the Rings," and a matching keyring that's a, you know, ring."

At the time I'd bought it I thought it was pretty neat and that he'd like it, from the moment I saw it. But here, with all my friends, I remembered how much money they all had and that they'd probably gotten him fancy electronics, or expensive clothes, or other things I didn't even know how to find that would outshine my little novelty gift.

But Pom's ears perked up and Dom grinned appreciatively. "Aw, that's cool," the red fox said. "I just got him a gift card to the Apple store."

"I got him a subscription to a music service," Dom said. "But hey, you're his best friend. Your gift should be better."

"I didn't know how to get a subscription to a music service," I said.

Pom put a paw on my shoulder. "Settle down, Rocky. Your gift's personal. He'll love it."

"Y'think?" I stared at the little pile and at my little gold-wrapped box in the middle of it. "I hope so."

Pom sniffed the air. Brittany had capped the rum a few minutes before. "Clearer now," the red fox said with a grin. "Come on."

So we joined the circle of people sitting on the floor. A little to my surprise, both Pom and Dom took drinks from the otter, though Dom sipped his and hadn't finished it by the end of the night. I could smell the rum just sitting beside them, but it wasn't as strong as when the bottle was open. I guessed it was okay for them, though both of them set their drinks behind them rather than hold them in their paws.

And though I felt weird about not drinking, nobody made me feel worse. And the foxes were right, it turned out. When Marquize got to my gift, the polite expression he'd worn while opening all the others melted away and he held up the money clip with a triumphant expression. "With this sword I will defeat all the villains of the retail world!"

Everyone laughed, in a boozy cloud. Marquize unwrapped the ring and loved that as well. He put them in his pocket, not into the pile that he'd set aside, and leaned over the circle to give me a hug, touching his muzzle against my whiskers. It wasn't anything that made anyone else take notice, but I felt warm enough for my tail to wag a bit as I sat back down.

Once Marquize had opened his presents and cards, we all sat back and drank, some of us with rum, some without, and the conversation turned to the school year, tennis, and the tournament coming up in a couple months. "Rocky's gonna win that," Bret said, getting up on his knees and pointing at me. "Bet you a hundred bucks. Anyone here." His paw swept the room. "He'd have won a match up at the juniors. Maybe two."

I expected a bunch of people to take him up on it, but nobody did. The two foxes looked at me, as did Kim, enough that I felt uncomfortable. "Nobody?" Bret sat back heavily and pointed at me again. "See? Frio's pet's gonna come through."

That brought more silence and an elbow in Bret's side from Kim. "Shut up, ass," she said.

My ears flattened, and Pom, next to me, leaned into my arm.

"Hey, Bret didn't mean anything by that. It's cool that Frio sees talent in you enough to spend time with you, y'know? If he thought any of us were that talented, he'd be spending time with them too."

"Yeah," Kim and the others said, and Marquize, on my other side, patted me on the shoulder.

"You're not better because he spent time with you," Marquize said. "He spent time with you because you're better."

My ears stayed flat. I didn't like being set apart from the group even in a positive way. "I bet if you'd been able to stay the summer with me, you'd be just as good," I said to the cheetah.

"Because it's my birthday, I'll believe that." He grinned at me and that set my tail wagging again.

After that, things went a lot better. We ended up staying up past midnight, though we turned the lights down at eleven in case someone came by. Nobody did. We watched videos on the Internet and laughed together, and Bret called up some terrible tennis shots that made us laugh even more. Marquize, citing his privilege as birthday boy, had a second rum and Coke, but nobody else did.

Pom was the first to take off, yawning. Brittany followed, then Dom and Bret a few minutes later. Kim stuck around until she saw me give a huge yawn, and then she grabbed my wrist. "Come on, Rock," she said. "It's past midnight. His birthday's done, and we've got class tomorrow."

"Yeah." I got up too, brushed out my tail, and when she let go, I extended a paw to Marquize. "G'night. Hope you had a good birthday."

"I did." He got up to walk us to the door. "Thanks, you guys."

Kim waved and walked out, and I turned at the door. "See you in class," I said.

Marquize stood about a foot away from me, our eyes right at each other's level. And then he leaned in and kissed the side of my muzzle.

I could smell the rum on his breath. I didn't know what to do. But he didn't follow it up, just leaned back and smiled. "Good night, Rocky," he said, and when I stepped back, he closed his door.

Chapter Eighteen

I didn't know what to make of that kiss. When I lay down to sleep, I felt the cheetah's lips against my whiskers again. He hadn't kissed me on the lips, but maybe that was because he didn't know whether or not I would like that. How could he? *I* didn't know if I would like that.

What did he want me to do in response? Maybe nothing. I thought about Ori, who the last time I talked to her had told me that her lion had kissed her. She said it wasn't a big deal, so maybe this wasn't a big deal either. I'd ask her about it. Looking forward to that let me get to sleep.

In the morning, Marquize said he had a bit of a headache. I asked if he wanted ibuprofen and he said he'd already taken some, and that the headache was worth it because the party had been so much fun. He thanked me again for the gifts on our way to class. I wanted to ask him about the kiss on the muzzle, but I couldn't quite figure out how to bring it up, and I remembered that I was going to call Ori and I kept quiet.

I was edgy for a lot of the day, though. Looking back, I guess I can tell why it occupied me so much, but that day I didn't quite get it. Part of me wanted Marquize to get that close again, and then part of me worried that if he did, Frio would find out and would start pressuring me again. I kept a reasonable focus on tennis, but as soon as we were done practicing, I ran in to change and told my friends I had to call my sister.

Even though it was near eleven at night back in Lunda, I thought Ori would be up. I called on my way to the fast food restaurant because this wasn't a conversation Ma should overhear, either.

Kamina answered the phone, angry. "Who is calling so late?" she demanded.

"It's Rocky," I said. "Rochi, I mean. Can I talk to Ori?"

"She's asleep."

"It's really important."

A long, angry sigh. "What is it? Is it about your mother?"

"Please," I said. "I need to talk to her."

She set down the receiver without saying anything else. I kept walking toward the Meat'n'Malt, the phone pressed to the side of my muzzle. A moment later Ori came on. "What are you doing?" she hissed. "She's awake now. I'll never get away tonight."

"Sorry," I said. "Did you want to get another kiss?"

"Ro." She lowered her voice. "Not so loud."

Kamina sometimes hung around the phone, and her jackal's ears could pick up the sounds from the speakers. I'd forgotten that our old phones back home didn't have customizable speakers. "Sorry. But I have to ask you about it."

"Why? Why now?"

I drew in a breath. "Marquize kissed me."

"What?"

Behind her, I heard Kamina's sharp voice asking what was wrong and Ori reassuring her that I'd only startled her with some news about the school. "How?" she asked when she came back.

"On the side of my muzzle. But he waited until everyone was gone, and it wasn't just a brush of whiskers, you know? It was a real kiss."

"It wasn't a real kiss if it wasn't on the lips." She whispered so low I could barely hear her.

"Maybe when boys kiss boys, it's not on the lips."

"Why wouldn't it be?"

"I don't know how any of this works." Stopped at a corner, I paced back and forth. Overhead, clouds gathered; tourists looked up while locals hurried to get to shelter. The Meat'n'Malt was a block away and I gauged that I could make it.

"So ask him."

I sighed. The light changed, and I crossed. "It was right at the end of the night, and he had been drinking a little. He didn't mention it at all today. I don't know if he's ashamed of it or what. When your—when it happened with you, did you talk about it after?"

"Kind of." She whispered again. "We look at each other and smile."

"He hasn't done it again?"

"No."

"Well." Fat raindrops splashed around me and hit my ears. I hurried to the front door of the restaurant amid the now-motivated crowd. "Marquize didn't look at me any differently."

"Ro." Ori's voice took on a new tone, more direct. I guessed that Kamina had wandered away. "Do you like boys?"

I got right into the shelter of the restaurant, in the outer lobby before you get into the restaurant proper, and I wedged myself to the side of one of the free newspaper racks, letting other people get by me as I waited there. Even all that didn't give me enough time to answer her question definitively. "Maybe," I said.

"Do you like *him?*"

A rabbit stopped in front of me and shook water from her ears. A fox and his little cub hurried around her, the cub squalling that he wanted ice cream, the father's ears flat. They disappeared into the restaurant.

"Yeah," I said finally. "I mean, I don't know…" The little space was clear of people for a moment, and I rushed the words out, "if I like boys, but…" A porcupine pushed her way into the space and I shrank back from her tail. "I'd try it if, y'know, if." She disappeared inside. "If he wanted to."

"So find out if he wants to."

"Ori," I said, "I can't just *ask.*"

"Why not?"

I exhaled. "Because he said that if he ever did want to talk about it, he'd come to me. I can't go talk to him until he does that."

"But he kissed you. Doesn't that count?"

"That's what I'm trying to figure out. I don't think it does. Wouldn't he have talked to me more today if it did?"

"Does he seem ashamed of it?"

I closed my eyes. "No. It's like it never happened."

"Well," she said, "does he know you might want to?"

"I, uh." I thought back to our conversation about Frio. Had I said anything about my own interest? Probably not. That was part of that whole incident that I'd tried to forget. "I don't think so."

"So kiss him back."

"Right," I said. "It's that easy."

"Isn't it?"

I held the phone to the side of my cheek as a family of wolves bustled through the small space. One of the cubs pointed at me and said, "Mommy, he smells funny!" His mother hushed him and pushed him through into the restaurant with an apologetic glance at me.

"It wasn't easy for him until he was a little drunk, I think."

"I wouldn't imagine you'd have to be drunk," Ori said.

That seemed very bold for her to say out loud. "Did Kamina go back to sleep?"

"No, she went to the kitchen to get a cup of milk."

For a moment I could smell the vegetables in the kitchen, taste the warm boxed milk, feel the cool humid breeze coming off the river. It might be true that Pensa was now my home, and Palm Gables specifically, but at times like this when I talked to Ori, sometimes the feel of Lunda came back to me in a powerful wave.

"She's looking for people to marry me off to again," Ori said while I was lost in my memory.

That snapped me back to the smell of frying burgers. "What?"

"I heard her on the phone when she didn't know I was there. But it didn't sound like things were going the way she wanted them to. She said, 'It's got to be worth more than a million francs.' I think she meant whatever they were going to give her for me."

One million francs was about a thousand dollars. I frowned. "Do you know why she said a million francs?"

"I suppose she knows how much I'm worth." Ori said it without affect. A year and a half ago, it had been part of our lives, but that time in the States had made it a lot less natural to me.

"How long do you think before she tries to sell you again?"

"I didn't know the first time. But I'm fourteen now, so definitely sometime in the next year. I heard her telling Ma that once I was sixteen she couldn't find as many males who would want me."

That felt familiar. "I'll have to start making money before that, then. I'll get good enough this year. This one guy I almost beat is off playing tournaments now, and everyone says I'm getting better fast. And my coach is spending more time with me." My voice faltered there, but I recovered quickly. "So if I win the tournament at the end of this year, I'll leave the school like he did."

"Not all the husbands will be horrible like the coffee guy." Ori sounded amused. "Ma won't let me be married to someone unsuitable. Maybe you can bring me and my husband over and we can have a family there in the Union."

"Wait, now you're all right with having your marriage arranged?"

"Our ancestors all had their partners chosen for them. It'll be fine."

I exhaled, and the smells of burgers and fries on the inhaled breath sparked hunger in me again. "As long as it's someone you're happy with."

"Whether I'm happy doesn't depend on who I marry."

"It does at least a little bit."

"No, Ro. It depends on me. That's something Raji and I talk about."

"Oh, Raji's his name."

"Yes, I told you that."

"You didn't."

"I'm sure I did." She exhaled across the phone, and her voice changed. "But Ro, really I must get back to sleep. Kamina is warning me that I'll be needing rest for my lessons tomorrow."

"Sorry I kept you away from Raaaaaji."

"Hush. Good luck, Ro."

"Love you, Ori."

"Love you too."

And I hung up the phone and slid it into my pocket, then went in to get some food. Ori hadn't really cleared anything up for me, but talking to her made me feel better. I decided I could wait and see what Marquize wanted to do. Maybe he'd just been a bit drunk and affectionate and it didn't mean anything. Or maybe…maybe I should kiss him back.

But the days went on and I couldn't ever find the right time to be alone with Marquize. I mean, we were alone a bunch, but mostly those times were on the tennis court. After tennis, we were showering and changing and there were often a bunch of us there. Besides, that wouldn't have been a good time. Not that I was uncomfortable with being mostly naked while showering with my classmates, but it wasn't the right time to return a kiss that might or might not have been an overture to a relationship.

I think Marquize felt a little awkward too, because once or twice he took off instead of walking with the rest of us to the park. I know it sounds weird that we played tennis, then showered, then went off to the park to play tennis again, but for one thing, the tennis in the park was more casual. We'd work on serves and shot placement and stuff, but we wouldn't run and chase shots down. For another, even if we did, I didn't get sweaty, just panted a lot. Pom and Dom and Kim and Veronica were the same way—canid biology—and sometimes we'd play games with more energy than the others.

On weekends, I continued to work at my job, which basically consisted of me sitting at the computer and processing orders. I'd asked them to let me help load since I was fifteen now, but Gen said first, "Maybe when you're sixteen," and later, "Frio said no physical labor. Doesn't want you screwin' up your knee or dropping something on your foot."

So when I was done with the orders and Gen wasn't in the office, I worked on my homework. And very occasionally, when even that ran out, I looked online for some of the kinds of pictures I'd seen Bret and Marquize looking at. Not that it was that hard to find—all I had to do on Gen's computer was open a browser and porn popped up almost right away. Gen had slightly different tastes than Bret, and very different from Marquize, but that didn't matter much. I looked at his sites with curiosity, and then went and found my own.

One time I found some gay porn, and the subjects were a jackal and a leopard, and though they weren't as athletic as we were, they still reminded me of myself and Marquize. The image stirred me in ways that the other porn didn't (and also in a few ways it did, of course). I lost that image because it was on Gen's computer, but it didn't leave my mind, not for a long time.

Sure, I probably shouldn't have been using Gen's computer. But I was fifteen, and I hadn't yet gotten tired of looking at naked aroused bodies on the Internet. You were fifteen once, weren't you? Remember what it was like? Can you imagine sitting alone in an office with a computer right there, knowing that a few clicks would take you to those images, knowing that Gen barely knew how to use the computer beyond the browser itself and some basic functionality? I mean, the problem was that I didn't really know much more, but I knew I did know a little more, and I thought with adolescent arrogance that that would be enough.

Anyway, I needed the job less because Ma wasn't asking me to pay for the groceries anymore. I bought one or two trips a month anyway, but she paid for the rest and for dinners out. She'd found a teaching job at a school a half hour bus ride away, where one of their teachers was having health issues and Ma assisted with the classes, taking them over when Mr. Velasquez wasn't healthy enough to teach. The pay was good enough, I guess, that our house bills didn't put as much of a strain on our money.

Ma also, I found out one day, knew about Ori's lion. The conversation happened completely by chance one day at the store. We were on our way out, arms full of bags, and a family of lions walked in past us. "Oh," Ma said as the door closed behind them, "I suppose Ori has told you about her lion."

"Her, uh, what?" I asked with ears askew, my knowledge plain on my muzzle, I suppose, because she chuckled.

"I have not told Kamina and I will not. Ori knows it will go nowhere."

"How did you find out about it?"

She smiled at me, eyes narrowed. "I'm not going to tell you all my secrets, Ro."

"But you're not going to tell Kamina?"

We walked out onto the sidewalk with our bags, heading back toward the apartment. "I said I wouldn't. Ori knows she will have to be married soon enough, and no cubs can result even if she is indiscreet, so it will do her good to have this little experience in the meantime."

"Wow." I shifted the bag against my chest. I'd taken the one with all the milk and orange juice in it, and it wasn't getting any lighter. "Then why not tell Kamina?"

"Kamina thinks too much of female virtue. It is important, but Ori understands it better than Kamina gives her credit for."

My thoughts returned to Marquize, and I shifted the bags again, out of confusion rather than weight this time. "Ma?"

She turned to look at me. I swallowed. "Do I have to get married, too?"

"It's different for you now," she said. "Back home, yes. You would have to get married soon and begin a family, to ensure your stability.

But here you have more freedom. When you start playing tennis professionally, you will have many, many opportunities to meet a wife."

"I know." That was a part of my tennis life that I'd touched on with Ma from time to time. "That's years away though, and I might want to go out with someone before then."

"Why? Is one of your classmates interested? That coyote?"

Kim certainly had seemed like she'd be open to going out with me, but after Shawna I wasn't so interested in coyotes, and at the moment I wasn't so interested in girls. But it seemed a good enough cover. "I was thinking about asking her out maybe," I said. "But I don't think we'd want to get married. I mean, I know you said that I could go out with a coyote and adopt, and I shouldn't be thinking about marriage, but if we did go out, would you be angry if we didn't get married?"

"You're being silly," she said, "and you're not making sense. I disapproved of that other girl because she wasn't a tennis player, not because she was a coyote. I'm sure she was perfectly nice. She just wasn't good for you."

I stopped at the corner, waiting for the light. Ma checked for traffic and crossed against the signal since the street was empty. I hurried to follow her. "So another tennis player would be good for me?"

"We've been over this, Ro." Her tail swished back and forth. "Ask her out. Why come to me with this?"

Home seemed far too far away now. My ears flattened and warmed, and though the day was cloudy, I felt Ma's curiosity and interest focused on me like a sunbeam. "No reason," I mumbled. "You keep talking about Ori's marriage and I was just wondering what if I never get married is all."

"You'll get married one day," she said. "But you probably haven't met the person you're going to marry yet."

Ma said a lot of things to me over the years, and many of them were right, and many of them were smart, and many were both smart and right. But that last sentence, though smart, was very wrong.

Chapter Nineteen

The longer I waited, the easier it was to put off saying anything to Marquize. And he didn't seem anxious to say anything to me, either. So I dove into the world of tennis, where I still had to guess what other people meant or were going to do, but at least I knew whether I'd guessed right almost immediately.

Coach Murphy had never talked to me one on one more than once a month in my first year, but as we moved through October, he started coming to my practices and watching. It unnerved me at first, because he stood there silently as I hit balls with Marquize, then went away without saying a word. The second time, he came over and gave me a few pointers. No compliments, just corrections to my form. He demonstrated and then made me repeat what he'd done, and called Marquize over to teach him as well. I think it was clear to both of us that he was mostly interested in me, but I thought it was really nice of him to include Marquize as well.

And then toward the beginning of November, Coach Murphy came to one of my training sessions instead of Frio. Marquize and I had been volleying back and forth when the white rabbit walked in. "Rocky," he said, before we could even stop volleying. "come with me. Marquize, wait here. Frio will be along with your new practice partner in a couple minutes."

"Okay," I said, and killed the volley. Marquize strolled to the net and I met him there to shake his paw as though we'd just finished a game.

"Moving up," he said.

"I'll still practice with you in the evening," I said.

"Hey." He smacked a paw between my shoulder blades. "I'm proud of you. Go kill it."

"Promise." I grinned and jogged over to Coach Murphy, who started walking right away, off the court.

The way Palm Gables is laid out, there's two indoor arenas with four courts each on them, and then three outdoor arenas with four each. At least, that's how it was then. They might've added more now or finally put a roof over those outdoor ones (Coach Murphy said the outdoor ones were valuable for teaching us how to play in outdoor conditions like most of the tournaments, but a bunch of venues are putting up roofed arenas now or are just plain indoors). Marquize and I had always practiced on the outdoor courts, but now Coach Murphy led me to one of the indoor arenas.

"Frio's done a good job with you," Coach said. "You need to get in some practice against different opponents, so I'm moving you up to the junior group."

"Which group?" I thought I'd misheard.

"The juniors. They're one year ahead of you this year, third-year students. You're better than most of the sophomores. This group will help you work on your overall game. From my observation and Frio's comments, it looks like your priority will be your return of serve and your court coverage. You're doing a good job of getting back to position side to side, but you're staying back too far. Take some of the court away from your opponent, give yourself a better angle."

"Yes, sir."

"Is there anything you want to ask me?"

I knew there probably should be, but my head was still trying to process my promotion to playing with the boys a year older than me. "Are you going to coach me now?"

The rabbit laughed. "Yes, I'll be attending your practices and taking over your individual coaching, but you'll also be working with Coach Kotten during the practices." We'd arrived at the indoor court, where he held the door for me to walk in. "That's him over there."

I'd seen the old kangaroo rat around the school but had rarely talked to him. He was older than Coach and probably older than Ma, and the only thing I could remember hearing about him was that he'd won a couple major titles with his jump serve back in the seventies. Now he stalked around the court snapping comments at the two players there: Yu and a ram named Cleve.

Fidgeting from one foot to the other on the sideline was a cacomistle who looked our way as we walked in and then came hurrying over. "Hey Coach," he said, "this the guy? Hey Rocky, I'm

Diaz," he said without waiting for Coach to answer. "Hope you're better than Spinner. You seen him? Can't return a serve for shit. Sorry, Coach." He ran to his bag and fished out a wallet, pulled a ten-dollar bill out, and ran back with it. "Here."

Coach Murphy took the dollar with a tolerant smile. "This is Rocky N'guwe," he said. "Rocky, this is Diaz Desol, who as you can see is dying for some competition. Let's put you two over on number three."

We walked to the only empty court in the arena. "N'Guwe, so you're from Africa, right?" Diaz asked. Before I even opened my mouth, he went on. "You know they're putting tournaments in Brasilia now but they still don't have a major one in Africa? Well, there's Cape Town, they want to start one up, but who wants to go there?"

"Where are you from?" I managed to break into his conversation.

"Iberia," he said proudly. "Came over four years ago because my teacher said I got better game than the students there. I learned clay court since I was six, but nobody over there teaches hard court well, so I came over here to learn. This is the best school for hard court, you know? Centro de Toledo is best in the world. Sorry, Coach."

"All right," Coach said as though Diaz hadn't spoken. "Rocky, you'll serve first. Play a match, figure each other out, and remember the things I've talked to you separately about. I want to see how you play each other, and then we'll work on things you can do to help each other."

It didn't seem to me like Diaz wanted to help me, but he did insist on slapping my paw before we took the court, and he said, "Can't wait to play you, Rocky N'Guwe. I heard a lot about you."

From whom? I took up my serving position wondering who had been talking about me when I wasn't around. What had he heard?

And then I tossed the yellow ball in the air and cleared my mind of everything but where it was and where I wanted to hit it.

Diaz played a similar style to Marquize, very energetic and mobile, but with more court awareness and more skill. I tried the same tricks I'd used to get past Marquize and Pom on him and almost none of them worked. He beat me pretty good in the first set, though we had a couple good long rallies and I got him to a break point once.

In the second set, he anticipated my serves better and I figured out some of his returns. It had been a while since I'd faced a new opponent, but I found myself adjusting to his movements without even thinking about it. On his side of the net, I'd never faced someone who figured me out as quickly as I did him. He was smart and experienced enough to spot the flaws in my backhand, to pick up on the patterns in my serve and rallies, and to start moving around them and hitting back to them.

It was exhilarating in a way I hadn't felt since those clay court matches: facing something new and figuring it out, like walking on the wall at the riverbank back home, when a misstep might plunge you into the mud. I played stronger in the second set and beat him in a tiebreaker.

"Woo!" Diaz said between sets. "You're good!"

"You too!" I returned, taking up my spot on the opposite court.

I expected, sort of, to win the third set because I had him figured out. But that's not quite how it worked. I knew how to play him now, but we'd run around so much and I guess I was so amped up from playing Diaz in front of Coach that I stumbled once or twice, got over-eager and mishit a few balls, and those few mistakes were enough to swing the set his way. I lost my serve once and that was it.

"Hey," Diaz said, reaching for my paw as we walked back to the bench. "Great match. We both gonna get way better."

Coach Murphy had risen to meet us, and heard this last remark. His ears twitched. "You are, yes. Now here's what I want you to work on. Rocky: watch how Diaz moves just before hitting his serve return. I want you guys to practice serving and returning to each other for an hour. Diaz: watch Rocky's backhand, how he sets and commits to it and follows through. I've told you this all year, but you have to slow down. You have an extra second you could be using before you have to hit the ball, and that's a ton of time. You can make up for it here in school because nobody's going to make you pay for that wasted time, but once you get out into tournaments they will eat you up. Rocky: Diaz gets here at seven a.m. for a calisthenics workout before school. I want you to join him. You've got to be in excellent condition if you're going to go pro. You two are going to be practice partners through the rest of the year. After that, we'll see what happens. Clear?"

We both nodded. "Right, then. Get serving." And he tucked his clipboard under his arm and walked around to the next court.

Diaz laughed. "Doesn't waste words, does he?"

"No," I said. "Better get to it, I guess. Oh! What was with that dollar you gave him?"

The ringtail grimaced and rolled his eyes. "I use bad words a lot, so my Dad asked Coach to get a swear jar going for me here. I put ten dollars in it every time I swear."

"Ten dollars? That's harsh."

"Dad wants to stop me swearing." He swung his racket through the air. "Parents, what'cha gonna do, huh?"

I thought about Ma and couldn't imagine her making me pay money to stop swearing. She'd just glare at me and say, "Ro, watch your language," and that'd be it. "Right," I said, and jogged to the opposite court.

I found out that evening that Marquize's new practice partner was a sullen rat named Dominic who resented being "demoted to the baby class" and spent their entire practice session trying to smash forehands past the poor cheetah. "After a while," Marquize said, "Frio told him he could only hit backhands for the rest of the session and then he got really upset."

"Jerk." I didn't know how to commiserate with him. "My guy is really excitable. And he has to pay coach ten dollars every time he swears."

"Tennis players." Marquize shook his head. "How did we get mixed up with them, Rocky? Oh, hey! You should see if you can make him swear more! That'd be really funny."

I laughed. "Maybe I'll try it. He's good though. He does this thing when he returns…"

We were on the courts, so I tried to show Marquize, but I couldn't quite get the motion right. Still, we hit the ball around and had a good time playing.

The others were there: Bret, Pom, Dom, Kim and Veronica; sometimes Yu and Brittany. But the others never wanted to play with me much after that. Yu would discuss the things we'd gone over in our lesson because he was now in my group, but he rarely actually wanted to play. He and Brittany worked together more often than not and he confided in me that she was going to start playing the tournaments at the end of this school year. "She's more than ready. I am not yet, but maybe by the end of the year I will be. And you?"

"I hope so. I need to start earning money for my family." Money for Ma and me to live, money for Ori to come over here: all those things weighed on me. Ma kept assuring me that we would be okay with money until I was ready, but I remembered her asking me to buy groceries for a while, a move which seemed stranger in retrospect because she hadn't told me why and I hadn't figured it out. Something that had happened once could happen again, and the sooner I was prepared for it, the better.

"I understand." Yu lowered his voice. "Brit doesn't understand, really. Most of these cubs haven't been without money ever. You and me came here because Palm Gables thinks we have talent and wants to be able to say we went here when we become famous. Everyone else is here because they have money."

"Some of them have talent, too."

"Yes." His gaze slid toward the otter and he smiled fondly. "But they do not understand playing for money."

I thought Marquize did, at least a little. He knew enough of my situation that he still offered to buy dinner most times we went out. "It's a dumb fast food place," he'd say. "My allowance covers it." But between my job and my stipend I had enough money to buy my own food, so I usually paid for myself.

At Thanksgiving, Ma and I came to a dinner given by the school. I thought she could've cooked a better one and she didn't disagree with me, but she thought it was important for me to spend more time with the people at the school, and she wanted to meet some of them herself as well. When I introduced her to Diaz, she didn't say very much to him beyond being polite and charming the way Ma always is when her mind isn't really on what she's talking about. It didn't matter, because Diaz chattered away like he does and I don't think he even noticed Ma was distracted.

We'd eaten our fill of dry turkey and sweet cranberry sauce, bland mashed potatoes and—well, the stuffing was good, I thought, kind of like an Anglic bread pudding except not sweet. I wouldn't have thought I would like that but I did. And the vegetables were overcooked but weren't bad. To be perfectly honest, I liked the cranberry sauce too, but Ma complained about how sweet it was so I did too.

(I resolved never to get her the Double Chocolate Shake at Meat'n'Malt because it would probably make her teeth fall out.)

"I don't see a ferret," she whispered to me as we were getting our food. "Is Frio here?"

"No," I whispered back. "I guess he went home. Marquize did too. Most of my class, actually."

I had a pretty good time sitting with Diaz and talking about this weird Union holiday that was all about eating food, and how in my home country this would have been considered arrogant. We had always had enough to eat, but very few people had more than that. In his country, Diaz said, at least a feast like this would have been associated with one of the saints. "Like San Tiago," he said, and told us about the two weeks of holiday leading up to that feast day.

"I hope I get to see that sometime," I said.

"Hey, if we're there for a tournament, I'll show you around." Diaz grinned. "I don't know if the tournaments fall near that day, but even if we're close, it's worth going down."

"It's a deal," I said.

Chapter Twenty

With December came the approach of the Christmas tournament. Marquize and I worked at least as hard during the evening as Diaz and I did during the day. The difference was that I learned more during the day because Diaz could push me in a way that Marquize couldn't: he was faster, more accurate with his shots, and more distracting. Like Marquize, he was always moving, but unlike Marquize, his moves were always purposeful.

This year, the tournament fell on the 19th and 20th, with the final on the 21st just before we were dismissed for Christmas break. Seedings were announced on the 18th while we were all in our last finals for the indoor classes we were taking, leading to a mad rush for the bulletin board outside the indoor courts when the final bell rang.

"Sixth," Marquize said, slapping my shoulder. "You really helped me out this year. But where are you? Didn't you get in?"

My throat was dry. "I'm on that list." My finger indicated the list next to the one Marquize was looking at, the one with the eleventh graders on it.

"Whoa," he said. "And you're fourth."

I was behind Cleve, who was first, and then Diaz and Yu. I didn't know most of the eleventh graders, and knew none of the ones below me. The thing was, and I didn't tell Marquize this, that I could beat Diaz about fifty percent of the times we played. And Yu hadn't played me much, but I'd watched him and I had a good idea of his strengths and weaknesses. I gave myself about an eighty percent chance to beat him.

Which left me somewhere between second and third best in the group of boys a year older than I was. I'd known that Yu and Diaz were good, but I didn't know they were among the best in their class. I thought about what it meant that Coach had paired me not only with eleventh graders, but with those in particular.

"That's pretty great!" Marquize hugged me. For a brief moment I thought he might kiss me again. But he let me go and ran to grab Pom and Dom, who were walking away from the board. "Hey!" he called to them. "Come check out where Rocky is!"

The foxes didn't seem to think it was quite as cool as Marquize did. "Huh," Pom said, and eyed me. "You're doing pretty good, I guess."

Dom did shake my paw and smile. "Nice job. Can't wait to see you play." But neither of their tails wagged, and when they'd said their congratulations, they just walked away again.

"Ah, forget them," Marquize said. "You're doing great. I hope our matches aren't at the same time."

I checked the schedule, looking at my opponent. "I have to play...Ollie. You know him?" Marquize shook his head. "It's tomorrow at ten. When's yours?"

He scanned the tenth grade matches. "I'm playing...Bret. But not until two. Cool! I'll come by in the morning and see you play. Now let's get a lot of sleep."

I'd called out of work that night specifically for that reason, so I was in bed by eleven. But I didn't get to sleep easily. I didn't even know what species Ollie was. And if I beat him, then I'd have to play the fifth seed (probably), another guy I didn't know, or maybe the 12th seed if there was an upset. Assuming I didn't get upset by Ollie. Even the 13th seed in the eleventh grade class was probably better than most tenth graders.

But not you, not according to what Coach thinks, I reminded myself.

Unless Coach was testing me, putting me higher than he thought I deserved to see how I did.

But no, I knew how good Diaz and Yu were. I belonged in fourth, or even in third.

Or did I?

Finally I did manage to fall asleep, and woke up sprawled at an uncomfortable angle on my bed the next morning barely feeling ready for a match, let alone a tournament. After a short morning workout, though, I shook the cobwebs off and arrived at the school slightly nervous and a little too hopped up to play, if anything.

Ollie was a bobcat who talked with a twang when he talked at all. "Seen y'all on the court," was all he said as we shook paws before the match, but the way he looked at me I could tell he thought I'd be an easy win for him. He was nearly a full foot shorter than me, shorter than anyone else I'd played at the school, so I was on the lookout for how he might use that to his advantage.

It turned out that the thirteenth best student in the eleventh grade was not necessarily better than any of the tenth graders. Ollie had a good serve return and great court coverage, but his serve was worse than any of my friends in the tenth grade and I broke him three times in the first set. After that he got sulky on court and the match was pretty much over.

"You were awesome," Marquize said when he and Ma met me off the court.

I glanced toward the coaches, seated in a box courtside, but they were already watching the next match. I didn't know whether I'd impressed Coach Murphy or not. "I'm off until tomorrow morning, anyway," I said. "Need to warm up before your match?"

"Sure, but let's get some lunch first. I mean, if you guys don't mind if I come along." He bent his head toward Ma.

"Not at all." She took him by the arm. "Ro won quickly, so we have time to go to Maria's."

Maria's sandwich shop was Ma's favorite place near the school, but Marquize and I didn't like it as much as Meat'n'Malt. Still, their sandwiches were pretty good and we didn't leave hungry. Then Marquize and I walked around for half an hour to stretch—me to cool down, him to loosen up—and got on one of the practice courts so I could hit balls back to him and help him warm up for his match.

"You're hitting every serve back," he complained after about twenty minutes.

I hadn't even realized I was doing it. This was his warmup, and a couple times he'd tried to blast serves past me, but I was getting to everything, even the ones he was hitting out. "Sorry," I said. "I've been working on my return game."

"Let a few go, okay?" he said, so I played the passive partner for the rest of his warmup.

Whether it was that warmup or something else I don't know, but Marquize was out of sorts when his match started. He was favored against Bret, if only by a little, but he made a lot of mental mistakes in the first set and lost it 6-2. I tried to meet his eye and encourage him as they took a break, and he managed a smile. It seemed to work: he took over the second set, blasting ten aces to win 6-3. Bret broke his serve in the first game of the third set, but Marquize caught fire and won four straight games before the poor cougar could get himself together, and Marquize won that set 6-3, and with it the match.

We ran into Diaz, who'd also won his match, and I introduced him to Ma—and to Marquize, when the cheetah stuck out his paw and said, "Hi, I'm Marquize."

"Sorry," I said. "This is Diaz. I assumed you guys would've known each other."

"Nah, never met. Good to meet you!" The cacomistle shook Marquize's paw enthusiastically and then turned to me. "Hey, you know, we might meet in the final. If we win out. You'd have to beat Cleve though, and, woo, not easy."

"Any tips for me?"

Diaz laughed. "Play your game, dude. But look, don't get all tense about it. I think it's cool you're in our bracket, but Coach really just wants to see how you'll play in a stronger tournament environment."

Ma cut in. "How do you know that?"

"Oh, I heard 'em talking, because Cleve was asking why a younger player was put in this bracket, and Coach said 'Rocky's been used to playing with stronger players, so putting him in his own age bracket would be unfair and wouldn't be a challenge to him. I want to see him handle strong competition.' And Cleve said he wasn't going to go easy on you and Coach told him that was fine." Diaz shrugged. "I guess Coach wants to see you compete, like, if you go out on the tournament circuit, you'll be playing against older better players, so he's gettin' you used to it? I dunno."

"Thanks," I said, not sure what to think of that.

"Hey, good to meet you all, but I gotta run." Diaz shook my paw. "Maybe see you in the final, huh? Don't matter what Cleve or Coach says. Only matters what you do."

"Yeah," I said, and shook back. "Maybe."

***

Ma took us out for dinner that night, where we talked about our upcoming opponents: Verid for Marquize and the fifth seed for me, a red fox named Jonathan. I knew Verid and told Marquize everything I'd learned from playing him, but neither of us knew much about Jonathan.

"Pity we don't have film of him," the cheetah said as Ma sipped coffee and he and I ate slices of an apple pie. "Can you imagine if we had film of everyone to watch?"

"Then they'd have film of us, too," I pointed out, still wondering if I'd been thrown into this bracket only because Coach didn't want me to beat all my peers. That didn't seem fair. I mean, I hadn't actually won a tournament of my peers yet. Wasn't I supposed to get better until I could beat everyone in my class and then leave the school?

"Oh, right." He chewed, thinking about that. "You worried about this guy?"

"I don't think so," I said cautiously. "But playing someone I have never seen is always interesting."

"'Someone *I've* never seen.'" Marquize still corrected me when I didn't use contractions.

"Yes. You don't know what he's going to do until you're playing him. I know Pom and Dom and Bret and everyone so well now that there's no mystery. So it's exciting."

"And me." He elbowed me. "You know me best of all."

"Right."

Marquize and I went back to the dorm after that. I'd chosen to stay there rather than go home to Ma's because I wanted to stay close to everyone during the tournament, but our suite was quiet that night. I guess Bret and Dom (who'd also lost) had gone somewhere else to hang out, and Pom was resting up for his match tomorrow the same way Marquize and I were.

I slept better that night, for whatever reason. Maybe knowing Coach didn't expect anything of me helped me relax. I was ready for Jonathan that morning and trying not to think about what would be my reward if I won: an afternoon match against Cleve, the #1 seeded ram. Worse, as the #1 seed, Cleve had a free pass through the first round of matches, so he had played the previous afternoon and was now free in the morning. Not only did that mean that he would be much fresher if we played in the afternoon, but it meant he could attend my match and watch me—and he did. But I couldn't worry about him, or anyone except the red fox on the other side of the net.

That fox, Jonathan, played angles really well. Several times I would think I had one side of the court covered only to watch as he skipped a ball onto the line out of my reach. The problem was that he was playing a game of percentages and his shots weren't quite as accurate as he needed them to be. We played a tough first set until I figured out that I could shade toward his angles and force him into harder and harder shots that he missed more often than not. If he tried to hit the court I was leaving open, I was far enough back that I was ready for him, and as that wasn't the shot he was lining up, he wasn't able to get it past me as easily.

That's not to say it was an easy match. We battled in the first and I rode a late service break to a 7-5 win. By then I started to see a pattern in his serves. I broke him in his first two service games of the second set and that was that.

When I came off the court, I hurried to find Marquize. He was locked in a third set with Verid, the groundhog implacably stroking forehand after forehand back to him, and I could see the cheetah getting frustrated. Like Jonathan, he had started trying more difficult shots to move Verid off his game. But that's not the way to beat him, I thought at Marquize silently. You have to be patient, match him shot for shot, move him to the side a little bit at a time, until he's off center; or you push him back and back and then hit him with the drop shot.

Later I found out that Marquize had tried the drop shot several times. It wasn't a reliable weapon for him, so I guess I could see where he'd give up if it wasn't working. But when he gave up, he pretty much let Verid stop worrying about it. There was a great rally in the second set, with Marquize desperate not to lose his serve, that went fourteen shots back and forth. Verid kept stroking those reliable forehands and Marquize kept trying to get angles, but he wasn't confident enough to try a sharp angle the way Jonathan did. Still, he got Verid off balance until the groundhog had to lunge for a return shot and missed it wide.

Marquize held his serve, and I'm sure hoped that Verid would be discouraged. But I don't think the groundhog had normal emotions like that. He held his serve easily and then went right back to returning Marquize's forehands mechanically. The cheetah was the one who got rattled; later he would tell me that he got down on himself because he'd hoped that rally would be a turning point.

You can come back from that sort of depression, but not when it puts you a break behind in the deciding set of a match. My friend struggled and managed to stay on serve through the rest of the match, but already being a break behind, he lost 6-4.

His shoulders were slumped as he came off the court. When he spotted me, he forced a smile. "Almost had him. Just that one game in the third set."

"You did really well," I said.

"You beat him last year."

"He's better now."

"So am I. So are you." Marquize squinted at me. "Did you win?"

It felt a little wrong for me to be celebrating in the face of his loss, but I couldn't very well lie. "Yes. Straight sets."

He slapped me on the shoulder. "Good job. Two more to go!" But he was not as animated as he'd been when we'd both won.

I didn't have a lot of time to console him, though, because I had to stretch and warm up and get ready to play the best in my class—or at least the one the coaches had thought would be best before the tournament.

Cleve didn't seem all that worried about playing me. The ram barely looked at me as he and I hit balls back and forth, trying simultaneously to figure out the other's style and to not give anything away of our own. We didn't talk at all on our way to the court, nor when we went back to the sidelines to wait for the match to start. I had very little idea what to expect from him as a player—or, for that matter, as a person.

The first set went very evenly. Neither of us took chances, except with our serves. We were watching each other's tendencies, probing. I tried to move him around the court, pushed him back and gauged whether I could get a drop shot down, but I didn't actually try it. He was doing the same to me, testing my backhand and my cross-court with some really well-placed shots.

Cleve was one of the first opponents who mixed up his styles the way I tried to, like Diaz but better. He'd wait patiently through a long baseline rally and then unexpectedly charge the net. The first time he did that, I got flustered and missed my attempt at a passing shot. The second time I was prepared enough to send the ball right into his body, so that he had to twist his arm awkwardly to get a racket on it, and his return went skidding out of bounds.

The third time he came to the net, I sent a forehand lob over his horns and dropped it right into the back corner of the court. He kept trying the net game, but I was good at not getting pushed too far back; I'd take his shots sooner than I needed to so that I didn't give up that part of the court.

I'd served first and was up 6-5, but Cleve didn't seem worried as he prepared to serve. Then his first serve came in not as fast as I think he'd hoped, and I smacked the return cross-court for a winner. He blew an ace by me next, and then I got a good return in, keeping him back on his heels enough that I set up an easy winner two shots later. And on the next point, we settled into a baseline rally and I decided to make a move. I hit to the right, to the right, to the right, and he kept hitting them back, waiting for an opening. Then I sent the ball to the left as hard as I could, got it a foot inside the line, and raced up to the net to wait for his return.

He didn't see me there until he was already turned to hit the ball, and by then it was too late. I watched his dismay as he sent an easy shot right into my forehand, and I smacked it to the right, out of his reach. That drew a clap from him—my first of the match, though I'd clapped twice for his shots—and many from the crowd watching, and it earned me two chances to win the set.

The crowd noise mounted, everyone excited at the end of a set no matter who they were rooting for. Cleve saved the first point with another ace, but I got a second serve to hit on the next point and I didn't waste it. It took me three shots to get a forehand winner down the line to win the set, and cheers burst from the crowd around me as Cleve and I walked to the sideline to get a drink.

I didn't look for Ma or Marquize, just sat and thought about what I was going to have to do to beat him one more set. He had a good serve, though not outstanding, and he moved really well. Coming to the net had surprised him, but that wouldn't work again if I started relying on it. If he became more cautious with his baseline play the way I was, we could have a lot of long rallies that would last until one of us made a mistake, and I was already feeling the effects of having played a match that morning. Playing a lot of long points, especially if we went to a third set, would give him a definite advantage.

So I tried to keep the points short. I ran him from one side of the court to the other as much as I could, which didn't work too well because he was doing that to me, too. I took more chances on the returns and won a few points and lost a few. Maybe as many as I would have anyway, but the points were over more quickly. And I changed up my serve to take advantage of where I thought he was going to be, getting a couple more aces in the process.

For all that, we ended the second set tied at 6-6 and went to a tiebreak. I could already feel my muscles protesting at the workout I'd given them today, and they betrayed me almost right away. I missed my first serve and lofted the ball to hit a safe second serve, only to feel the racket not catch the ball quite right. It fluttered and clipped the top of the net, and dropped back onto my side. Double fault.

Cleve didn't need more than that to close out the set. "Great," I told my arm as we headed for the sideline. "If you'd just held up for ten more minutes, this could be over. Now we have to play a whole other set."

I'd been exhausted many, many times in Palm Gables, of course, but usually those times were during workouts or at the end of classes. I'd never been this tired and then had to go out and play another whole set of tennis. It reminded me more of several times at home, when I'd been playing all day and could barely lift the racket, but stopping play meant Ori and I would have to go home. Not that we didn't like Ma or didn't want to spend time with her, but it was much more exciting being pretend tennis stars than being actual jackal children living crammed together with a whole neighborhood of jackal children, where it was much harder to pretend that the worlds on the other side of the television screen were reachable.

Now here I was in one of those worlds, and yes, I knew that staying or leaving didn't depend on whether I won this one set against a ram who was very good. Coach only expected me to make a strong showing, and I'd done that. I could coast in the third set and nobody would be disappointed in the outcome except for me. But Ma had told us often, "Don't save for the future what you need today." Not in a money sense, but in the sense of doing our best or giving extra effort. And so I thought, well, if I let fatigue win today, then it will be that much harder to defeat the next time I have to face it. Coach Murphy and Frio had told us on many occasions that we would have to play through fatigue. Here was my first real test.

I gulped another half-bottle of water. Cleve was already on his way back to the court, so I stood and jogged back to my place. The jog was for my own spirits, to put a fly in the eye of my fatigue and tell it I wasn't going to give in without a fight.

And then of course in my first service game I double-faulted again and lost my serve.

The crowd muttered and I knew what that meant: they thought that was going to be it. Well, it wasn't, not if I had anything to say about it.

The question was, what was I going to do? I searched for anything Coach or Frio might have told me about playing fatigued, but all I could come up with was a warning from Frio not to panic when I made one or two mistakes. The double faults had cost me the tie-break and the first game of the third set, but those had nothing to do with the style of play I was adopting, trying to shorten the points and make Cleve run. That strategy had kept me even with him. So I would keep doing it.

My legs felt like lead by the sixth game. Cleve was serving, up 3-2 and that one break. A couple points had been long rallies, which he was trying for, but more of them had been finished quickly, and I'd discovered that if I reserved my energy, I had enough to run for one or two points in a game—enough to surprise him maybe when he wasn't expecting it.

Cleve also looked to be tiring, at least a little. I might have been imagining it, but there were at least a half dozen times I could swear he hit the ball a fraction of a second late. He was strong and sure enough that it didn't matter much, but I noticed it: he wasn't placing it exactly where he wanted. On the first point of his serve in the 3-2 game I guessed he'd be going out wide, to pull me over to that side of the court and make me run more. As he tossed the ball, I edged a couple steps out wide; he saw me but not in time to change his motion.

The ball came out wide and I was ready for it, slamming a

forehand down the line to catch the corner before Cleve had time to do anything but watch it go by. He shook his head and walked to the ad court, pulling another tennis ball from his pocket.

The logical thing for him to do here would be to go down the middle. But he hesitated, and I knew he was trying to out-think me. So I took a chance and shaded wide on his second serve (after the first went into the net), and it came down right in front of me, hanging there perfectly for me to send it cross-court.

To his credit, Cleve, who had immediately run to protect the shot I'd made last time, reversed direction in time. But when he lunged and swatted the ball back over the net, he wasn't fast or agile enough, not like Marquize or Diaz, to reverse direction again. The whole court was available for me to hit a winner, and I didn't miss.

Two points later, I was sitting at 15-40 with two chances to break him back. And when he had to fade back to cover my strong forehand return of his serve, I eased a drop shot over the net, spinning back toward me and away from the ram, who just stood staring. He clapped for the shot as the crowd cheered, and we were back on serve at 3-3.

That was the moment I knew I could beat my fatigue, that even though I felt like dragging my feet across the court and my racket felt like it was made of stone, I could still play with him and even beat him. When I broke his serve again at 4-3, giving me the chance to serve for the match, I didn't even feel nervous. I just felt like getting it over with. And when he netted his service return at 40-15 to give me the match, I let my knees go and they dropped me to the court. Just like when Braden Longacre won his first major final on TV three years later, except the cheering crowd was a few hundred people rather than tens of thousands. Also, I hadn't actually won the tournament.

Cleve had come to the net and waited there patiently as I struggled to my feet. "Good game," he said, one arm around my shoulder as we shook paws.

"You're terrific," I said honestly. "I want to practice with you more."

He gave a strained sort of laugh as we walked off. "We'll see."

From the hugs and cheers Marquize and Ma greeted me with, you'd think I had just won the tournament. But I had one more match to play. So after I stretched and changed, I joined them in the stands and drank two more bottles of water as we watched Diaz beat Yu, 6-1, 6-4.

The cacomistle saw me, too, and as he came off the court he flashed me a smile and pointed a finger at me. "Tomorrow," he said, and I nodded.

***

It seems weird to say that the tournament final was an anticlimax, but it felt that way. Diaz and I had played each other enough that I went into the match a little nervous because it was the final, but mostly reminding myself to execute on my shots. As it turned out, I got lucky twice in the first set, once when one of Diaz's shots clipped the net cord and gave me an easy winner, and again when he double-faulted on break point. Once I'd won the first set, the cacomistle tightened up a little, like he was feeling the pressure of the final, and I got lucky midway through the second set when one of my passing shots barely clipped the line.

When I held serve at 5-4 to win the game, the set, and the tournament, it was on a very ordinary forehand down the line that Diaz watched go by. I walked to the net to meet him, barely hearing the cheers of the crowd, thinking that it was strange how the whole match had ended on such an ordinary shot. It would've seemed more fitting for that net cord ball to be the last shot, or one of my service returns, which were improving, or a furious rally like the one we'd had in my third game. But no, it was: serve, return, forehand, backhand, forehand winner. And there I was at the net shaking paws with Diaz and he was grinning at me and saying something.

"What?" I said, shaking my head.

"I said I'm not even mad at you, bro, you won! Look at you!"

And then I took in the cheers, the applause, Ma and Marquize on the sidelines and even Frio and Coach Murphy coming over to the court as Diaz wrapped an arm around my shoulder and walked me to meet them. I started to realize what it was I'd done, and elation bubbled up from inside me, banishing any weariness from the match. My tail wagged as everyone surrounded me, paws reaching out and patting me, squeezing mine. *I won the tournament*, I thought in a daze. *I won a tournament against players a year older than me.*

"Great work," Coach said, shaking my paw, and Frio shook my paw as well and tried to say something, only I saw Marquize running toward me, his eyes and smile lit up with joy, and I tore myself from Frio and ran over to hug the cheetah.

"So proud of you," he said, his voice muffled in my neck fur, slapping me on the back as he did.

I had my muzzle pressed against his cheek. Overcome with the excitement of the moment, I kissed him there quickly, so close to the fur that nobody else, not even Ma who was right there, could see. But I knew he'd felt it because his eyes widened a little and I think he was going to say something before Ma swept me into a hug of her own.

And then Coach Murphy was pulling me away again. "You know there are two other brackets that played..."

I gulped, and his big ears twitched. "If you really want a moment to yourself, I can make another announcement here. I mean, you won a bracket of players a year older..."

"No, no," I said. "I didn't hear the announcement, I'm sorry, I thought you were going to tell me I had to play another match."

He laughed and shook his head. "No, just be back here this afternoon at two for the trophies."

"I can do that." I gulped again and looked around for my water.

***

The trophy presentation was surreal, at least to me. Marquize said later that it felt a little boring to him, or maybe he was impatient for the part where Coach would say my name. I stood next to Brittany and Verid, who'd won my year, along with the girl who'd won the eleventh grade year and two younger players who'd won the ninth-grade tournament. Coach introduced all of us and said an extra little bit about me. "I want to call out Rocky N'Guwe, who came here a year and a half ago from Lunda. He lost his father to the wars there and had to leave his sister behind, but his mother was able to come along and ease his transition to this country. As you can see, both she and he did a pretty good job."

The crowd applauded. I folded my ears down, but looking at Ma in the front row, I put my ears up again and tried to bear the praise with good humor. "You may not know," Coach went on, "that Rocky

is actually a sophomore. He's been practicing with the juniors, so we put him in the junior bracket, and again, as you can see…" He gestured back toward me. "He did pretty well."

More applause. Ma beamed at me. And Coach moved on to the next winner.

We all got little trophies and then there were cheers and photos taken and families and the other students were let in to mingle with us. Coach took the time to congratulate all the winners again, and said a few words to each of us. To me, he said, "You're staying over Christmas, right?" When I nodded, he patted me on the shoulder. "Come to my office in the morning and we'll go over the tournament. Lots of good things to take away from it, lots of things to work on, too."

I nodded. "Thank you, sir."

"Good job." He smiled broadly enough to show his buckteeth, and moved on.

"Let me take a photo to send to Ori," Ma said, and so I posed with the trophy while she took a picture with Marquize's phone.

I gestured to the cheetah as she was giving the phone back to him. "Take one with me and Marquize." Marquize hesitated, but I said, "Really, you practiced with me all those times and I owe a lot to you."

"You owe it to yourself," he said, his ropy tail flicking, but he came over to stand beside me anyway. It felt good to be beside him, our arms around each other's waists as Ma took the picture.

"Tomorrow," Ma said, "We'll go to the amusement park to celebrate. Marquize, can you come along?"

My friend disengaged himself and shook his head. "Sorry. I'm on a plane in about four hours. I already rescheduled it so I could stay for this."

"We can still hang out for a few hours though, right?" I wanted to keep sharing this giddy elation with him.

"If you want to ride with me to the airport, you can hang out until I go through security," Marquize said with a wide grin.

I glanced at Ma for permission, and she nodded, so I said, "Yeah, sure."

"Wait, really?" Marquize's laughter subsided as his gold eyes gleamed into mine.

"I'm not doing anything else." I hefted the trophy. "Just let me get this home."

"Home to the dorms or to your ma's place?"

"Ma's place."

"Ah, sure. Hey…" The cheetah's grin came back. "Why don't you go drop that off? I've got some packing to do. I'll meet you back at the dorms in, say, an hour?"

"That sounds good. Ma, let's get something to eat."

She nodded, watching Marquize as he walked off toward the school. "All right."

I held the trophy out to her. "I couldn't have done this without you, Ma. You want to carry it on the way back?"

Her ears flicked back and then up. "Are you trying to get out of carrying it?"

I laughed and pulled the trophy back to my chest. "I'll carry it if you want."

"No, no, I can bear that burden for you." She took it from me and cradled it in her arms as we walked back to her apartment.

***

Marquize texted me as I was on my way back to the dorm. *Cab out front*, he said.

I hurried down the street and found him leaning against a cab texting on his phone. When he saw me, he slid the phone into his pocket. "Hey, you ready to go?" He opened the door.

I jumped into the cab and slid over on the back seat. The cab smelled weirdly smoky and funky, mostly of the immense elk crammed into the driver's seat, his antlers cut off near the base. But when Marquize slid in beside me and said, "Phew!" I smiled anyway, because then it was a thing we shared. I put a paw over my nose and he rummaged in his bag for a Neutra-Scent tissue, but I waved him off.

"How you getting back from the airport?" he asked.

"There's a bus. I looked it up online."

The cab driver offered to take me back, but I told him I'd be fine on the bus. And then Marquize lowered his voice and pulled something else out of his bag, a small box. "I know we said no Christmas presents, so this isn't a Christmas present. It's a congratulations-on-winning present."

"Uh." I took the box. "You didn't have to. I got a trophy, you know."

"I know, but…" He zipped up his bag, looking down. "Look, it's really not much. Just open it, 'kay?"

Inside the little box, I found a small strap woven in blue, red, and yellow. "Those are the colors of your home country, right?" Marquize peered at me. "I looked it up."

"That's about right, yeah." It was clear that he hadn't just bought this on the spur of the moment, but also clear that he didn't want me to make a huge deal of it.

"I noticed you talk about your sister a lot but you don't have a lot of stuff from your home and I thought this might remind you of her."

I picked up the strap and let it dangle from my fingers. "That's really nice of you. How does it, uh, work?"

Marquize took the strap from me. "Hold out your wrist." When I did, he pulled the ends together around it and tied them.

The cloth felt light on my wrist. "How do I take it off?"

"You don't. You keep it on."

I shook my arm. "It won't affect my game, will it?"

"You've got plenty of time to get used to it before the May tournament. But if you don't like it, you can take it off. I put it on your left wrist so you won't have it on your serving arm." He hesitated there, looking at the colorful strap against my dusky brown fur.

"I do like it," I said, and reached over the seat to hug him. "Thanks, Mar."

He hugged back, awkwardly across the cab seat. "I'm glad you like it."

The closeness to his muzzle, his breath on my fur, gave me the courage to go a step further. "Um. Hey. I wanted to ask you something. I don't know if you remember the night of your birthday party…"

"Not here," he whispered.

I pulled back from the hug. He was smiling, but a little awkwardly, and he wasn't meeting my eyes. "Okay," I said. "So when do you get back?"

"Oh, day before classes start." He rested a paw on his bag.

A gruff voice interrupted us. "What airline you need?" The elk had half-turned as the cab headed up the ramp to the airport.

"Oh," Marquize said. "Sun Flyer."

"Right." The elk turned and swerved one lane over, cutting off a hotel shuttle bus.

"I guess this is about it," the cheetah said, getting his bag ready.

I hadn't been to the airport since landing there a year and a half ago. The international flights came in at the small terminal at the very end, so I'd assumed we were going to one of the larger terminals where the domestic flights went. But the driver took us past all those and down to the international terminal. "I thought you were going to Port City," I said.

"Sun Flyer goes to Port City now?" the elk chimed in.

Marquize opened his mouth, shut it again, and then said, "I guess so. I mean, that's what I'm taking."

He felt weirdly on edge, different from the relaxed cheetah who'd given me the cloth bracelet fifteen minutes ago. I didn't know anything about Sun Flyer, so I had no idea what might be going on and I kept quiet.

"Hey," Marquize said a moment later, leaning forward, "where does the bus pick up?"

"Back at the transport center," the driver said.

The cheetah checked the meter and dug in his wallet as the cab pulled up to the curb. "If I give you forty bucks, will you take Rocky to the bus pickup?"

"Oh," I said, "thanks, but I thought I was going to walk you to security."

"My flight's really soon," Marquize said. "I'm gonna have to book it. So let's just say good-bye here and I'll see you on the 10th."

The driver got out to get Marquize's bags from the trunk. I hugged him there in the back seat again. "Have a good Christmas," I said, and then, because his attitude was worrying me, I added, "and I'll be happy to see you when you get back."

"Thanks. I'll text ya." He nuzzled me but didn't kiss me, and I didn't kiss him. I did roll down the window and wave to him on the curb as he gathered his things and walked into the airport.

For a moment, I thought about following him like in one

of those spy movies. I could tell the driver to leave me here and I'd hop out and make my way through the airport terminal. But I dismissed that idea even before the elk got back in the driver's seat. Marquize was going home and all I'd do was stalk him to security and then not be able to say good-bye. I had a home to go back to and a dinner with Ma, and just as Marquize was on his way back to his home, I should be getting back to mine.

***

The day before Christmas we went to OswaldWorld as a prize for winning the tournament and spent a day riding amazing rides and eating terrible food ("terrible" meaning "delicious but loaded with fat and sugar that made me feel queasy"). I texted Marquize with descriptions of the rides, and wasn't surprised when he didn't answer right away; he was busy with his family too. When Ma and I left the park, I took out my phone to ask Mar how his day had been, and still he hadn't answered. That, I thought, was a little weird. I felt the prickle in my fur that I hadn't felt for so long, the one I used to get at home when I hadn't seen a friend of mine in days. So I wrote, *Everything okay?*

It wasn't until late that night, as I was lying in bed trying to sleep, that my phone buzzed. I picked it up.

Sounds like you had a fun day, he'd typed.

Pretty good. Can I call?

Not now. On Christmas.

Marquize's family celebrated Christmas, sort of, but not in a religious sense. I told him I'd call him late on Christmas or on the 26th. But the prickling in my fur didn't entirely subside.

***

We had a nice Christmas, me and Ma, and we called Ori early on as well. She told me in confidence that her lion had come to the Christmas show to see her perform in the choir, which wasn't unusual because anyone was welcome to the show. Many Muslims came to see because their holy days were at a different time of the year. But it was special to Ori that he'd come.

I didn't tell her that Ma knew about her lion. Ma hadn't told me not to, but I figured it would be easier not to make Ori wonder who else there was talking to Ma, at least not until I could figure it out.

And then Ma and I had a baked ham in the light of the little artificial tree she'd bought, and we sang a couple Christmas songs ourselves.

I missed the pageantry and celebration of Christmas. There were shows at churches around Palm Gables, but most of them had been the weekend of the tournament, so we didn't get to see any of them. On Christmas Day, Ma found a Christmas Mass on TV, and we watched that, but it was too solemn for us. We couldn't bring ourselves to turn it off, but we did migrate to the kitchen to cook until it ended.

Ma's next attempt, Christmas movies, worked better. There were several on TV, and we flipped around channels until one came on that carried us away with its story. Another came on after that, and another, and soon it was dinnertime and we both felt cheerier.

I called Marquize the next morning. He sounded totally normal, at ease and annoyed at his family as usual. I asked what he'd been doing on the 24th and he said, "Oh, family outing. I was out of phone range for most of the day."

It wasn't until I'd hung up that I thought it strange that he hadn't told me where they'd gone or what he'd done. After all, we'd gone to an amusement park and I'd sent him maybe half a dozen texts about the rides I was on. But then again, Marquize didn't get along very well with his family, so maybe there'd been a fight and he didn't want to talk about it. That I could certainly understand.

***

On the 28th, I met Coach Murphy in his office. He waved me to a chair, and I sat. "Quiet today," Coach said. "I like the holidays, not because I have family, but because I get two minutes to think in here."

I wasn't sure what that meant. "Should I come back later?"

"No, no." He laughed. "I'm glad to have the time to focus on important students. Winning a tournament a year ahead puts you in the level of someone I need to pay attention to. Last student to do that…"

"Braden Longacre?" I asked when he paused.

He peered at me. "No, Braden ripped through his class and took off for the pros. I didn't put him ahead because he didn't need the confidence boost. That's part of what I wanted to talk to you about."

"Confidence?"

"Confidence and going to the pros. And what you need to do to get there."

I sat up straighter. "Like…now?"

"No. Well…no." He hesitated. "You could go now, but you'd benefit from another semester here. I think if you work on a few things this spring, you'll be in much better shape this summer. There's a series of tournaments that a lot of the graduates from this school go into, so I can give you some information about them—where to stay, who the organizers are, things like that. Help you get your feet under you for the tour."

"Thanks," I said. "I'd—that'd be great."

He leaned forward. "The things I want you to work on with Diaz this spring are your footwork, your return game, and your net play." He ticked off the items on his fingers. "Footwork because you will never stop improving your footwork. Get your feet stable and in the right place and your shots are more dependable. Your return game is improving, but in the match against Cleve you could've won it in two sets if you'd gotten a few more returns in. Right now it's one of the weakest parts of your game. And your net play is a surprise tactic right now. It works because your opponent isn't expecting it. But it can be much more than that. You need to incorporate it as a regular weapon in your arsenal. Show improvement in those three areas and I think you'll be ready to enter the tournaments. I'll continue to work with you, of course."

"I'll keep practicing with Diaz?"

Coach nodded. "He'll challenge your net play. We'll do footwork drills three times a week with Coach Kotten, and I'll talk to Cleve about working on your return game. He's a better server than Diaz."

"Thank you," I said. "For everything you've done."

The rabbit smiled at me. "When you get closer to the professional circuit, we can talk about the ways you can give back to Palm Gables."

"Of course. I'd be happy to. This school has been a second home to me."

"We're glad to hear that. You know, we take a chance on foreign students. It's more of a risk than cubs from this country, but people who devote themselves to tennis and adapt successfully make us more inclined to take that risk again." He cleared his throat. "Anyway, that's not really your concern right now. Just letting you know that your performance here has ripples beyond your life."

"I am very interested in helping other students from foreign countries," I said, and I thought about Ori. Was she too old already? I knew though that she wasn't as good as I was. I suspected that Ma had sent tape of both of us and that Palm Gables had already seen her and turned her down.

"Good." Coach Murphy's smile widened. "In about twenty years when you're ready to retire, come back and we'll talk about you becoming an ambassador. But that's a long way off. Let's focus on getting your career started before we worry about how it ends."

***

I said good-bye to 2009 and hello to 2010 with Ma and a bottle of sparkling apple juice. Marquize texted me Happy New Year, and we chatted back and forth while I talked with Ma about my goals for the upcoming year. And then I went to bed to get up early to go practice, feeling like my life was back to normal for the first time in a couple weeks.

The night Marquize got in from the airport, a week later, we went to the Meat'n'Malt and talked for over an hour. I mentioned the outing with his family and he looked confused for a second and then said, "Oh, that. It was fine, it was out of the way is all." But he didn't meet my eyes when he said it, and little prickles traveled up and down my fur, so I changed the subject.

As the other students came back, my feeling of something being a little bit wrong remained. Everyone was nice, happy to see me, but they all felt more distant. Not a lot; we all went out for dinner that first night, and everyone talked about their Christmas vacation. There wasn't anything I could point to and say, "That remark made me feel like something was wrong." But I had a sense at the end of the night that they'd all shared some experience that I hadn't been a part of. Or, perhaps, that they had decided to share some experience that I wasn't being told about.

But it wasn't even something concrete enough that I'd ask Marquize about it. I figured maybe it was everyone coming back from Christmas and getting used to the school again. Kim, for example, told me privately after the dinner that her parents spent the whole holiday fighting and she had "shut down" by the end of it. "I'm really glad to be back here," she said, "but Mom's texted me four times already tonight. This is gonna suck."

"I'm sorry," I said, trying to imagine a father living in the apartment with Ma and fighting with her. "What do they fight about?"

She flicked her ears back, and I apologized immediately. "I'm sorry, I was—I don't know. I only have one parent."

"It's okay." Kim sighed and her ears came back up. "They fight about money. We have enough but Dad wants to invest it and Mom wants to enjoy it, or something like that. And it's not only that. There are times they'll start to say something and then look at me and change the subject right away. Like when Mom wanted to keep taking golf lessons and Dad said he knew why she really wanted to take golf lessons."

Not wanting to say the wrong thing, I didn't say anything, and Kim smiled at me. "They think I don't know about Mom sleeping with the golf instructor. I'm not stupid. Or blind. And this," she tapped her nose, "works just fine."

"She cheated on your dad?" I couldn't help saying that; it just came out. I mean, I knew from movies and the guys at the warehouse that people cheated. But it was always an abstract thing, something "those other people" did, not something that happened to people I knew, or parents with a family.

Kim flashed me a smile. "They cheat on each other all the time. Dad used to 'work late' until Mom made him fire his secretary. And before Mom was learning golf, she had late nights 'showing Jake the ropes' at her real estate business. I always wondered if that was literal."

I shook my head, bewildered. "Don't they love each other?"

The coyote blinked at me and her smile faded. "You know," she said, "I really don't know."

As nice as Kim and Marquize were to me, all the other friends I'd grown accustomed to hanging out with definitely showed more distance in that first week. I joined them after school at the park, but after Marquize and I had hit for a bit, nobody else got up to use the courts. I asked if any of them wanted to hit around, and nobody did. They said things like "I'm still recovering from vacation" and "I'm not feeling it right now."

"I guess we're the only ones still in game shape," I said to Marquize. "Want to keep going?"

The cheetah hesitated, and Dom picked himself up off one of the benches. "I'll hit with you, Rocky," he said with a look at the others.

The next night, not everyone showed up at the park. Yu and Brittany did, but didn't play any tennis; Dom and Kim came, too, but Bret, Pom, and a couple of the others were absent. "Everyone's lazy this semester," I said to Marquize.

Dom, nearby, perked his ears up. "It's not that," he said, ignoring Marquize's efforts to shush him. "You've moved on."

"What?"

The arctic fox tilted his head. "You played in the juniors tournament—and won it. You're not really in our class anymore."

"I'm in your classes every morning! We had World Cultures and Trigonometry today, remember?"

"I know." Dom held up white paws as if to calm me. "I mean, tennis-wise, and that's why everyone's really here, isn't it?"

Kim spoke up. "Come on," she said. "When you get to the tournaments, you think all the players hang around and practice together after the matches? You'll have a few friends, sure, but not on the court. Everyone's clinging to whatever little edge they can get over everyone else."

I wanted to say that that sounded terrible, but as I was opening my mouth it occurred to me that I had done exactly that all last year, studying my opponents to figure out how to beat them. Braden's advice had been good for my game, but not so good for friendships. "It's not like most of them are going to end up facing me in tournaments," I said, feeling hurt. "I mean, really."

"Probably not." Dom wasn't fazed by my words. "But they're jealous, too. When you were in our group you were one of us. Now you're not." He shrugged.

"Did you know about this?" I demanded of Marquize.

"Sort of?" He shrugged too, wiry shoulders rising and falling. "They didn't come to me and say they were leaving the group."

"Veronica asked if I was *really* going to hit around with you." Kim flicked her ears.

Dom looked around and his eyes settled on Marquize. "We

could sort of play mixed doubles," he said.

The cheetah didn't look amused, and I didn't quite understand what he meant. I didn't care, because I was still processing all these people I'd thought were friends, people I'd thought would celebrate my accomplishments, all turning their tails to me. "That's shitty," I said, using a word I didn't often have recourse to.

"Hey." Marquize put a paw on my shoulder. "We're here."

"Yeah." My mind flicked through wanting to call Ori about it and imagining what she'd tell me, which was something close to what Marquize had said. My ears came up and I looked around at them. "Thanks. I'm glad you guys don't think I'm not in your class anymore."

"You're definitely not in our class," Dom said. "At least, me and Marquize. But you're still our friend."

The cheetah's fingers squeezed my shoulder. "Yeah," Kim said. "Screw those guys."

"All right." I exhaled, trying to let go of the hurt. "So, mixed doubles, yeah?"

***

Two weeks into the semester, I felt more and more like I had my first few weeks at Palm Gables, when I didn't know anyone and Marquize was about my only friend. It wasn't entirely that bad, of course; everyone still talked to me and I did a World Cultures project with Bret, studied math with Pom and Dom, ate lunch with everyone. But then my day separated from theirs; I went to practice with Diaz and sometimes Yu; Cleve refused to practice with me unless Coach Murphy specifically ordered him to.

"Don' worry about him," Diaz told me. "Look, I know his type. Burn himself out before he ever gets to a major."

(He was not completely right about that, by the way, but close enough that I'm inclined to credit him for it.)

And then in the evenings, it was mostly me and Marquize. Sometimes Kim came to hang out with us; she never explained why, but we enjoyed her company. Sometimes Dom came, and when he didn't he often apologized to me the next morning. Frustrated, I said one evening when he wasn't there that he should pick one side or the other.

"Hey," Kim snapped. "Don't put that on him. He's trying to keep all his friends happy and he didn't ask to be caught in the middle."

"I didn't ask to be put outside!"

"No," she said, "but you could do something about it."

"What?"

"Go back."

I blinked at her. "What?"

"I mean, it's probably too late. But you could stop practicing with Diaz, come back to our regular tennis lessons, stop worrying so much about your career."

I looked at Marquize, but he'd fixed Kim with a curious look as well. "But Coach told me to practice with Diaz."

"Coach wants you to become a star. I mean, that's what most of us want too. But if your friends are more important, then you could coast through the rest of the school term here, become an assistant coach like Frio or Kotten—not necessarily here—and eventually teach other cubs tennis."

Marquize looked down at the picnic table, no help to me. I struggled with this unexpected choice that I hadn't even realized I had. "I...I would like to teach cubs, maybe in foreign countries..."

"No!" Kim smacked my shoulder. "You want to be a star. That's why we're all here. Your friends here aren't going to be friends forever anyway. Frio and Kotten weren't going to compete in major tournaments ever. You don't set out to be a coach at 25; you *end up* as a coach at 25. You," and here she poked me in the chest, "can compete in major tournaments. Don't you hear everyone around here comparing you to Braden Longacre?"

"Usually in how much better he was than I am."

"Pah." She waved my words away. "They all talk about him now because he's successful. He was great here, sure. He made it to the main draw at the Ocie Open this year, sure. When you start making it into the main draw of majors at the age of 21, Coach will compare all his students to you."

"Wait, Braden made it to the main draw?" I'd watched the open, as much coverage as I could fit in between my classes and training, but I'd missed him. I hadn't even known he'd left the Challenger circuit, though with the way he'd been winning tournaments, I wasn't surprised. "Who'd he lose to?"

"Some panther, I forget." Kim waved a paw. "That's not the point."

"The point is," Marquize said, looking up, "fuck those other guys. You're gonna be great."

"The point is," Kim went on, "cut Dom a little slack. He likes you and he doesn't care so much about tennis. Everyone else wants to be a star and they're jealous of you."

It made me feel a little better, but I still wanted to find something else to do with some of my evenings. So on Thursday night I told Marquize and Kim that I was going home to spend time with Ma and study my schoolwork, and even though they knew the real reason I was skipping out on the evening social, they let me go.

My path home took me near the mall, and then my ears picked up the noise of basketball. I followed it a couple blocks down and found Marcus and his friends in their pickup game, playing four on four. I wasn't sure how to approach them, but after a few minutes of watching, I got bold enough to walk up to the court. Marcus saw me and gave me a head bob, so I hung around.

When they took a break, Marcus came over and asked me what was up. I nodded at the courts. "You guys need another player?"

"Maybe." He nudged me. "You miss it, huh?"

Some of his friends came over and a few remembered me. "Hey, it's Jackal Eye," another coyote said, patting me on the back. "You wanna shoot some?"

"Sure, but I don't want to push anyone out of the game."

"Nah, Dab there gotta go early."

The marmot named Dab said, "I could stay another ten minutes," but nobody seemed to listen.

So I shot around with the guys for forty-five minutes. It was a lot of fun and relaxing. I didn't have to worry about whether I was eventually going to play basketball for the FBA or whether any of the other guys there was going to be jealous of me. I wasn't the best player there by a long shot; I was maybe the second worst. But the guys liked my passing. "Real crisp," they said. "Great court vision," Marcus said. And I didn't need to be a good shooter to play tennis, so I wagged my tail at those compliments.

At the end of the evening I was panting pretty hard, but I also felt more relaxed than I usually was after a tennis session. The process of analyzing how I'd played, what I needed to do better next time, and what my opponent had done had become so automatic that I hadn't realized how much energy they took. After the basketball game, I could enjoy the fatigue, the flexing of well-used muscles, and the camaraderie of the other players.

"You guys play here every night?" I asked.

"Tuesday, Thursday. And Saturday afternoons." Marcus held out a fist for me to bump. "You should come back."

"What about Dab?" I asked.

"We can play four on five if we need to. Or someone sits out."

"Yeah," the other coyote said. "Rather have more people if we can."

"All right," I said. "Is it okay if I bring a friend?"

They said it was fine, so the next time I felt restless I dragged Marquize to the court with me. He was worried about Marcus, and it turned out when he showed up, Marcus was worried about him, too. The coyote took the first step, apologizing for the fight at the party, and offered to let Marquize take a swing at him. The cheetah turned him down (of course) so they shook paws and kept an eye on each other for a bit and nothing happened. Eventually they relaxed.

Marquize enjoyed basketball and was much closer to the other guys in skill level. He admired my passing and I admired his shooting. We made a good team when we were on the same side, because he knew where to set himself up for a good shot, and after a couple times I started looking for him there. When we were on opposite teams we guarded each other and he was much better at blocking me than I was at stopping him. But it was fun all around, more fun with Marquize than without him.

We told Coach about the pickup games; I hadn't even thought to, but Marquize said he'd want to know about anything we were doing outside the school. He didn't care, as long as we didn't injure ourselves. "It's good cardio," he said, "and good for you to be doing different exercises. Be careful, that's all."

"The playground guys aren't that rough," I said, but Coach said a guy could get hurt messing around and basketball was rougher than tennis.

Still, we played with those guys through January and February without suffering anything worse than a banged knee on the basket pole (me) and a jammed finger (Marquize). We had fun with the guys and I felt like at least I got better at basketball.

I'm not sure whether or not that translated into tennis. I definitely improved at tennis, but I was following Coach's regimen and Diaz challenged me in ways none of the other students ever had, so it might have been no more than that.

The cacomistle and I developed a pretty good friendship-rivalry. We did drills but always played one competitive set a day. He kept track of the score as the days wore on, so I took his word for it that I was winning. I invited him out with me and Marquize, but he wanted to spend evenings with his family and he never took me up on it.

Meanwhile, things had more or less stabilized with the other students in my class. They remained aloof, at least where tennis was concerned, but in the classes we shared they were friendly. I didn't ask them why it bothered them so much that I'd been pushed ahead a level in tennis, but Kim tried to explain it to me once.

"This sport is all shitty and competitive," she said when I happened to run into her outside the tennis courts at the end of one afternoon of practice. I'd asked her how everyone else was doing and I must have had my ears down or something, because she picked up on my sad mood. "You saw how they were with me after I went to Porter Colliere's camp."

I blinked. "They teased you about...about her."

"None of them got invited to a professional's tennis camp." Kim smiled, a long, smug smile. "So they tried to tear it down. My mom says that when people are envious like that, they'll shit all over you to make themselves feel better."

"Why can't they be happy for me?"

She laughed. "Rocky, you might just be too sweet for this game."

"I don't think I am. I can compete on the court."

The coyote shook her head. "I'm not talking about that. I mean...in this country we get all hyper-competitive about stuff, and people have a hard time being friends off the field."

"I've seen the movies." I sounded stiff, so I tried to relax. "I know there are competitors who are friends with each other."

"Sure, but we're not in that culture yet." She leaned back against the wall of the courts and watched the other students walk by. "You know the top two tennis players in the world?" I nodded. "They're actually friends. They have this fierce rivalry on the court, but they are good friends off it. But if you asked most of these guys," she waved to the students, "they'd say those two hate each other because they're competing so hard. We have this culture that says you can only be great at the expense of others, and lots of people don't realize that doesn't mean you can't be friends with people outside of tennis. Or whatever."

"But Bret talked to me after math class," I said.

"Yeah, I think they finally realized you're still their friend. They just don't want to help you get any better at tennis because you're already way better than they are. They envy your talent and success, and, honestly, the time Frio spent with you."

You know what that reminded me of, but Kim didn't need to know about it and I didn't want to talk about it anyway. "That's dumb."

"That's us." She waved an imaginary flag. "Woo! Our culture. But don't let it get you down. You've got an amazing school supporting you. Coach knows how good you can be and he's going to make sure you get the best tennis education, with or without those dolts."

I peered at her. "So why are you being so nice to me?"

She laughed and patted my shoulder. "Because someday when you're famous, I'm totally going to sponge off you. Come on, you want to get something to eat or are you playing basketball again?"

Chapter Twenty-One

In early March, Ma asked if I wanted to do another birthday party. I said yes, and figured that I'd keep tennis out of it so my old friends felt okay coming. When I called Ori next, I complained to her about the people who couldn't put their competitive natures aside for friendship, and asked what she was doing to celebrate her birthday.

"Kamina is going to make me a sweet potato cake and plantains," Ori said. "But I may have to go out of town."

"What? Why?"

"She got a request today delivered by messenger from the head of a village about fifty kilometers from here. These things go slowly so it might be months before anything happens, but he also might want to meet me in the next few weeks. Kamina says he's considering six different potential brides."

"That's not so bad," I said.

"Kamina says he might buy all six."

That seemed normal to me for a moment, and then it seemed completely wrong. "You deserve to have someone all to yourself," I told her.

"I'm not sure I get a choice. Besides, if there are six of us, then each of us has to do less, right?" In the background, I heard Kamina's voice, and Ori snorted. "Kamina says it doesn't work that way, but there aren't six of him, right?"

"I don't think so. I don't like this, Ori. If it takes months, then maybe I'll be playing tournaments for real money by the time it happens and I can fly you over here."

"That'd be great, Ro, but look, I knew I was going to be married sometime. It's not the worst thing in the world. So tell me, what are you doing?"

I told her about the party. She already knew about the situation with my class. "Are they all coming?"

"I think so. Most of them have said yes. We're not doing it in the park this time, but Ma won't let me do it in the dorm, so we're going to have it here."

"In her apartment?"

"Our apartment." I rested an arm on the arm of the couch that was my bed.

"You live at the school." She laughed. "Is Ma going to make plantains and sweet potato cake?"

"I think she's making a peanut butter cake," I said. "It's hard to find those around here. You can get chocolate cake easily, and I like it, but she wants to do something more traditional."

"It's your sixteenth. You're grown up now."

I thought about that after the call, lying in bed. I didn't feel any more grown up, didn't feel like I was approaching being grown up. But in a few months I'd be playing in real tournaments for real money, I wouldn't be taking classes, and I'd be supporting Ma and hopefully Ori. Back home, I'd be looking for a wife and starting a business, maybe taking over some of Ma's trade since I didn't have a father to succeed. Here I had a little more freedom—although when I thought about it, maybe not so much. I pretty much had to keep up with tennis or else we'd be poor and eventually have to go back.

Fortunately, I loved tennis—not only the game itself but getting better than everyone else, too. Kim was wrong; I wasn't too sweet for the game. I was sad that my former friends couldn't handle me getting better, but her theoretical choice of keeping my friends while giving up the advanced lessons? Wasn't even a choice.

***

All my friends did come to the birthday party. Ma bought chips and salsa and chocolate chip cookies in addition to the food she was making, in case some people didn't like her cooking, but not many people went for them. The peanut butter cake was especially a hit, gone before the first guest had left.

Last year I'd had the little figure of a fox with a tennis racket on the cake; this year at my request, Ma left the cake plain. We avoided any mention of tennis and maybe as a result, the party went smoothly. Bret brought over his video game console and a couple games, so we took turns playing some game called Final Fantasy and then sang karaoke for a couple hours. It was warm and fun and I felt for a while like it was still 2009 and none of them resented me for skipping ahead of them.

After that, Bret said he had to get home and packed up his video games. Brittany and Yu and Veronica left then too, but Kim, Marquize, Pom, and Dom stayed. "Wish I had a console," Pom grumbled. "But Dad says it'd be distracting."

"Of course it would be." It had been fun, but I could see where I wouldn't want it around every night. I wasn't sure I'd be able to resist it.

"I don't guess you'd have to worry about it," Pom said.

"Hey." Dom jumped in sharply.

"What?" The red fox glanced at me. "I just meant...he didn't grow up around video games, that's all." But his ears were splayed to the side. I remember understanding that he meant that I was too devoted to tennis to be distracted by video games, and that somehow he meant that as a bad thing; not bad that I was dedicated, but bad because he was jealous of my dedication. I would confirm this later with Marquize, but I got it and I felt sorry for Pom. I knew he wasn't going to be a tennis star, that he didn't have the same drive that I did.

He and Dom didn't stay long after that, but Kim and Marquize stayed until we got hungry again and Ma allowed me to order a pizza delivered with the toppings I wanted on it. I still felt guilty because I knew she didn't like pineapple on her pizza, but she told me not to worry about it and because it was my birthday, I actually listened to her. Besides, pineapple is amazing.

When Kim left, Marquize yawned and said he should probably go home as well. I was tired too, but had been hoping we might have a little time to talk. I didn't want to press it, because I was having a really good time and if I asked Marquize to talk and he said no, I'd feel bad and might ruin the evening. But as he was getting his rain jacket on, he said, "Mind walking me out, Rocky?"

I pulled my own jacket on and wagged my tail as I followed him to the door. We went downstairs in silence and then he stopped in the entryway to my building, looking at the light rain outside.

"So you're sixteen now," the cheetah said.

He knew all the uncertainty around my birthday, so I nodded.

"Sixteen. I can…what, start learning to drive a car?"

"Pah." He grinned. "No big trick to driving a car. My dad let me drive his around. You have to be aware of what's going on around you, that's most of the trick."

"I'm getting better at that." I watched the cars pass outside. "Here the roads have curbs and lines to keep you on them. It seems easy."

He stayed leaning back against the wall of the entryway, silent. "Did you want to talk about something?" I asked, my heart beating.

"This is a lot harder when I haven't had a couple rum and Cokes." He chuckled nervously. "Look, I don't know if I've been imagining it or what, but you know the stuff you found on my computer?"

My fur prickled. "Uh-huh." I shut up quickly because he was already finding it difficult to talk and I didn't want to say anything to make it worse.

"I, uh, I know that what happened with Frio—that you didn't want it—but I was wondering if you maybe…"

"Yes." It came out before I could think about it.

Marquize met my eyes and relaxed, and I thought he was almost smiling. "You haven't even heard what I was going to ask."

"You were going to ask if I wanted to kiss you again." I kept my voice low. "Or maybe if I was interested in the stuff that was on your computer. The thing with Frio, it was—I wasn't interested in *him*. It felt strange and Ma told me why it wasn't right. But if you want to—I've thought about it." My ears flattened and I turned away. "I don't mean, like—"

He grabbed my muzzle and pressed his lips to mine. No polite brush this time, no mistaking; it was a kiss like the ones I'd shared with Shawna. I made some kind of noise in my throat and slid my arms inside his jacket to hug him.

It had been—wow, more than a year since Shawna. I'd been so focused on tennis for that year that I hadn't really been thinking much about what I'd given up: that closeness to someone else, the excitement, my blood racing like it did, tingles running from my ear tips to my tail tips. I don't know that there were any thoughts going through my head except maybe *this is amazing, this is really happening*. I remember he was wearing that green Ultimate Fit shirt under his jacket, how smooth it was under my paws, how warm and strong his body felt under my fingers.

"Ah." He broke the kiss and stared at me, the smile fully on display in his spotted muzzle. "So you're—you like—I mean—"

"Uh-huh." My heart raced, my sheath felt harder, it seemed, than even that time Shawna had grabbed it, and I couldn't look away from Marquize's eyes.

"I was actually just going to ask if, uh, if you might want to go on a date sometime. I mean," he hurried on, "you're sixteen now so it's not illegal. Well, we're really close in age so probably it's not illegal anyway, but it's safer if you're sixteen. If we're both sixteen."

I laughed. "I didn't know what the laws were, but I'm glad you looked them up. Yes, I would like to go on a date."

"I'm not going to distract you from tennis." He sounded rushed, like there were a thousand things he wanted to say and couldn't get them all out in time. "And I'll be respectful. But I've been thinking about you, too, and I'd like to see if…you know, I think we could have fun together."

"I'd like that." I was smiling and I couldn't stop. "You're my best friend and I'm really happy you kissed me. And asked me."

His smile matched mine. "It's so cute how your tail wags. I've never seen it so active."

"This is pretty exciting." I pushed my muzzle forward to his and we kissed again, softer but longer.

A noise sounded on the stairs and we both broke the kiss at the same time, turning to stare at the door. Nobody came out. "I guess we can't really tell anyone about this," I said, my ears back.

"Probably not." Marquize took my paw. "But I don't mind having a secret. Screw the rest of them."

"Yeah." I thought privately that I might tell Kim, but I didn't say anything about it then. "I'll…probably have to tell Ma. I tell her everything."

"We can talk about that." But his ears flattened again and I knew he was thinking of his own parents.

"Uh-huh." I glanced back at the stairs and then outside at the rain. "So, uh, when did you want to go out?" I couldn't quite bring myself to say *on a date*.

"You work Friday and Saturday nights. How about next Thursday?"

"Sure." My tail got its wag back. "After school?"

"Dinner. I'll find us a place to go."

"Deal." I reached out again and hugged him, and he hugged back, but we didn't kiss this time.

"So," he said. "See you tomorrow."

"Yeah."

"Happy birthday, Rocky."

I smiled again. "Thanks."

And then he was gone, out in the rain. I skipped back up the stairs to the apartment.

"Did you have a good birthday?" Ma asked.

"Yeah." I was still smiling, but she would think it was just from the party. I helped her clean up and then she retired to her bedroom and I lay on the couch, stared at the ceiling, and thought about Marquize. The cheetah lying beside me on the couch, pressed up close, holding me; the two of us going around in the tournaments being boyfriends without anyone else knowing, winning title after title, taking the tennis world by storm; the two of us in a more private bed, doing some of the things I'd seen on his computer and, later, on mine…

That was, and still is, my favorite birthday of all time.

Chapter Twenty-Two

That Thursday was one of only three times in my life that I couldn't focus on tennis. Diaz beat me in our set so badly that he asked if I was feeling all right. I told him I was fine and hurried off to change for my dinner with Marquize.

I didn't know what to expect. Would he be dressed up? Would he bring flowers? Should I bring flowers? I'd gotten them for Shawna once or twice, but in my head they were something a boy got a girl, and neither of us was a girl, so how would that work? In the end I was so worried about doing something wrong that I decided it would be easier to do nothing and let Marquize take the lead. He knew more than I did, after all. Then I wondered, did that make me the girl? And did that in turn mean that I would have to...well, let's just say I hadn't pictured myself in *all* the positions I'd seen in Internet porn.

But that wasn't likely to come up at dinner, or anytime in the near future, for that matter. The dorm had thin enough walls that we made each other wear earphones when listening to music, and the only other place I slept was on Ma's couch. Ma never went out of town, so unless some hotel would rent a room to a sixteen-year-old, it might be summer before Marquize and I got to do anything more than fantasize about each other.

Thinking that out, part of me was disappointed, but part was relieved. The idea of doing things with another guy was still strange to me, and having it be Marquize was also a little strange. I'd known him for a year and a half as a friend, and now we were adding this other layer to it. How would that go? I was more nervous than I could remember being except for maybe that first time I went on a date with Shawna. But if I thought about it then I would make myself more nervous, so I was trying not to. Just dinner with a friend, I told myself, and tried to simultaneously think and not think about the

extra dimension that had been added to it on my birthday.

I had a lot of time to imagine it, or at least it seemed like I did. When I checked my phone I found that only twenty minutes had passed between the time he'd texted he was on his way and the time he showed up in the mall where we'd agreed to meet.

"Hi," I said. I couldn't think of what else to say through my grin, and Marquize wasn't much more articulate.

"Hey." He raised a paw to me and then extended it to shake, and as I reached out to take it, he laughed and pulled it back. "Maybe I should hug you?"

"Sure," I said. "That's fine too."

"Okay." So he hugged me, and I hugged back, and it wasn't as tight or as exciting as the hug on my birthday, but it still made my tail wag, and he noticed.

"That's cute," he said as we walked up toward the food court.

"I'm not doing it intentionally. I mean, I can, but I'm not." The fact that he liked it made it wag more.

"Oh god," he said, "I just called you 'cute.'"

"It's okay." I laughed. "I liked it."

But it made me think again about how this was different from all the other times I'd had dinner with him, and that made me quiet as we made our way to the food court.

"I was thinking about going to the Meat'n'Malt," he said, "but I wanted this to be different. I know the food court isn't really romantic, but it looks out over this artificial lake, and it'll be sunset soon. It was pretty nice when I was here Tuesday…"

He stopped, and I wouldn't have noticed anything if his ears hadn't flattened. Then I thought about what he'd said. "Did you come here to see what it would be like?"

The cheetah reached up and rubbed his ears. "I kinda went to a few different places. It was tough between this one and The Palm, but The Palm was all old people and plus we can come here twice for the same money, and I'd rather do that."

"Yeah, that makes sense," I said. "I don't really care as long as we're at dinner together."

"That was my thinking." He smiled at me and his ears came up.

We got Xiaqinese food, salty noodles and stir-fried vegetables and meat, and sat at a plastic table by a window overlooking the lake. The sunset was pretty, and for the first few minutes we sat and watched it while eating. I don't know what he was thinking, but I was wondering if we should talk like normal. Finally I asked, "How was practice today?"

"Oh, the usual." And he told me about his day, and I told him about my day, and we eased into the conversation like we usually did. By the time we'd finished our food, we were sitting comfortably and laughing together, and it all felt natural. But it also felt less like a date.

Marquize realized that, too. I know because he told me, lowering his voice. "So I know this isn't much of a date," he said.

I smiled. "It is a little different. Most of the dates I went on with Shawna, we went to dinner and talked, but we didn't have this much to talk about. And it's different because at other dinners with you, if Dom walked by, I would say he could come join us. But if he came by tonight I'd ask him not to."

The cheetah's smile grew. "I feel the same way. It's private. This is just for us."

I looked around. There was a fox two tables over facing away from us, and with us canids you can never tell, but his ears seemed politely focused on his own conversation. Nobody else near us seemed to be listening. Still, I lowered my voice even more. "And previous dinners didn't end with a kiss."

"Oh." Marquize kept that wide smile on, resting his paws on the table. "I'm glad to hear that. I mean, that you think this one will. I mean, I want it to, too." He laughed and looked down at his empty plate briefly. "If I had a jackal tail, it would be wagging."

"Good." I took a breath. "I don't know how to do this. I wasn't any good with Shawna, but I learned a little. I don't know if the same things work when it's…" I gestured to him.

"I know." He reached over and squeezed my paw. "I have a little more experience."

That was a surprise. Where had he gotten experience? Who had he dated in the year and a half I'd known him? Someone before that? My surprise must have shown. "I mean, not personal experience, not dating," Marquize said. "I mean, I've read more about…*gay* dating…" He whispered those last words.

That was the first time I think either of us had said the word "gay" in reference to ourselves, at least in my hearing. When Ori had asked me if I liked boys, that was something personal, something just about me. Knowing that something was part of you and giving it a label were different things, and I could acknowledge that I enjoyed looking at all-male porn, that I enjoyed kissing my best friend, and that I wanted us to hold hands (and more), but putting that word on it associated it with all the times I'd heard it out in the world. It was a word that described a whole other group of people, of which I guessed I was now one, but being part of that group was something outside myself, different from the inside feelings that made the word apply.

And then I looked up at my friend with the spots and teardrop lines down his face and realized that I wasn't alone, and that was the best feeling.

"Okay," I said. "So if you know so much, what do we do after dinner?"

He laughed. "We get up and take a walk."

So we dropped our trays off and walked out of the mall into the light evening rain. Neither of us said very much, and then we passed a movie theater and talked about the movies that were out that we wanted to see. "Maybe we can see that one next week," Marquize suggested.

My mouth went dry, thinking about Shawna's paw in my lap. I imagined Marquize doing that. How would I react? Was it too soon for that? But we'd gone to the movies together before. "Sure," I said, because he was still waiting for an answer.

That easily, we'd planned a second date. My tail swung behind me again as we reached the dorms and walked up to our floor. There was nobody in the common suite when we got there, so I leaned in to Marquize, but he pulled away. "Not out here," he said, keeping his voice low.

"Why not?" I matched his tone, ears perked in case someone decided to come out.

"They have cameras in the public areas." This was almost in a breath at my ear. "For our safety."

"Really?" I turned around to try to spot the cameras. "How do you know?"

"I found out a couple months ago," he said. "They don't have cameras in the rooms; that would be a violation of privacy. But out here, yeah."

"Okay," I said, opening the door to my room, "then come in."

So he came in and we closed the door, and there, quietly, he kissed me again. It wasn't as intense as the one in Ma's apartment foyer, but it was nice and warm. And then he hugged me and we studied together for a little while, with my door open, before the bell sounded for lights out.

In the dark, I lay in my bed and thought about the dinner, the walk, and the kiss, and my tail wagged again, thumping against the sheets.

That first week, and especially the Friday after we'd had an official date, I thought that everything would feel different. But I got up in the morning, cleaned up and dressed, went to my classes, where Marquize and I tried hard not to catch each other's eye, and then we both had lunch with our friends. We didn't say anything about the date, but it looked to me like he was as happy as I was.

And tennis in the afternoon felt better. Leaving lunch, Marquize patted my shoulder and said, "Go get 'im," and I ran out onto the court with Diaz and Coach Kotten, putting everything else out of my mind. I beat Diaz that day pretty soundly, and he shook his head as he walked up to the net to shake paws. "Don't know what got into you today, bro," he said, "but bottle that shit."

"If I could, I would." I grinned and thought about Marquize and the feel of his lips against mine.

I met the cheetah in the locker room as we were cleaning up from our afternoon sessions. "I'm going to shower," I said, "because I have to go to the warehouse tonight." Normally if we were going to meet Marcus and his friends to play basketball, neither of us bothered showering.

"Aren't they all gross and smelly anyway?" Marquize pulled his shirt off.

"Everyone's smelly." I tapped my nose. "That's why I don't want to be."

"Ha." He swung his towel over his shoulder. "I'll shower too, then. Don't want you wrinkling your nose at me all the way to the warehouse."

"What, you're walking me to my job now?" I stopped in the middle of taking my own shirt off, then went ahead anyway. It was a little strange to be undressing now that we were dating. But after all, we'd been shirtless around each other a bunch.

Marquize flicked his tail. "Sure," he said. "I've never seen this warehouse. And now…" He shrugged and flashed me a quick smile. "Anyway, I'm gonna shower."

He picked up his towel and soap in a hurry and padded off to the stalls. I flicked my ears and got my own things together, but then I caught Frio's scent and turned to see him behind me. "Hey, Rocky," he said. "How's it been going?"

"Fine," I said. "Uh, and you?"

"Not bad. You were great in the tournament. Nice footwork, and good work on your return of serve. You came a long way."

"Thanks."

He seemed a little uncomfortable, but he kept smiling, so I did too. He went on. "Coach says you're thinking about going pro at the end of the semester."

"Maybe." I nodded. "Depends on how I do, I guess."

"Okay, well. I wanna make sure we keep in touch. You're a special guy." His smile broadened.

"Of course," I said, and made a movement toward the showers. "I should…"

"Don't let me keep you." He stood aside, that smile remaining fixed on his masked face.

I worried that he'd try to follow me to the showers—I don't know why. It had been months since the clay court hotel. But that memory came back to me strongly then, and my tail curled between my legs as I hurried to the showers. I hesitated by the curtain behind which Marquize was showering (I could smell his distinctive soap). Maybe in a few months we'd be at a point where I could talk to him like this, where I could open up about feeling weird for no reason. Or talk to him at all while he was in the shower. For now, though, I'd leave him to his shower and I'd try to wash away the feeling in mine.

When I came out, Frio was gone and I was telling myself I'd been silly, overreacting because Frio hadn't talked to me much all fall. He was just being friendly, reminding me he still liked me. Maybe he couldn't figure out how to approach me without being a little creepy. Maybe he was feeling awkward about that hotel room, too. That idea made me feel better, and when Marquize playfully swiped at my tail as I was pulling my shirt on, I forgot all about Frio and focused on hanging out with the cheetah.

***

I kept doing better at my tennis, energized by the dream of me and Marquize taking the tournaments by storm, but the cheetah didn't quite feel the same effect. I overheard Frio yelling at him one day, and though I folded my ears down so as not to catch the exact words, I did hear the ferret saying, "…like you don't care anymore."

Marquize did care about tennis, for sure, and after that I asked him if he wanted to practice more with me. He said, "I'm always happy to spend more time with you, but I don't want to hold you back."

"Then get better," I said.

He didn't quite know what to make of that. I'd meant it as a friendly challenge, but it felt like he was taking it really seriously. "I might just not be as good as you, you know?"

"Hey." I put a paw on his arm. "What did Frio say about us last year? We've both got a lot of potential?" I lifted my paw into the air. "High ceilings, he said, right? So I think we're still way below your ceiling."

The cheetah's expression darkened. "He doesn't say that about me anymore."

"So what? You wouldn't be at Palm Gables unless you were good. So let's see how good you can be—how good we both can be."

That brought a determined smile to his muzzle. He held out a fist and I dapped him (Marcus had taught us that word). "All right," he said. "I'm in."

So we stepped up our after-hours practice. Honestly, he wasn't that bad. Certainly he was better than half our class. I tried to teach him the things Coach Kotton worked on with me that day, but Marquize didn't get them as quickly as I did. It helped me anyway because I could repeat the lessons and learn them again as I was trying to teach him.

He got frustrated sometimes, but he made sure to tell me he wasn't going to let that affect the other part of our lives. Which was funny, because I'd been more worried about the reverse of that. But unlike with Shawna, my dates with Marquize slid easily into the fabric of our lives at Palm Gables and didn't interfere with our practices.

And maybe because of that, it didn't feel like there was a whole lot to our dating life. We went to dinners together, talked about slightly more intimate things, and kissed in our rooms after hours. We didn't dare do more, but as the days went on, we started talking about wanting to. I know I was getting more eager, especially after I went to a site Marquize pointed me to where boys talked about their first times having gay sex. It wasn't that the stories themselves were arousing; it was that they were awkward and completely normal. They made me feel like I could be one of those boys, as long as Marquize was the other, and that even if neither of us knew quite what to do, it would be all right.

And then in late April, after we'd been dating almost a month, Marquize arrived at school and held out his phone. "There's a tournament two hours away next weekend. Futures series, one of the ones we might play next year. Probably will, actually. Want to go?"

"Go?"

"Yeah." He smiled. "I asked my parents for bus fare and, uh... hotel money."

"Oh." His eyebrows rose, and I smiled. "Oh! Sure. Let me ask Ma."

We asked Coach Murphy first, and he thought it was a great idea. In fact, he had three other students who were planning to turn pro soon whom he thought would benefit from seeing the tournament. "I just need to find someone to chaperone all of you, and then I'll approve it."

"Chaperone?" I asked.

"Someone to keep an eye on you so you don't get into trouble." He smiled around his buckteeth. "Your behavior reflects on the school. Can't have you partying too much while you're there."

"We wouldn't," I protested.

He laughed. "I'm sure you wouldn't. What teenage boy, on his own two hours from home, would even think about having a rowdy party with his friends?"

I'm sure Marquize wasn't thinking that, and I know I wasn't, but what we were thinking would have gotten us in even more trouble, so I kept my mouth shut and so did he.

"Don't worry about the chaperone," Marquize told me over dinner that night. "We can get our own room with my parents' money, and they'll have to stay with the other cubs for at least some of the time. We should have some privacy."

My heart pounded. I reached out and took his paw. "Can't wait," I said.

"You scared?"

I nodded. "A little."

"Don't be. It'll be fine. We'll have fun."

I searched his eyes. "Are you scared?"

"No." He ducked his head. "Maybe a little."

"Good." I squeezed his fingers. "I'd rather be scared together."

***

Three days before the trip, we found out who the chaperones were going to be. One was Coach Collings, a gazelle we didn't know well. And the other...

"I was happy to accept," Ma said. "This way I can see what you will be doing next year, and spend more time with you."

Marquize and I talked for two dinners about that. I thought Ma would definitely want to stay in the room I was in. Marquize thought that because he'd be paying for the room, he could tell her she had to stay elsewhere. "I don't think Ma will listen," I said, but Marquize talked himself into believing we'd have some privacy. He said he'd stand up to her but I told him not to, because the idea of a confrontation between Marquize and Ma made my stomach churn.

The trip down did not start out promising. We rode with Ma in a car she'd borrowed from one of the coaches and she insisted on talking tennis the whole time. Marquize was fine, but I felt self-conscious; she told him very frankly about some of the things she and I had discussed. Like: "Rocky feels that his serve lacks the power of some of the best players. What do you think?" or "I think confidence is the most important trait for a tennis player. Rocky needs to work on his."

To his credit, Marquize diverted the conversation to more general topics, giving me reassuring smiles whenever I looked at him. He praised me whenever Ma asked, which was nice but also made me feel a little uncomfortable, because he was my…boyfriend? Maybe? And I didn't know if the praise was sincere. I thought it was but I wondered if he felt obliged to take my side.

I also felt self-conscious because I was worried about saying anything that might give away our relationship. I planned to tell Ma that we were dating, but on my terms and in my time, not have her find out because I blurted out something in the car. So when we finally got to the hotel, she took me aside and asked me if I was feeling okay.

"I'm fine," I said.

"Are you angry because I came along with you?"

I shook my head. "It's fine."

She was pretty good at detecting my lies, but she missed that one or let it pass. "All right," she said. "The school has provided three rooms. We will put Janette and Haylee in one room, Marquize and Terrence in another with Mr. Collings, and you and I will share the third."

"Uh," I said, "actually Marquize's parents got him his own room. I was gonna share it with him."

"You can still go sit with him and Terrence in their room until bedtime. Don't flatten your ears, Ro, you're not sharing a room unsupervised."

"But Janette and Haylee are," I pointed out. "Why aren't you sharing their room?"

"We will be in an adjoining room to theirs. Don't complain. You get a bed to yourself, while Marquize and Terrence will have to share one."

That made me feel worse, if anything. At least if Marquize and I had been sharing in a room with Coach Collings, we could wait until he went to sleep and... "Can't Terrence stay with you?"

"Ro!" Ma frowned. "The arrangements have been made. This is over."

And it was. Marquize protested that he'd reserved his own room, but both Coach Collings and Ma told him that the school wasn't going to let him go on an official trip without supervision. "But this trip was my idea!" he complained. "You can't stop me from staying in my own room."

"You can be disciplined by the school and forbidden from taking any more school trips," Coach Collings said. He probably wasn't waving his horns threateningly, but Marquize and I both took it that way. "You think you invented field trips, hah?" The cheetah sent me a pained look and shut up.

The tournament itself was fine. While we were watching the games, I sat next to Marquize and we looked at the techniques of some of the players. "I'm pretty sure you could beat most of these guys," he said.

"Maybe not most," I said, "but I'd have a good chance against some of them."

They were all good, don't get me wrong. But I saw in many of their games the same flaws I was trying to correct in mine; in others I saw Diaz and Cleve. Four stood out to me as clearly above the rest, and three of those four ended up in the semifinals, so I felt good about my eye for tennis skill.

Ma overheard us talking, but the only time she addressed it was to ask me, "You're serious, Ro? You think you could beat many of these players?"

"I'm sure he can," Marquize replied quickly.

Ma waited for my answer. "Yeah," I said. "I think I could."

Chapter Twenty-Three

Marquize and I got exactly one moment alone that whole weekend, when we offered to run down to the convenience store to get soda pop for the group. I volunteered and before I could even give him a meaningful look, he said he'd come along.

On the way there, I said how sorry I was that Ma and Coach had taken over everything and we hadn't gotten a moment to ourselves. "It happens," he said, and then he pulled me down into an alley and pressed his lips to mine.

Out in the open, or semi-open, it felt dangerous and exciting. I kissed back, and when we finally parted, hearts pounding (at least, mine was, and I could see the matching excitement in his eyes), he said, "I won't stop trying."

"We won't stop trying," I said, and squeezed his paw.

On the car ride home, I talked more and the conversation was much more fun and comfortable. When we dropped Marquize off at the dorm, Ma asked me if I wanted to stay, but I said I'd have dinner with her. So we returned the car and took the bus home, and Ma talked through all the things I would have to do at the school to be able to leave at the end of the spring. My mind was on Marquize and our missed opportunity now that he was gone and I didn't want to concentrate on tennis for these moments, so I lapsed back into short, dull responses. I also did it partly to annoy Ma because of her chaperoning, and it didn't take long for my sullen conversation to have an effect.

"What's wrong with you?" she asked finally. "This is what we came to this country for."

"It's months away," I told her. "The tournament's in a month and if I do well there, maybe going to the Juniors at the States Open in the fall, then turning professional, that's forever away."

"Months you cannot waste. All those other players you saw today, the wolf, the rabbit, you think they wasted their time in school?"

"I don't know," I said. "Maybe they all did. Maybe the ones who spent every minute planning went crazy and couldn't make it to the tournaments."

"Don't be stupid. Is that what that Braden Longacre would say?"

No. Braden would say that I should put everything else aside, even Marquize, that tennis was all there should be in my life. But Marquize helped me with my tennis and so he was part of it. I wished I knew another gay tennis player, a Braden Longacre who could advise me on how to have a relationship and a tennis career, but there weren't any gay tennis players—none that admitted it, anyway. There was that female one whose camp Kim had gone to, supposedly. I wondered if Kim would introduce me and then maybe I could ask her...but no, that was even stupider than what I was trying to say to Ma.

So I changed the subject. "I'm worried about Ori," I said. "I haven't talked to her in a while. It's morning there now, so she'll be up."

Ma narrowed her eyes but nodded. "All right," she said. "Tonight we call Ori. Tomorrow we plan your spring."

"Fine," I said, and picked up my phone.

Ori talked to Ma for a little and then Ma handed me my phone back. "She misses you." And as I took the phone, she added, "The better you play in tournaments, the sooner we can bring your sister over here."

Like I didn't know that, like I didn't want that more than anything, more than a room alone with Marquize or a tennis career. I put the phone to my ear as Ma retreated to the kitchen. "Hi, Ori."

"Hi, Ro."

If I'd been quiet and withdrawn after the car ride that weekend, that was nothing compared to the flat, unemotional voice of my sister. My ears perked up right away and I lowered my voice, facing away from the kitchen and Ma. "What's the matter? Did Raji..."

"He went to fight. To Andush. There was a massacre of Muslims there, and he felt...he had to..." If Ori had sobbed or cried, I would have been less worried. But her voice held no emotion at all, only a terrible resignation as though the lion she loved were already dead.

"Oh no," I said. "And...you heard?"

"No. Nothing."

"Ah, Ori." There was nothing I could say for her. "Did they take him?"

"No. He went. His family...he wanted..." She cleared her throat, and a little more life came back into her voice. "He said good-bye to me. He told me that we both knew nothing could ever come of this, that I would be married off to that jackal from the village and he would be matched to a pride by his family."

"But you knew that," I said.

She was quiet for a long few seconds. "I thought..." Her voice cracked. "I thought that maybe if we both could come to the States..."

I was wrong. I wasn't less worried when she cried. "Ori," I said, "listen, it'll only be a couple months, and then I'll start playing in tournaments. We went to see one this weekend and I'm as good as a lot of the players there. I'll be better soon."

"That's great."

"That means..." I shifted position on the couch.

Ma poked her head into the room. "I'm running out to get tomatoes," she said. "Do you need anything?"

I shook my head and waved to her. "That means," I told Ori, "that soon, maybe even this year, we'll have enough money to bring you over here."

"That'll be great." Her voice flickered with a little more life.

"I mean it. Even if you get married, you can run away."

Now she sounded alarmed. "I can't break a marriage contract."

"Then stay out of one. Stall, do whatever you can."

"I might not be able to—"

"Ma will fix it."

"All right." She still spoke quietly, but without that flat affect. "Thanks, Ro."

"Listen, I need to tell you something." The front door had slammed, but I still paused and listened, making sure Ma hadn't remained behind in the apartment to listen to my private talk with Ori.

She spoke into my silence. "What?"

I took a breath. "You remember I told you about Marquize kissing me?" She did. "I kissed him back. And we're—we're dating. But nobody knows yet, not even Ma."

"That's wonderful." Ori didn't have quite the enthusiasm I'd imagined she'd have when I told her, but I understood why. "How is it going?"

"I think it's going well. I'm not sure. We don't get much time alone, so mostly we go to dinner and then we kiss in our dorm rooms and that's all. We were going to try to have some time this weekend, but…" I told her briefly about Ma and the tennis tournament.

Ori chuckled softly. "I bet Ma knows already."

"She doesn't."

"You know her. She finds things out."

"She can't know. How would she?"

"I don't know, but don't be surprised."

"Hmph." I shook my head.

"So you wanted to have time alone this weekend? You haven't… you know…?"

"No." I leaned against the couch back and closed my eyes. "I want to. At least, I think I do. It's scary, you know."

"I don't really think you'll go to Hell."

"I don't either. But there's so many people saying it's wicked and wrong…"

Ori snorted. "Don't listen to people, Ro."

That was one of Ma's sayings: *Don't listen to people, listen to me.* I flicked an ear. "But there are other people who tell the story of how it changed their life and it made them feel whole."

"Don't listen to those people, either."

"I know." It was a comfort to hear her say it. "I have to find out for myself."

"But be careful when you do. There's diseases."

"Not so much over here."

"They're everywhere. And there are people who get killed for that. Not so much over there, I know, but still."

"I'll be careful."

We were silent for a few seconds. "Tell me how it goes," she said presently.

"Really?"

She snorted again. "Not *how* it goes, but how you feel about it."

"Oh, of course. I just don't know how we're going to do it."

"You'll figure out a way."

There was more silence, and then Ori said, "I should go. But thanks for calling, Ro."

"Hey, Ori? Raji's going to be okay."

"Thanks," she said, and hung up.

It wasn't until I was helping Ma slice tomatoes that I thought about the conversation again and wondered if Ori had been upset that I'd been talking about my dating life when her not-boyfriend had gone off to fight a war and maybe die. The thought came to me in a flash and stayed with me all through dinner, keeping my ears low enough that Ma asked me again what was the matter and I had to make up something about having a headache.

Ma gave me a couple Advil for the bus ride back to the dorm. I thought about Ori all the way back, and when I got to my suite, Marquize was studying, so we kissed quickly and then I went to my room to do the same.

The first thing I looked up was whether taking ibuprofen when you didn't actually have a headache could be harmful (nope). Then it occurred to me that maybe I could find out some information on where Ori's lion was fighting. I didn't know where Andush was, but I could find it easily enough. If the fighting had stopped, then Raji might be okay; I could call Ori and tell her that. I didn't think I could find out anything specific about him, but even general updates were more than she had now.

Andush was toward the eastern part of my country, and I knew there were Muslims in the area. Marquize's home country was in that direction, though several other countries away. But as I looked for information on a massacre, I found that it wasn't a religious issue. It wasn't Muslims who'd been killed, but lions. Rather—it might be a religious issue, but religion wasn't mentioned. It was one tribe of lions killing another tribe.

And not only a village, I found, clicking through links, and not just lions. A whole group of villages, a small community twenty kilometers north of Andush. Lions, hyenas, bat-eared foxes, and anteaters were the primary species listed. *Warning: graphic images*, one link said, and I clicked it anyway.

Smoking clay huts, burned wooden structures, worn and pitted trucks ablaze. Piles of bodies, tawny fur streaked with red, severed paws, ugly patches of muscle and bone amid rent fur. A severed tail, one of the worst pictures because of the simplicity of it, my eye starting at the tip of the tail and traveling up, expecting to find a body and finding instead only a white bone and a small pool of dried blood.

I closed the page and stared at the text of information about the massacre. With the images burned into my head, the numbers were somehow worse: 244 confirmed dead, the body count believed to be at least 300. That page was four days old. I watched the international news and I'd heard nothing about it. More recent updates confirmed that the group of lions, called MS (speculation was that that stood for "Mapigano Simba," Fighting Lions or some variant) were fighting in the hills north of Andush, that they had gotten aid from the neighboring government, and that further casualties had occurred but were as yet uncounted.

As yet uncounted. Was that was Raji was, as yet uncounted? And if not him, how many others? The massacre had been unprovoked as far as the writer could tell, or it could have been provoked by any of a hundred other recent incidents, both in my country and the neighboring ones. The war my father had died in was nominally over; so too was the war in each of our two eastern neighbors, but splinter groups with grievances against the winning side continued to take out their hatred on the people in this area. I hadn't known that any of these wars had names, nor beginnings or ends; there was always only "the war," a word whose translation into English had confused me. In my History classes, wars ended, wars had winners and losers. It felt as though that word didn't match the Kikongo word I'd grown up with, and here again I felt the disconnection between the two.

While the lions from neighboring countries particularly hated the lions in Lunda, inter-species violence was much more common: lions killing foxes, hyenas killing lions, anteaters killing everyone. And there were mixed-species groups, too, anything you could imagine, a carnival of violence and warfare. So far from the capital, my already-weak government could do nothing, and the United Nations was there but doing not much more.

There were other links in the sidebar under "Violence in Lunda," and each one looked to be about a different incident. I couldn't help but picture the same images repeated over and over behind each one of those links, a different set of villages each time, the same violence going on all over my country. I knew that it had happened; that earlier war was what had taken my father, and even though we'd been told about its "end" a few years ago, people kept leaving to fight, returning wounded or dead or not at all. But as a cub, Ma had shielded us from the reality of it as best she could. We knew that people were taken from us, but the way they died and the causes they died for were left to our imaginations and the vague pronouncements in school. The ongoing fighting was sometimes for our religion, but mostly for our country, against tribes in the far-flung areas we would never see who were trying to destroy us. The causes were noble, the deaths clean and heroic. When I'd imagined my father dying, I'd imagined a wide battlefield like in the movies, rows of uniformed jackals and lions running at the enemy. I hadn't pictured severed tails, dead cubs, burning homes.

My paws shook slightly as I turned the computer off. Ori was still there, safe—for the moment—but still there. And Raji had gone off to fight. I wondered whether he would be fighting in a government uniform or as one of the militia groups. The causes didn't matter to me; Ori cared about him and he was gone.

I clasped my paws together. The swell of emotions left me unable to think about anything else. I could call Ma, but Marquize was right here, across the suite. I got up and hurried to his door, knocked once, and stood there.

He opened quickly. "Rocky? What's up?"

I gulped. "I saw some stuff…on the Internet. Can I come in?"

His spotted muzzle glanced up and down the hall. "Yeah. Hurry up."

I wouldn't remember until later what he'd said about the cameras. At the moment I was still trying to get those images out of my head. "What did you see?" he asked as he closed the door behind me.

There was a spare chair and his bed. I plopped down onto the bed, my tail still wound tightly around my hips, paws still interlocked. "The fighting back in my home country." I took a breath and told him about Ori and Raji, and how I'd never really gone back to look up what was happening in Lunda from here, even when I had access to much better news sources.

He sat beside me and listened. "That sucks," he said. "But look, you're here and you're okay. Your sister's going to be okay. There's bad shit happening in my home country too, but there's nothing I can do about it."

I wanted him to hug me but it felt like he wasn't quite sure how to handle the situation, and I didn't want to press. "There is something I can do about this, though."

"What? You're only sixteen."

"I can get my sister over here. And maybe I can find out what happened to her lion."

Marquize shook his head. "You don't even know this guy's last name. How are you going to find him?"

"I don't know. I'll write to one of the reporters covering the war."

The cheetah did rest a paw on my wrist at that point. "Rocky, I don't know that they answer e-mails. They seem to be pretty busy with not dying."

That didn't help. It only reminded me that Raji, and to a lesser extent Ori, were in the same danger. "There has to be something for people who want to find out what happened to their family. Ma found out that my father died. How'd she do that?"

"Ask her," Marquize suggested.

"Maybe. But she's over here now. She might not be able to…" And she wasn't supposed to know about Raji, and this was something Ori had confided in me.

He sighed and squeezed my wrist. "I don't know what to tell you. I can't help."

"Can I just…" I lifted my muzzle. I didn't want to cry, but I felt shaky. "Can I sit here for a bit while you study? I want to be around someone."

"Sure. You want to study together?"

"I can try." I wasn't sure how good I'd be at it. But when Marquize asked me math questions, I forced myself to focus on them. After fifteen minutes, I was doing better, and after thirty, the images had mostly faded in favor of sines and cosines and unit circles.

That was also when I started feeling tired. So I stood and said, "I should get going."

"Feel better now?"

I nodded. "Thanks."

He came over and took my paws and kissed me on the lips,

softly. "Anytime," he said.

***

Monday, my fear had been replaced with purpose. If the only thing I could do was to get better at tennis, then by God I was going to get better at tennis.

I started the next day with a fierce determination that lasted me all the way through that afternoon and to lunch the next day. It wasn't like I'd been slacking off by any means; I'd already been working to get Ori over here, and the additional urgency gave me a restless energy that didn't jibe well with the repetitive nature of tennis lessons. After hours of numbing drills, I took to my game with Diaz and promptly sprayed my serve all over the court, double-faulting three times in our set. I still won, because I chased down every single ball he hit, but when the set was over my heart was pounding and I was still buzzing, and I was exactly one day closer to getting Ori back, just as I had been one day ago and would be at the same time tomorrow.

Practicing with Marquize was more frustrating because I was still going full-bore and that made it obvious that he couldn't keep up. I saw his frustration and suggested we stop before he did. We went to dinner and everything was all right after that.

I started Tuesday with the same determination, eroded somewhat by the frustration of not having gotten appreciably closer the previous day. The coaches told us over and over that repetition was key, that we had to teach our bodies and minds the right movements and patterns so that they became second nature, and that there were no shortcuts to that process. If will and drive could speed up our learning, I would have been winning tournaments the next week, but I had to bring myself back to the patience that had served me well for the previous year and a half.

Even so, I hadn't gotten over my angry energy by lunch on Tuesday. It was something else that distracted me then.

Kim often sat with me and Marquize, and when she did, Dom usually came over too. It was the four of us that Tuesday, with Pom and Bret and some of the other guys at the next table. Kim finished her burger before any of the rest of us, licked her fingers, and announced, "I have news."

"You're pregnant," Dom guessed.

"No, I always make your dad use a condom," she said sweetly.

(Kim believed that if guys could joke about fucking each other's moms—which, by the way, nobody had done with me since that first birthday party—that she could joke about fucking their dads. None of the guys quite knew what to do with that, which was probably the effect she was after.)

"So what is it?" Marquize asked. "You're going pro?"

"Like those are the only two pieces of big news someone could have." Kim sneered at him, but her annoyance told us all that he'd been right.

"Wait, really?" Dom put his half-eaten burger down. "Already?"

"What, already? I'm ready. Coach Bellina as much as said so. And Porter Colliere says I'm as talented as she was at my age."

"Was she winning tournaments at your age?" I asked.

Kim flicked her ears. "Yes. Or...a year or two later, but close enough."

"But why now, why in the middle of the term?" Marquize leaned across the table.

"That's my other big news." She smiled from ear to ear. "I've been talking to a lawyer for the last week and I'm going to file to become an emancipated minor."

"What's that?" I realized what "minor" meant as soon as I'd asked the question, but I still didn't know "emancipated."

"It means I'll be treated as an adult. I won't have to listen to Mom and Dad. Also they won't pay for me to go to school here anymore."

"Again," Marquize said, holding up a finger, "why in the middle of the term?"

"Because I think they want to take all the money I make from tournaments. I won't get any of it."

"Why do you think that?" Dom's question was mild and reasonable, I thought, but Kim turned on him as though he'd criticized her service game.

"Because they told me. Okay? You want to hear it all? We had a big fight two weeks ago over Skype. I told them I wanted to stay here another year and they said they wouldn't pay for it, that they needed the money I was going to bring in by winning tournaments. And I said that was going to be my money, and they said 'not until you're eighteen,' which is why they wanted me to start playing tournaments before then."

"So." I tried to work this out. "You're making yourself legally an adult...right?" She nodded, and I went on. "So that you won't have to leave school early. And that means you have to leave school early?"

Her anger turned down to a low simmer. "I know, it kinda sucks. But Mr. Colavito—the lawyer—he and I talked about it for a while. They were going to force me to leave early anyway, so there's no way for me to stay. This way at least I get to keep the money I earn." The satisfied smile returned. "And I really am ready. I wanted to stay so I could keep getting better. I mean, realistically I probably won't start winning right away. But I'll be learning on the road, and Porter Colliere did say I could stay with her to cut down on expenses for a year or two."

"Oh-ho, really?" Pom leaned over. "Rent paid in bed time?"

"Don't be gross." Kim stuck her tongue out at him. "Lots of pros let younger players stay with them."

"Yeah, but not lots of pros were kissing other girls on TMZ."

"Anyway." Kim turned away from him and back to the rest of us, "Mr. Colavito says the paperwork shouldn't take more than a week or two, and he knows a sympathetic judge. I have a recording of the Skype convo in which they pretty much say they're going to use me for my money, so Mr. Colavito says it's a one hundred percent slam dunk."

"Slam dunk" I knew because of our basketball with Marcus. It was something I was teased for not being able to do even though I was as tall as the tallest of them. "Good luck," I told her. "Don't forget us when you're famous."

That was something people said to me a lot the last couple months, and it made Kim smile. "Never," she said. "We'll always have Palm Gables."

"We'll always have Palm Gables." I used the Bogie voice.

Marquize looked between us. "Is that from something?"

I stared at him. "You haven't seen 'Casablanca'?" He shook his head. "Okay. My turn to show you something. We'll rent it this weekend."

"Can I come?" Kim asked. "I love that movie."

The cheetah and I exchanged glances. "Um, sure," Marquize said. After all, we both knew, it wasn't like we were going to be doing anything while watching the movie.

I took Kim aside on our way out of lunch, when Marquize and the other guys had gone on to their tennis lessons. I was supposed to be going too, but I wanted to talk to her first. "You're sure about the tournaments?" I said.

Her long muzzle dipped and her ears lay back. "Not as much as I made out," she admitted. "I'm a little scared. But I talked to Coach Bellina, too, and she says I know how to learn, and that's the important thing."

I cocked my head. "What does that mean?"

"You know." She nudged me. "Find the flaws in your game, practice over and over again, keep getting better. It'll be rough the first year because I can't afford to hire a coach, but Porter Colliere... honestly, I couldn't do this if not for her. Getting into her camp was the best thing that happened to me. She says she'll mentor me for a year. Not full time, like a coach, because she's got her own career still, but she takes on two or three young female players a year."

"That's great," I said, and wondered if there was anyone who took on young male players.

"But they taught us pretty well here. I can keep doing the drills, and Coach Bellina said she'd keep an eye on my matches too. So I'll have a support network."

"If I can help, let me know," I said.

"Thanks, Rocky." She took my paw and squeezed it. "I'll miss you and Marquize. The other guys not as much, but you two are pretty awesome."

"I'll miss you too. Hey, if I give you my Skype, will you call me?"

"Sure!" She laughed, took out her phone, and sent me her Skype username.

And as I was heading to my practice session, I thought again about Ori and about all the battles in Lunda. The best thing I could do, I realized, was keep working patiently and efficiently. There was no telling when something might happen and I might lose my Palm Gables education, so I should make the most of it while I could.

I wasn't going to lose my redoubled drive to get my sister home. I was just going to be smarter about it.

Chapter Twenty-Four

Marquize got annoyed at me over the next week or two because all I wanted to do was practice. I'd rush through dinner and want to squeeze in another hour of practice before bed, and he wanted to relax and think about things we could do together. I pointed out that we played tennis together and had dinner and he said he wanted to do other things.

"We don't have anywhere we can do 'other things,'" I told him as we were wrapping up a late afternoon snack one evening in the food court. "So we might as well play tennis."

"I don't just mean that." His little ears flicked and the spots on his muzzle scrunched up. "Like go out to a movie, or head down to the parks or something. You were going to show me 'Casablanca.'"

"I need to get my sister—"

"I know, I know." He leaned forward. "It sucks over there. But you lived there for years, and you survived, and she's survived until now."

"Every day she's over there, she's in danger."

"We could get hit by a car!" He got a little more animated, waving out the window at the street.

I didn't look at the street. "You didn't see the pictures," I said, staring down at my plate. There was one noodle left. I picked it up and licked it off my fingers. "It's bad there. And they're trying to marry her to someone."

"Okay, I don't know about the situation there but your aunt, right? Your aunt isn't going to marry her to some crazy murderer like in Bluebeard or something."

"You don't know my aunt." The sunset, which had seemed so pretty on other days, now looked like a slash of blood across the sky.

"She's family. She's got to keep your sister safe."

"You don't even know what 'safe' means over there!" I didn't know why I was angry at Marquize. None of it was his fault, but he didn't understand and I didn't know how to make him.

He pushed his chair back but didn't get up. "Don't yell at me."

That he was right and calling me on my behavior made it worse. "You're telling me how to act now?"

"I'm—" He did get up then, grabbing his tray. "You know, I'm tired. I'll talk to you later. Go shoot hoops with Marcus or something."

"Mar!"

He turned. "I can't deal with this," he said. "You're obsessing over this and I don't know why. Nothing's changed."

"It *has* changed!"

"The only thing that's changed is that you know about it. Seeya tomorrow, Rock."

I wanted to charge after him, and I almost did, but then I saw myself punching him and that scared me. So I sat and stared at my empty plate until he was gone, and then I got up slowly, emptied my tray into the garbage, and walked out. As I pushed the door open, I thought about how I looked forward to coming to the food court ever since that first date, how it seemed special to me, and how now I would always remember the fight. Damn Marquize for not understanding, for running out on me.

Normally I would go back to the dorm, but home wasn't too far, and I didn't want to go back and sit alone in my room until it was time for a late night snack, which Marquize and I normally would get at Meat'N'Malt. That was probably where the cheetah was, and I was worried I'd yell at him again.

So I called Ma to tell her I'd be coming home and would eat a little dinner with her if she held off for an hour or so. The theory was that that would give me time to cool down, because I was still in as foul a mood as I'd been in days. I reined in my temper around Ma out of habit for the hour we were in separate rooms, while she was making dinner and I was doing homework. But once we sat down at the dinner table together, my hope that my mood would magically get better proved futile, because when Ma asked me about my day, I didn't think about my classes or my tennis practice.

"I had a fight with Marquize," I grumbled.

Her ears perked up and her eyes narrowed slightly. "Did he hit you?"

"No. I just yelled at him." I shoved food around my plate, not wanting to eat any of it. "He was being a jerk."

"About what?"

"About Ori!" That was when I broke. "About Ori being there in the middle of all those wars, people burning villages and cutting each other into pieces and we're just sitting here letting it happen! We left her behind."

She put down her utensils and looked steadily at me. "Where is this coming from?"

"You left her behind!" I pointed. "I wanted to bring her along! Why couldn't we?"

"The visas—"

"You can fix it, I know you can."

"Ro." She said it with rock in her voice and I stopped. "Do not interrupt me. You think I am not doing all for Ori that I can? The truth is she may never be allowed to come over here."

My ears flattened against my skull. "What?"

"There are rules and regulations. We can seek asylum, but Ori is not the only young girl, or even the only young jackal, in an oppressive society. You got special dispensation through the school. They have money and connections."

"So we'll get them to help. Coach Murphy would do that. He says I'm special."

(But it wasn't Coach Murphy who'd said that.)

Ma shook her head. "They owe us nothing. If anything, we owe them."

"She can play tennis. She can…" I trailed off. Ma's expression didn't change; her ears weren't down like mine, but she wasn't smiling. Her paws rested on the table in front of her and she gazed steadily at me. I saw the words in her eyes before she said them.

"I am not telling you to give up hope," she said. "We may be able to do something. But you are old enough now to understand the reality. Believe that I will do everything I can to bring her over. Know that it may not be enough."

"I'll be able to," I snapped. Ma's steadying tone only calmed my surface; underneath the anger and frustration roiled, curling my tail and grinding my teeth. "I'm not going to leave her to be raped and burned."

"Rochi!" Ma's ears did go back now as her eyes flared and her teeth showed. "Ori lives with Kamina in the same neighborhood where you spent a mostly peaceful childhood. Do you think because you've seen these pictures of war that now you have put Ori into them? The wars are hundreds of miles from where she lives, and life in our city goes on as it always has. What brought you to look at those pictures? Did something happen to Ori's lion?"

"Maybe," I growled. "She doesn't know. He went off to fight in a war."

"Ori is not in danger," Ma repeated. "I am sorry if her lion is caught in this fight, but Kamina knows her duty to her family."

"Can you find out whether he's alive or not?"

She shook her head slowly. "Ori has no future with this lion."

"God." I shoved my chair back and got up. "You're just like Mar. You don't understand."

"Sit down."

I didn't. The act of disobedience felt good because it was something I was doing, it was an action that was having an effect right now. I was tired of doing what people told me to do. "I'm going to save her," I repeated. "Even if you can't."

Ma stayed seated, her paws folded on the table, her eyes fixed on mine. "Sit down and finish your dinner. We will talk about this later."

"I'm going to Burger Royale," I said, and walked to the door.

I wanted her to try to stop me so I could yell and push her away. But she didn't say anything as I yanked the front door open, walked out, and let it slam behind me.

***

I wanted to fly home across the ocean, take Ori on a plane, and bring her back, like a movie action hero. But movie action heroes had reserves of cash for plane tickets, or they had pilot friends, or a mercenary friend who warned them darkly that they were on a foolhardy mission. I had a mother and a friend-boyfriend who didn't seem to get how urgent it was. Ori wasn't their sister, wasn't the jackal they'd spent most hours of most days with, at the tennis center, in school, at home, playing by the river or in the market or on the roof of the house. Ma trusted Kamina, but Kamina had almost sold Ori to that plantation owner.

The Burger Royale sat at a corner two blocks from the basketball court where we played with Marcus. It was empty at this hour, everyone probably at home with their families eating dinner. Their *whole* families. I didn't feel like eating; I'd long since burned off my noodle dinner, but there wasn't room for food around the tight, angry knot in my stomach. My paws curled into fists and I punched the chain link fence as I walked by.

Another block, and broken glass sparkled in the gutter. I watched where I put my feet, but most of it had been swept off the sidewalk. In the better parts of town, there were stiff fines for "hazardous littering," but here there was nobody to enforce that; at least there was a cleaning crew here. The warehouse where I worked was on the edge of another part of town like that, where boards and iron grates covered windows and the smell of urine was worse than anything I'd smelled back home. Gen had warned me against walking too far south of the warehouse, though he wouldn't say why. Marcus had told me that gangs littered the streets with broken glass, creating mazes that only they could navigate without cutting the pads on their feet to shreds. The police in that area wore foot armor like soldiers, he'd also told me. I'd heard of that, vaguely; one tennis player who'd torn a muscle in his foot had worn a "pad" on both feet (because on just one it would affect his balance).

I didn't have any foot armor, but I kept going, not sure what I was looking for until I smelled the thick odor of some coyotes and rats around one corner. When I focused, I could hear them talking over the hiss of the wind and the far-off growl of traffic. Then the spatter of rain joined the other noise and I lost the voices, but the smells persisted. These guys hung around this neighborhood a lot, and the water on the ground and in the air carried their scents well.

The streets were mostly empty of people, so I headed for the smell. I wanted to confront *someone*, to yell, to get into a fight the way I couldn't with Marquize or Ma. That urge led me to an abandoned row house from which low conversation emanated. Broken glass littered the steps, but the path through it was clear enough for me to recklessly stomp up them and push open the hanging door.

"Hey," a voice said sharply, "who the hell are you?"

The voice came from a shadowy closet to my right missing its door, and the speaker was a rat about a foot shorter than me. His voice lost some of its confidence on the "you," as he emerged and his eyes traveled up to my head.

In the few seconds I was pondering how to answer, a shirtless, scruffy coyote scrambled in from the hall with a loud clatter of beer cans scattering. "Is it—" He, too, stopped when he saw me, and his paw went to the back pocket of his jeans but stayed there. "He's not a Cinco, is he?"

"I don't know what that is." I didn't give the rat a chance to answer. The smells of the house, the coyote, and the rat sank in as I stood there, both of them staring back at me. I wasn't quite sure where I was, I was hungry, and although I towered over both of them and outweighed them by ten or twenty kilos each, there were two of them and more within earshot, and the coyote had something in his back pocket that if I was lucky was only a knife.

That didn't relieve me of the desire to punch something. If I couldn't punch the rat or coyote, I could punch the wall to my left, whose moldering plaster had fallen away in patches. I curled my damp right paw into a fist, and as the coyote took another step forward, I slammed the plaster wall.

It didn't give as much as I'd thought it would, but it did crack. Not enough. I punched it again, and a third time, and then a thin paw grabbed my wrist and forced it behind my back. A hard shove sent me out the door. "Go fuck up your own house," the coyote snapped.

"I can't!" I yelled, and slumped against the wall to the side of the door.

"Fuckin' Cincos," he said.

"Hey." The rat sounded muffled, behind the coyote. "I'm pretty sure he's not a Cinco. Maybe he needs help."

"So go buy him a burger." The coyote scuffled and left, beer cans clinking around as he did.

Shame washed over me. I'd walked into someone else's house— at least, the house they lived in, if not owned—and cracked their wall. I pushed off from the wall and stumbled down the stairs, ignoring the rat behind me calling, "Hey, you okay, guy?"

Only three blocks away did I register the stabbing pain in my foot. Lifting it, I pried out the shard of glass lodged between two of my pads. The rain washed away the small amount of blood on my fingers and my foot felt better right away: still sore, but at least not in sharp pain.

At the Burger Royale—not the one I'd meant to go to, but another, dirtier one I found on the way—I grabbed a stack of napkins and tended to the cut in my foot. It bled, but was already matting up the fur. Ma and Marquize and Coach would be mad at me. I didn't care.

And then my phone rang. Ma, I thought, or Mar, but when I picked it up to see who I would be ignoring, I saw an international number. So I answered.

"Ro?" Ori's voice. "Where are you?"

"I'm...in a burger place. Where are you? Isn't it..." My brain refused to process numbers. "Really late?"

"It's ten past midnight. Ma called me. She's worried about you. She said you stormed out."

"How are you doing?" I clung to the phone.

She sounded half-amused, half-exasperated. "I'm fine, Ro."

"Have you heard from—"

"I'm *fine*. Kamina sends her love as well."

I took the hint. "I'm going to get you out of there."

"I know you will. But in the meantime, I'm fine. Ma says—"

"Ma left you there." My muzzle twisted into a snarl.

"Ma says," she went on patiently, "that the best way to bring me home is for you to work hard and win tournaments."

I leaned back into the unyielding plastic seat. "She told me that you might not be able to come over, even with money."

"Maybe." She sounded perfectly at peace with that. "But if you become famous and people print the story about your sister...Ma thinks that could help as well."

"So I have to become famous now as well as earning money?"

She laughed softly. "Isn't that what you were going to do anyway?"

A grey fox in a shabby flannel shirt and torn cargo pants shuffled in through the door, wiped rainwater from between his ears and along his whiskers, and shot me a look as he fished in his pockets. "Yeah," I said to Ori as the fox stumbled through the tables toward me.

"Hey," he rasped when he got closer. "Got any change? I need to get dinner. I'm really hungry."

I nodded to him and reached into my pocket as Ori said, "Then go ahead and do it. I'll stay well, I promise." The fox held out a paw and I dumped the coins into it.

"God bless you," he said, and his breath smelled sour and sick. Instead of going up to the counter, though, he headed back to the door.

"Hang on," I said to Ori, and put my paw over the phone. "Hey," I called to the fox. "You're not going to get food?"

He flicked an ear but didn't even turn his head as he walked out. I looked back at the clerk, a cacomistle who was grinning at me. "He's going to buy booze," she said. "He comes in here three times a day, never ordered once."

I stared after the fox and settled back into my booth. "I'm back."

"What happened?"

"Oh, I had to buy booze for this fox, I guess." I squeezed my eyes shut. "But Ori, the war, the fighting…"

"Lundara is just as you left it," she said calmly. "There's not much war, and none of it comes into the city now."

"Ma knows about Raji," I said quietly.

Ori exhaled. "I told you, she knows things."

"She still doesn't think it's urgent."

"It isn't. I have enough to eat, and Kamina is looking diligently for the best husband for me."

"If you're married, that's already too late."

"I asked Ma. She says you'll be able to buy me back. Didn't she tell you?"

For a flash of a moment I regretted giving my change to the homeless fox. "No," I said, "she didn't. How much will it cost?"

"I don't know, but I'm sure you'll be able to afford it. Just win one major tournament."

Ori and I sitting in front of our little black and white television, watching the BBC broadcast of Wimbledon as they showed the prize money for the winners, running to Ma because we were sure they were making up numbers, that no single person had earned that much money in their life, let alone in one fortnight. "Even just reaching the quarterfinals."

"Probably. But to be famous, you have to win."

I let out a long breath and sank back into the seat. "And you have to stay safe."

"Deal," she said.

Chapter Twenty-Five

I called Ma on my way back to the dorms. "I'm sorry I walked out and yelled at you," I said.

"I'm glad you listened to Ori, at any rate." She hadn't even asked whether Ori had called; she just knew. "Are you coming back home?"

"No. I'm going to go to the dorms." I paused. "Ori said I would have to buy her back from her husband."

"Most likely."

"You didn't tell me that."

"It didn't seem important. The amount will be less than the airplane fare. By the time you are prepared to bring her over, the government paperwork will be much more difficult than the money."

Finding my way back through the streets was tricky, but a ways away I spotted an office tower I recognized and I made for it. "You have a lot of confidence in me."

"Do you not have so much in yourself?"

"Maybe a little." I sighed. "When it was only money—I can win some tournaments at the junior level, get a few thousand dollars together. But now..."

"Now it may take a little longer. Now you understand why I want Ori married in a good situation to someone who will be well disposed to selling her to you in a few years."

"A few years." I laughed. "Braden Longacre was the best student at this school and he's not even winning major tournaments yet. He was here..." I tried to work the math in my head. "I don't know, what, four years ago?"

"So you will have to be better than him."

My laugh got deeper and more bitter. "Is that all I have to do?"

"Ro." She was calm. "If you can do it, you will. If you cannot... we will figure something out. I have never lost hope, and neither should you."

There was the basketball court, deserted. I walked past it more confidently as the streets around me took on the familiarity of a tennis court, lines guiding me to where I needed to go. "You told me she might never be able to come over."

"Hope and reality are not incompatible."

"Incompatible?"

"You can hold both in your head at once." When I didn't say anything, Ma went on. "Think about your tennis match against Cleve. You knew it was possible you might not win. But you hoped you would, and you did all you could to win."

And I had. She didn't have to say that part. "I'm not going to look up wars at home anymore. I think that's a little too much reality for me."

"You should continue to learn," Ma said, surprising me. "But use that knowledge well. Don't let it take over your life. Focus on the things you can control—and control them."

"Like what?" I kicked at a can in the road, sending it clattering past a red panda talking on his phone as well. He shot me an annoyed glance, but I ignored him. "Tennis. That's all."

"That's right. When you're on the court, you're in control. So work on that. Leave Ori's situation to me."

All that did was remind me that Ma had left Ori back with village chiefs looking for harems, back in a world of conscriptions and severed tails and burned huts. I clenched my teeth and then forced my jaw to relax. And in that moment I remembered Kim, how she was cutting ties with her parents, finding a way to control her life that I hadn't thought was possible. Not that I wanted to cut ties with Ma, but the idea that there might be angles I hadn't thought of yet comforted me, eased my tension, set my tail to swinging more freely. "I'll try."

It took me another half hour to work my way back to the dorm, through dark empty streets. I saw a couple other people, dressed in rags like the fox who wanted booze, but they didn't bother me and I didn't approach them.

When I got back to our suite, Marquize's door was closed. I paused and then rapped quickly twice.

Five seconds passed. The gravelly rolling of his chair sounded, and then the click of his claws on the floor. The door opened a crack and I stepped back to give him room. His spotted muzzle held a guarded expression, his ears back.

"Hi," I said.

He looked me up and down. "You play hoops?"

I shook my head. "They weren't there. I went home and I, uh. I yelled at Ma."

That got his eyes wide and his ears up. He leaned forward and sniffed around my shoulders. "What?" I said, stepping back again.

"Trying to smell where she cut you," he said. "You don't smell like blood. Did she only throw you across the table?"

I pushed him away with a laugh. "I walked out, and I called her to apologize. Ori called me and she calmed me down."

"Ah." He leaned against his door frame.

"So, uh." I looked at the floor, the words harder than I'd expected them to be. "Sorry for yelling at you, too. None of this is your fault."

"Okay," he said. "Thanks. I figured it must be pretty hard with your sister over there, and I saw how much the wars upset you."

"Yeah, it's..." I pressed fingers to my eyes. "Ori reminded me that she's safe where she is. Ma reminded me that she is doing everything she can."

"She's."

"What?" I looked up at him.

"I keep telling you, use your contractions."

Pressure built behind my eyes. I stepped forward, then again, and wrapped my arms around him as I drove him back into his room. He closed his door and pressed me against it, holding me tightly in his arms. We didn't kiss, just held each other as I let myself relax into his warmth and the reminder of how much he cared about me. My tail, pressed against the door, still found a way to wag.

"I wasn't really mad at you," the cheetah said in my ear. "You were going through some stuff and you know, it was like when I came down with my parents. I get in a bad mood around them and I can't get out of it sometimes. I figured it was like that for you."

"Yeah." I hadn't cried or anything, but I did have to wipe my eyes. His arms stayed around me, his body against mine, and even though we hadn't kissed or anything, we were both reacting to being so close against each other. I ignored that for the moment. "And Ma said…"

I told him about the complications of getting Ori out, and you would think that would've dampened our physical reactions, but it didn't really seem to. I guess that the same way I was thinking about how close he was in the back of my head while talking, Marquize was thinking about it in the back of his head while listening.

He did okay listening despite that. "You're going to be famous," he said. "I know that for sure. So you'll get her out eventually. It might take a few years, but you'll get her out."

Everyone else seemed more confident in my abilities than I was. Winning a tournament at school had drained me. How would I feel after playing the best players in the world? "It seems so far away."

"And where were you two years ago? Did you think you'd be winning tournaments at a school in the States, getting ready to be a professional tennis player?"

"I dreamed about winning Wimbledon," I said. "But the more I learned about tennis, the more I realized how far away that is, how much work it takes."

"Look how much you've already done." He nuzzled my cheek and whiskers. "Look at what you came from and where you are. You're a legit star here, and the rate you're learning, you'll be a star on the circuit before too long."

"So will you," I murmured back.

"Maybe. I don't know. I'm having trouble keeping up with you now. Can't imagine where I'll be in a year."

I squeezed him. "Right here, I hope."

He laughed in a soft breath past my ear. "Yeah."

At that point, the physical pressures between us forced out thoughts of Ori, tennis, and anything else. "And…and I want to find a way to do other stuff with you. Not just 'Casablanca.'"

"Yeeeah." That one was a lot more breathy, a lot more needy. His paws slid down my back toward the base of my tail.

"Maybe we can rent a hotel room some weekend?" I nudged up against his cheekruff with my muzzle.

He leaned against me. "I could rent one but my parents see the credit card statements. Dad's already told me he'll take it away if I abuse it. So we could have one or two nights—if he's not watching the statement online, which he probably is—and then I wouldn't have a credit card."

Marquize's credit card came in handy for dinner sometimes and for occasional shopping. In my head at that moment, I would have given all that up for one night in a room where we didn't have to worry about anyone spying on us or listening at the adjacent wall. I wanted to know what it would be *like,* being with him like that. But the credit card was important to him, I knew, so I said, "I don't want you to lose your credit card."

He was quiet, maybe thinking about it as well, and then he rubbed against me and said, "We'll figure something out."

The rubbing wasn't helping. I let my paw drop to the spot where his tail hung over his pants and rested it there, and for what seemed like forever we stood like that, panting and touching and pressing, until Marquize stepped back. "Okay," he said, his chest heaving. "This isn't going to, y'know, end well. The cameras saw you come in here, and if we keep doing that I'm gonna..."

"Me too." I wanted more but was aware of how dangerous it was. My paws slid along his arms to catch his fingers. "But we'll figure something out. Or I'm gonna explode."

"Yeah." He laughed and leaned forward to kiss me. "You better go."

"Uh." I adjusted my pants. "How good are those cameras? Maybe we should talk about Math for a bit."

We did, but it didn't help; as soon as I got back to my room I had to ease my tension the same way I was sure Marquize was easing his. When I lay back to sleep, my initial thoughts were of Marquize, the two of us lying in a bed together in a hotel room, but before long I was remembering our comfortable, dirty mattress at home, and picturing Ori curling up on it. I was being selfish wanting to have a boyfriend here, wanting anything that distracted me from tennis.

Only, I reminded myself, Marquize didn't distract me. He was helping me, encouraging me, making me believe in myself. That movie Marquize had shown me, about the cub who played chess, whose parents decided it wasn't healthy for him to be nothing but a chess player—that was the situation I was in, wasn't it? Wasn't it important that I not be *only* a tennis player, that I have a life as well? Marquize was part of that life and Ori would tell me that a relationship was important—had, in fact, told me that.

Still, sleep didn't come easily that night, nor the rest of that week, no matter how much I wore myself out. By Friday night, I was feeling like maybe I had a handle on things, and then Ma had to go and rattle me all up again.

We were eating dinner, spaghetti with meatballs and sauce and plantains for dessert, and it was over those that she said, "How are things with you and Marquize?"

I gulped down the mouthful of sugared fruit and stared down at my plate. "They're, uh. Fine."

"You made up after your fight?" I nodded. Ma tapped the table with a claw. "It sounded like a serious fight."

"I was upset," I said. "I got over it when Ori called."

"Yes." She kept her eyes on me, and all I could think was, *Of course she knows.*

"Is he helping you with your tennis?"

"Yeah."

"Good."

There had to be something I could say, some other conversation to draw her into. My mind was blank. "These are good," I said, taking another bite of the plantains.

She sighed. "You're being careful?"

"Yes," I said, spraying bits of plantain over my plate, and then swallowed. "I mean, what about? In tennis? We have all this guidance from the coaches on how not to be injured, and we do our stretches before every match, and we're...careful with the rackets..."

When I finally dared to look up at her, my ears flat, she was smiling. "Good. But I also want you to be careful when you go on dates. There are people around who would not look kindly on two boys dating, and it might affect your career."

I gulped again. "I don't know—dates? Me and Mar? No, we're— we're not—"

She shook her head, still smiling. "He is better than Shawna. At least you don't spend every night on the phone."

"We see each other at school." I blinked, realizing I was admitting she was right. "Not that, I mean, uh..."

"Relax. I have talked to Ori about it. I don't think it is a bad thing. If you care for someone, that's what is important." Ma reached out to me across the table. "But do be careful. You are young. People may take advantage of you."

I knew who she was talking about. "Marquize isn't like that," I said.

"I am not talking about Marquize. But now that you mention him, I want to meet him."

My tail curled around under the chair, and I squirmed. "You've met him a bunch of times."

"Not since I knew what he is to you." She tapped the table again. "We will have dinner."

"All right." I sighed. "I'll tell him."

"Good." She smiled, and then reached across and rested her paw over mine. "It's a good thing. I'm glad you have someone else to care about you. Especially someone who understands that tennis comes first."

I didn't think about the implications of those words until I was lying on the couch trying to sleep. It seemed to me that Ma was saying not only that Marquize wouldn't let our relationship become a distraction, but that if my career was threatened, he would understand if our relationship had to end.

Could Marquize really affect my career? If it got out that he and I were dating, would that stop me from getting into tournaments? What would I do if that were the case? I felt tight around my chest, like I was having to choose between him and Ori. Stop it, I told myself. This is just imagination.

And it was worse because in my heart, I knew which way I would choose, and it wasn't even close. Even if it were only my career set against a relationship with Marquize, the cheetah would come in second. I felt terrible about that, and only marginally better by trying to convince myself that he felt the same about his career.

Chapter Twenty-Six

Marquize wasn't sure he would have much of a career; that was the problem with my hypothetical scenario. But it became important to me that he do as well as I did, so I kept relaying to him the lessons I was learning. He was frustrating to work with; he would have flashes where he would play terrific, rallies and points and even whole games when he was moving well and placing his shots well, when the things I was trying to work on clicked for him. And then he would go back to relying on his speed and reflexes and would forget about footwork and court coverage.

But after yelling at him that night in the food court, I didn't want to yell at him again. I mean, not unless I had a really good reason, like he was ignoring the way I felt about my sister. For something like tennis, I tried to stay calm and focused. And after repeating the lessons I'd learned and watching him make mistakes, I came back to Palm Gables focused and clearer about what I needed to do myself.

Diaz commented on my progress after I beat him every set we played one week, a couple weeks after that bad night. "Damn, son," he said. "Coach gonna take you and put you with the seniors if you keep that up."

"I got lucky," I said, to be polite, but I smiled and wagged at the compliment.

Coach Kotten didn't say anything, but he must have noticed, because the week after that, Coach Murphy called me into his office for a meeting.

The room still smelled of sweat and rabbit, a familiar smell that set me at ease. The calendar on his office wall had changed to May, an image of the arena in Lutèce with flower gardens in the foreground. Coach, in a Palm Gables polo shirt, leaned forward across his cluttered desk as he talked.

"We've got a month until the end of school tournament."

Coach's paw tapped papers on the desk. "Coach Kotten reports that your progress has been good. I'd like to talk to you about starting up some lessons that will prepare you for your life as a professional, and to ask if you'd be willing to skip the tournament."

"Not play? Why?" My ears perked up and my fur prickled. Had he seen me going into Marquize's room on the security cameras? Was that why he wanted me out of the tournament?

Coach grinned, showing his large front teeth. "I'd rather build up the confidence of a couple of the other students. You're going to leave the school anyway and you've won the tournament already. I never intended for you to compete in it again."

My tail uncurled and my shoulders untensed. "Then why wait…?"

He waved a paw. "It's good for you to finish your classes this year, and I thought you'd need about this much time. You never know what's going to motivate someone, but usually cubs at your level can't wait to get out there and start playing the real talent."

I hadn't thought of it that way, but when he mentioned it, the prospect of playing different people with different styles, people who were better than I was, got me pretty excited again. Nervous, too, but I'd been beating up Diaz and understanding that there wasn't much left here to challenge me. And it would be a big step toward getting my sister to safety. "Yeah," I said. "Can't wait."

"All right, then." He chuckled. "Coach Planza will be teaching you the lifestyle lessons. He was on the tour for a decade and only retired two years ago, so he's pretty up to date on the tour. Things change so fast."

"Yes, sir," I said.

"And you'll meet with me once a week. If you're going out there to represent the Palm Gables name, you're going to do it right."

So I started the last phase of my education at Palm Gables. Coach Planza, a wiry wolf who still had enough energy that he rarely sat still during our lessons, talked to me for an hour each day about hotels, hiring coaches, travel, and saving money. And once a week, Coach Murphy and I sat down and watched film of matches in Challenger tournaments.

And in the evenings I talked to Marquize about all I'd learned, tennis and otherwise, and we played tennis and made our plans for what would happen when we went out onto the tour. We could learn together, support each other, share expenses by staying in hotel rooms together.

We came back to that one a lot.

About a week after my first meeting with Coach Murphy, I finally got up the nerve to tell my boyfriend about Ma inviting him to dinner. We'd finished a practice match and were leaning against the chain link fence gulping water because it was over thirty degrees out. I knew I was going to have to tell him, and I'd rehearsed a couple ways to lead into it, but what came out when I crushed the empty water bottle in my paw was, "Ma wants you to come over for dinner."

Marquize kept drinking as though I hadn't said anything, but when he put down his water, he nodded. "Okay. Why?"

"Because she knows we're dating." I'd meant to dance around that one as well, but none of the words I'd prepared sounded right.

He stared, opened his mouth and shut it with a snap, and then said, "Rocky—"

"I didn't tell her. She just knew somehow."

He put a paw on my shoulder. "I'm not mad. But I would've thought you'd tell me when you were going to tell her."

I shook my head. "I didn't, I promise. I mean...I told her we had a fight, and that was the night I stormed out. When I got back and we talked...no, it was the next day, I guess. She asked me about you, and then said some stuff about dating, and I told her we weren't but it was like she didn't hear me."

He squinted at me. "That was like a week, week and a half ago."

"Yeah."

"You're just telling me about dinner now?"

My ears folded down. "It's not that important. She didn't say, like, right now."

"But what if she thinks I didn't want to go to dinner and that's why it's taking so long?" Marquize's tail lashed. He picked up the water again and finished the bottle. "I don't mind going to dinner. I like your Ma. I don't want her to come after me with a knife."

"She won't. I mean, unless you attack me, I guess."

"Then I won't attack you." He put his arm around my shoulders and hugged. We'd worked out this "friendly hug" that we could do in public to satisfy our urge to hug each other. I'd been nervous about it at first, but nobody cared when we did it, so I'd relaxed by this point.

"I promise I didn't tell her," I protested. "I mean, I didn't mean to."

"I believe you." Marquize nosed my ear and let me go.

"But it's good that she knows." I sighed. "On the tour I'll probably be living with her a lot more of the time and it'll be hard to keep a secret like that. And...I wouldn't want to. I like that she knows."

"Yeah," the cheetah said, "I do too, kinda." When I looked at him, he said, "It's nice you can share it with your family. Don't expect to get invited to *my* place for dinner anytime soon."

"No, I know." I relaxed back against the fence again. "Is it being gay that's the problem with your family?"

We hadn't talked much about his family before this point, and I wasn't sure how he'd take it. He didn't really react at first, then started gathering up his stuff. "No," he said. "It started before then. Normal cub stuff, I guess. They wanted me to be more religious, and I never felt it the way they do. They didn't like the friends I hung out with. Partly I think they sent me to this school to get me away from some of them. They promised they'd stay in touch—my friends, I mean—but we really haven't. So it kind of worked."

"Oh. I thought you wanted to come here."

"I did." He smiled. "I'm glad I did. It's complicated, that's all."

"Okay." I started to gather up my stuff as well.

"It'll be simpler once I get out on tour, maybe next year. Then you won't have to room with your Ma, and we'll have hotel rooms. And when we're eighteen, nobody can tell us what to do."

I hefted my bag over my shoulder. "I don't want to wait that long."

"Oh, no. I just meant things'll be a lot easier then." He walked alongside me as we left the court.

"Right. But I was thinking..." I took a breath. "That night, you know, I went into your room and I was in there for a while. We could've been doing...anything."

His ears perked, and then he shook his head. "We can't. I mean, people would hear."

"We'll be quiet."

"They'll smell it."

I grinned. "Um. I don't want to burst your bubble, but I can already smell when you're doing stuff without me in your room. I mean, if I go over to the garbage can. It's not like a thick smell in the room or anything."

It was funny how uncomfortable he looked. "Rocky."

"What? I do it too. I spray Neutra-Scent in the trash when I'm done, though. I'll bring mine over."

"O-okay…" He stared ahead as we walked, and I knew he was thinking about it. "When?"

The dorm buildings rose in front of us. "How about tonight?"

Chapter Twenty-Seven

We talked about it more on the way in, all very vague: "Are you sure?" "I really want to," and so on. But we'd been dating for two months at that point and there wasn't much doubt that it was something we both needed (we told ourselves). And we'd exhausted all the possible alternatives (we told ourselves). And after all, it wasn't like we didn't both do "stuff" ourselves in our rooms, so what was the harm of doing "stuff" together (we told ourselves)?

Still, from the moment I'd said "How about tonight?" there wasn't much doubt in either of our minds that it would happen. Those words had crystallized it from a distant longing to a reality, and though all of our conversation before and during dinner sounded as though it hadn't been decided yet, the truth was that we had already boarded that bus and there was no way we were going to jump off it.

We both sat out in the suite with the others after dinner, supposedly studying, though I was mostly keeping my textbook in my lap to keep my thoughts hidden. I can't even remember what textbook it was, but it was a heavy one, so maybe World Cultures. I stared down at the pictures on the page, but all I saw was me and Marquize, Marquize and me, finally doing the things we'd wanted to for weeks.

Finally, finally, Bret stood and said he was going to sleep. I checked my phone and found that what I'd thought was like six hours had only been an hour and a half. Marquize and I exchanged looks across the couch and neither of us moved, because Pom and Kim were still chatting. Kim hadn't left the school yet, but her filing was going to be heard by the court the following week and so she had basically given up on schoolwork and was dedicating her remaining time at Palm Gables to training and distracting the other students.

When Pom fled to his room to get some actual work done, Kim turned her attention on me. "Rocky, do you have a coach lined up for when you go pro?"

"Uh, no." I stared down at my book, pretending I was trying to study.

"You really should. Here." She brought out her laptop. "These are the boards with the accredited coaches. Porter's going to mentor me but I still need a coach who can watch my game film. I can't afford one without my parents helping, of course, not until I win a few tournaments, but there are coaches who will take you on part time, and Mr. Colavito is going to put some of his own money into me."

"Sounds gross," Marquize said from across the room. When I looked up, he was almost glowering at Kim.

The coyote stuck her tongue out at him and kept talking to me. "I don't want to use it all to hire a coach because there's hotel rooms, equipment, lots of other expenses. And I know you won't have a lot of money either. So someone like these guys," she waved a claw past a list of names on the screen that might as well have been a blur for as much as I was paying attention to them, "might be good for you, too."

"Thanks," I said. "That's great."

"I know you don't need this yet, but when you're ready, let me know. It's going to be weird for me, sharing a coach with someone else, you know? I don't mean that to sound, like," she waved her paw. "I know you didn't have all the advantages I did. It's kind of exciting getting to go out on my own and having to earn everything myself."

"Yeah."

She kept on chattering about how she was going to be eating cheap, "but not fast food, that's not good for you," as if we didn't know that from our Nutrition classes (Mar and I always heavily modified our dishes at the Meat'n'Malt to get rid of the worst stuff) and about what it would be like to be professional. I didn't know how to get out of it, and finally Marquize stood and said, "I'm going to finish up studying in my room."

I stared longingly at his door after it closed. Kim and I were the only ones left. I didn't want to abandon her, because she was so excited to talk to me about being a pro, and I knew that some of that came from her being as scared to leave the school as I was. But even though I knew all of that, it was only about ten minutes before I closed my book and said, "I oughta get some sleep, too."

She didn't seem annoyed, thankfully, and stood at the same time I did. I kept my textbook in front of my pants and hurried to my room.

How long should I wait? What if Kim was still studying out there? What if someone else came out while I was hurrying from my room to Marquize's? I paced back and forth along my bed and then stopped to listen. It didn't sound like anyone was moving outside.

I hurried quietly to the door and put my ear to it, but as soon as I did I caught footsteps outside. As I stepped back from the door, it opened a crack and a golden spotted muzzle poked through.

"Hurry up, come in!" My heart pounded as Marquize slipped through the door and we closed it quickly.

For a moment we stood there, muzzles a couple inches apart, staring at each other, and then he grabbed me and pressed his lips to mine. We twisted and stumbled our way across the floor to my bed and half-sat, half-lay back on it, our paws going to all the places they were familiar with and now daring to move beyond those boundaries. And yet we were still unsure, taking turns pushing each other further as we kissed and pressed together. I was first to put a paw under Marquize's shirt, touching his bare stomach, and he pulled my shirt free of my pants as soon as I did. He was the first to put his paw on the front of my pants, and then he put his other paw on my muzzle when I made a noise involuntarily.

"Sorry," I whispered, though it felt like my entire body was vibrating, agonizing over the heat of that touch.

"It's okay," he whispered back with a smile, and tightened his fingers as he did. "I wanted to make a noise too."

I reached out to touch him back, but his fingers felt so good that I hesitated, worried that if I interrupted him he'd stop. And I didn't want him to stop.

And then his paws were unfastening my pants, and I had to reach over and put my paw on him so I didn't fall too far behind. The act was as quick as a tennis shot, accomplished without thinking once I knew how to do it. Except in tennis you went right on to the next shot, back and forth, and you established a rhythm, and all your actions were forgotten as soon as they were done. Here, we were volleying back and forth, but as soon as I'd touched Marquize, even through his pants, I couldn't think of what the next move should be because the awareness of what I was doing exploded all through me. I forgot everything except what was under my fingers and the way Marquize froze, the feeling of his fingers on me at the same time. Time slowed the way it did on the court when things were going really well.

Marquize let out a long, slow breath. His paw moved again, and I pulled at his pants as it did. Time sped up and accelerated as we pulled at pants and shirts. Clothes flew to the floor and then we were pressed together fur to fur on my narrow bed, panting. We stopped again there and looked at each other, tracing the patterns in each other's fur, boldly going everywhere with our fingers. And through all of this we met each other's eyes and smiled, and as our petting got more and more urgent, we started talking.

"So, uh, how do you want to…?"

"I don't have condoms."

"Oh yeah, we're not ready for that." Nervous chuckles from both of us.

"So…?"

"Um." Marquize licked his lips. "We could try…"

"I, uh."

"If you don't think you're ready…"

"No, I mean, if we…I mean, if you want…but this, uh, this feels good too…"

"It does yeah."

"Good enough to…um…?"

"Oh yeah." Pause. "You?"

"Y-yeah." My voice shook. And so did I.

We stopped talking then. Our paws got busy and, well, it didn't take very long.

Afterwards we were both a little embarrassed, cleaning up. But we were happy, too, and Marquize hugged me and I hugged him back. We panted together and then he reluctantly edged away. "I should…I shouldn't stay too long."

"No, I know." But I clasped his paw, and he leaned in to kiss me. It wasn't our longest kiss, but it was our most passionate to that point.

He pulled his clothes on quickly, but when I started to dress too, he stopped me. "Stay like that," he said. "I like looking at you."

So I stayed sprawled out on the bed naked and waved at him as he disappeared out the door. Then I rolled over and buried my head in my pillow. I'd just…I'd just had *sex*. Sort of.

It counted, though. I was pretty sure it counted.

Chapter Twenty-Eight

The glow from that night stayed with me through the next morning, as if Marquize's fingers were still roaming my body. When we met in the hall that morning, we looked away from each other at first. I could feel his smile, as bright as mine, and when I looked up he was looking back at me. We didn't say anything as we walked to class together, staying quiet in the usual chatter of our friends around us.

"You okay?" Dom asked me as we walked through the morning drizzle to our first class.

"Yeah." I couldn't stop myself from glancing at Marquize, and the cheetah grinned back at me, his tail flicking from side to side.

"It's just usually when I talk about Longacre, you get bristly."

"Oh." I focused on him. "What about him?"

"He won at Manula last weekend and Li, the guy he was playing, said Braden was trash-talking him and made an inappropriate comment. But nobody else heard it and he won't say what it was."

"That figures," Marquize said. "That fox is a dick."

"Yeah, he can be." My first thought was that Marquize was still mad at Braden for the fox's slight on me all those months ago, and how sweet that was. Then I remembered Braden's e-mail to me and wondered if he really was that abrasive all the time or if that was a persona he developed to look tough to the outside world.

Dom's eyebrows rose. "You've forgiven him for dicking you out of a point?"

"It was a while ago," I waved a paw.

"Winning's going to make him worse." Marquize's voice had a growl to it, and he wasn't looking at me anymore.

"He's already been winning tournaments."

"Yeah, but Manula's one of the top Challenger tournaments."

"Oh, shit, that's right. What's his number now?"

"It was 82 before the tournament. Going up for sure." Dom didn't even have to look at his phone to know the number.

"What was Li?"

Dom knew that one, too. "Fifty-one. Longacre beat him in four sets, 7-6, 2-6, 6-1, 6-3."

"Too much to hope he'd just flame out, I guess." Marquize bumped my shoulder, and his tail flicked against mine.

That distracted me into wagging again, and as Dom went on to talk about the trajectory of Braden's career, I snuck a look at Marquize and saw his annoyance at Braden melt into a smile.

Neither of us had talked about getting together again that night. It was in my mind, though, all through that first class, the way it had felt, the intimate smells of him and the warmth of lying by his side. I wanted not only to have sex again but to find some way for him to be able to stay with me afterwards, to lie side by side in bed and fall asleep. For today, though, I'd settle for a repeat of last night.

Somehow we got through that morning. I don't think either of us took a single note; I stared at my laptop screen and didn't type. I know the one time Marquize was called on for an answer, he stammered until the teacher called on someone else. We exchanged glances and my tail wagged whenever I forgot to stop it, and once when he caught me looking, he dropped his paw to his lap and I flattened my ears and buried my nose in my laptop, grinning hugely.

We couldn't really talk at lunch because all our friends were around, but after lunch, Marquize said, "I'll walk you to your practice." Still there were people around, so he pulled me into a little side hallway outside the indoor practice courts.

"I thought maybe tonight," he said in a low voice, "maybe we could try…"

"Sure," I said.

"You don't even know what I'm going to say."

"I don't care." I squeezed his paw. "But I bet I do know."

He brought my finger to his muzzle and licked it, eyes on mine.

"Yeah," I said. "That's what I thought. I still don't know, but…I want to try."

"Okay." He dropped my paw and his eyes flicked over my shoulder.

I turned and saw an ocelot I didn't recognize. "Hey, you guys are

Rocky and Marquize, right? Coach Murphy's looking for you."

"Why?" Marquize asked, a little sharply.

The ocelot shrugged and gestured toward Coach's office. With an uneasy glance between us, we followed.

Frio stood alongside Coach Murphy's desk and greeted us with a nod. The rabbit himself sat with his elbows on the desk and barely moved as we entered, his eyes fixed on the laptop on his desk. "Rocky, sit down," he said. "Marquize, go with Coach Young."

"Are we in trouble?" Marquize asked as I put my paw on the chair.

I thought that was rather obvious. Frio was smiling, but the smile wasn't a happy one; it was the tight smile he used when we'd done something wrong on the court, like really wrong. And Coach wasn't smiling at all. But in response to Marquize, he said, "Not right now."

So I sat as Frio led Marquize out of the office. Coach Murphy kept staring at his laptop and then reached up with a paw and ran it back over his ears. They popped up again and he started over from the base, running his paw down them. "Look, Rocky," he said finally. "We've done the best we can to prepare you for life as a professional on the court. And Coach Planza has been talking about all the practical aspects of life outside the tournaments."

My heart raced. They'd seen us on the cameras, I knew they had. For some reason, maybe they hadn't been watching the other night, maybe we'd done something last night to tip them off, *somehow* they knew what we'd done. My claws scraped the arm of the chair.

Coach Murphy paused, and I wasn't sure if I was supposed to say something, so I kept quiet. After a moment, he went on again. "But there are other parts of that life that we haven't really covered with you. Being here at Palm Gables, you're insulated from a lot of what goes on out there. The first few years you won't have to worry about it that much, but if you continue on the path I think you will, you're going to have reporters sniffing around, people prying into your private life, people trying to take advantage of you. And I don't know what your situation is." He held up a paw. "But Coach Young has some concerns about the time you've been spending with Marquize lately. And he says Marquize has been going into your room after hours."

Again he paused, and this time he looked up at me, squinting like maybe I was out of focus. Again I waited for him to talk, squeezing my paws against each other, tail tight against my hips. Finally he took a breath and let it out. "So, look, if you're—" He drew in another breath, and the next sentence came out in a rush. "If you're gay, it's none of my business. Or just experimenting, or whatever. Hell, at your age—" He held up a paw. "I don't know, and I don't want to know. But something like that can really ruin your career. You have to live with a hundred other guys on the tour and it can be a really hard place. Once you start winning majors, hell, you can do whatever you want. But until then, you want people to notice you, but only in a good way. You're going to have articles written about you. Talk about escaping the poverty in your home country, how great the Union is. Those always go over great. Talk about your respect for the top players, your idols from the past. And it wouldn't hurt you to hang out with one of the female players from time to time."

Now, when he paused, I cleared my throat. "We were just studying," I said, but even to myself my voice sounded weak and unconvincing.

Coach Murphy nodded. "I don't want to know," he said, and pointed to his door. "The point is, those people out there, they'll eat you alive—if you let them. Don't give them anything to hold onto. When you get more successful, you'll have a manager who'll work on your image, but until then…be careful."

I swallowed. "Yes, sir."

"And," he said, "whatever you do, don't do it in the dorms. You've probably figured out there are cameras there."

"I know," I said before I could stop myself. "Marquize told me. But we didn't think—I mean, we were just studying so I didn't think there was anything wrong."

Coach's eyebrows lowered. "He told you about the cameras?"

It was too late for me to deny it, but I tried anyway. "I—I think? Maybe it was someone else. I think it was, actually. I think…" I scrabbled in my memory for a name. "I think Coach Young might've told us both."

Coach shook his head. "You're a good cub, Rocky. And you're talented. But you need to wise up if you're going to make it."

"Yes, sir." My paws were still pressed together, but I couldn't feel them anymore. Everything had gone numb.

"All right, go to practice. And come to me if you have any more questions, okay?"

"Yes, sir." I got up and made my way out of the office mostly via muscle memory.

I looked for Marquize but didn't find him, and I was already late for my practice, so I ran over to where Diaz was waiting. "Hey, where you been?" he asked.

"Coach's office," I said, and went over to Coach Kotten for our lesson without saying anything else, even when Diaz trailed behind me asking if everything was okay.

I lost the set we played after our practice because I was worried about Marquize, and every time someone came in or out of the arena, I looked up expecting to see the cheetah. "Good game," I said as I netted the last point, and hurried to the bench to put away my racket.

Diaz usually took his time getting to the locker room, but this time the cacomistle threw his gear into his bag and grabbed my arm as I crossed the court. "What's up? You going pro?"

I sighed. "It's complicated."

He laughed and slapped me on the shoulder. "Shit, everyone around here knows it. Ah…" He dug around in his bag and pulled out a ten-dollar bill. "Here. Give this to Coach next time you see him."

I took it because he was holding it out to me. "Sure."

"So when are you leaving?" We fell into step together down the hallway.

"I don't know."

"What did Coach want to see you about, then?"

"He wanted…" A spotted figure crossed ahead of us, and I sped up for a step before my mind caught up to warn me that it wasn't Marquize. "Just to warn me about some stuff out there on the tour that we hadn't talked about before." I waved a paw. "People taking advantage of me."

"Oh yeah, people are shitty. Ah, shoot." Diaz pulled another ten-dollar bill out and gave it to me. "Anyway, you can't trust anyone. I wouldn't even trust me if I were you."

"I trust you," I said. "What do you want from me?"

"Nothing now." The cacomistle waved his paws. "But later on, you never know, I might come around asking you to put me up in a room, or do some publicity with me, stuff like that. I don't know, I don't need anything now."

"Okay." His chatter was putting me at ease, at least distracting me from worrying about Marquize. "I'll be careful."

"That's the spirit." He slapped me in the small of the back.

I showered and got dressed and still couldn't find Marquize. So when I was done, I texted him.

At the Meat'n'Malt, he texted back some fifteen minutes later, which was funny because I'd already decided to head there to grab dinner. So it was only five minutes after his text that I walked into the bright white tiled restaurant and saw the cheetah sitting alone at a two-person table against the wall.

I went to sit across from him without even ordering. His head was down over a crumpled wrapper and he was sipping from a cup. As I sat, I smelled that it wasn't diet soda. "Are you having a shake?"

He looked up and tilted the cup toward me. "Vanilla. Want some?"

"Um, I shouldn't, but..." A taste wouldn't hurt. So I took the cup, sucked a bit of cold shake through the straw, and let it slide down my tongue. "How'd it go with Frio?"

He took the shake back and sucked down another mouthful of it. "Well," he said, "I guess I'm turning pro with you, ready or not."

"That's..." I wanted to say "great," but it was clear that that wasn't the right word, or at least that wasn't what Marquize was thinking. "So Frio thinks you're ready?"

"Ha." He put down the shake. "I'm being expelled from Palm Gables."

The words clattered about in my head for several seconds, making no sense until I put them back together in order and inspected them. "What? Seriously?"

He nodded. "For 'conduct detrimental to the school' or some bullshit like that."

I fingered the two ten-dollar bills in my pocket at the swear word and tried to figure out what to say. "We were going to go pro anyway. This is just a little early."

"I guess." He shrugged. "I'm going to see what tournaments are going on in the next couple months."

"Good thing you have that credit card."

He buried his head in his paws. "Ugh, I'm going to have to tell my parents."

My fur prickled. "Is the school going to tell them what you actually did?"

"I don't know." His voice was muffled.

"How do they even know? Coach Murphy said they didn't know what happened last night."

Marquize didn't say anything, so I went on. "If he didn't know, then how could…" How could Frio know, I was going to say, but then I remembered Frio walking naked through my hotel room, sitting on my bed. Of course Frio would suspect what two boys were doing in a closed room together.

"You're the special one," the cheetah said, lifting his head. "You're the one who's going to represent the school. I'm the one distracting you."

"But you're not," I protested. "I'll go tell Coach Murphy."

"Don't." He put a paw up. "Don't get in any more trouble. I'm done, but you're not."

I stared back into his eyes and wanted badly to take him behind a closed door and put my arms around him. "You're coming to dinner Friday," I said. "Maybe Ma can help."

"I'll come to dinner," he said, "but I don't think your Ma can help."

"Well, I've got to do something." He'd set down the shake, so I took it and slurped down another mouthful. "This is all my fault."

"Your fault?" His eyes widened and he grabbed the shake back from me. "How is this your fault?"

"It was my idea!" I pressed my paws together. "I said we should… and you were the one who wanted to be cautious."

The cheetah laughed, relaxing for the first time since I'd sat down. He covered my paws with his. "Rocky, I wanted that as much or more than you did. If you hadn't suggested it, I would've for sure. I was going crazy every night lying there, thinking about you just across the suite. Don't blame yourself. If anything, it's my fault."

"It's not more your fault than mine." He didn't answer that, staring down as though the answers to life were written on the plastic lid of his shake, and I leaned forward, turning one of my paws over to hold his. "Marquize?"

"Yeah," he said, "I guess."

A couple wolves in letter jackets from the local high school walked by us on their way out. "Get a room, faggots," one of them said, and they both laughed.

We pulled our paws back quickly and then looked at each other. "Assholes," Marquize murmured, but neither of us reached out for the other, even after they'd gone.

"You hungry?" he said after we'd sat quietly for several minutes.

I nodded. "Maybe I'll grab something."

"Nah," he said, and got up. "Let's go to the food court."

So we went and had early dinner and sat looking out over the lake. We didn't talk too much until Marquize said, "Frio said I have until the end of the week to get my room cleared out. I guess I'll go home for a while until I can figure out where I'm going to join the tour."

"Wait." That hadn't even crossed my mind. "You're going back to Port City?"

"Where else am I going to go? I can't afford to live in hotels. I need to see if there's anyone who'll share a room with me for a while."

"I will."

"Yeah, but you've got months until you're on tour, and you won't be able to afford hotels either. We're both going to have to room with other people early on."

"So it's going to be even worse than it is here." I sighed, my ears flattening.

"Maybe not. I mean, we can ask to have the room for a night or something, you know? We won't have cameras filming us all the time. We won't have..." He trailed off and looked out over the lake. "I'm tired of this place. I'm glad to get away, to be honest."

When I thought about leaving with him, the prospect excited me. Traveling around the country, around the world, playing tennis in different cities, no Math or History (though I enjoyed History) or anything but tennis all the time...that sounded like a wonderful life. I was itching to grow up, to start winning money and saving it against the day we could bring Ori back. To be moving forward, finally.

"Yeah," I said. "I know what you mean."

***

Marquize had told me not to cause trouble, but I couldn't stop myself from going to see Frio the next day. I didn't want my boyfriend to have to go back to Port City to wait until we were both ready to strike out and go pro, and after a night spent thinking about it, I thought I'd come up with a plan that might work.

It took me two tries to catch the ferret, first before my afternoon practice and then after. When I did find him in his office, I had to wait for him to be done with another student. Finally he stood and welcomed me in. "Thanks for waiting, Rocky," he said. "What can I do for you?"

"It's about Marquize," I said, closing the door behind me.

His smile didn't waver. He didn't sit down either, though, just stood next to his desk leaning on it. "You don't have to worry about that," he said. "I understand you might be upset, but it's all over. Trust me, we at Palm Gables know what's good for you."

Again, the image of Frio walking naked into my hotel room, in almost the same posture he was holding now, flashed through my mind. "I wanted to talk to you about that. Is there any way you can let him stay? At least until the end of the semester?"

His muzzle stretched into a wide, tolerant smile. "Rocky," he said. "I know you think you're friends with him. But he was only using you."

"No, he—"

"Trust me." He held up a paw to stop me from talking. "I've seen a lot of boys come through these halls. I know what they're about. You're only sixteen. You've never run into someone like Marquize before."

He started to go on, but I saw the opening and I cut him off. "I have, actually."

That stopped him. I went on, but I'd barely gotten two words out before his expression closed down and his ears flattened. And yet his smile stayed fixed on his muzzle. "I seem to remember a hotel room by Pelotas Rojas."

"I'm sure you don't want to bring that up," Frio said. His smile could have been made of plastic.

"I am bringing it up." I cleared my throat, not sure how to proceed now that I was at the moment. I bulled on ahead anyway.

"Believe me, I would prefer just to forget it."

"I should think so." He straightened his shirt. "I never told anyone about your behavior that night. I'd hate to have to file a report with Coach Murphy."

"My—*my* behavior?" I stared at him.

"I don't know what it's like where you come from, but being a homosexual on the pro tennis tour would make things a lot more difficult for you. I know that we had a very close relationship, and I didn't hold that night against you, but if it were made public, some other people might."

Words were not coming to me, not even in Kikongo. I gestured with one paw and made some sounds. Frio waved soothingly at me. "Hey, I don't want to do this. But you're the one who came in here trying to threaten me by making up stories."

"Making up? But you—I was—it was—"

He stepped toward me then and I took a step back. "Look, Rocky," he said. "Why don't you head on out and we'll forget that this ever happened. Don't worry about Marquize. His family has money. He'll be fine. He'll go pro maybe or he'll find another tennis school—that's actually what I'd recommend, but he'll do whatever he wants to do and I can't control that. I do appreciate your concern for him, because I think you know as well as I do that he's not ready to go pro yet, but sadly we can't keep him here at Palm Gables any longer."

His confident assertion of the way things had happened made me doubt my own memories. Had he just been wandering out of the shower and I'd watched him too long? Stared at his body? No. No, he'd definitely come to sit on my bed. But... "I don't understand how you can keep me but not him."

"Because that's how things are. If you want that to change, I can go talk to Coach Murphy. After what just happened, I'm sure he'll believe me."

He let that threat hang there. I tried to find some way out, but I kept running up against his willingness to lie to get me in trouble. And there had been no cameras in that hotel room.

The unfairness of it stayed lodged in my throat even after I'd left Frio's office, even after I'd showered and changed, and especially after I'd met Marquize. We walked to dinner in silence, both of us lost in our own thoughts. I didn't want to tell Marquize what I'd done, because it had gone so badly and because he'd told me not to. I'm not sure what he was thinking, because he wasn't telling me either. Maybe he'd gone to Coach Murphy to plead his case.

We talked more as we packed up his stuff Wednesday and Thursday night. It didn't take long, but we wanted to spend time together. And even though we had to leave the door open and be careful about what we said, we enjoyed each other's company.

Chapter Twenty-Nine

Marquize hadn't wanted to tell the rest of the class that he was leaving, but I said, "What are you going to do, just not show up on Monday? Then I'll have to tell everyone about it."

"I guess that's not fair," he said. "But would you do it anyway?"

I thought about that. "I could say…I could say your parents made you come home. But I mean, you're still going to talk to those guys, right? They've all got your number. They're going to text you anyway."

"I could throw out my phone." He had it in his paw and stared down at it.

We were in his room with the door open, but there wasn't anyone outside. I reached out and put a paw on his shoulder. "Hey, don't do that. Tell them your parents need you at home. To…to run one of the stores." I searched my memory. "Didn't you say your parents have three? What if one of the managers quits?"

The cheetah's lips were thin and tight. "I guess." He nodded and then slid his phone back into his pocket. "Yeah, I'll tell them that. It's easy and simple. Thanks."

I forced myself to smile, and so did he, and we went on packing as though he were only going away for a weekend. When we weren't talking, though, I couldn't stop myself from thinking about the situation and grasping for anything I could do to make it right. I'd already failed with Frio, and I didn't want to risk my relationship with Coach Murphy, who'd been much nicer than Frio about me possibly being gay. I hated the feeling of not having any power to help Marquize; it felt like Ori's situation all over again, only Marquize was right here in front of me and I couldn't stop him from going away.

***

Friday after he'd told the class, they wanted to take him out to dinner, but he'd already agreed to come to dinner with me and Ma, so they settled for skipping some of the afternoon practice and hanging out at the Meat'n'Malt for shakes. I wasn't going to come, but Marquize said it would be okay, so I tagged along.

It was a sad gathering, but awkward for both of us, because people kept asking Marquize about his family's shops, and I knew he was making up lie upon lie. At least he kept them simple, and I helped where I could by trying to change the subject whenever they pushed too hard at him. They were all really nice and solicitous and everyone promised to keep in touch with him. Brittany promised to come by the store when she was in Port City, and Dom said he'd keep him up on tennis videos as they kept learning.

We escaped after an hour and rode the bus to Ma's apartment. "That was harsh," Marquize said as we got on the bus. "They kept asking me questions."

"It was nice. They all like you and they're sad you're leaving." I slid my paw over his, behind the seat back where nobody could see it.

"I'm sad I'm leaving, but mostly because of you." He looked past me, out the bus window. "This place is full of people who'll shit all over you. They'll pretend they like you and then they'll just…" His muzzle dropped.

I squeezed his paw. "They aren't that bad. I mean, they were jealous of me but things settled down and we're mostly friends, right? Was someone bad to you?"

He met my eyes and then looked away again. "It's no big deal. It's the way things are."

"We'll still be…" I couldn't quite find the right word. "You still want to…date and stuff? When you're back home?"

"Oh yeah, I do." He came alive, engaged and smiling at me. "It'll be harder, but we can text and Skype."

By the time we got off the bus, we were talking ourselves into a future that wasn't all that bad. Skyping every night wouldn't be as good as regular dinners and tennis practices, but it would be something at least. We wouldn't completely lose each other. And it would be only temporary, until we could both get set to become tennis professionals.

The smell of dinner as we walked into Ma's apartment brought a smile to my muzzle, and a slower one to Marquize's. "Smells awesome," he said. "What is it?"

"Pork loin," Ma told him, "and a recipe from home made from things I could find at the supermarket here."

"It smells like barbecue sauce, only different." Marquize extended his paw. "Thanks for having me over, Mrs. N'guwe."

"It's nice to see you again. Please have a seat in the living room. Dinner will be ready in about half an hour."

When we sat down, Marquize's ears went back and his tail went limp. I nudged him. "What's wrong?" I hissed.

"We're going to have to tell your mom about..."

I tried to hush him; he wasn't used to jackal ears. But it was too late. "Tell me about what?" Ma came in from the kitchen and leaned against the doorway, ears up, arms folded.

We silently tried to figure out which one of us should talk. She was my ma, but it was Marquize's news. It affected both of us, and neither of us wanted to speak, so we sat with paws in our laps and tried to pick up on cues from each other that neither of us was giving.

Finally, Ma made the decision. "Rochi," she ordered

I sat up straighter. "Marquize got kicked out of school," I said.

Her eyes widened. She turned to the cheetah, who hunched over and stared down at his knees. "What happened?"

This time, I looked at Marquize, but he didn't look back at me. I swallowed. "We were in my room together late at night."

Ma's ears went down. She walked over to me and before I could move, cuffed me on the cheek. "I told you to be careful," she snapped. "Did you get expelled as well?"

"No," I said, ears flat.

"Why not?"

Now Marquize lifted his head. "I think because he's better than me at tennis."

"Hum." Ma rubbed her chin, then turned and went back into the kitchen.

Marquize stared after her, then leaned over and whispered to me, "Are we in trouble?"

"Probably," I whispered back.

"Should I go?"

"Oh no." I glanced toward the kitchen. Ma was stirring

something on the stove. "She'll tell you if you should go."

He followed my gaze and nodded, and then asked more questions about the food until Ma came back in and told us dinner was ready. We trooped into the kitchen after her, Marquize following my lead as I picked up a plate and served myself from the pork chops simmering in a spicy brown sauce, then from the stir-fried green beans and almonds and from the mashed sweet potatoes. "Feels almost like Thanksgiving," Marquize commented as we sat at the small table.

"I very much like Thanksgiving," Ma said, cutting a piece of her pork.

Marquize hesitated, but when I did the same he picked up his utensils. "I guess you don't say Grace or anything."

"No." Ma had her mouth full, so I answered. "We remember God in our daily lives and we don't have any ritualized prayer before meals. We go to Sunday Mass sometimes, but not every week."

"Only when the spirit moves us," Ma said. "You don't say Grace?"

Marquize shook his head. "My parents say a *du'a*, but it's personal. They just recite it to themselves, we don't say it as a group the way people say Grace. A *du'a* is a short prayer," he told me, seeing my expression.

"Rochi knows about Muslim prayers," Ma said.

"I didn't know what they were called."

Marquize laughed. "It's weird hearing you called 'Rochi,'" he said. "I know it's your real name, but you're Rocky to me."

That made Ma smile, though I wasn't sure why. We talked for a little while about the Muslims in our country, and I tried not to think about Raji. I hadn't heard anything about him from Ori since we'd last talked, and I didn't want to bring up the subject if she wasn't going to.

"So," Ma said to Marquize as we were finishing up our meals. "What are your plans?"

He set his fork down. "I'm going to go home to Port City. Stay with my parents for a little while, save up some money, try to make connections online for the Futures circuit."

"What connections do you mean?"

"Oh." He glanced at me. "I mean, my parents can pay for some of my expenses, like travel and stuff, but until I start winning, I need to keep things cheap. So I'll look for people who can share housing—sometimes the tournaments have housing, but not always—and I'll need to find a coach. Rocky and I were talking about sharing a coach maybe."

"That is a good idea." Ma rested her elbows on the table and looked across at us. "And you will be playing doubles together?"

We faced each other and grinned. "We haven't talked about it," I said.

"You should. Doubles means more matches, more chances to win money. You will need all of it."

"Yeah. Okay," Marquize said. "Doubles partners?"

"We'll need to practice somewhere." I couldn't even think of who we would be able to find to play doubles against. "Oh, and you'll be in Port City."

"Not for long. I'll look up the tournaments and when you're ready to go, we'll join up. Until then, I can practice with local clubs like I was doing over the holidays…"

"No." Ma put her paws down on the table, drawing our attention. "You'll practice here."

"I can't stay at Palm Gables," Marquize said, but Ma cut him off with a wave that ended with her pointing at the living room and the couch on which I slept during the weekend.

"You'll stay here," she said. "You'll help with groceries if you can, and you'll practice with Rochi—with Rocky—after his classes. When his semester is over you and he will start playing in tournaments. I will help you get organized, and we will see where we can get money from until you start winning."

"Are…are you serious?" Marquize gaped.

"Perfectly." She fixed me with a stern look. "But the two of you must be on best behavior. No visiting in rooms at Palm Gables. No more sleeping here, Ro. You will stay in the dorm every night."

"Yes, Ma."

"Yes, ma'am."

"And you." She turned her gaze on Marquize. "You will spend days practicing and researching tournaments, and you will continue your lessons. I will help. There's a certificate you can get that says you have the equivalent of high school education that you will both pursue. I'd intended for Ro to get it anyway." She smiled, showing her teeth. "I will help you study."

I hadn't realized until that moment how much Ma had actually been planning for my career. Knowing about doubles play, planning for my equivalency certificate, being ready to accommodate Marquize into these plans—I would have been overwhelmed if I'd had to face all that alone. "She's a tough teacher," I told Marquize, to cover my embarrassment and gratitude.

"That's okay," he said. "I'll work hard."

"Good," Ma said. She stood, her tail flicking back and forth. "Now bring your plates to the kitchen. There's almond cake for dessert."

Chapter Thirty

I couldn't find the words to thank Ma the next day. I stammered out a few thank yous when Marquize was in the bathroom, and Ma accepted them with a smile. "I'm glad that I can help," she said. "You will do your part as well."

"I will, I promise." I would have promised her anything in that moment. I wasn't even sure what she was specifically talking about, other than keeping up practice and not getting caught with Marquize in compromising situations, but I was going to do my best at it. That was how I felt I was doing my part in rescuing him. "And Coach wants me to skip the school tournament anyway, so maybe I'll start looking at tournaments."

Her eyes narrowed. "Coach Murphy said he didn't want you to play in the tournament?"

"He said I already won and he knows how good I am. He thinks I'm ready for the circuit."

She nodded and relaxed. "I'll talk to him about it. Do you feel ready?"

"I've been thinking about it a lot." Marquize finished in the bathroom, so I waited until he came out and joined us. "I'm ready. I'm pretty sure I am."

"He is." Marquize came to stand beside me.

"All right." Ma wagged a finger at me. "You can start investigating tournaments. But you don't have to make the decision yet."

"We have a few weeks," I said.

With the weight of Marquize leaving lifted, the next week was much more enjoyable. We moved his boxes out of the dorm, though we decided not to tell anyone that he was staying at my Ma's place. He said he'd found a place with a friend nearby and he was going to stick around and keep practicing tennis.

On Saturday we looked at the tournament schedule and saw

that the Futures tournament we'd gone to nearly a month ago had been the first of a series of three in Pensa. The next set of three were all out in Golden, on the opposite side of the country. But they were all $15,000 tournaments instead of $10,000, and when they were over there were a bunch around the Midwest that were all tens again. "Does the winner get fifteen thousand?" I asked Marquize. "That'd pay for a lot of stuff."

"No." He pulled up a tab he'd found that showed that the winner actually received about $1300. "The fifteen thousand is the total prize money. So if you get to the round of 32, you get like a hundred bucks. Get farther, you get more."

"That's three weeks away. Can we still apply for it?" In three weeks, the school tournament would be under way. Technically the school year didn't end for a month, but if we had to leave early to get to these tournaments…Ma could probably leave her part-time job and come with us.

"Um." He clicked through a bunch of webpages. "Until Thursday. And we have to register and get something called a TPIN."

"A tee-pin?"

"Tennis Player Identification Number." He pulled up the page and we looked at it. It looked so official to me that I couldn't quite believe we could do it all ourselves from the computer.

"This is all we have to do? Just pay them money and then we can enter tournaments?"

His spotted muzzle squinted up at me. "Don't you have a coach who's teaching you all about being out on tour and stuff?"

"Yeah, but…" I gestured. "It's things like showing up early, getting along with other players, finding the right places to eat in the cities, whatever. It's not all this practical stuff like how do I register for a tournament."

"Oh, well." He tapped the screen. "Here's how. Should we get our numbers?"

"Let's do it."

So first Marquize and then I went through the process of registering for the world of professional tennis. My TPIN was—and still is—USX2010052503, which is a handy reminder of the day I joined the circuit. Marquize is USX2010052502. We never found out who the US player was who got his number first that day. We had to enter a whole bunch of stuff about our playing record, our emergency contact, and a lot of personal information. They then sent us to a profile page where we could fill out things like hobbies, place of birth, and coach's name.

"What should we put there?" I asked as we both hesitated at that section.

"Blank for now," Marquize said, and we went on.

It occurred to me that Braden might have some advice about finding a coach, and so once we'd finished that up, I logged into my e-mail and wrote him a quick letter congratulating him on his win at Manula, telling him I'd be on tour soon, and asking how he got his first coach. I was sort of hoping he'd refer me to someone directly, but then again, I reminded myself, this was Braden, and he wasn't great at taking hints.

***

I told Kim and Dom on Monday that Marquize was going to be staying around at a friend's place. Math was the first class of the morning and Kim grabbed my paw as I was going off to it. "Why you bothering? Come on, let's hang out," she said, and I couldn't think of a reason not to.

So while everyone else was learning algebra, the coyote and I stood in a hallway by the soda machine. I confided in Kim that I was going to be joining the tour maybe sooner than the end of the term. "You might beat me to it," she said sourly. "My parents are fighting the motion and my lawyer says it might be another month."

"Why are they fighting it?"

"They want to keep me." She flattened her ears and sagged back against the wall.

I leaned back next to her. "That sucks. For the money, right?"

We were alone in the hallway, but she looked to the left and right and spoke in a very low voice. "Kind of. They're getting divorced."

"What?"

"Splitting up," she clarified. "Ending their marriage."

"No, I know." I shook my head, wanting to give her a hug, not knowing whether that was proper or not. "I'm surprised, that's all."

"Why? You don't know them."

"No, but…"

"Sorry." She bumped her shoulder into mine. "I don't mean to snap. No, they've been fighting for a while and it's finally over, I guess. But they both want to keep custody of me, and I think it's not just for the money I might make; it's because they want to be able to hold that over the other one or something. It's fucked up. They're fucked up. I want to be out of that family so bad."

"I'm sorry," I said. "Sorry you have to go through that." I couldn't imagine a parent not wanting the best for their cub.

"Yeah, I am too." She straightened and her tail wagged. "But Mr. Colavito says it'll be soon now. I'll catch you in the Midwest if not out in Golden, right?"

"Right," I said, and met her raised fist with mine. "I'm not sure if I'll get out to Golden, but...hoping."

"You will." She flashed a bright smile. "Come on, want to hit around?"

"I've got History in half an hour," I said.

She put her paws on her hips. "You're out of here in a week, and I want to hang out with someone. Come on, I just told you about my parents' divorce."

I thought about telling her again that I hadn't decided if I was going to the tournament in Golden, but I didn't think it would make a difference. And while I liked History, I wasn't sure how many more chances I'd have to hang out with Kim. "Yeah, yeah, okay."

We both felt better after hitting around, and by the time we were done, it was 11, so we cleaned up and went to sit in the lunch room and wait for everyone else. "Too good for classes, huh?" Pom said when he walked in and saw us.

"Cheers." Kim raised her water glass to him.

"Rocky, I thought you were going to finish out the term at least." The red fox sat by me. "Isn't your mom a teacher?"

"She's getting me some kind of equivalency certificate," I told him. "Anyway, I'll go to class tomorrow. Kim wanted to hang out this morning."

"We'll see about that," she said, and got up. "Come on, let's get food."

***

That evening, I was surprised to find an e-mail from Braden in my inbox. I opened it and read.

Rocky,

I'll be near Palm Gables next week. If you want to talk I can spare half an hour.

Braden

I stared at the screen. It seemed implausible, but I read it three times and it didn't change. So I wrote a quick reply back saying that of course I would be happy to talk to him and where would he like to meet? And then I stared at the inbox until I told myself that of course he wasn't going to be sitting there waiting for my answer—

Ping.

A reply came in. I opened it up.

How about a match at the Palm Gables courts?

Again, I could hardly believe what I was reading. I sent back an acceptance and then called Marquize.

"He wants to humiliate you," the cheetah said.

I hadn't even thought of that, but as soon as he said it, doubt gnawed at me. "No, he probably wants to see where I am. In my development, I mean."

"Why would he even care?"

"I don't know." I walked to my bed and sat cross-legged on it. I hadn't washed the sheets since the night Marquize had come over, and I could still smell him there. It made me feel good when talking to him. "But he does. He e-mailed me this summer and I talked to him on the phone."

"Yeah, but all that was through Frio."

"Not the e-mails. And he told me not to listen to Frio all the time."

"Okay, well, I didn't know about the e-mails."

His tone was faintly accusatory, and it made my fur bristle a little. "They were private, and I know what you think of him. Do I have to tell you about all my e-mails?"

"No." He sighed. "Sorry. But he's such a jerk. I'm worried that he'll..."

"What? That he'll be a jerk to me?"

"I was worried about that, but..." He clucked his tongue and paused. "You've done really well. And you're ready to hit the tour, I know you are. The thing is, Braden's really good. And he might be a lot better than you, and might make you doubt yourself. You see what I mean?"

"Kind of? You mean, I might think I'm not good enough anymore?"

"Yeah. Not everyone on the tour is as good as he is. You have to remember that if you play him."

"What do you mean, 'if'?"

He sighed. "You're going to, aren't you?"

"Of course I am."

"All right. Just remember, Rocky...you don't have to let him define who you are."

That seemed like a weird thing to warn me against. I wasn't sure what he meant by it, but it was easier to say, "I won't," and then we could talk about how much we missed each other.

Chapter Thirty-One

Braden asked that I not tell anyone he was coming back. "Even Frio?" I asked, and he replied, "Yes." I told him my best friend Marquize wanted to watch the match and he said that was fine. We set the time for Friday night at eleven, when most of the people should be gone from the school but Braden said he had a friend who could get us into the courts.

I was going to quit the warehouse job soon, I was pretty sure, though I didn't know exactly when. I hadn't yet, so I called Gen and told him I'd be late on Friday. We chatted a little more and I mentioned I was playing a tennis match as preparation for going pro, but I stayed mindful of Braden's warning and I thought that Gen might know who he was, so I didn't mention his name.

Gen asked again when my last day was going to be. I felt bad leading him on, but I still didn't know what I was going to do or when. Was I going to the tournament in Golden with Marquize? Or was I going to wait for Coach Murphy to tell me I was ready sometime this summer? I hated the idea of giving up a hundred dollars a weekend for an uncertain future in which my income relied on my tennis skills. Part of me bragged that I could beat anyone; another part of me wanted to hold on and see how the match with Braden went; another part pointed to the statistics of all the students who left Palm Gables and struggled in the Futures tournaments for a couple years before giving up. As long as I hadn't quit my job, I could still return to my safe life at school.

The rest of the week I mostly went to my classes except when Kim convinced me to skip (and taught me the term "playing hooky") and we sat in the dorm looking out at the city beyond Palm Gables. We sometimes talked about the tour but more often about movies and music, TV and food and all the great things about life in Pensa (and we also talked about the weather). Her lawsuit was progressing slower than she'd hoped but her lawyer kept assuring her that things were moving along. There were a lot of complicated words that I didn't know and she confessed that she didn't really understand all the intricacies either, but her lawyer had told her that he was asking the judge to hurry it up because her future rested on his decision.

In a way, I envied her. It would've been nice to have someone else in charge of the decision. Me, I was the only one who'd decide when to leave Palm Gables. So I couldn't chafe like Kim at someone else's boundaries; I could only worry over my own decision. And Marquize's; I thought he might have stayed at Palm Gables, given the option, but then again, he'd agreed to come on tour with me after this semester anyway, hadn't he? So it wasn't as though what had happened with us had disrupted our lives in a major way.

We'd registered, gotten our numbers, and were acting as though we were going to go out to Golden to play in the Futures tournaments. And yet I hadn't mentioned that to anyone at the school except Kim.

***

Marquize and I waited for Braden in the brick archway of Coball Pavilion where the fox had told us to meet him. Marquize squeezed my paw. "You nervous?"

"Nah." I smiled and wagged my tail. "I'm excited. This is like my first real match on tour, you know?"

"I guess. First match against a professional. It is nice of him to take you seriously," he added grudgingly.

I hefted the duffel bag with our rackets in it on my shoulder. "I'll show him I'm worth it," I said.

Marquize nudged me into the shelter of the archway and kissed my nose. "Yeah you will."

I touched my nose to his and moved to kiss him, but then I caught the click of claws on stone and stepped back. Marquize knew my senses well enough to trust them, so he leaned against the wall and looked around.

A moment later, Braden Longacre came around the corner. It had been a year since I'd seen him, but he hadn't changed much: still striking with his dark mane and russet fur, his green eyes bored, ears back. He wore casual clothes, which was a little jarring: a black collared short-sleeved shirt and khaki pants. But he stuck out a paw with some kind of cloth bracelet around it and said, "Hi there."

I shook, noting that he wore his bracelet on his dominant paw rather than on the opposing one, as I did with the bracelet Marquize had made me. "Hi. Thanks for coming."

"No problem." His eyes flicked to Marquize, then to the locked door. "You ready?"

"Yeah." I peered behind him. "You said a friend was going to let us in…?"

He reached into his pocket and pulled out a key. "Here's my friend."

As he unlocked the door, Marquize asked, "Where'd you get that?"

We filed into the dark building. Braden didn't answer until the door closed behind us, and then he set off to the left. "I got it from the coaches while I was here, and I forgot to give it back when I left. Court Four okay with you?"

"Sure," I said. Marquize touched me on the shoulder and nodded his head at one of the empty rooms we passed, a grin creeping up his lips. I caught his meaning and smiled back with a nod. Yeah, if only we'd had a key like this, we could've come in here. I didn't see any cameras in the public areas like they had in our dorms, so maybe we wouldn't have gotten in trouble at all. Then again, it would be odd if they didn't have cameras on the courts, I guess.

Braden unlocked the door to the courts and held it open for us. "I'm going to change," he said, eyeing my athletic shorts and t-shirt. "That's what you're wearing?"

"Uh-huh."

"Okay." He raised a paw. "Back in five."

"Want me to help you warm up?" Marquize took my duffel and pulled his racket out.

"Let's do it." I grabbed mine and a pair of tennis balls and jogged to the other side of the court.

Braden came back three rallies into our warmup wearing a white shirt and shorts, carrying a black and orange racket in his right paw. He didn't comment, but moved to Court Three and began practicing his serve, firing rockets across the net. When I took the time to glance over at them between rallies, they looked less intimidating

than they had a year and a half before. I might not be able to return them all, but I'd get to a good number of them, I thought. Braden served four, then walked to the other side of the court, gathered the balls calmly, and served them back to the side he'd come from.

"Want to switch?" I asked after a while. I'd gotten warmed up and could use the chance to practice my serve. In addition, I wanted him to see how I was serving now, maybe put some doubt in his mind.

"Sure," he called back. He happened to be on the opposite side of the court from me; he left the four balls on the baseline and walked toward the net.

"Don't I get a say in this?" Marquize asked, but Braden ignored him.

I walked to where he'd left the balls. "You don't have to rally with him if you don't want to," I said.

Marquize grumbled and set himself, waiting for Braden to hit the ball over.

358

Those minutes practicing felt strange in the big empty pavilion. The smack of the ball on the court, the zing of the racket strings, the click of our claws, our grunts of exertion, all those echoed in the huge space. Hundreds of seats sat empty, benches and seat backs in neat, orderly rows. But when I was serving, or when I'd been rallying, I concentrated and my world shrunk to the court, and then it didn't matter if there were zero or a thousand people watching.

Because of that focus, I never looked over to see if Braden was watching me serve the way I'd snuck glances at him, and when I asked Marquize later, he said he hadn't noticed. But Braden would be seeing my serves up close soon enough.

The echoes of serves and rallies hid the sound of footsteps approaching, and the residual scents of students hid the scent of someone coming, so the first indication we had that someone else was in the pavilion was when we heard Frio's voice. "You boys aren't supposed to be here," he said.

I lowered the ball I'd been about to toss and turned around. He was standing there in the doorway, paws stuffed into his pockets, and he wasn't looking at me. "Hello, Braden. I heard you were going to be in town, but didn't know you'd be coming by your alma mater."

Braden shot a look at me. "You told him."

"No!" I protested. "I didn't tell anyone."

He leveled a finger at Marquize. "Then you—"

Frio raised a paw and cut him off. "No, no," he said. "I didn't know you were going to be here. Rocky called in to his job and his boss told me there was going to be a tennis match. I've been going around to all the outdoor courts, and only a few minutes ago did I realize you might have broken into this building. Court Four, huh?"

Braden scowled and swung his racket at air. He looked back at me. "I'm ready when you are."

"All right." I looked back at the ferret.

"Oh, go ahead," he said. "I'm not going to stop you. I'll wait until after to have a few words with Mr. Longacre here."

We started with me in the court nearer the door, which was where Frio was sitting, and I saw Braden's eyes flick to him before his first serve. The moment the ball left his fingertips to rise to his racket, though, he was all game.

I got a racket on his first serve but sent my return into the net.

We crossed to the ad court without a word and he focused on the ball, then lofted it again. This time I got the return over the net and we settled into volleying.

That first game I was too focused on holding my own to try any of the tactics I knew, and I lost at love. When it was my turn to serve, I met Marquize's eyes, sitting on the sideline. He didn't talk, mindful of the etiquette of tennis, but I took confidence from his gaze. Time to force that fox to play my game.

I got two serviceable serves in and split the points. On the third, I watched to see which side he was expecting me to serve to, and it looked like he was leaning wide just a bit. So I aimed right down the middle and caught the line with one of the best serves I had. It clipped the line and zipped past Braden's outstretched racket.

He stared down at the line, then walked over to the deuce court and set up without a comment. I exchanged grins with Marquize, and we went on to play.

He broke my serve anyway that game, but I had some confidence. I started placing my shots, moving him around the court and trying to cover as much ground as I could. I lost the set 6-1, but I won my lone game near the end of the set and my confidence was up. "Good set," I said as I came to the net after the final point. "Are we playing a full match?"

"No, I think I know what I need to know." Braden's ears flicked back toward where the ferret stood leaning against the stands, examining his phone as though he didn't care at all what we were doing. "You mind if I get that out of the way before I talk to you?"

I nodded. "Go ahead."

The cross fox walked over to Frio. I only heard the ferret say, "It's been a long time," and then Braden growled something and they walked out into the hall and shut the door.

Marquize gave me a water bottle. "You played really well."

"Not the first couple games, but I was getting better." I emptied the bottle, handed it back, then stretched out my legs while I talked. "He's really good, though. I think he wasn't trying hard at first, but there were a few points…"

"That one where he went to the corner and the cross-court—?"

"And the drop shot."

"Oh, and when he got to your service return, the one in the deep corner." The cheetah pointed to the court. "He's fast."

"Fast isn't our problem." I worked on my arms. "It's knowing what to do with it."

He leaned against the fence as I finished up my stretches in the empty court. The single bank of lights illuminated the court well but cast shadows all around it. "Why did he want to play you?"

"I still don't know." I shrugged, sitting down, my tail resting on cold concrete. "You've been here the whole time. Did you hear him say anything?"

"He doesn't say much." Marquize folded his arms and looked toward where Braden and Frio had left. "He's not as good as he thinks he is."

"How do you know how good he thinks he is?" I reached for the water and took another drink. "He's pretty good, Mar."

"You're just as good." He paused. "Or, well, you're going to be."

"I'm a ways off. And I don't think he was doing his best."

"He wasn't at first, but as you got better, he tried harder too. That last game he was playing all out."

It was a nice thought. If I were close to Braden, even a little close, then I was ready to go out to the tournaments. I might have a chance to be successful and famous, to justify all the trust Ma and Ori had placed in me. I looked up at Marquize, his spotted muzzle shadowed by the bright overhead lights. He trusted me too, as a partner and a boyfriend to make this transition with.

There were a lot of people relying on me, and I was relying on myself, too. And now I reviewed the match in my head. I thought I'd played pretty well—not at first, but I'd adapted to his play and I'd formed a strategy. I don't think I'd have won a second set, but I'd have won more than one game if we'd played one. On his serve, he was hard to beat. He got serves into the corners with amazing precision, and even when I got to them—my return game still needed work—he was dictating the entire point. I'd won three points on his four service games.

On my serve, he was good at reading my body language, so I'd have to work on that in the pros for sure. But my serve got past him a few times and although I wasn't as good as he was at controlling the point, I had had a couple exchanges where I'd kept him off balance. I'd have to figure out what was different about those times. I wished

I'd told Marquize to film the game.

"Rocky?"

I looked up again. Marquize's head was tilted to the side, his eyes in shadow from the overhead lights. Over my own panting scent, I breathed in to catch his. It was familiar but also stressed, which was strange because I was the one who'd been playing a professional player. I perked my ears forward to show I was listening, and he went on. "This is gonna work out, right?"

"Sure." My tail flicked back and forth as I recovered some of my energy. "We're good enough to succeed at the next level, at least, and we'll keep learning, right?"

"Yeah. I know we have a long way to go."

"And we'll go together. That's what's important."

I still couldn't make out his eyes, but his smile stretched upwards. "That's right."

The door to the hallway opened. I scrambled to my feet and turned in time to see Braden walking from the shadows into the light of the courts. He paused with a paw on the switch. "We gotta go," he said, and cut the lights before Marquize and I were even a quarter of the way to the exit.

Marquize cursed, but it only took a second or two for our eyes to adjust, and then we hurried through the dim gloom to where Braden waited. The cross fox held the door as we walked out and then let it shut, following us through the deserted hallways.

"Everything okay with Frio?" I asked.

"It's fine," Braden growled.

I wanted to know what they'd talked about, but there was no polite way to ask. Next to me, Marquize stared down at his paws as he walked. "Asshole," he muttered, and I thought he was maybe thinking the same thing.

We were all quiet after that until we got to the outside door, and then Braden put a paw on it as I moved to open it. "Wait," he said.

I turned. In the light of the streetlights coming through the door glass, his fur seemed monochromatic, but strangely patterned, not like Pom's red and white muzzle with the black smudge on it. Braden appeared to have a perpetual shadow over his forehead. He glanced over my shoulder, then down at the floor, and finally back up at my muzzle. "The reason I wanted to play you," he said in a low voice, "is because Frio said you had a lot of potential and I thought you might be leaving school too early. You're going to be one of the youngest players, even on the Futures. If I beat you badly, you'd stay another year, come out later, and get better."

My heart tightened. I leaned back against the door and tried to hide my disappointment. "So you think I should stay."

"No. You're good. You should get the hell out of here. Start making a living. If I had to bet..." He stopped himself. "You'll win a Futures before the end of the year."

"Thanks." I met Marquize's eyes and swallowed. "I mean, I only won one game."

"Yeah, but you were adjusting. That's what I was looking for. Lots of people come out against a celebrity, they're intimidated."

"Hardly a celebrity," Marquize put in. "Minor one maybe."

Braden went on as though the cheetah hadn't spoken. "But you shake it off after a game or two and you play. That's what you did. You're raw, but you're not going to learn any more here. Get out on the courts."

He made as if to move past me, and I said, joking, "Want to be my coach?"

The cross fox snorted and pushed the door open. But the joke had reminded me of why I'd written him in the first place. "Wait," I said, hurrying after him. "Actually, do you know any coaches who..."

He stopped, tail flicking. "Yeah. I'll shoot you a couple names."

"Thanks!" I extended a paw. "And thanks for coming all the way down here."

Braden looked at my paw. It took him a second to extend his own and shake it. "You're welcome," he said. "And...good luck."

"I'm going pro, too," Marquize said, stepping up beside me.

Braden did look him up and down then. "Good luck," he said, but with a far more sarcastic tone. And before the cheetah could respond, the cross fox had turned on his heel and was on his way down the street.

Chapter Thirty-Two

B raden Longacre says I'm ready to go pro," I said to Ma, shaking the rain out of my fur.

I'd walked to Ma's apartment first thing in the morning. After the match, I'd gone right to the dorm to sleep. But Saturday morning I was up not too long after sunrise, and I texted Marquize to make sure he was up before I headed over.

Ma didn't say anything other than, "Come chop onions."

"I can do that," Marquize said.

"Ro knows how." Ma pulled me into the kitchen. "You can go get us some fresh bread from the market."

"Oh," Marquize said. "All right." He pulled on a light rain jacket and left the two of us alone.

I took the onion from the counter, set it on the cutting board, and sliced off the ends. "I played a set against him. He's really good, but I won a game and I was getting better."

"You don't want to wait for the end of the term?" Ma cracked eggs into a bowl as we talked, facing different directions in the small kitchen. I kept my tail tucked so it wouldn't brush hers.

"For what? To get grades on a bunch of tests that won't matter?"

"They may matter in the future."

I took a breath. "There's a set of tournaments out in Golden. Marquize and I registered—sort of—anyway, we can cancel this week if we want to but I don't really want to. I want to start playing."

Ma shook spices into her eggs and stirred. "And how will we get to Golden?"

"We?"

"I will come with you, of course."

"Oh. Oh, well." I thought about that. "It'll cost more money. And I mean, I've been helping pay for groceries..."

"That's over. We will have enough money to get by if we're

cautious."

My ears perked up. "What's over?"

She was quiet. I got the sense that she hadn't meant to say that and was now debating whether or not to tell me the rest. "Ma," I said, "I'm sixteen. I'm old enough to know."

Her paw kept stirring in a regular back and forth motion, and she stared at the bowl. Finally she seemed to come to a decision. "You remember that coffee plantationer that Kamina wanted to marry Ori to?"

"Sure."

Now she stopped stirring and set down the bowl. "I want you to understand that this is not about your aunt. This is how things are done there. Don't be angry at Kamina."

I frowned, my ears flattening. "What did she do?"

"She would have gotten a million francs for the marriage. So I paid her that amount. It's about a thousand dollars. I needed to send it to her in installments, and so I needed your help with household expenses for a while. But that's been paid off now."

"Wait." I set my knife down. "You bribed her to not marry Ori into a dangerous situation?"

"You may use that word if you like, but it's not accurate. Kamina was told to marry Ori into a good situation. She found one, and according to her argument, if I didn't like it, I should compensate her for what she lost."

My fingers pressed into the counter, claws hard against the wood. Kamina had often taken care of us while Ma worked, played games with us, walked with us to the market or the tennis center. I remembered her fussing over one of Ori's shirts, trying to get it straight while Ori laughed and wagged her tail. "She..."

"The word you may be looking for is 'extorted' but that is also not quite right." Ma seemed very calm. "Listen. I knew there would be costs when I chose to accompany you here. I could have sent you here by yourself and stayed to ensure Ori's future. But there was very little I could have done that Kamina would not."

"She was going to sell Ori to a guy who needed a new wife because his last one was killed!"

Ma put up a paw. "I had been helping Kamina a little when she needed it, more lately. Now that I'm over here, I told her she would have to make do without my assistance, and that she could keep half the money from Ori's marriage. That money is important to her, and there is no guarantee that Ori would have been killed on the coffee plantation."

"Can't she just marry someone in Lundara?" I asked. "There's nowhere safe anywhere else in the country."

"Most of the west is relatively safe."

"Relatively." The word sounded bitter in my mouth.

"There are too many jackals in Lundara. Kamina would not get enough money from anyone."

Of course it all came down to money. "And that's more important than Ori's happiness."

Ma frowned. "Your happiness depends on you." She poked my chest. "And that goes for you as well as for Ori."

My voice was rising despite my attempts to keep it down. "Ori's happiness also depends on not being shot."

"And she's not going to be." Ma gripped my wrist. "I did what I had to. It serves you nothing to fight with Kamina. You should be worrying about your own career."

I relaxed, and she let go. "Sorry," I said, though my fur was still bristled and my tail couldn't stay still.

"Now. What are our plans for going to Golden?"

"I have some money saved up, and Marquize has a credit card."

"I see." Now she did turn, coming to stand beside me. "Marquize is going with you."

"That's the idea." I got a better grip on the onion, turned it to slice it longways. "We're going on tour together, I told you that."

"Mmm. Yes." She sounded amused. "Tell me about these tournaments."

So I told her about the fifteen thousanders, the prize for winning each one and the prizes for just getting to the round of 16. I told her they were all in the same general place and that we'd been looking up people offering places to stay, and that we'd been looking for a coach, and all the things we'd been doing to prepare. When I was done, she looked at me over her slender muzzle. "It sounds very impressive," she said. "Good research. You think you are ready?"

"Coach says I am, and Braden says—"

She put a paw on the wrist holding the onion. I stopped

chopping. "Do you think you are ready?" she asked again.

"I think so." I didn't have to hesitate. "Yes. I'm ready."

She searched my eyes and then nodded. "All right. Then we will buy tickets out to Golden."

And just like that, the decision was made. I told Marquize when he came back, and he whooped and hugged me, and then let me go quickly because Ma was in the next room, but Ma called from the kitchen that she didn't mind us hugging as long as it didn't last longer than three seconds.

***

So on Monday I officially told Coach Murphy I was withdrawing. We'd booked flights out to Golden the following weekend, so I said I could stay in school until the end of the week. "What's the point?" he asked. "No, you can have this afternoon's practice but then you should spend the week studying the other people on the tour. You can get all that information online pretty easily, you know."

"I'll look, thank you," I said. "And I have to find a place to stay."

He pulled out his phone. "Let me call a couple people. If I turn up something I'll let you know."

"Thank you, sir." I stood. "And thank you for the opportunity to come here and learn. It's been a wonderful time."

He showed a bucktoothed smile. "It's been a pleasure working with you, N'Guwe. Now go out there and prove that our school is the best."

"Yes, sir," I said.

And then I had to tell all my friends over lunch. At first it was only Dom and Kim, whose case was still inching its way through court, but at their exclamations, more of our original group perked their ears or came over to our table, and soon I had almost a dozen cubs sitting around me as I explained that I'd be leaving for professional tournaments.

"We'll miss you," Bret said.

"Kill 'em out there," Pom said.

"I can't believe you're getting out there before me," Kim said.

And Dom reached out and squeezed my paw. "Good luck," he said with a smile. "Keep in touch."

"Yeah," everyone echoed.

"Keep in touch."

"You have my number?"

"Here, let me get my phone."

"Text me on Skype."

"I'm on ScentBook. Are you on?"

I got my phone out and spent a good long time trading contact information with people, feeling good about my time at Palm Gables coming to an end. Until I saw Frio watching me across the room. I couldn't read his expression; he looked like he was smiling, but he had a paw to his muzzle partly hiding his lips, and I didn't want him to think I was staring at him, so I looked away quickly.

That was one part of the school that I would not miss. Certainly there were probably terrible people like him out on the tour, but nobody would ever have that kind of power over me again. I swore that.

Kim walked me to my practice and nodded at my phone as I was putting it away. "You know most of them will forget you in a year. Maybe not Dom, maaaybe not Bret. And not me. But the rest? They're going on with school. If you run into them on the tour, sure, it'll be great and you'll reminisce about good ol' Palm Gables. But they're not going to be chatting with you every night like BFFs."

"How do you know?" I was a little annoyed that she was spoiling the good feelings I'd had after lunch.

"Porter told me. We were talking about my friends here and she told me not to get attached, that none of the people from tennis academies stay in touch. It's not like we all went through some big crisis together. We were competing most of the time, and you got pushed ahead, so everyone else resented you."

"But you and me will keep in touch."

"Sure." She laughed and draped an arm around my waist. "But we're friends already, right?"

"Bret's my friend. So is Dom." But I hadn't really talked to Bret in months, not the way we used to do things together. And Dom and I had had a few close moments, but not a lot.

She waved a paw. "It goes both ways. I bet you're going to be crazy busy those first few weeks out on tour, prepping for matches and playing matches and getting to know a whole new group of guys." My ears folded back, and she punched my arm. "Don't ear-flat.

It's gonna be great. I want you to tell me all about it."

"I will," I promised. "And you'll be playing those tournaments soon enough. Only the girls are separate, I think."

"Yeah, a lot are. I won't see you a lot. Not until we're both in the majors."

I matched the grin on her long canine muzzle with one of my own, holding out my paw. "So about six months, right?"

She slapped her paw into mine and squeezed. "Deal."

The last person I said good-bye to was Diaz, after our practice and a fiercely fought set which I won. "Hey, good luck," he said. "I don't know if I'll see you out there on tour. Might never be good enough, you know?"

"You're about as good as I am." His comment took me aback. "Did you not see how close that set was?"

"The one you won?"

"Yeah, but…"

"You haven't noticed you won nearly every set except when you really upset?"

"Well…I mean, you beat me…" There was that time I was having the fight with Marquize, but that counted as being upset. And before that… "I'm sure you beat me a couple times."

"Look." Diaz put an arm around me. "You won't get better here. Don't care what the coach says. You gotta get out, you gotta play against lots of other people. And you're gonna do great. I might not be on the court but I'll come to your matches."

And that left me with a good feeling as I cleaned out my locker. The school was bustling with people on their way to and from the courts; few of the coaches were about, and none met my eye as they roamed the halls. I threw all my stuff into my bag and looked around again at the tile floor, the cream-colored walls, the red clay accents, and the big double doors thrown open at the end with the afternoon light streaming through. I walked past eager students, tails wagging; I was passed by intent, determined students. Every step, every click of my claws on the tile brought me closer to the doors. And then I was at the doorway.

I paused to look back at the interior, now dim and shadowy as my eyes adjusted to the outside light. I'd spent almost two years here and had learned so much, and barring a Braden-like return, probably would never set foot in these halls again. But my name was on a plaque up on the second floor with the other tournament winners, and maybe one day a replica of a trophy I'd won would sit in the alumni pride case across from it.

A deer pushed past me, mumbled an apology, and was gone. I smiled back into the halls and then turned my tail to Palm Gables.

Epilogue (2015)

That feeling. When you lose yourself in the flow of the game, the back and forth, and your mind is analyzing the situation, and gets you to set up a shot, and then your body executes and the ball flies off your racket and you can tell from the moment you hit it that it's going right where you aimed it, and it skids off the baseline two inches past your opponent's racket...that's one of the best feelings in the world.

Braden shoots me a look and an approving nod and walks back to the ballboys to get a few balls to serve with. We're 2-2 in the second set and even though he's won the first set, I feel my feet a lot more firmly under me. I know Braden, and I know he didn't mean what he said on the changeover. Even though he broke me on the next game to win the set, he understood that conceding the set didn't mean I was conceding the match. I proved it, challenging him hard on his first service game, winning both of mine handily. Maybe I had been too much in my head that first set, thinking about the history of it all and how I didn't want to be the guy who stopped him from a historic Grand Slam. I got away from that after the first set and started thinking about how it could be cool to be the one guy who managed to stop Braden Longacre this year.

He plays a little flat in his third service game, clipping the net on his first two first serves. I jump on the second serves; knowing how good he is at handling quick returns means I have to be unpredictable, and while he's ready to jump to either side, the first time he isn't prepared to handle a return right to the body. The second time he backs up, so I follow a deep return with a run to the net and a winner into the open court.

He doesn't get rattled, of course. He wouldn't have won three majors if he got rattled when he was down love-30. As well as I know him, he knows me, and he catches me off guard with an ace wide on the deuce court. Then he gets a first serve in on the next point, I manage to return it, and we settle in to volley.

I'd tried in the first set to make something happen, but Braden is amazing at seeing angles, especially this year, and he slapped back everything I sent him, often for winners. This set, I'm more patient, opting for quality returns instead of creative ones, and it pays off: Braden tries to catch the corner and paints a forehand wide of the line. I have two break points.

Should I point out here that Braden's only been broken on his serve five times this whole tournament, and three of those were in his epic five-setter? He doesn't like losing his serve (who does?), so he bounces the balls a whole bunch preparing for this next point. I can feel the thoughts in his head: another ace and I'm right back in this. So I move a bit wide, preparing for the same ace he'd sent earlier, leaving the middle tantalizingly open.

Of course he doesn't take the bait. He thinks I'm going to jump toward the middle as soon as he moves the racket. So he slaps the serve wide, and it's a good one, but I'm already ready for it. I whip my racket around and send the ball right down the line, landing an inch inside the corner. Braden doesn't even lunge, just pulls up and stares at it.

I go to the ballboy to collect balls for my service game, listening to the official call, "Game N'guwe," and getting a brief warm flush in my chest. But you can't take the last game into the next one, so I tell myself to get back to business. The service break gives me a fighting chance to take the second set, and whether or not I *do* win it, now I know I *can*.

When I turn around, Braden's still staring at me. Maybe he's forgotten, but he was the one who taught me tricks like that.

The balls feel warm in my paw. I skip one back to the ballboy. Braden's strolling back into position, still looking my way. I salute him with the racket, and then, finally, he grins and gets into position. And I know that he knows it too, that he's not just going to roll through this match in straight sets.

It's on.

Patreon

Love Match was created with the help of Patreon, a web site that allows fans to support their favorite creators with monthly donations. Every week, another segment is posted on my Patreon site, with extra content available for those supporting at higher levels. If you'd like to continue to read about Rocky's adventures before the second volume appears, you can find them at http://www.patreon.com/kyellgold, where the first part of the next book is highlighted so you know where to begin. If you'd care to join the support for this book series, I'd greatly appreciate it! Patreon helps my income be more predictable and allows me to do things like commission more interior illustrations for this book than I've had in any of my others. And there are many other excellent creators on Patreon, so browse around and see who else you might find there.

(URL for first part of book 2: https://www.patreon.com/posts/love-match-part-5180483)

My deepest thanks to all these contributors to the Love Match Patreon as of the conclusion of book one in April 2016:

Silverfox 361
Courtney
Strangewolf
Austin (or) Aus
William A Cook
Tame Adams
Aleksandr
Anonymous
Mad as A March Hare
David B.
Barium45
Baylei
Kade Beatty
belladann
Chris Beningo
Chelsie Bergnaum

BlackMoon
Jace Blades
Jason Blake
blargh
Abigayle Bode
Jered Bosco
Tiller Brown
Christopher Bryan
Kingy Buizel
buu38
Trevor Bygland
Dustin Byrd
Frost Byte
Wesley Capelle
CasuallyFoxy
Guillaume Cauvet
Weidz

Chandra
Corvo
Cory
Crimson
Cyle
Korel Dagh
ole dahl
DatGingerCat
Dave
Maarten de Vos
Jack Devries
Shakal Draconis
Drew
Dunkelpfote
Dynaphus
L E
EgoSaber

Shane Elfield
Donovan Elk
Em
Evandill
Bryan Ezawa
Fabi
Dale Farmer
Farrgo
Felrnn
Bobby Ferry
FlatFootFox
Floxee
Aiden Fox
K Fox
Scamp fox
Unknown Fox
Zerda Fox
Kevin Frane
Riley Frits
Mu Gamma
Jeffrey Gardner
Geemo
Glassan
Marc Gold
Reilly Grant
Grey
Grims
K H
Sean Hanson
Harelfaz
Edward Haynes Jr
Shanon Hodkiewicz
Nate Hopp
Imnobody
Brandon Ingalls
iqbunny
Ashley Jade "Blaze"
Wiles

Jakebe
James
Alline Jaskolski
Jem
JLeet
JS
karmakat
Kato
Keone
Sirberus Khaos
Curtis Kihlmire
Travis King
Kittopherson
Marcelino Klocko
Chris Knox
Kogawakenji
Jens Krogh
Ammitzbo
Snow Kruzer
Michael Laforest
Connor Laleff
Colin Leighton
Texas Lion
Peri Llwyn
Rei Loire
Christian Lopez
Yifan Mai
Marcwolf
Nathan Martinez
Vinnie McGlynn
Ryan McKown
Michael
mightyferret
Mikasi
Mino
Flann Moriath
Randi Mueller
NegaImage

Alexander Nelson
Nicholas
Nina
Noctiffe
oseyeris
Ottah
Kairan Otter
Diego P
Dmitry P
Thomas Peters
Phenris
Phief
Pockets
Prator
ProwlingPaws
Qball
Ragnar9
Rankine
Skandranon
Rashkae
Rennec
Michael Reyes
Reyfar
Tom Romsang
Rooth
Canis Rufus
Ryan
Benjamin Ryder
Sean
Senimantas
Felix seven
Chris Shannon
shirou14
Silver
Foxon Silverfur
Silwer
Nielas Sinclair
thomas smith

Hitsu Solo
Kaily Spensor
Spirit
A Strange One
Streaks
Tiger Stripes
Cole Stryker
sunkawakan
Lennon Surcot
Tau Switchblade
Taylor

Tiago
Semilico Tiger
TomLeo
Selah Trantow
Tyde
UltraFennec
Demetri Upton
Vaska
Wanderer1708
Joey Watts
Bill Welsh

Setsune Wiefel
Matt Wills
AJ WOLF
Buck Wolf
Fuzz Wolf
Sketchy Wolf
Wolfbite
Pescetarian Wolfe
Wolfi
Xevious
Ysegrim

Acknowledgments

This book was my first experiment with Patreon, and great thanks are due to all the folks who signed up and contributed during the year and a half this novel was written (listed in the Patreon section). Many of them commented on the story, helping me catch mistakes, but more importantly, helping me keep up my enthusiasm for this project.

As always, I owe a great debt to my writing group: Ryan Campbell, David Cowan, and Watts Martin. They provided invaluable feedback and support as always.

Rukis not only illustrated the book but has read in advance and has also offered feedback and suggestions along the way. She's been very much a partner in this story and has been terrific to work with.

And as always, my thanks to Kit and Jack for their support not only of this project, but of my writing career and me in general. Without them, none of this would be possible.

About the Author

Kyell Gold has won twelve Ursa Major awards for his stories and novels, and his acclaimed novel "Out of Position" co-won the Rainbow Award for Best Gay Novel of 2009. His novel "Green Fairy" was nominated for inclusion in the ALA's "Over the Rainbow" list for 2012. He helped create RAWR, the first residential furry writing workshop, and was one of the instructors at its first session in 2016.

He lives in California and loves to travel and dine out with his husband Kit Silver, and can be seen at furry conventions around the world. More information about him and his books is available at http://www.kyellgold.com.

About the Artist

Rukis lives on a farm, where she spends most of her time working on art, caring for her animals, and hanging out doing tabletop gaming with her friends. She is a huge fan of old school D&D, White Wolf, and Warhammer, as well as studying and collecting exotic fish (Cichlids, mostly) and drinking a lot of Dr. Pepper. Her menagerie includes a rabbit, some fish, two wonderful dogs, and a whole mess of chickens.

She is the author of *Heretic,* the *Off the Beaten Path* trilogy, and *Legacy*, which take place in the world of *Red Lantern*.

About the Publisher

FurPlanet publishes original works of furry fiction. You can explore their selection at *https://www.furplanet.com* and find their e-books at *https://www.baddogbooks.com.*

CPSIA information can be obtained
at www.ICGtesting.com
Printed in the USA
LVOW13s2250230217
525298LV00007B/110/P